PRA
THE CAI

the first novel in The Justine Trilogy and winner of the Silver Nautilus Award and the Bronze IPPY Award, 2014

". . . A rather remarkable diary—one with profound implications for religious communities already roiling with discontent . . . the novel delivers a tautly suspenseful historical tale. In particular, Lambert sharply ties together early Christian beliefs with the plight of females in traditional societies, and effectively depicts the fears unleashed when entrenched beliefs are challenged . . . She keeps a sure hand on the romance plotline, letting it percolate and flare . . . An engaging thriller/romance, and a smart evocation of modern Egypt."

—*Kirkus Review*

I loved Linda Lambert's daring novel, *The Cairo Codex*, winner of the bronze Independent Publisher (IPPY) award for historical fiction. Her knowledge of the religious and political struggles in Egypt is uncanny, as well as timely. It will make a great movie!

—Jim Barnes, Editor and Awards Director
IndependentPublisher.com

"This page-turner will keep you on the edge of your seat! The contents of the codex are so startling to both Christian and Muslim faiths that their disclosure triggers violent reactions. The Muslim Brotherhood is further provoked to action as it prepares to take over the political reins of the country. This discovery will challenge accepted belief in history and religion. It will also raise questions of just how much knowledge the world deserves—or is prepared—to receive. THE CAIRO CODEX is the first in what will be THE JUSTINE TRILOGY."

—*Arab Vistas Today*

The
ITALIAN
Letters

Also by Linda Lambert:

The Cairo Codex
A Rapture of Ravens
The Constructivist Leader
Who Will Save Our Schools
Women's Ways of Leading
Building Leadership Capacity in Schools
Leadership Capacity for Lasting School Improvement

The ITALIAN Letters

Linda Lambert

WEST
HILLS
PRESS

West Hills Press
Atlanta • San Francisco

PUBLISHED BY WEST HILLS PRESS

Cover images ©123rf.com/Aleksandar Mijatovic

All of the characters and events in this book are fictitious, and any resemblance to actual persons, living or dead, is purely coincidental.

ISBN-13: 978-1933512471

Printed in Canada
10 9 8 7 6 5 4 3 2

DEDICATION

I dedicate this novel, *The Italian Letters,* to my husband, Morgan Dale Lambert, and to our magnificent memories of Italy. He is my friend, mentor, muse, and lover, as well as father, grandfather and great-grandfather to our shared and extended family members. Whatever role he assumes, he does so with tenderness, grace, and empathy. Morgan is that rare and exceptional human being who knows how to love unconditionally. His circle of care radiates out like a wave from the most intimate of personal relationships to the country and the world.

CHAPTER 1

—&&&—

Italy is a dream that keeps returning the rest of your life.

—Anna Akhmatova, Chechen poet

VILLA CELLINI, FIESOLE, ITALY, MARCH 2008

HER WHOLE BODY shakes as the ancient pillars pull loose from their Corinthian crowns and plunge into the crypt, trapping her beneath rubble. The dust of shattering sandstone smothers the oxygen in the dank air. The earth shivers ferociously. She bends with a pillar, barely catching herself as she falls to the convulsing floor, large stone slabs undulating, one slicing into her leg. All light in the crumbling crypt is extinguished. Cold sweat covers her body as she struggles for air. Turning her head violently from side to side, she grasps her injured leg, determined to stop the bleeding.

"Justine! Justine! Wake up." Bolting upright, she struggled to focus on the intruding voice.

Fear still gripped her trembling body; light flooded through the windows, blinding her. "Where am I?"

"In your room in Fiesole. You're home." Her mother softly coaxed her into wakefulness. Justine had spent many a summer in this small, terraced bedroom with its embossed, baby blue wallpaper. The ancient, wobbly bed was still cozy and comfortable; but if she stayed, she would shop for another one.

"The nightmare keeps returning, Mom. Ever since St. Sergius." Justine's nightgown clung to her wet skin, and her hair stuck to her face like the damp ringlets on Botticelli's Venus. "They've gotten worse since the churches were burned and Zachariah was killed." Remorse and a nagging sense of guilt and shame distorted her lovely face.

"It might help if you talked to me about it. You've told me so little of how it ended." Her mother sat down at the foot of the bed, placing her hand on her daughter's ankle and turning the leg so she could see the damage. "How is it?"

"The leg is fine," Justine said, wiping her damp face with the sheet. "But I'm humiliated. Here I am, twenty-eight, unemployed, living in my mother's house. Am I starting over?" She swung her long legs over the side of the bed, revealing a scar nearly the length of her right calf. Despite her injury, healed now, she moved toward the bathroom with the litheness of a runner, which she was. Observers found Justine Jenner to be striking and warm, but with a brush of reserve, an occasional distant expression that arrested onlookers, as though she harbored mysterious convictions and memories.

Her mother sat there wide-eyed, mouth gaping. "Humiliated? Starting over? Those are harsh statements. Talk to me."

"Later, Mom," Justine called from the bathroom, "I need to take a shower to clear my head. Go for a run."

Lucrezia pushed herself back onto the short bed, drawing her legs up under her white kaftan. She decided not to push—just yet. "Your father's coming to breakfast," she said.

In the bathroom, Justine looked in the mirror, shocked at her spent appearance. The nightmare receded in the wake of this news. "Father? As in Dr. Morgan Jenner, man of adventure? I didn't know he was in Italy." Just before Christmas, shortly after being expelled from Egypt for revealing the unthinkable, Justine had met her father on holiday in Rome. He was on the verge of returning to his archeological dig in Peru. Neither had expected to see the other for some time. Their time in Rome had not gone especially well.

Justine's parents had divorced when she left California for graduate school, and yet, over the years, had remained friends. But she rarely saw her father, who was often on the road, digging somewhere or other for treasures. Justine had given them little to worry about, until Egypt.

—∞∞∞—

The morning room of Lucrezia's Cellini villa provided a panoramic view of the Arno River valley. As they gathered for breakfast, dark green cone-tops of cypresses, introduced to the land by the Etruscans, danced across the vista. The crown of Brunelleschi's Duomo popped up through the mist like a cardinal's hat, suspended in midair.

"I've got news," said Morgan as he strode into the room, hugged his daughter, wedged into his favorite chair at the head of the table, and rested his feet on a small needlepoint stool. "I'll be here in Italy a while." He was wearing what he considered proper attire for an archaeologist: khaki shirt and pants, both thinning at the elbows and knees. The Peruvian sun had tanned him to a rich golden tone and bleached his hair nearly blonde, save for a brush of gray at each temple. Some considered his Roman nose unattractively long, others found it regal.

"For how long?" asked Justine, watching her father as though he were one of her subjects. She was often amused by his predictability, such as the casually worn, yet intact, field uniform. As an anthropologist, she prided herself on her analytical abilities, though they had sometimes failed her where men were concerned.

"More than a visit this time, honey. I'm coming here to work. A new project at an Etruscan UNESCO site. Very exciting!" he said, pausing in expectation of excited or complimentary responses.

Justine felt surprised—and confused. She smiled, choosing to provide her father with the positive response he desired. She knew that she would now have to deal more directly with the misogynist tendencies she had put up with since adolescence.

Lucrezia gave him an indulgent smile and waited for details. She picked up her fork and pushed a strawberry round and round through a dollop of yogurt.

"Archaeology is a crowded business here," Justine cautioned. "Everyone and his sister wants to live and dig in Italy, so I'm assuming you have something good up your sleeve. My father, the famous archaeologist, would hardly be interested in a typical Roman excavation," she said, reaching for a croissant. Maria, the family cook, had prepared a spread fit for the visiting royal she considered Justine's father to be. Forever enchanted with Dr. Morgan, Maria—much more than a family cook—inevitably treated him like a nobleman; he reciprocated with gallantry and compliments to her cooking.

Morgan stood, stretched his muscular arms, and walked to the carved nineteenth-century buffet table, methodically filling his plate with cold cuts, tomatoes, eggs, and a large piece of banana bread, Maria's specialty. "You're right, honey. Not the usual Roman dig." He placed a whole egg in his mouth before returning to the table.

"Tell us about it," coaxed Lucrezia, falling effortlessly into her familiar role as attentive Creta, as he often called her. Her backlit black hair gleamed, and her arched eyebrows shadowed luminous green eyes that reminded Justine of a silent movie star. Only direct light revealed the hairline wrinkles around her eyes and tiny creases above her lips.

It seemed to Justine, even now, that her mother needed Morgan to find her attractive. What woman wouldn't, especially one who had shared his bed for so many years?

"Thanks for the invitation, Creta." Taking a large bite of banana bread, he assumed a relaxed pose at the head of the table, and smiled charmingly when Maria reentered the breakfast room with a large plate of fruits. Like her mother before her, Maria had worked for Lucrezia's family all her life. Justine always felt reassured by Maria's maternal presence—round face, generously curved body. Even her feet were round. She was all that "round" implies: warmth, connection, accessibility. Good food.

"It's an Etruscan dig at a UNESCO site in Cerveteri. Do you know the place?" He gazed at Lucrezia, and his temples flushed with excitement. "Teams from the local superintendent's office have been excavating there for a couple of years, but now they may be onto something new. Startling, really. UNESCO insisted on an international team, so they called me. The superintendent resisted hiring a foreigner at first, but I think she's come around. Or will." As a professor emeritus at the University of California, Berkeley, Morgan knew he had choices.

"I know Cerveteri a little," said Justine, refilling her coffee cup and taking a heaping spoonful of the fruit salad. "About an hour's drive north of Ostia, isn't it? Charming little town." She paused. "Not much is known about the Etruscans, I understand. Not sure why."

"What's going on there?" Lucrezia asked.

"That's the strange part. I know little. They've been very mysterious . . . which makes me think this is something big."

"You wouldn't take the job unless it was promising, Dad. You know something," challenged Justine. "Another origin myth?"

"They didn't mention origins, but yes, I suspect that's what they have up their sleeves. Finding evidence of the genesis of the Etruscans—or the source of their isolated language—could change the course of history!"

"Ah . . ." Justine studied her father's sculpted face. "Now that is something worth getting excited about. Are we Neanderthal or Turkish? Or Egyptian?" adding the last option for fun. *He knows more, but is holding back.*

"The Etruscans are hotly debated in European history!" exclaimed Lucrezia. "Herodotus claimed they came from Lydia around 800 BC, but that theory has been nearly debunked by recent studies. At least we do know they taught the brutish Romans how to start an empire."

"I'm impressed," said Morgan, winking at his ex-wife. "I don't think you can call yourself a casual scholar of ancient Italian history anymore."

Lucrezia shifted uneasily in her chair and smoothed the lap of her linen kaftan.

Justine noticed her mother's self-conscious move. *They're both such unremitting charmers. This flirting probably means nothing. Would I want it to?* As these perplexing thoughts whirled through her mind, the eastern light penetrated the drawn gauze panels of the French doors. She forced her thoughts back into the room. "I thought no Etruscan artifacts had been discovered in Italy dating back earlier than eight or nine hundred BCE."

"That's what makes this hunt so appealing. And, of course, my favorite daughter is now in Italy."

"Your favorite and only daughter, I assume," said Lucrezia, one eyebrow arching.

"As far as I know," Morgan teased. He stood up and circled the table, snatching grapes from Justine's fruit salad. "For now, I'm concerned about the composition of the damn team. I haven't been able to choose anyone to my liking, and they've now added a historian. Damn historians! Worse than anthropologists, if you ask me. What I need is a couple of seasoned archaeologists, like Ibrahim." Morgan's Egyptian mentor, Ibrahim El Shabry, was well into his eighties now, his arthritic knees barring him from archaeological digs.

Justine refused to take the bait. A few years ago she would have swiped at it like a kitten batting a ball of string. Not now. She smiled sweetly and picked at her fruit salad. "So what is it with you and historians?"

"Historians have theories. They try to make connections that aren't supported by the facts." He sat down and spread lemon curd on a second piece of banana bread, which he then devoured in one great swallow.

"All people have narratives, Dad." Justine cut open her croissant before meeting her father's intense cobalt eyes.

"Facts. That's what's important. The evidence should speak for itself. Find the evidence, verify its authorship and timeframe, and display it in museums so the public can understand how the ancients lived. Scientific. Straightforward."

Lucrezia sighed. "That's why museums are so lifeless, except for the one in Orvieto, perhaps. Generally the evidence is presented without a narrative. I find it tedious."

Morgan laughed. "I see my girls are ganging up on me again."

Lucrezia's face recoiled. She had no intention of allowing her former spouse the pleasure of infantilizing and possessing her again. The spell of his charm was broken.

Maria reappeared in the doorway. "The phone. It's for you, Justine."

"Who is it?" Justine asked, feeling rescued by the interruption.

"A Dr. Andrea LeMartin. Calling from Paris."

CHAPTER 2

‑‑‑oxxo‑‑‑

We would like to live as we once lived, but history will not permit it.

—John F. Kennedy

"WHO'S DR. LE MARTIN?" asked Morgan, folding his napkin and placing it on the left side of his plate.

Does he plan to stay? Justine wondered. She had mixed feelings about the possibility.

"A colleague of Justine's from Egypt and long-time friend of mine," Lucrezia answered, also taking notice of Morgan's gesture with the napkin. "I'm sure you've heard us talk about her."

"The name's familiar," he said, staring appreciatively at Lucrezia, his eyes warm with memories of their youth together, making love on the summer porch in Berkeley.

"She's coming to Italy in a couple days," offered Justine. "I've invited her to join us to discuss the codex that dropped into my lap in Egypt. As far as I know, the original hasn't shown up in the black market. Perhaps we'll take a little side trip to Rome."

"It'll show up. Probably in Milan or Rome," said her mother, helping Maria to clear the table.

"Catch me up here," demanded Morgan. He already knew about Justine's discovery of a codex during the earthquake in Cairo and the involvement of the infamous Supreme Antiquities Director. What he wasn't sure of was where things stood now.

A soft morning breeze carried the fragrance of damp grasses and early spring plantings from the garden below. At Christmas, Justine had told him about his old mentor Ibrahim El Shabry's complicity in the theft of the codex from the Supreme Director's safe in the Egyptian Museum. At very least, Ibrahim had known about the theft and hadn't done anything to stop it.

"I found it hard to believe that Ibrahim was involved. Impossible, really. Not the man I know." Morgan and Ibrahim had been colleagues during several digs in Egypt, particularly a notorious one at Darshur. Friends and colleagues for thirty years. He was pensive for several moments. "Come work with me, Justine. After the Egyptian fiasco, you could reestablish your reputation as a fine anthropologist."

Justine cringed at the word *fiasco*. "I thought you didn't need an anthropologist. We just muddy the water."

"*Touché*. We'll figure out a role that you'll find appealing. Think about it."

"Okay. I will."

"What can you expect from this Andrea? Will she bring more translations? Whatever you two reveal about this codex, you can expect all hell to break loose," he said, concern washed across his face.

"It already has. Hell, that is. No telling what will happen next." Justine attempted to sound casual; she knew efforts to prevent further findings from surfacing could get much worse. *Who am I kidding? Myself? Or am I trying to comfort my parents?*

"You haven't tackled the Catholic Church yet, my dear," said her mother, leaning across the table to refill the coffee cups.

Justine sat back in her chair, watching her mother's face closely. For several moments she watched the morning sunlight dance across the crystal glassware still on the table. *Is that worry? Is she afraid of what the Catholic Church could do to me?*

"How about your own work, Dad? No small controversy there. Many Italians insist Etruscans are native to Italy. If we challenge that, maybe we'll both be thrown out of Italy!" She reached over and patted his arm.

Morgan squeezed her hand. "Italy tolerates controversy a little better than Egypt, my dear. What we uncover about the Etruscans might shake things up, yes. Are you ready for that? But too, Cerveteri has already been combed pretty thoroughly. And Mussolini's long gone."

"What does Mussolini have to do with it?" asked Justine, slowly withdrawing her hand from her father's grasp.

"Mussolini and a few archaeologists, Massimo among them, tried to reestablish the Roman Empire during the 1920s and '30s," said Lucrezia, sitting back down at the table, taking up her coffee cup. "Part of those efforts was to portray the Etruscans, who taught the Romans how to build, as militaristic warriors ... and indigenous Italians, of course. But I don't think this portrayal of the Etruscans is accurate. They seem very unlike the Romans and the Greeks, I would say." She paused and let her eyes linger on Morgan, forgiving him for the earlier slight.

Morgan and Justine remained silent. They knew when other thoughts were simmering in Lucrezia's mind. "I'd like to think women played a greater role in Etruscan society. And yet some things never change," she said finally. "Look at today. We're saddled with Berlusconi, who considers women playthings. And he's corrupt, yet he's bound to be elected president again next month!"

"I doubt women held as much sway or played as powerful a role among the Etruscans as your mother suggests," Morgan said to Justine. "The Greek and Roman women who followed them certainly didn't have as much power as their male counterparts."

"We know that, Dad! But what if it really was matrilineal culture?"

"Never!" Morgan almost shouted. "And I, for one, am willing to give Berlusconi another go." He turned toward his ex-wife and displayed the grin that had once swept her away. "By the way, Justine. This Andrea. Is she my type?"

"Decidedly not your type," Lucrezia answered for her daughter. "She's a tad independent for your taste."

"*Buon punto!*" said Morgan, grabbing the last remaining piece of banana bread as Maria left for the kitchen.

Justine wondered when her parents' predictable script would morph into tediousness. They could combine forces when it came to protecting her, but they couldn't bury their individual competitive natures for long. As they sought to arouse one another's jealousy, Justine slipped into her sandals and extricated herself from their sport.

✑

Gripping the warm terrace railing, Justine stood on her toes and leaned backward, drawing in the fresh scent of lemon. Exhaling slowly, she released the tension that had accumulated during breakfast. Just below, in the garden, the first hint of new growth beckoned. Creeping thyme moved up the stairwell and spread around the stepping-stones. The path led her between widely planted cypresses and the scented jasmine and honeysuckle that filled the air. Lemon and olive trees stood like soldiers on watch among the zucchini and lilies. The plantings were not random.

Tuscans tended to separate objects of all kinds into their respective spaces. Moving further down into the garden, Justine found a newly planted herb garden of oregano, winter savory, sage, and chives, ringed by a low hedge of rosemary. This was the secret place she remembered so well . . . a small, intimate blanket of grass with table and chairs, hedges, hydrangea, and boxed topiaries. *This could be the place where I write in my diary.*

She did not stop to enjoy the private place of her childhood, for this morning she was looking for Prego. Turning right through blossoming green bean and catalogna chicory, she approached the small potting shed of glass and faded oak siding. Spiders and webs drooped everywhere.

"*Ragno*, spiders, keep me company. Eat the aphids and beetles," Prego intoned, as though he were picking up in the middle of an ongoing conversation with Justine. He had not seen her for several weeks, although they had spoken briefly on her return from Egypt before Christmas.

"Thinning the tomato seedlings?" she asked as she spied a box of uprooted sprouts.

"*Prego*," he said in agreement. "Babies need room to grow. One by one. *Pomodoro-pantano Romanesco*. Harvest in June if the weather keeps comin' good. Need lots of sun."

"May I help?" she asked. Without waiting for permission, she buried both hands into the moist soil and lifted a fragile seedling from the flat of miniature tomato plants as one would lift a child from its cradle.

They worked side by side in silence for some time. Justine watched as a spider descended on a long fiber of webbing. "How long have you worked here, Prego?"

"All my life, my child. Father came as a young man. My mother, just a girl, worked upstairs. *Prego*." In Italian, *prego* means please, and thank you, and yes, and excuse me, and just about anything, depending on the context. Prego scattered the word about in the way some people overuse "you know"—thus he had been called "Prego" for as long as Justine could remember. She didn't remember his real name.

"This house, Prego. How was it used during the war?" Justine watched the spider as it crawled back up its web, a geometric tapestry. *Nature! Entrancing.* Sunlight caught the fibers, and they shone like stained glass windows.

"I was a boy. No memories. Only gardens. See arugula, *signorina*. Seeds itself. Plants have memory, not Prego." Blue veins on the backs of his hands bulged ever so slightly as his fingers tightened around the wooden ledge of the table.

She watched his hands, knowing that memories were buried there, deeper than the plants he loved. "What did the visitors wear, Prego? Were there boots?"

"Boots. *Si*. Many boots."

"Fiesole remained in German hands until the end of the war. Right? You would have been . . . what? Ten, eleven?"

"Twelve, *signorina*." His shoulders moved closer to his neck, his unkempt hair rising above his collar. A weathered hand touched his forehead as he crossed himself. "This house, so beautiful. Much art. Picasso everywhere."

Justine looked at the man she had known all her life. His body had grown smaller. Always short, he was now shorter. She towered over him. His coveralls with rolled up cuffs, his plaid shirt with frayed collar, were familiar to her. His face was a portrait of a wrinkled, contented man, one who didn't allow himself to worry . . . or recall the unpleasantries of life. The twinkle in his eyes that had once signaled mischief had quieted, for he had spent those thoughts that life could be something grand. The garden was enough for him, was satisfying in the way old age brings contentment for those who are fortunate enough to embrace it.

Prego trusted Justine. He trusted who she was. He trusted that she would always be gracious. He trusted that she would always return. Yet he trusted no one with his deep secrets—secrets that, if disclosed, could disrupt his quiet regimen.

Justine understood this. She wiped her hands on a nearby towel, gave Prego an affectionate hug, and climbed the steps toward the terrace. Their conversation about World War II could wait for another day.

CHAPTER 3

‐◦◦◦‐

**The two of us are a country under embargo, living on parentheses and si-
lences, on blackouts, so that when the lights finally come on again, we have
already forgotten what to say to each other.**

—Elisa Biagini, Italian Poet

IN 1927, TWO IMPORTANT visitors came to Cerveteri: Benito Mussolini and
D.H. Lawrence. Mussolini demanded that a road be built between the village and the necropolis so that visitors could access the tombs of the great
Etruscan warriors, forebears and teachers of the triumphant Romans. D.H.
Lawrence came in search of *Etruscan Places,* his loving tale about the Etruscans he loved—destroyed, he felt, by the crude Romans. Both men were captivated by the Etruscans, but they came with different assumptions and left
with disparate idealistic convictions.

Like all Etruscan towns, Cerveteri—or Caere, as it was called then—sat on
a craggy hill overlooking a valley and the sea beyond. The volcanic rock, or
tufa, wall surrounding the village was now nearly smothered by trees and
vines growing up the escarpment from the ravine below. Three major volcanic
actions had loosened and split the tufa walls and the tumuli—domed structures that housed multiple tombs—beyond. Partially buried under these natural concealments were ancient carved lions, horses, birds, and the tools used
to make them. A citadel rose above the wall, created in the classic design that
has marked the Italian landscape for 2,500 years.

During the Middle Ages, a huge iron gate secured the wall. As centuries
passed, the gate opened and the town welcomed visitors—although few came.
Even today, at the tourist bureau, no one spoke English. Shop owners seemed
surprised by other languages, and residents watched outsiders with curiosity,
even though UNESCO promoted the Necropolis of the Banditaccia of

Cerveteri as the "patrimony of humanity, an exceptional testimonial to the Etruscan civilization."

Having spent the night in Viterbo, two hours to the northeast, Justine drove up the sharp incline to the ancient town appreciating the late March warmth. She parked her sapphire 2004 Alfa Romeo Spider across from Santa Maria Maggiore Church. She stood for a moment, examining the city map. She walked north across the bridge leading up to the Piazza Risorgimento. A Renaissance clock tower rose on the west end. To the left, a restaurant glowing pink and yellow in the morning light, matching turret and potted trees surrounding outdoor tables and umbrellas, which protruded into the square. An adjacent pharmacy and a vegetable market shared an edifice painted with elaborate murals of medieval life. A contrasting, stern gray government building towered over the piazza's south side; Justine wondered if it still hosted dungeons and guillotines.

She had agreed to meet her father at one of the tables under the clock tower, an imaginative structure of marble and bricks with double pillars that felt reminiscent of Disneyland. A coat of arms boasted a wide-antlered buck.

A young woman emerged from the corner café and took Justine's order for two double cappuccinos.

❧

"Love those boots," she said as her father approached. "Cappuccino?"

"You always know what I like," said Morgan, sitting down and flinging one leg over his knee so she could get a closer look at the boots. "Had them made in Cuzco."

"Are we going out to the dig this morning?" she asked, running her palm over the polished buckskin surface. "These won't look so new in a couple of hours."

"They clean up easily enough," he said, brushing a slight residue of dust from the toes. "But let me fill you in before we head out. Yesterday big equipment was brought in to dig ten feet down around two of the tumuli identified as interesting by aerial photos. So . . . we might be able to get into the troughs today."

"What made the photos interesting?"

"Formations deep under the tumuli. They look like geometrical designs. But I've been fooled before. From the air, ordinary rock can form outlines that look man-made."

"I love being in on the beginning of a mystery . . . what do you expect to find?" She moved her chair slightly to avoid the direct sun and took off her sunglasses. Her amber eyes glistened.

"Probably not much." Morgan was forever understating his excitement. "The tombs there already stretch over four centuries. Caere was an active community in the ninth century BCE and 200 years later it dominated the Tyrranean coast, including the Tolfa Mountains and Lake Bracciano, which you would have passed yesterday coming into Viterbo. But I'm hoping for a few surprises. Perhaps the tomb of an Etruscan king." He laughed.

"I didn't think you liked surprises." She was incredulous.

"Only in archaeology, honey." He grinned, finishing off his cappuccino, picking up his clipboard, and pushing back his chair.

They rode in his jeep to the necropolis five miles away. Sycamore, oak, and cypress created a canopy over the road into grounds adorned by white narcissus and salmon and ivory lilies, once known as asphodel. Persephone, the daughter of Zeus, had claimed the asphodel lily as her own during the half of her life she could spend on Earth. Abducted by Hades, she was condemned to spend the other half in his underworld. Justine compared the fable to her own life. *Maybe Egypt was my underworld. I was smothered in an earthquake, run off the road, kidnapped, and kicked out of the country. But there were exquisite moments as well. Amir . . .*

Morgan parked the Jeep near the miniature train and tourist center. They walked through the public area. Mounds of verdant earth ran wild with dandelions and green brambles. A door on each side of the tumuli led to two separate tombs. The tumuli themselves rested on four-foot-high stone foundations crusty with lichen and fungi. Set about twenty feet apart on either side of a common walkway, they fashioned a comely neighborhood. No other necropolis in Italy lived so lightly on the land.

At the end of the path they stepped over a low-lying fence and approached two tumuli whose foundations were ringed by a deep trench.

"Olives were actually found in this one," a young man was saying as he stepped out of a nearby tomb. "That's why it's called the Tomb of the Olives. *Furbo*, clever." He held out his hand, stepped forward, and took Justine's hand into his. "Riccardo," he said.

"Riccardo Chia, our historian," offered her father, by way of further introduction. He dug the toe of his boot into the earth.

Justine read her father's fidgeting as contempt. "Delighted to meet you," she said. "I'm always eager to meet a historian. So tell me, how difficult is it to work with my father?"

Riccardo blanched, but quickly recovered. "He's son of a bitch," he said in broken English. An open khaki shirt revealed a chest of dark brown hair and a small scar near his trachea. A careless ponytail rested on his shoulder like a squirrel's tail. His eyes were a little too

close together, and that and his scraggly eyebrows, almost touching, gave him a look of intense concentration. Two days' growth obscured his narrow chin. "But I expect to learn an enormous amount from Dr. Jenner." He shifted his feet like a boy who has overstepped his authority.

Another charmer, she thought. *If rather odd-looking.*

Her father touched the rim of his hat and raised his left eyebrow, obviously uncomfortable with Riccardo's portrayal of him.

"And what is it you're hoping to learn from this dig, Riccardo?" Justine asked.

"In the best world, God willing, we find a house with scrolls of poetry and a few plays. But I'm dreaming, since no literature remains—burned by early Christians, mostly. And only a couple of Etruscan towns have been found."

"Riccardo's a romantic," said Morgan. "Typical historian . . ." he muttered.

"Why do you think that is, Riccardo?" Justine asked, raising her voice to drown out her father's rudeness. "That so few verified Etruscan towns have been found?"

"Most of the buildings were made out of wood so didn't survive. Probably destroyed by fire or dry-rot. Later generations probably used the wood for cooking fires as well. But tombs tell us a great deal about what the homes probably looked like. Come on, I'll show you." Riccardo led Justine back over the low-lying fence and toward a nearby tumulus. Her father reluctantly followed.

Riccardo led them into the Tomb of the Shields and Chairs, its large vestibule adorned with intricately carved shields. Chiseled from the rear wall, funeral beds of stone that once held sarcophagi. Nearby, two chairs with footrests gave the enclosure the homey appearance of a bedroom. "Look up," Riccardo pointed. "This painting of a home with a thatched roof supported by capitals and columns tells us something about how they lived. And, think about it, this tomb was built more than 2,700 years ago. Notice these tools for everyday use sketched here and on many of the other tombs. Clearly, they thought they stayed here for a while before traveling on to the afterlife. So they brought along what they needed for daily life."

Justine noticed the carving of an ornate mirror as well, and an arched comb with small, graduated teeth. *Clearly women were expected to continue their beauty regimens in the hereafter.* She grinned to herself, then pointed to the finds.

"Speculation," grunted Morgan. "There are conflicting theories about how they viewed the afterlife. I can't imagine that vanity held sway."

"Many theories," confirmed Riccardo, unruffled. "I'm drawn to D.H. Lawrence's . . ."

"The biggest romantic of them all," interrupted Morgan. "He didn't know a thing about the Etruscans. A novelist," he added dismissively.

"Why don't you come to dinner this weekend and tell us about Lawrence and the afterlife?" Justine extended the invitation without looking at her father. "A friend of mine from Paris is coming in."

"Love to," Riccardo nodded, the morning light streaming in, dancing dust particles alive in the air. "I'm sure Dr. Jenner will tell me how to get there."

Morgan turned away and walked into another chamber.

"Perhaps you can ride together," she suggested, turning to climb back out into the full sunlight. *Maybe they can get to know each other a little better.*

Justine following, Morgan led toward the newly ploughed trough and scrambled down a small wooden ladder. Justine followed. Riccardo returned to his work site. Father and daughter sat yoga-style on the damp earth. Morgan removed his gloves and ran his hands over the newly cut earthen wall as though it were a thoroughbred. "This is the moment I love," he said. "Virgin soil hiding her treasures like Michelangelo's marble."

Justine watched her father with fresh insight. "You're a poet," she charged.

"In some ways," he admitted. "When I'm close to the treasures of history, I try to seduce them into releasing their secrets." He continued to run his palms over the dark earthen wall with witching sensitivity.

"If you seek the treasures of history, why do you give historians like Riccardo such a bad time? Aren't you after the same thing?" Justine's hand followed the motions of her father's, searching for the sense of mystery he felt.

"Not at all. Riccardo would connect finds together and create a story. The story may or may not be true. What we can infer today may not be how people thought back then. For me, each artifact can have value in and of itself. Then I look for patterns. If I find enough artifacts of the same expression, of the same utility, I know it was in routine use. If I find a piece of technology, I know the level of progress of the civilization. There is a valid history of technology, although sometimes even that can be misleading."

"Such as?" She brushed her hands together to loosen the clinging soil, then wiped them on her pants.

"Well, for instance, the indigenous Americans used rounded objects to grind corn and make pottery, yet they never invented the wheel for transport. Amazing."

"Amazing indeed." She nodded. "Which led to a number of misinterpretations of native uses of technology . . . Regardless of some faulty assumptions, though, wouldn't you say that some histories are defensible?" In spite of the heat, the damp ground soaked through her khakis and chilled her.

"Defensible histories that are straightforward, linear, that use the pieces of knowledge necessary to achieve the next level of advancement, yes. But not quixotic histories that speculate on human motives and emotions. Too subjective for me."

"Psychological profiles are important to anthropologists. Otherwise, we couldn't reason out the stories of civilization, understand human motivation. Perhaps there's a niche for me there." She shifted from side to side to loosen her slacks from the grasping earth.

"The female brain is hardwired for such endeavors. I'm not." Morgan was unaffected by the growing dampness. He was in his element.

"Let me see if I get this straight: I'm an unrealistic girl who goes around with her head in a cloud wearing rose-colored glasses."

"Something like that." He tipped his hat playfully.

She stood abruptly, brushed herself off, and climbed the ladder. "I'm walking back," she called down from above. *Should I even consider working with him? He insists on such unimaginative thinking.*

"I had more to show you, Justine. Don't be angry. I was just playing with you." He climbed the ladder two steps at a time, walking rapidly after her, unable to catch up.

As she emerged from the tree canopy into the heat of the day, her scalp began to sweat. The walk back into town didn't soothe her frustration with her father's chauvinism. He was either dismissing her work or trying to get her goat. Testing her all the time. She knew he was kidding, but it got tiresome.

Justine opened her car trunk, threw in her jacket, changed out of her boots, grabbed her purse, and brushed the dried mud off her slacks. She headed toward the east side of Cerveteri and a gray stone castle that housed the Etruscan museum.

A small sign indicated the entry through a ground-floor archway underneath the ramparts. She handed three euros to a young woman in a glass booth and stepped inside. An incline led to the upper ramparts and wound into a parapet and eventually a turret with barred windows. Crevices from missing stones offered homes to dozens of pigeons.

In the darkened room, strategically placed lights beamed down on sarcophagi, pottery, tools, and delicate votive offerings behind glass walls. Light streamed in through the barred window onto ancient carved metal mirrors, one decorated with the Etruscan god Tinia, known in Greece as Zeus, holding a feather umbrella and touching the gown of a maiden wearing rose- and disc-shaped earrings and bracelets of gold filigree and granulated crystals. Long rows of perky ducks walked across brooches and fibula. Fingers of light caressed black Bucchero pottery scattered about, designed to serve both utilitarian and decorative function; amphora and drinking cups dedicated to the Etruscan god Fufluns; vases and funeral urns engraved with the names of men and women. Bronze tableware, bowls and pitchers, ladles and strainers. Halfway down the room she came upon a terra cotta sarcophagus that drew her attention with such intensity that chills moved up her bare arms. She stood mesmerized for several moments by the mystery of this scene of profound union. A man and a woman lounged in each other's arms on stone pillows, legs extending the full length of a royal bed. He was naked above the waist; she wore a tunic and long braids. His right hand rested tenderly on her shoulder, the forefinger of his hand extended as though pointing toward something they were viewing together through peaceful, yet lively, almond eyes. His left palm remained open as though it had once held a treasured offering of his love. *The intimacy of this poised couple makes me feel like an intruder in an ancient boudoir.* Behind the sarcophagus were four framed drawings of the floor plan and sketches of the inside of the tomb in which the sarcophagus was found. This Sarcophagus of the Married Couple from the necropolis nearby had been dated to the second half of the sixth century BCE.

She turned around slowly, riveted by a growing consciousness of the story around her. She stared again at the images of men and women on the mirrors and black pottery, some etched with names for both partners, at amphora with dancing partners regarding each other without guile or modesty. She swirled, seeing the room with new lenses, her eyes the shutters of a fast-firing camera. Men and women were in conversation, touching, relaxing together, a natural part of each other's world. The men assumed no dominance or superiority—no semblance of diffidence or timidity defined the women. The room came alive with the communal existence of humans on a shared journey. If any moment in time can bring an awareness powerful enough to inform everything that comes after, this was such a moment for Justine. Her eyes narrowed, her long fingers formed into a tent that she drew in wonder to her lips. *A goddess culture, this extraordinary civilization began as a goddess culture!* She felt with great avouchment that she understood the relationship between men and women in Etruria.

CHAPTER 4

—∞∞∞—

"Unrequited love is the only possible way to give yourself to another without being held in indentured servitude."

—Bauvard, Some Inspiration for the Overenthusiastic

HER HEAD STILL SPINNING from the museum visit, Justine parked her Spider in front of Chez Anna and checked in. She climbed the stairs to her room, threw open the shutters, and gazed out on the valley below, the sea beyond. Her mind floated back to the carved mirror in the ceiling of the tomb, the married couple in a warm, respectful relationship on the sarcophagus lid in the museum. Riveting images of men and women together . . . what did she know now?

The iron four-poster bed, covered with a white quilted coverlet, coaxed her to take off her shoes and dirt-encrusted khakis and relax with her latest purchase—D.H. Lawrence's *Virgin and the Gypsy*, a quick read that the author had written for his stepdaughter, Barbara. She was again surprised by Lawrence's ability to write with such sensuality without explicitly describing sexual consummation (until Lady Chatterley, that is):

> . . . And through his body, wrapped round her strange and lithe and powerful, like tentacles, rippled with shuddering as an electric current, still the rigid tension of the muscles that held her clenched steadied them both, and gradually the sickening violence of the shuddering, caused by shock, abated, in his body first, then in hers, and the warmth revived between them. And as it roused, their tortured semi-conscious minds became unconscious, they passed away into sleep.

An hour later, Justine was awakened by a cool air drifting in from the sea. Stretching and shivering, she took a warm shower and dressed in a white silk blouse and clean khaki slacks. She was ready for dinner with her father.

⚮

It was a short walk back down a narrow street, hugged by fourteenth-century stone houses, to the fish restaurant Morgan had suggested. The theatrical owner and chef came from Napoli, and therefore was immediately held suspect by locals. The Ristorante Vladimiro ai Bastioni boasted the best Napolitano seafood outside of Rome . . . and Napoli, of course. Two diners at the table in the intimate room. One was her apprehensive father.

"Good evening, Dad," she said in a lighthearted tone. "I see you've started on our bottle of wine."

The other man turned toward her. She gasped. "Oh . . . Amir! What a surprise! I didn't know you were here." Her voice sounded slightly accusatory.

Morgan looked puzzled.

Amir met Justine's questioning stare. "Do you think I'm following you?"

Justine blushed. "It entered my mind."

"Whoa! Hold on here!" Morgan nearly shouted. "If I'd thought there was something between you two, I'd never have hired Amir without talking with you, Justine."

"There is nothing between us." Justine's voice was confident.

Amir looked wounded. He turned toward the mustard stucco walls, dotted with framed photos and commendations to the owner as a much younger man. "Quite an array of accomplishments," he noted, and picked up his wine. "Your father's offering me a job. Archaeologist on the new dig."

Morgan glanced at each of his guests, one at a time. He squinted. "You do know that I've known this young man since he was a mere whippersnapper."

"Of course, Dad. I was just caught off guard."

"Now for the wine. A little celebration," Morgan said. "Mastroberardino *Lacryma Christi del Vesuvio Bianco*, tears of the Christ. I thought it apropos. Made from the *Coda di Volpe*, tail of the fox, to be exact." He poured them each a glass. "Did you get some rest?" he asked, cautious with his daughter.

"I couldn't rest until I went to the museum. Remarkable!"

"How so?" asked Amir.

"I visited it on my first day in town," Morgan interrupted. "Impressive structure, but not much of a museum. At least, it doesn't live up to the reputation of the necropolis itself." He sipped his wine, watching them closely over the rim of his glass.

"You asked why I found it remarkable, Amir," she said, ignoring her father. "I found it not only informative but moving. Particularly the Sarcophagus of the Married Couple. There seemed to be such an equal, respectful relationship among Etruscan men and women." Picking up her wine glass, she held it suspended in her right hand until she concluded her impassioned description, then she took her first sip.

Amir nodded, captivated by her passion.

"You read too much into things, honey," said Morgan. A flicker of regret moved through his eyes.

"Perhaps you're right." Her comment surprised both of them. Morgan relaxed into a familiar grin. He didn't anticipate what was coming.

"Women are gifted with intuitive powers denied to men. Perhaps men are just defective women." She saluted the two men with her glass, winked, and suggested that they order.

Amir laughed wholly, a laugh that Justine loved, and looked around for the menu.

"So true, Justine. So true." Morgan also laughed with unrestrained fullness. "We don't order here. Giuseppe tells us what we want to eat." He motioned to the owner, who walked toward the table, his majestic stride practiced for a more abundant audience. "What delightful dishes do you have for us tonight, my friend?" Morgan had become a regular patron, one who was treated with the reverence of family.

"*Calamari Ripieni* and *Pescespado o Tonno Alla Stemperata, signore.* Giuseppe's best. Only for you." He clustered his chubby fingers into a bud and pressed them to his pursed lips. His smile stretched from cheek to cheek.

"Squid and tuna?" Justine asked, turning toward her father.

"Tonight, no tuna. Swordfish, my lovely *signorina*. Calamari stuffed with pecorino and prosciutto," Giuseppe said in his rich Genoan accent. "And who is this beauty with you tonight, *signore*?"

"Ah, forgive me. Meet my daughter, Justine." Giuseppe bowed deeply and kissed Justine's hand. His gallantry charmed her. "And, this young man is my colleague, Amir El Shabry."

Amir smiled and bowed slightly.

"Everything sounds wonderful," Justine assured him, flashing her most beguiling smile.

The chef came to stand next to Giuseppe. "My friend here prepares the swordfish with olives and raisins and capers. Delicious," said her father. The rotund chef hurried back to his open kitchen.

Two hours later, compliments about the glorious seafood paid, the three of them exhausted from speculating about the work to come in Cerveteri, the evening was winding down. With the second bottle of wine, tensions had relaxed and the three had become playful, recalling the years Morgan had taken Lucrezia and Justine with him on dig assignments in Egypt. Amir had tagged along, fascinated by Justine's buoyant crinoline skirts, at children's parties at his family home in Cairo. Morgan's partner and mentor, Amir's grandfather, Ibrahim El Shabry, had brought the families together on festive occasions. Being Egyptian, Lucrezia had forever been the guide and the star of any occasion.

Justine watched Amir closely as he picked at his dinner. Both Justine and her father knew that Egyptians tended to shy away from exotic cuisine. She had almost forgotten how handsome he was with his rumpled, curly black hair and piercing dark eyes. So sensual, so sexy.

"I'll walk you back to Anna's. That's where you're staying—right?" asked Amir.

"Thank you, Amir. Dad—you coming?"

"I'll nurse my brandy." Morgan pointed to the owner. "Giuseppe and I have some lies to exchange."

"Why did you say there was nothing between us?" Amir asked as they turned the corner and started west down the narrow, darkened street. "We've been through a lot together. How about the kidnapping? Finding the Virgin Mary's comb? My brother's death?"

Justine shivered. He was right. They had been through a great deal together. Perhaps she didn't want her father to know how intertwined they really were. They had desired one another, but refused to act on those feelings. Besides, she knew she wasn't entirely over her affair with her betraying Egyptian lover, Nasser. Her father had been pressuring her on the details. "I know, you're right, Amir. I'm sorry. But why didn't you tell me you were coming? Going to be working with Dad? You have my e-mail."

Amir took a deep breath. They had arrived in front of Anna's. "I'd like to come up for a few minutes. At least try to resolve some misconceptions."

Justine let the comment pass. She opened the outside door with her key and started up the stairs. Amir followed. The door to her room was unlocked. Inside, she turned to face him. "So, what's the story here?"

"I assumed your father would tell you—and, frankly, as you said at dinner, I feared you'd think I was following you."

"Were you?" she challenged.

"Justine, you know I've wanted to get back into the field for a long time . . . but there is some truth in your hunch. I did want to be nearer to you." He stepped closer, moonlight catching the side of her face, her white blouse.

"So you relied upon my father to be the intermediary? To inform me of your intentions?" Her voice rose, eyes flashing. She reached over and turned on the table lamp. "I think you know I don't like being treated like a little girl, especially when my father is concerned. Please don't communicate with me through him."

Amir looked confused, miserable, angry. "Why are you overreacting like this? I thought you'd be glad to see me!" He grabbed her by the shoulders. Their fiery eyes met, and held. Her body stiffened—then, breathing deeply, relaxed.

She let her head drop onto his chest. He softened his grip, wrapped his arms around her, holding her, and both began weeping, exhausted by the old desire that now seized them. They began breathing together, the near panting that marked longing. Finally, he raised her chin to meet his and kissed her tenderly, the embrace long, delicious, leading to hunger, then to demand. Shivering, she pushed him back, enveloping him with her eyes. He was handsome, sensual beyond belief. Slowly she began to unbutton her blouse.

He took her in his arms, spun her back toward the bed and let them both fall, press into her quilt. He kissed her with near desperation, born of unrequited obsession.

She held him tightly as they embraced, her legs wrapped around him now, and rolled on the bed. They slowed as they flourished in each other's bodies, exploring with touch, caressing, finding the heat of buried passion. Shadows danced across the walls, then stilled. No words were spoken before they fell into a deep sleep.

CHAPTER 5

Do you know how it feels to want something you think you can't have; Or to awake in the morning only to find the day does not belong to you?

—L.S. McFadden

JUSTINE SPED NORTH from highway A1 across Florence toward San Domenici. It was another one of those glorious days, morning mist clinging to the cypress like billowing skirts. Turning the convertible onto Via Giuseppe Mantellini, she ascended the main road climbing up to Fiesole. The vibrant and abundant foliage reminded her of the Nile Delta in early summer. Her body shuddered as she recalled making love with Amir the night before. She was a little embarrassed by her initial immature behavior. She had left Cerveteri early, sneaking out before either Amir or her father were awake. What would it be like now to work with her father—and Amir? Last night she'd had a long, satisfying evening with both of the men in her life. Now it might be difficult to face Amir when they both came to dinner tonight.

At Largo Leonardo Da Vinci, just below Villa San Michele, Justine squinted into the sun and turned onto Via Maiano, a narrow street hugged by ten-foot-high stone walls. A left turn into the third driveway with its towering cypresses brought her to the winding road that led home, up to Villa Cellini. Before she could turn off the motor, Prego opened her door.

"Good morning, *signorina.* Your friend here. Come in last night. *Prego,*" he said, reaching for her small suitcase.

"*Grazie,* Prego. Is my mother home also?"

"In the garden, *signorina.*"

"Andrea!" Justine cried out as she burst through the door, dragging her bag. She had not seen Andrea since their meeting at the Cairo Marriott the previous fall. Andrea was the visiting professor of linguistics at the American University in Cairo whom Ibrahim had drawn into translating the codex. Justine had been surprised to learn that Andrea had known Lucrezia for many years and had occasionally co-hosted salons with her in Paris and Fiesole.

"Justine!" Andrea walked out of the breakfast room, still in her lavender dressing gown. Even without makeup she looked much younger than her forty-eight years. She often reminded Justine of the French actress Juliette Binoche with her high forehead, over which she had taken to wearing half bangs, which complimented her pronounced cheekbones and impish grin. Andrea's father had sculpted her when she was a teenager, but both of her parents had died in a car accident before she was out of secondary school.

"How did you get here so quickly? Never mind. It's wonderful to see you. You look like a real anthropologist in those khakis. Just great." She pulled Justine to her and kissed her profusely on both cheeks, then held her at arm's length, her chocolate brown eyes twinkling.

Justine hugged her fiercely in return. "So what's new, my friend?" she asked as she leisurely removed her boots and wiggled her toes. "Have you fallen in love? Translated more secret diaries? Been followed by cloaked villains?"

"*Touché*, my beautiful friend. Your mother and I caught up on our secrets last night, I am now ready to hear yours." Andrea folded the length of her dressing gown between her white legs before sitting down. "You were with your dad in Cerveteri?"

"I was. He's back from Peru and is part of a new UNESCO team searching for Etruscan ruins. He and another member of the team will be joining us for dinner tonight. Also, to my surprise, Amir is here, as Dad's new archaeologist."

"You mean that dashing, sexy man with the curly hair and flashing black eyes? Ibrahim's grandson? I could eat him up," said Andrea.

Justine blushed. "The very one," she said flatly, turning toward the stairs.

Andrea stared at her but changed tack. "Well . . . that gives us the day together—I've so many questions. And a few ideas."

Whatever you know, I'm bound not to hear all of it at once, thought Justine with affection. Andrea revealed information slowly, a habit that had driven Justine crazy until she'd taught herself to tolerate the power play as an affectation. "I'll change and meet you in the garden. Mom will want to be part of this conversation."

Once back, in black linen shorts, a white cotton shirt, and carrying her buckskin sandals, Justine moved gingerly down the stepping-stones into the garden. Her damp hair corkscrewed into ringlets around her face. In the small patch of lush grass halfway down the garden, Andrea stood talking with Lucrezia, who was on her knees weeding a patch of herbs: oregano, winter savory, sage, and chives.

"Put on your sandals, my dear. You know bare feet are scandalous in Italy," cautioned her mother without looking up. Lucrezia seemed consumed by her renegade herbs.

"I have trouble following rules that I don't understand." Nonetheless, she sat down on a stone and slipped into her sandals. "This is nonsense."

Her mother ignored her.

"Justine, the independent woman," Andrea teased, ignoring the frowns from both women. She changed the subject. "All right. I want to know what was in that little brown package you left Cairo with. Either answer will be scandalous." She grinned and leaned back in the garden chair, drinking in the warmth, her pale blue blouse falling in folds around her. "Paris is still dreary this time of year."

Lucrezia raised an eyebrow and turned to Justine. "What is she talking about?"

"You already know the answer. The day before I left Cairo, Amir brought me a package from Ibrahim. By the way, Mom, Amir is here. He'll probably join us tonight for dinner. I didn't know until I landed in Florence what was in the package. Was it the actual codex, or a copy?"

Lucrezia relaxed; she knew the answer.

Andrea fidgeted with impatience. "And??"

"I'm afraid it's a copy—but a good copy. Fortunately, it had been almost entirely translated, so it gives us much to work with for our requested article for *Archaeology*. Did you bring the translations? Hopefully we'll find time to write while you're here."

"I don't see why not—although I only brought one file of the translations. I thought we'd start when Mary was yet a young girl."

"I'm going to need a copy of those translations, Andrea. I'm certainly not a linguist, so having the copy in and of itself will do me little good."

"I realize that, Justine," Andrea said, lifting her hand in a mock salute. "Those pages should give us a good start, and I do have to go to Rome for a few days."

"I'll come with you. Dad expects me to work with him, but we haven't found a slot for me yet—and Cerveteri is close by."

"But you'll be here for dinner tonight?" Lucrezia interrupted, waving a small spade in her gloved hand.

"*Absolutement!*" exclaimed Andrea, as though it was the only thought worth harboring.

Prego moved unsteadily down the stepping-stones, balancing a tray with three cups of tea. "Prego," said Lucrezia sharply, "you must let Maria do that. I don't want you breaking your neck . . . or my good china." Before she could stand, Justine stepped in front of her to take the tray from Prego and kiss him softly on the cheek.

Andrea paid no attention to the tea drama. "If we had the original codex," she said, "we'd be able to digitize it, which would make it much easier to read. Stanford has a Synchrotron Radiation Lab X-ray scanner that can strike ink on parchment or papyrus and cause certain elements in the ink to glow. These detectors pick up each element's distinctive wavelength of fluorescence and a computer converts the data into images. Isn't that amazing?"

"Doesn't the fluorescent glow come from the iron in ink?" asked Lucrezia, brushing dirt off her knees to attend to the tea. "I don't think Mary's ink could have contained iron, since such technology wasn't in use until about 700."

"Very astute," acknowledged Justine. "But isn't such X-ray action needed only if the ink has been scraped off and the paper reused? In this case, the equipment might show us the original text closer to the way it was written, imaging the missing formations, completing the words, so to speak, like bringing the binary code of computer language into full formation." She said casually, thinking it through and adding a squeeze of lemon to her tea as she spoke, "I hate to dampen your enthusiasm, but this is just not to be, Andrea. At least for now."

Andrea nodded and added two lumps of sugar to her tea before looking up at the scrutinizing stares of her friends. "I like sweet things," she said defensively. "I know. I know. We'll get the original back one of these days, perhaps sooner than you think," she said, rather mysteriously, not looking them in the eye.

"You seem uncharacteristically optimistic," said Justine, narrowing her eyebrows while balancing her teacup on her knee. "I'd like to reread the few translations you brought before we start writing."

Andrea ran both hands under her long, dark hair, lifting it off her neck. "It's beginning to get very warm." Then, as though reading Justine's mind, she said guardedly, "It's not as though I'm unaware of my secretive tendencies, dear friends. But my suspicions can be quite useful. A strength, really."

Justine rolled her eyes and grinned. She knew Andrea only too well. At least, she thought so.

Lucrezia laughed fully. "The heat will soon be unrelenting, too intense to sit out here without an umbrella," said Lucrezia, ignoring Andrea's confession. "But spring weather in Northern Italy is so unpredictable. Hot one day, cool the next." Soon she was back on her knees, digging among the savory. "How long can you stay?"

"A week—perhaps longer, if things get interesting."

"And you must be Morgan," said Andrea, stepping forward to take his hand in both of hers. She had dressed in her favorite traveling outfit, a red linen suit with matching heels. She stared into his deep blue eyes with unguarded curiosity. Morgan blinked.

It was evening now, and family and guests had gathered for dinner. A ribbon of tangerine trimmed the horizon, buffering the deep purple sky. Amir had not accompanied Morgan and Riccardo. Justine was disappointed, hurt. *Does he regret last night? Or . . . ?*

The still-humid air flowing through the French doors warmed Andrea's jacket, which she slowly removed to reveal an almost sheer white camisole. The sweet scent of lilacs and honeysuckle arose from the garden, blending with the garlicky aromas of roasting wild boar.

Justine paused momentarily in the doorway, watching her father and Andrea, a gentle evening breeze claiming the tender chiffon of her mauve dress. She noticed the slight flush at her father's temples and was amused to realize that Andrea had rendered him speechless. She had seen her mother accomplish this feat a few times, but Lucrezia was not in the room at the moment to enjoy the rare occurrence. She walked in just as Morgan spoke.

"May I get you a drink?" Morgan managed to say, assuming the role of host. He busied himself, trying to regain his composure. "And Riccardo," he said, turning toward his neglected guest. "What can I get you? Sorry. Creta. Andrea. This is my colleague Riccardo Chia, a member of our team."

Riccardo stepped forward and shook hands with the two women. His dark hair was tidily pulled back into his signature ponytail, which fell stylishly over his black linen shirt. His easy smile revealed near-perfect teeth, yet did not improve on his rather odd expression, his tight-set eyes, or his shelf of undomesticated brows.

"Campari and soda for me," Andrea said, walking to the buffet bar to assist Morgan. She stood close, her smooth arms feeling cool against his arm, beneath a thin cotton shirt.

"I'll have the same," echoed Riccardo, realizing that no one was listening.

"I've heard so much about you from Creta and Justine," Andrea said, turning to face Morgan. "I must say, you exceed my expectations."

"How so?" he asked with a dry mouth. He expected to be embarrassed by whatever answer was forthcoming. And he was right.

"I expected the tanned, dashing archaeologist, but you're somewhat more handsome. A little taller. More hair."

"I'm glad I don't disappoint," he said, sighing deeply, as though his breath had been arrested by alarm, and raising his glass to toast his palpable relief.

"Not at all." Andrea smiled at him as she turned and walked toward the historian. "Tell me, Riccardo, are you part of the renowned Chia family of vintners?"

From across the room, Justine noted that her father stared at Andrea as though he'd been left standing naked. She walked toward him, brushed his cheek with her fingers, then turned and poured herself a glass of champagne.

Morgan put his arm around his daughter's shoulders and hugged her lightly. "This was your idea, honey."

Justine wondered just what he meant by that. She watched him walk across the room to join Andrea and Riccardo. *My idea? Is he talking about Riccardo . . . or Andrea?*

"Exactly," Riccardo said, answering Andrea, pleased at the attention. "Are you familiar with our wines? We've been making Brunello at Castello Romitorio for more than two decades."

"Has your family been affected by the recent scandals about doctored wine and olive oils?" asked Morgan, joining Andrea and Riccardo. He had not been pleased that Justine had invited Riccardo for the weekend, nor that they had been forced to ride together. Not that he had anything against the young man. Decent sort for a historian, he'd told himself.

"Not directly, although in Italy you're guilty until proven innocent. With our slow justice system, by the time you're exonerated, you're out of business."

"I'm sorry to hear that," said Andrea, her brown eyes on Morgan suggesting that she was wondering why he brought up the scandals. "Your wines are excellent. Surely this will blow over."

"It is difficult to see wine written about in the way you'd write about terrorism. Even in *The New York Times*," Riccardo said, his voice intense, his accent becoming more pronounced. His hand tightened around his glass of Campari. "Not in tune with our world. Italy is a land of subtleties and innuendo. Fortunately, I have a day job."

"Dinner is served," Maria announced from the hallway. Lucrezia motioned everyone to a chair. She and Justine were on either end of the redwood table, Riccardo and Andrea together on one side and Morgan alone on the opposite side. Candles and a chandelier lighted the room, over which presided *The Woman with Long Hair*, Picasso's painting of Justine's grandmother.

"Will you do the honors, Morgan?" Lucrezia handed him a bottle of Tommasi Classico '98. She had forsaken white linen this evening for a delicate black silk with wrists trimmed in miniature black satin roses. Small emerald earrings, the color of her eyes, shone when she turned toward her ex-husband.

"Not a bad wine for a competitor," grinned Riccardo. "Women call it earthy."

"And men call it complex," added Morgan, offering Andrea the first taste. She held the wine in her mouth for several moments before swallowing, her cheeks closing in under her high cheekbones. "Lingering sweet cherry," she said, drawing out the words, then licking the corner of her mouth with the tip of her tongue. She nodded her approval.

"The Etruscans may have been the first to make wine," Riccardo said after he'd swirled the liquid around in his mouth. "The vines . . . they were over thirty feet high, some of them climbing up into trees. At that height, they could catch sea breezes."

"What is this I hear about an Etruscan appellation near Naples?" asked Lucrezia. "Do you know anything about that, Riccardo?" She and Riccardo had met when he and Morgan arrived, before they dressed for dinner. She found him unassuming and warm, a man who would not bend easily to her ex-husband's expectations.

"I think you mean Asprinio di Aversa, one of the world's smallest and most obscure appellations. They've planted less than 150 acres," answered Riccardo, continuing to savor the Tommasi. "Nearly 2,000 years ago, Pliny the Elder wrote about the wine. As I recall, it went something like this: 'The vines espouse the poplars and, embracing their brides and climbing with wanton arms in a series of knots among their branches, rise level with their tops, soaring aloft to such a height that a hired picker stipulates in his contract for the cost of a funeral and a grave!'"

"Bravo!" exclaimed Andrea. "Bravo. Very sensual."

Morgan was uncharacteristically quiet, watching the wine swirl in his glass as he turned it slowly by the stem. "Pliny the Elder wrote extensively of the Etruscans in *Naturalis Historia*," he said casually, still twirling his wine. "I've been most impressed by his observations on Etruscan hydrology. He pointed out that the system they built under Rome was perhaps the most stupendous of all, 'as mountains had to be pierced for their construction.'"

"And the Tarquinians built the canals through Capitoline and Palatine hills wide enough for wagons full of hay to drive through," added

Lucrezia, her hand gently turning her single-strand emerald bracelet like a wagon wheel.

Maria set down the first course, a *nudi gnocchi*—Morgan first, as usual. She paused, drew her cheeks into an embracing smile, and straightened her slightly frayed white apron before returning to the kitchen.

"Tarquinius, from Etruria, was the first king of Rome. It was during his reign when much of the historic city was established," said Riccardo, watching the new pasta dish make its way down the table. "The low-lying marshland was unbuildable before Etruscan hydrology drained the area. Today, this master plan is attributed to the Romans and taken for granted."

"I hear that Chuisi is also a remarkable achievement. Is that right, Riccardo? Have you seen the underground water system there?" Justine pushed her hair behind her ear, the delicate gold filigree Etruscan earrings she'd purchased in Volterra catching the light.

"*Si, signorina,*" said Riccardo. "I've been there . . ."

"The three-tiered tunnel complex once provided drinking water as well as sewer drainage to Chuisi," Morgan interrupted, finishing off his gnocchi. "Great gnocchi, Maria," he called toward the kitchen. Turning back to the other guests, he added, "But the Chuisi water system fell into disuse after the Romans conquered the town."

"First, King Porsenna of Chuisi defeated the Romans," Riccardo went on, nonplussed by Morgan's interruptions. "He should have destroyed them right then and there instead of returning to his throne. Anyway, now the complex under the city has been reclaimed. You can go down into the bowels of the hill and view the well and the canals. Dozens of sarcophagi!" He was either oblivious to the tightening muscles around Morgan's mouth or choosing to disregard his nemesis's competition. Morgan appeared to find competition with an underling tiresome.

Justine watched Riccardo with fascination. *What an unpretentious man*, she thought. *He's himself, even when he ruffles Dad's feathers. I like his courage.*

Riccardo would have been surprised by Justine's thoughts. He didn't think of himself as courageous; he saw himself as an ordinary man who took life in stride, a practice he'd learned from his father, a successful man with few pretensions. And as for Morgan, he'd realized by the second day on the site that his boss couldn't be pleased. Eagerly watching Maria enter with a platter of steaming roasted boar wreathed by onions and baby carrots, he quickly scraped his pasta plate to make room for this succulent second course.

"What's this?" Andrea asked suspiciously.

"*Cinghiale*. Boar, my dear," answered Lucrezia, forking a generous amount onto her plate, making sure that the carrots didn't touch the boar. So Italian.

"Maria's *cinghiale* is the envy of local chefs," Morgan assured the guests, and he smiled at Maria, who bowed and blushed.

The diners ate in silence for some time, eagerly devouring the tender game, the sweet and savory roasted carrots and onions. Small side conversations consumed the table. Justine leaned toward her father. "What are your plans for tomorrow?"

"Riccardo and I will be looking over some more of the aerial photos, and then we'll consult with Amir when we get back to the site about some applications for the team linguist position," he said softly.

"If I can be of help, let me know," she said.

He nodded agreeably. "It's been a long day. I'm turning in," he said. He laid his fork alongside his plate and pushed back his chair. Grabbing his half-full wine glass, he made for the door.

"No *crème brulee*?" Lucrezia called after him.

"I need to go to Rome for a couple of days, *chérie*. Would you still like to come?" asked Andrea. The light from the eastern dawn flooded the terrace where Maria had laid out a small breakfast of croissants, coffee and cream, pecorino, and fig jam. Andrea opened a croissant, spread jam on one side, and topped it with a thin slice of cheese. "You remember Blackburn?"

"The codex thief? How could I forget?" Robert Blackburn was an infamous, slippery thief who owned the Tut Tut Bazaar in Cairo. It was rumored that he had stolen the original codex, but Justine suspected that was a ruse to protect the real villain, the Egyptian Supreme Director of Antiquities. Still full from the night before, Justine settled for a cup of coffee. She had already dressed in her running clothes and carried her tennis shoes.

"Exactly. I have reason to believe that he might be in Rome."

"I thought he was still in an Egyptian prison," Justine responded, surprised. "Is that who you are going to see in Rome? So, if you find him, you'll walk right up to him and ask for the original codex? Or tell him Stanford is waiting with their new fangled machine?"

"Don't be cute!" said Andrea. "He's been a prickly thorn in Egyptian sides for some time, so I understand they released him with the agreement that he would leave the country. All rumor, of course."

"How will we find him? In the phone book, perhaps?" Justine began to put on her running shoes.

"In a little antiquities shop, I'm led to believe."

"You have the most interesting informants. Tell me, do you seduce all of them?" Justine cocked her head and glared at Andrea.

"Agitated this morning, aren't we?"

"What are your intentions toward my father?" Justine drained her coffee and picked up a small piece of pecorino. She stood and stared down at Andrea. Waiting.

"I'm not that proactive, my friend. Except where my work ambitions are involved. As for your father, I find him attractive. You object?"

"I don't want him hurt, Andrea." Justine didn't wait for an answer.

CHAPTER 6

⚬⚬⚬

THE LONG ROAD FROM TARQUINIA, the Etruscan city more than two days' ride northwest of Rome, was muddy from the spring rains. The damp riders and their entourage had camped the night before near Ostia, to the west. But now the warm afternoon sunlight of early spring reflected off the golden chest of Achilles as the Greek god received armor from his mother, Thetis. This finely embossed imagery of Achilles in bronze was carved across the fashionable chariot, its long pole issuing from the head of a boar and ending in the head of a beaked bird that protruded between proud black steeds. This magnificent chariot carried Lucumo Tarquinius Priscus and his wife, Tanaquil, a haruspice learned in the ways of divination. Had she not known, when the eagle crowned her husband with a cap, that he was the chosen one? That a new city would give them a chance to claim the glory that was rightfully theirs?

As Lucumo drove their lathered horses up the rise to the foot of the Palatine Hills, he cried out, "Ah, this place will host my games. Horse racing and boxing in a Circus Maximus!"

"But first the swamps will have to be drained, my husband," said Tanaquil, who had more mastery in mind than childish games.

⚬⚬⚬

The first Tarquin king of Rome, Justine thought, continuing her musings as she steered her Spider into Via Cristoforo Colombo toward the Coliseum. Her imagination often entertained her, especially this morning, as she was once again captivated by the majesty of Rome. Justine forced herself to fast-forward twenty-eight centuries and turn her full attention to the chaotic traffic. *Not so different from Cairo,* she thought. *The Coliseum, the world's best-known monument to brutality . . . yet now in the twenty-first century, as if in irony, it is lighted all night when a death penalty is commuted or abolished anywhere on earth.* She turned right onto Via La Spezia and swung into Cavour Boulevard, heading toward the middle of Rome.

Andrea had left Fiesole the day before, coaxing Justine to Rome with rumors of Blackburn, shopping . . . and a certain baroness. They would meet near the Piazza Navone, at the Chiesa di San Luigi dei Francesi, where Andrea planned to meet the daughter of an old classmate. A baroness. *I wonder what she'll be like?* Justine mused. *An elegant diva? Reserved? Haughty?* According to Andrea, the family history of the Baroness Miranda Taxis and her husband ran to daunting. Justine braced herself as she approached Saint Maggiore Piazza, where human and vehicular traffic made inroads impenetrable.

Justine finally pulled into the Piazza Navone, with its baroque palazzo, magnificent fountains, street hawkers, artists, musicians, and tourists. The enticing aromas of sausage pizza and sizzling pigeon rose from the street-side cafés. Built to be used as an arena 2,000 year earlier, it had been paved over in the fifteenth century and was now a community market. Bernini's Fontana dei Quattro Flumi, his Fountain of the Four Rivers, depicted the Nile, Ganges, Danube, and Río de la Plata flowing together, connecting the known world.

In front of the boutique Hotel Michelangelo, situated in the southwest corner of the piazza, Justine unloaded her single buckskin bag and handed it, with her car keys, to the waiting bellman. She would not take time to check in, as she was expected at the church by noon. Following the bellman's directions, Justine walked gingerly across the piazza and turned into an alleyway that ended in a smaller piazza housing the church—and, across the narrow street—the French Embassy. In spite of herself, she was looking forward to a day of adventure with Andrea, who was always good for a surprise or two.

Andrea was sitting on the church steps, her white linen slacks protected by a copy of *Italia,* a spaghetti strap hanging down over her sunburned shoulder.

"Waiting long?" asked Justine, sitting beside her friend and giving her a light squeeze. "Where's the Baroness?"

"Just got here," said Andrea, kissing Justine on the cheek. "Before Miranda gets here, let me tell you a little bit of her intriguing history. Her husband, William Taxis, earned his title and surname from a distant uncle in Austria who invented the notion of paid transportation. Hence, the 'taxi.' And, her great grandfather, Sir James Rennell, was the British ambassador to Rome during World War I."

"Impressive!" exclaimed Justine. She wondered whether Sir Rennell had known her great grandparents, Ahmed and Isabella Hassouna, when they were stationed at the Vatican. They probably would have known each other, as the ex-patriot world then, as now, was a small one.

"Miranda's grandfather," Andrea continued, gently pulling a spaghetti strap up over her sunburn, "was Lord Francis Rennell of Rodd. I think he became Governor of Sicily when the British and American forces retrieved the island from the Germans in World War II . . . Wait. See that sedan just pulling up? That's Christine Lagarde, our finance minister. I met her once at a reception. Sharp woman. She's rumored to be the next IMF director." A tall, slender woman in a gray Givenchy suit stepped out of the car. Two embassy officials welcomed her and escorted her into the embassy. "And here is the woman we've been waiting for." Andrea nodded toward a young woman walking toward them with the gait of a horsewoman.

The Baroness Miranda Taxis bobbed, auburn hair swaying across her pixie face, as she walked, willowy and relaxed. She wore a tan khaki skirt, silver flats, and an aqua cotton blouse with a lace collar. Baroness Miranda picked up her pace as she waved and cried, "*Pronti!*"

As the baroness drew closer, Justine noticed that her eyes were the same color as her blouse. *A bit of an avocation for me*, she grinned. *Eyes.*

Miranda hugged Andrea tightly and turned to Justine, taking her hand with the spontaneity of someone at home in the world.

Not at all what I expected, thought Justine. *So natural, unassuming.*

"I want to show you my favorite painting," said the Baroness, hardly pausing for proper introductions. "In here." As she led them into the church, she talked with Justine about Caravaggio. "Almost every major event in his life happened within a five-minute walk from here. He hawked his first painting in the piazza and killed a man over a tennis match. Then he went into exile and it took years for the Pope to forgive him. Look here."

They were entering the Contrarelli Chapel, where a gathering of people anxiously crowded in front of a darkened alcove. A young man placed a euro into a rusting machine nearby and light sprayed across three magnificent scenes. "My Caravaggios!" said Baroness Miranda with personal pride of ownership.

Miranda took Justine by the elbow and moved her closer while Andrea made her own way through the crowd. "These are called the Matthew cycle," Miranda said. "Almost photographic images of miracles in progress, aren't they? That one on the left wall is *The Calling of St. Matthew,* my very favorite. It's based on a verse from St. Mark: 'And as he passed by, he saw Levi, the son of Alphaeus, sitting at the receipt of custom, and said unto him, "Follow me." And he rose and followed him.'"

On the left side of the painting, three young pages were elegantly dressed and crowned with feathered hats. In the center table, an older man in spectacles and draped in fur peered over Levi's shoulder. Standing on the right of the painting was Jesus, hand outstretched toward Levi, who would become Matthew.

"Look at the dusty light on Jesus' outstretched hand. So real! So vivid!" observed Justine, taking her host's arm just as the lights went out and the small crowd dispersed.

"Quick, another euro," cried Miranda, taking the coin from Andrea's hand and walking toward the coin drop. The soft spotlights shone and she turned back toward the paintings. "Caravaggio's recent biographer, Francine Prose, points out that this is the moment when a man's life changes forever and becomes something else completely. Levi becomes Matthew—we don't know why the name change—and he enters a world completely different than the counting house. Notice that Matthew hesitates and points at himself as though to ask, 'Me?'"

"I imagine because 'Levi' is Jewish," Justine offered, unable to draw her eyes away from Jesus' face.

Miranda looked momentarily puzzled, then nodded in agreement and turned back toward the paintings.

Justine was suddenly flooded by memories from the Virgin Mary's diary, allowing the warmth of her intimate knowledge about this great savior as a boy to flow freely through her trembling body. Mary had transcribed provocative conversations with her young son into her diary. Many were explicit about values and behaviors, like when they talked about equality and Jesus challenged, "If God wanted everyone to be equal, why didn't he make them so?" "I believe," answered his mother, "that this is God's test of us—to look past the exterior differences and find the human inside." Justine couldn't help but notice that Caravaggio had captured the compassion and gentleness of Jesus that the codex had led Justine to expect.

"Matthew can look across this chapel to the scene of his own martyrdom," observed Andrea, moving forward to put her hand on Justine's shoulder. "Perhaps he had a premonition."

"Perhaps," sighed Miranda, her smile almost beatific in the filtered light. "Perhaps . . . Shall we go? I'm hungry."

The Baroness led the two women back through the Piazza Navone and into an alley on the opposite side, where they spotted a small bistro called Trattoria Bernini. Its checkered tablecloths and red umbrellas reminded Justine of a movie set. "I like this place," the baroness declared. "The lasagna is just terrific!"

Justine thought that Miranda was surely more sophisticated than she let on. She grinned. "I adore lasagna too."

Andrea nodded, scanning the area as though expecting to see someone else. "Are we near the antiquities area?" she asked—and, to the dismay of the waiter, claimed a table that was not yet cleared, selecting a chair that faced the alley.

"I guess you could consider it the antique section. Via dei Coronari starts there," Miranda pointed down the adjacent alley, "crossed by Via del Governo Vecchio and Via dei Banchi Nuovi. All nearby." She pronounced the Italian streets crisply, with a charming British accent.

Justine peered over her sunglasses at Andrea, whose face creased with edginess. Back at table level, her attention was captured by a wrinkled cocktail napkin inked with a rough sketch of an ancient airplane with broad, heavy wings and twin propellers, headlights like insect eyes, and little curtains drawn in eight small passenger windows. *A DC-2*, she thought, brushing the napkin into her purse without comment. *Is this what Andrea was looking for? What is going on here? Why am I feeling uncomfortable with Andrea?*

Justine turned back, asked Miranda, "What brought you to Italy from England?" It was midday and the café was full. *As many Italians as tourists*, she thought gratefully, picking up her menu.

"The sun," began Miranda. "Opportunity. We just barely sold our home near London. Titles don't necessarily bring riches, you know. We found this darling old farmhouse between Arezzo and Cortona. William is exceedingly good at remodeling. The girls love it here. We have room for horses and a garden . . . The house wine is quite drinkable. Shall I order a carafe?"

"Please," said Andrea distractedly.

"I'd love to see your home sometime, Miranda. I'm fascinated with the reconstruction of old homes throughout Europe." Justine picked up the menu.

"When the kitchen is finished!"

"I'll hold you to that," returned Justine. Miranda's exuberance was catching. "As soon as we finish lunch, I'd like to go to the Villa Giulia, if you don't mind. I'm looking for something."

Although Miranda had decided on lasagna, Justine buried herself in the extensive menu.

❧

After lunch, the three women caught the Termini bus to Flamino, traveled across town through the Piazza de Popolo, and exited at the bottom of the hill leading up to Il Museo di Villa Giulia. As they stepped from the bus, they encountered the first beggar they'd seen in Rome, a dignified, one-legged, elderly man. Justine placed a euro in his hand as two Romas holding a young girl and a baby moved toward them. Miranda placed her hand on her purse; the other two women followed suit. Justine still knew Romas as Gypsies, a term that her mother had used to describe her own wandering life. That and "vagabond."

The premier Etruscan museum in Italy occupied a garden-enclosed, eighteenth-century, rose-colored villa that had been used as a hospital during World War II. "To understand the Etruscans, you must understand the Greeks," Miranda called over her shoulder. "The reciprocity cannot be untangled." Justine would one day discover the profound significance of that simple statement.

Justine found what she was looking for on the second floor, the Sarcophagus of the Spouses, sixth century BCE, in terra cotta. She looked at the inscription and found that it had been discovered in Cerveteri. "Are these sarcophagi only found in Cerveteri?" Justine asked Miranda.

"No," replied Francesca Boitani, the museum director, entering the room behind them. "These are molds that could be purchased. Like a tombstone. Nonetheless, there are very few of them in existence."

A wave of disappointment moved through Justine. She didn't want to know that the sarcophagus was a common mold.

"Is Dr. Andrea LeMartin here?" asked the director.

"That would be me," said Andrea, puzzled by the recognition.

Dr. Boitani stepped forward and took Andrea's hand. "Thank you for leaving your names in the gift shop. I'm familiar with your work, Dr. LeMartin, especially your translations of some of the Dag Hammadi finds in Egypt."

"Andrea, please. I'm honored that you know of my work."

"Etruscans are my specialty, Egyptians my avocation and passion. Your translations are thorough, detailed. Very professional. I am curious about some of your findings. Won't you ladies join me in my office for tea?"

CHAPTER 7

"Cicero smiled at us. 'The art of life is to deal with problems as they arise, rather than destroy one's spirit by worrying about them too far in advance. Especially tonight."

—Robert Harris, *Imperium: A novel of Ancient Rome*

LATER THAT EVENING, a taxi drove the three women to the end of Via Veneto Boulevard to a stone wall surrounding the city. On the left stood Ristorante Harry's Bar. A golden crest signifying the name hung amid a row of amber lanterns that lit a large patio of formally prepared tables. The name, Harry, was about the only consistent feature of the famous saloons found in New York, Paris, and Venice. The Roman Harry's was Victorian in style. The interior featured delicate lights in the form of lilies, velvet curtains, and gold-embossed walls. Its waiters wore tuxedos.

"The drink of the house is the Bellini," said Miranda, who was modestly attired in a city where women wear stilettos to pick up their children from preschool. She had changed at the hotel into a tailored salmon dress and small gold earrings for the evening, defying Justine's expectations of royal glamour. "A blend of champagne and peach liquor. It's yummy."

Without waiting to hear Justine's preference, Andrea turned to the attentive waiter and ordered three Bellinis.

"That conversation we had with Dr. Boitani was unexpected and welcome," said Justine. "Kudos to you, Andrea. She was almost gushing about your work. And her belief that the Etruscans created literary works is exciting, even though such remains have not yet been found. Dad and Riccardo will want to talk with her."

"I'll be glad to arrange a meeting," said Andrea. "I could pick up your father in Cerveteri." She winked at Justine.

Justine stiffened at the thought of another liaison between Andrea and her father. "Aren't you returning home soon?" she grinned, fingering the four strands of pearls at her neck that complemented her black linen dress.

Miranda looked from one woman to the other, clearly puzzled by the exchange.

"That I am," Andrea admitted. "But just now, I want you to know that Miranda has been working with the Italian Culture Minister, Riccardo Rutelli." Andrea slowly lifted her napkin and set it across her silk slacks. "I think she can fill us in on the Marion True story."

"Marion True? I've read a couple of things in the *International Herald Tribune*," said Justine, pushing the previous moment's apprehension to the back of her mind.

Miranda shook her head, her auburn hair swinging from side to side. "Andrea overstates my importance in the ministry. I occasionally assist with translation, but my primary occupations are teaching two English classes and raising my two lovely daughters. Okay. Here's what I know. Marion True was the Getty antiquities curator from 1986 to 2005, when she was released from her duties—fired, as you Americans would say." She went on to explain that Marion True had represented one of the world's most aggressive collectors, and had worked endlessly in the international markets, assessing and acquiring Italian and Greek antiquities. Italian authorities investigated her for years and charges were finally filed in court in 2005.

"So she was dismissed because she was guilty?" asked Justine, squinting at her friend. *Andrea never pursues a story without a reason. So why Marion True?*

"Really, no. The public reason was that she had taken a loan for a second home from a client. But I think it was because the Getty wanted an excuse to disassociate itself from her before the trial started in Rome."

"Back up, please," said Justine, confused but engrossed in the story. "Isn't this case a bit extreme? After all, unprovenanced trafficking has been going on for centuries."

"I know. I know, but things in the field of museum acquisition have changed dramatically in the last few years," said Miranda. "At one time, asking

'Where did you get this?' would have been poor etiquette. And provenances were often unknown or shaky."

The musicians started to play "La Vie en Rose." Andrea shivered as though old memories encircled her. She held the sleeves of her beaded sweater and interjected, "As far back as '72, I remember, there was a case of a vase involving the dealer Hecht." The vase had been the work of the Greek ceramicist Euphronias, found in Cerveteri.

"Dad is working on a new dig in Cerveteri," Justine explained to Miranda. "I've heard that the Etruscans were the largest importers of Greek vases."

Miranda nodded. "The New York Met was charged with plundering many Etruscan sites. They focused on aesthetic qualities and didn't ask too many questions about provenance. Today that wouldn't do. Countries want their artifacts returned, so museums have to know where they came from."

"True got caught in the crosshairs of history with some questionable characters, dealers such as Hecht, a collector named Symes, and Giacomo Medici, who was convicted in '04, sentenced to ten years in prison, and fined a lot of euros," said Miranda, now in her element. "There were letters, purchases, ample circumstantial evidence, plenty of *prova di contorno*, information to adorn the edges. Enough to suggest that Marion True knew what was going on. Or should have known."

"Do you think she was guilty?" asked Justine. "Will she be convicted?"

"I think she was careless. Perhaps she couldn't imagine what can happen with authorities in Italy once the competition starts. It's my hunch that they'll drop all charges, now that they've got what they wanted," said Miranda. Her nose wrinkled involuntarily when she knew she was particularly clever. "Conforti has retired."

"Who's Conforti?" asked Justine and Andrea simultaneously.

"I'm hungry," said Miranda, noticing surprise on the other women's faces. "I'm very active!" she added defensively.

Justine laughed, amused that such a willowy woman could have such a voracious appetite. "Please go on . . ."

Miranda pursed her lips, then continued while she studied the menu. "General Conforti became personally obsessed with this case, so he and the

Carabinieri started investigating True in the late '90s. There was tremendous rivalry among the ministries, each trying to make *la bella figura*, to look good. When such competition gets going in Italy, the evidence can get lost in the shuffle. You see, Conforti was particularly obsessed with the return of the Aphrodite, the most disputed piece at the Getty. And he and the Carabinieri were unimpressed by the museum's pretense at diligence in returning other items. They became determined to pursue this case to its conclusion. To create an intimidating example."

"What do you mean by lost in the shuffle?" asked Andrea, fingering an engraved silver cigarette case that she never opened in Justine's presence.

"The process is more important than the outcome," explained Miranda. "Looking good, getting promoted, playing the game, outdoing your rivals. As long as the evidence is enough to bring a passable case to court. After all, it might all be dropped anyway. Usually for political reasons."

Andrea laughed in recognition. "Men are more alike than different."

"Did you ever meet her?" asked Justine, indifferent to the menu.

"Once, at a party," said Miranda. "A woman in her mid-fifties, gracious, confident. Well-dressed, an Armani suit and furs. Blond hair, probably not natural. She told me, quite casually, that you're not really important in Italy unless someone is investigating you. Actually, I liked her."

"Sounds like a sophisticated woman," observed Justine.

"I'd say so," said Miranda, "Ironically, many of the reforms that Marion talked about are now in place. Many in the field have argued that if museums hadn't picked up on and collected unprovenanced finds, they would have ended up in private collections. But things have changed. Museums have stopped buying these antiquities for the most part. Many items have been returned, and museums are engaging in loans. Ownership isn't that important anymore, as long as loans can be liberally arranged."

For nearly a half hour, Justine had been trying to piece together Andrea's motive in pursuing the Marion True story. Andrea did few things without reason. "What does this story have to do with the codex, Andrea?" Justine finally asked, almost sharply. "There's always a purpose behind your curiosities, *n'est-ce pas?*"

"You know me too well, *cherie*. I wanted the inside story so we'll know what to expect from the Italian authorities regarding the codex."

Protecting me—or herself?

Miranda placed both her hands firmly on the table, palms down, and demanded to know what the codex was.

Andrea and Justine stared at each other. After a short silence, Andrea said, "Let us order first. A true Roman dish, *baccalà*, cod with raisins and pine nuts."

"And *puntarelle*, a salad of chicory and garlic-anchovy sauce," added Justine.

Andrea touched her forefinger to her nose and called the waiter. "I'll have the *nudi gnocchi*. And another Bellini," added Miranda. For several minutes, the women listened to the music, watching people come from and go into the underground station situated between the restaurant and the stone city wall. Street lamps gave the remains of their Bellinis a pearly luminescence.

"I'll start," Justine said finally. "A year ago—I can't believe it was only a year ago—I visited St. Sergius Church in old Cairo. The cave, now a crypt, under the church, was supposed to have been the resting place, for some years, of the Holy Family." Justine heard Miranda inhale sharply. "I entered the cave just before a major earthquake hit. I was trapped. But with help, I managed to get out, carrying with me a little book that wasn't mine . . . that had apparently fallen into my bag in the chaos."

"An ancient codex," interjected Andrea, coolly. "The diary of the Virgin Mary."

Miranda opened her mouth but was unable to form a word. Then she managed, "Where is it?"

"It was stolen," whispered Justine, just as dinner arrived.

CHAPTER 8

—∞∞∞—

The market in antiquities is perhaps the most corrupt and problematic aspect of the international art trade.

—Marion True

T HE NEXT MORNING, Justine lay on her bed in the Hotel Michelangelo, staring at the cocktail napkin in her hand. An hour passed as a kaleidoscope of haunting scenes raced across her mind. The earthquake in Cairo, her disappointing love affair with Nasser, being expelled from her mother's home country. *But Amir is here . . . where do I want that relationship to go?*

But it was the story that Andrea had told her in Alexandria that flooded her mind most prominently: the story of Andrea's fiancé, Francois, landing in Algeria the night before he was kidnapped, tortured, and killed. His Foreign Legion uniform perfect in the afternoon sun, shining buttons and metals. His blinding smile. Francois had written to Andrea that last night. On the letter, he had doodled a sketch of the plane he'd flown across North Africa. So eager was she for news, his voice. Justine was convinced that the plane was a DC-2. The same plane, she'd come to learn, that was flown over Africa by Hal Blackburn, the codex thief's father. So many questions she'd had for Andrea. But not asked. Had Francois expected Algeria to be like India—safe? So innocent, so unsuspecting he was. Andrea's only grand passion, and the one from which she still hadn't recovered.

A wave of guilt washed through Justine. How could she resent Andrea? Her secretiveness; her efforts to find momentary happiness with Morgan. Forcing herself to get out of bed and stop whining, Justine walked unsteadily to the bathroom and stood under the hot shower for several minutes while she made her decision. *Oh, those Bellinis!* She would go to the antiquities area alone.

Andrea didn't need to know . . . not yet. Although Justine was convinced that Andrea suspected something, she would protect her friend until she was sure.

She quietly opened her door, glanced across the hall to Andrea's room. No light was coming from under the door; she heard no sound. Justine headed for the stairs, avoiding the noisy elevator.

Light swarmed into the narrow alleys off Piazza Navona. Bicycles wound their way by grocers filling bins with spring squash, carrots, and chard, alongside imported bananas and peaches. Street grocers gave way to shops distinguished by black brick and brass entrances. Justine stepped into a coffee shop and ordered an espresso, which she drank quickly before returning to the alley.

She walked more slowly now, staying in the portion of walkway still shaded from the searching early light, examining each antiquities shop in turn. Unknown to Justine, another figure moved rapidly, running toward her, south across Ponte San Angelo, turning briefly onto Tor di Nona, then continuing south, nearing Via Coronari. The two collided violently. Justine fell on the cobblestones, cutting her left elbow. The runner grabbed a cornerstone and kept her balance.

"What are you doing here?" demanded a breathless Justine, struggling to sit up.

"I could ask you the same thing," answered Andrea, clearly angry that she was being left out of some adventure, even if concerned about her friend's injury. "I often run in the early morning too. Just started up again recently. Trying to stay in shape." Andrea held out her hand to help Justine up. "Weren't we going to meet for breakfast at the hotel?"

Justine accepted the extended hand, brushed herself off, and examined her bleeding elbow. She pulled a handkerchief from her jean pocket and held it to the wound. "You run with the power of a train, my friend. Don't you watch where you're going?"

"People rarely lurk in the shadows on the left side of the street. What were you looking for?" Andrea asked even as she looked up and noted the row of antiquities shops. "Ah."

"All right. I was looking for Blackburn. His shop, anyway. Thought I might recognize something."

"Like a codex displayed in the front window?"

"Smartass. Let's go back to the hotel. I need another shower and a bandage."

The two women walked silently back to Hotel Michelangelo and entered their separate rooms.

Andrea called back over her shoulder, "Let me know when you're out of the shower. I've got a small first aid kit."

⸎

They chose a table in the hotel breakfast room by a bank of tall windows with lace curtains that overlooked the piazza and fountain. A young woman brought a tray of coffee and hot milk, motioning to a side table with pecorino and cold cuts, hard rolls, butter, and jams. Justine handed Andrea the cocktail napkin she'd found at lunch the day before and told her what she knew about the ancient DC-2. "And, of course, Francois flew . . ."

Andrea stared down, stirring her coffee, listening carefully, occasionally looking out at the Fountain of Four Rivers.

Justine stared at her friend across the table—an adventuress, daring and self-possessed. Capable of getting herself in over her head. "He'll recognize you," she said flatly. "I'll go."

Andrea grinned, as though she had hoped Justine would be enticed to confront Blackburn.

"One shop particularly interested me. It had many Egyptian artifacts, a bust of Horus, Isis with her sparrow hawk wings, amphora, a gold-plated chair, its back painted with hieroglyphics and poppies. Most of the other shops had Italian period furniture and lamps and an assortment of small Roman and Greek replica statues. However," added Justine, "it seems too obvious."

⸎

"May I speak with the owner of your shop, *signore?*" Justine asked a crumpled older man behind the cases of Egyptian jewelry, scarabs, and knives. The gentleman beheld a young woman in a dark gray suit, spike heels, and pearl earrings. Her hair was pulled into a chignon. The overall effect reminded him of Kim Novak in *Vertigo*. He loved American movies. "I'm Dr. Justine Hassouna with the Medea Foundation."

The small man bowed slightly and walked to the back room. Calm voices could be heard through the curtain. Shortly, an erect man with long, lanky arms and legs and a wide girth emerged from the back of the cluttered shop. He was probably in his seventies, although his face was surprisingly free of wrinkles. Even though Justine was more than five foot eight, this man towered over her. He looked down, taking her hand. His blue eyes sparkled but revealed the pain that must have accompanied the scars on his left cheekbone and neck. "I am Enrico Lamberti," he said gently. "How may I be of assistance?"

"I'm pleased to meet you, Mr. Lamberti," she said, shaking his hand. "Dr. Justine Hassouna. I've been commissioned by the Medea Foundation to find a certain codex, recently discovered in Cairo. When I saw your Egyptian displays, I thought you might be helpful."

"Interesting. A codex, you say? What more can you tell me?"

"According to the acquisitions director of our foundation, the codex may have some connection to the Christian Holy Family. I believe it was found in St. Sergius Church."

"Cairo, then. Remarkable," said Lamberti, narrowing his eyes so that his full gray brows nearly touched. "Now that would be quite a find. But I'm afraid I can't be of help. I do have in my keeping a small codex found near Jerusalem from around 200 CE, but it lacks provenance. A serious problem these days."

"Indeed it is," laughed Justine with delicacy. "The authorities no longer turn their heads when a significant discovery is traded. I sympathize with antiquities dealers such as yourself. It makes life difficult."

"I'm impressed that such an obviously accomplished woman would care. I deeply appreciate your gesture of sympathy." He bowed and took her hand once again, raising it slowly to his lips. "Is there any way that I can reach you if I come across information of interest?"

"I'm embarrassed to admit that my purse was taken last night, Mr. Lamberti, by Romas in Piazza Popolo. As a consequence, I have none of my cards with me. But I've written my cell number on this slip of paper."

Blackburn grinned, accepting the paper without turning his eyes from hers.

♊

"It was Blackburn all right," she said, vividly remembering Andrea's description. "I wasn't fooled by him, and of course he wasn't fooled by me. You were right, he certainly is a charmer." Justine took off her jacket and placed it over the wrought iron chair in the coffee shop near Chiesa Nova. She vigorously rubbed her arms.

"How's the elbow?"

"Better." The Neosporin had been cooling.

"How did you come up with the Medea Foundation?" asked Andrea. "I haven't heard of it."

"I made it up," grinned Justine. "This adventure reminds me of a multi-headed monster." They both laughed. "What will we do with the information about Blackburn? Contact the Carabinieri? Egyptian embassy?" asked Justine, stirring her coffee with unusual vigor.

"What information?" Andrea asked.

CHAPTER 9

Spaghetti alla Puttanesca

     2 small (14–16 oz) or 1 large (28 oz) can crushed tomatoes

     4 cloves of garlic, halved

     4 or 5 anchovy filets, chopped

     3 T olive oil

     10–12 black olives, stoned and coarsely chopped

     2 T capers, soaked and drained

     2 T Italian parsley, chopped

     1/2 to 1 small red chili, chopped

     Salt

     1 lb spaghetti or spaghettini

"WHAT ARE YOU MAKING, Mom?" asked Justine as she pulled out a stool snuggled under Lucrezia's marble island, which was large enough to service ten chefs. Without waiting for her mother to answer, she sat down to survey the remodeled kitchen. The marble counter featured a six-burner stovetop beneath a stainless steel hood. Copper pans hung beside Tuscan baskets. A yeasty aroma floated in the air because two domes of *focaccia* dough sat rising under warm red cloths. Mammoth timbers crossed the high ceiling like protective arms, supporting two stories of living area above.

"*Puttanesca*, Justine. What do you think of my new kitchen?"

"Terrific! But since when did you become a chef?" Justine wore jeans, a blue cotton shirt, and her sandals. She had corralled her long hair with barrettes that she'd found in her old dresser. To her mother, she looked sixteen again.

Lucrezia dug her fingers into a large jar and removed a dripping palm full of capers, then dropped them into the giant crockery bowl in front of her. "I think of cooking as art," she said. "But if it becomes routine, I find it drudgery. Besides, Maria is in Bologna with her family and since I took Lorenza's cooking course at Badia a Coltibuono, I've been trying my hand in the kitchen occasionally. I remodeled this kitchen to look very much like hers. Hand me the anchovies."

Justine carefully lifted the bowl of anchovies bathing in brine and moved it to the island beside her mother. "I didn't know Lorenza de Medici was still giving classes. Isn't she gallivanting around the world selling her cookbooks?" Justine walked to the sink and washed her hands, even though she hadn't touched the salty creatures. "Stinky little things," she said over her shoulder.

Lucrezia smiled as she sank her hands into the brine. "Her son, Guido, teaches most of the classes now, but Lorenza hosts a few friends from time to time."

"So, what is *puttanesca*, anyway?" Justine asked, watching her mother mash the small sardines with a mortar.

"Juice those lemons for me while I tell you the story." Lucrezia wiped her hands on a towel. The shiny patina on the surface of her skin glistened in the late-afternoon light.

"How many do you want?" asked Justine, slicing each lemon in half and turning it upside down over the juicer, forcing the liquid into the bowl below. More pungent aromas filled the room.

"Four will be plenty. Now listen . . . this tasty sauce is related to the world's oldest profession. It originated in Naples and the official name, *Pasta alla Puttanesca*, means 'Pasta the way a whore would make it.' Quick and easy, between tricks. I love it!"

"Devil!" Justine laughed at her mother's delight in all things sensual. The late-afternoon sun caressed the casement windows and a crystal vase full of yellow bougainvillea.

Lucrezia grinned without turning around. "In the 1950s, brothels were state-owned and these 'civil servants' were only allowed one market day. So this dish, made quickly from common ingredients kept in the larder, fit the bill. With three of Italy's choice cooking ingredients—anchovies, capers, and black olives—it's a salty, saucy taste worthy of a king. A naughty king, perhaps. You think the men will like it?"

"I don't understand men much anymore, Mom. Not since Egypt." Justine slid the jar of black olives nearer her mother.

Lucrezia glanced at her daughter, who chose not to return her gaze.

Instead, Justine moved her stool to the opposite side of the island and set the bowl of dough in front of her. Only then did she look up.

"What's going on? I hadn't realized your self-doubt was so strong." Her mother pulled up a stool as well, giving her full attention to Justine. Without looking down, she started to cut the peppers into thin slices.

"I'm still having trouble trusting myself. I got it all wrong with two men, one in love and one in work. Maybe three. How much worse can it get?"

"A lot worse. You could have married one of them."

"Good point, Mom," she laughed. "But you know how much I pride myself on being able to read people."

"Yes, the work of an anthropologist."

"That's right. Well, my abilities failed me this time. I blew it."

"You're too hard on yourself, dear. Surely there were reasons."

"Amir suggested that both reasons related to Dad. Ibrahim was Dad's friend and colleague. And as you know, Nasser claimed to be Dad's student, so I . . ."

"So you didn't apply your usual rigorous screening," her mother interrupted. "Makes sense to me."

"It makes sense, but how can I trust that it won't happen again?"

"You can't trust that life isn't going to throw you curves. Anyway, I understand that Amir is here."

"To work with Dad as an archaeologist." Justine took a deep breath.

"Well then, what's going on? What does Amir have to do with any of this? Cute little kid, but I haven't seen him since he was a child. Tell me . . ."

Justine told her mother about the night before: the dinner, her outburst, their making love. She kept her eyes on the *focaccia*.

"Ah. I see. Is it men you don't understand, or yourself?" Lucrezia sliced into a red onion and tears ran down her cheeks.

Justine hammered at the *focaccia* dough with both fists. "Both, I guess."

"I don't mean to confuse the two. I've always been puzzled by men's egos, their need to compete, to win. Sometimes at any price. But I've also learned that you can't generalize about men, or women for that matter. The best you can do is be aware, be present. Keep your antennae up but don't be overly suspicious."

"Like Andrea?"

"Like Andrea."

Justine was quiet for several moments as she methodically rolled out the dough, placing it into three waiting oiled pans, pressing thumbprints across the surfaces. She had learned the traditional way to prepare *focaccia* from her Grandmother Laurence during teenage summers with her.

Lucrezia scooped richly scented rosemary from another bowl and handed it to her daughter, who scattered it evenly over the surface of one of the breads. She placed sliced tomatoes and grated pecorino on another loaf, and red onion and kosher salt on the third. Satisfied with the colorful *focaccia*, they looked up at each other, quietly savoring the bond that often grows between women who cook together.

"Where did you get your wisdom, Mom?"

"The Etruscan goddess Menrva, of course," she laughed, taking her daughter's face into both hands and wiping away her tears with her thumbs, leaving a residue of oil on each cheek.

Justine took the stairs to her room two at a time. She needed to run. Running was her emotional equalizer. When she was stressed or worried or angry, it cleared her vision and released muscle tension; when she was happy, the run heightened her joy, her energy, opening up possibilities. She slipped into her black running shorts, remembering how violated she'd felt on her run that first morning in Cairo when a stranger's hand had reached between her legs. After that incident, she'd worn only loose clothing on the streets of Egypt.

Justine started up the pathway leading across the Fiesole hills, behind the Villa San Michele, and upward into town. At first her pace was uneven, her heart beating wildly. Wild sweet peas, poppies, and orchids reached for her ankles, and the scent of lemon and mulberry trees filled her lungs. Honeysuckle and wild roses clung to terraces nearby. *Glorious*, she thought. Such beauty inevitably rested Justine's life in perspective. Her heart slowed and her pace evened. She knew that life was uncertain, and wondered why she had to be reminded.

I create my own cages, she thought, taking a deep breath, pulling her shoulders back, and stretching her arms forward onto her knees. She turned to watch the late-afternoon sun being pulled toward the Arno and reflecting off the ochre dome of the Duomo. After she'd run herself out, at the crest of the hill just below the Aurora terrace, she turned back for home.

Justine entered the parlor at twilight, her cobalt blue dress resplendent in the evening light. Her chestnut hair was combed back from her face to show off sapphire earrings, a graduation present her father had brought back from India. She was meeting him; he had driven up from Cerveteri with Riccardo once more for a traditional glass of sherry. Once again, Amir had chosen to stay behind. He had used the excuse that he needed to meet with the regional superintendent.

"Amir is better at politics than I am," Morgan said.

When Justine filled Morgan in on the visit to Rome, he casually revealed that Andrea had stopped in at Cerveteri on her way to Rome. Justine chose not to comment on this news. She and Morgan both seemed to get involved with sudden affairs. She wasn't sure where she stood with Amir; he'd sent but one casual e-mail, was clearly avoiding her.

By eight o'clock the sun had abandoned the mountainside, leaving behind ribbons of purple and rose. The table was set in the china and linens Justine preferred: beige ceramic plates painted with whimsical willows. The tablecloth and napkins were bright yellow linen, and clusters of daffodils sprung unevenly from crystal vases.

This was Andrea's last weekend in Fiesole for a few weeks. Lucrezia had invited Marco de Marco, the director of the Zona Archeologica in Fiesole, and another friend of hers, Alessandro Cardini, a manager with Ferragamo in Florence.

Radiant in her flowing kaftan and turquoise jewelry, Lucrezia began serving the *puttanesca*. She was one of the few women in Italy who would risk eating pasta in white linen.

Andrea sniffed the pasta dish, wrinkled her nose, and turned to Morgan. "What is this?" she whispered. He hunched his shoulders.

"What you smell is anchovies," whispered Justine. After learning from her father that Andrea had stopped by to see him in Cerveteri, she was puzzled by her feelings, and pondered how she would respond to her French friend this evening. *What is it about daughters and fathers? Jealousy?* She turned her full attention toward Marco and her mother.

Lucrezia slowly curled her spaghetti around her inverted fork as Marco quizzed her on the legacy of Benvenuto Cellini and her villa, and the repair of the Chimera.

"Delightful story, as I recall," said Alessandro. "About Zeus and the winged horse Pegasus. Perhaps I should persuade Ferragamo to add wings to some of our shoes. Love this *puttanesca*, Lucrezia." His deep tan complemented his cream-colored linen suit and matching buckskin shoes, a magnificent representation of his company.

A strikingly handsome man, Justine mused, though she noted that his ears were slightly too large for his head. *A petty observation.*

"*Grazie.* Another helping?" Lucrezia asked. Marco grinned and shook his head.

"You know I love your cooking, my beautiful friend, but I'm not crazy about these smelly little fishes," whined Andrea. "But this wine . . . ah, *paradiso*. Did you bring it, Alessandro?" She tilted her head to one side, a gesture that rarely failed to captivate.

Alessandro noted the flirtatious gesture and smiled broadly.

Morgan's dimples tightened, and his eyebrows moved closer together. His fingers grasped his fork, momentarily turning pale pink. But almost as quickly as his reactions to Andrea's flirtations arose, they dissipated.

"*Si, signora.* The wine is called Asprinio de Aversa, from one of the world's smallest and most obscure appellations. Like an exotic perfume of jasmine and wild mint, don't you think? Crisply acidic and dry, yet with a hint of almond," offered Alessandro with the pride of the vintner himself.

"Well described, my friend," said Riccardo. He raised his glass and smiled, whereupon his discordant facial features settled into a more attractive arrangement.

"Riccardo, how did you ever get involved in history and archaeology in the first place? I understand it's not a family tradition."

"Not a direct tradition, no, but in a way it's all about aesthetics."

"Aesthetics?" asked Justine. She would soon learn that the answer to her question led to deeper roots and some old wounds.

"Beauty, art, the sublime—the soil, the vine, the wine," said Riccardo, pleased with his poetic turn of phrase.

"In Italy, beauty has meaning beyond the smell of the rose, beyond the visible," remarked Marco, swept up in Riccardo's lyrics. "The desire for beauty permeates everything."

"More to the point of your question, as Dr. Jenner would say, when I was fourteen I read D.H. Lawrence's *Etruscan Places* and became fascinated by his interpretations. So rich. So imaginative," said Riccardo. "After being pummeled by Dante in Catholic school, I appreciated the Etruscans' ideas about death."

"But surely you don't subscribe to those ideas?" challenged Morgan, feigning amazement. He had dismissed them the first time he'd read them.

"I think I do," said Riccardo, without apology. "For the Etruscans, everything is about life. Even death. Life for them was a thing of ease. And they felt no need to force the mind or the soul in any direction. Death was a pleasant continuance of life. This is what Lawrence taught me."

"A most romantic view, I'm afraid," interjected Morgan without looking up. He finished off the remaining mozzarella and salami in the antipasti.

"I'm afraid I must agree with Dr. Jenner on this point, Mr. Chia," said Marco, slowly sipping his wine. "A significant amount of evidence indicates that the Etruscans were frightened by death and the afterlife."

"What evidence?" asked Lucrezia over her shoulder, slipping out to the kitchen to snatch serving plates of *Pollo Arrosto* with roasted peppers. As she reentered through the swinging doors, Justine took the steaming plates from her mother and placed them in front of their guests.

"The recent finds of La Tomba della Quadriga Infernale," said Marco, preparing to slice his chicken into thin strips.

"Please translate," asked Andrea.

"It means 'The Tomb of the Devil's Chariot,' *signora*," said Marco. "A *quadriga* is a chariot drawn by four horses. This discovery at Sarteano is exceptional. The paintings are vivid and beautiful, typical of Etruscan work in the fifth to fourth century BCE. The Devil drives the dead to the boundaries of Hell, where they are met by a three-headed snake."

"Hadn't heard of the discovery . . . remarkable," exclaimed Riccardo, separating the peppers and sprig of rosemary to one side of the plate and plunging his knife into the roasted chicken. "But the Etruscans were often merely amused by Greek myths, legends, portrayals. Perhaps these creatures were playful cartoons, like superheroes."

Marco laughed wholeheartedly. "The Greeks were not the first to portray the afterlife as frightening. Images similar to theirs appeared in Tarquinia and Vulci before Greek art and myths were brought to Etruria."

"Snakes were often depicted as symbols of rebirth, new beginnings, Marco," said Lucrezia. "Consider also the Snake Goddess of the Minoans. She ruled without fury or spite. Hindus and Buddhists consider snakes to be guardians . . ."

"In Egypt, the cobra was the patron and protector of the country, and the pharaohs," added Justine. "They also possessed the all-seeing eye of wisdom and vengeance." She peered at Marco. "On the other hand, for Abrahamic religions, snakes represent deceitfulness. Am I right?"

"There is truth in what you say, ladies," responded Marco, convinced of the veracity of his argument. "The snake is not always a loathsome image, but the preponderance of monsters and devils in Etruscan tombs suggests to me that fear accompanied death." He turned to the multicolored peppers.

"Well said, professor," said Morgan. "Fear of the afterlife is universal. The Incas prepared for death just as the Egyptians did, and they feared their gods, as well as the consequences of death. No argument there." Morgan often declared that no argument could exist in the presence of his conclusions.

Lucrezia and Justine glanced at one another and smiled.

Riccardo, unconvinced, set down his fork and wine glass, preparing to speak. "Lawrence's essays convince me that the Etruscans joyfully embraced what would come after death. They were not like any other people. However, I have high regard for other points of view, especially yours, Dr. de Marco." He bowed his head slightly.

"The faces on the sarcophagi certainly don't express fear," said Justine. She felt an urgent desire to defend Riccardo, although he had little need for defense. "They appear peaceful, even amused, or perhaps merely stoic."

"Portraiture, Justine," said Marco gently. "The Etruscans were the first to sculpt themselves as they were, without pretense at perfection."

"How do you account for the serenity?"

Marco smiled, raising his palms and hunching his shoulders.

"Ah, beautiful discourse is rarer than emeralds . . . an old African proverb . . . yet it can be found among the servant girls at the grindstones," said Andrea.

Morgan stared at her, cleared his throat, and repeated, "Beautiful discourse is rarer than emeralds." He smiled and paused. "Anything is possible, I guess," he said with uncharacteristic tentativeness.

"For Lawrence, death was a dance—a festival," said Riccardo.

"Death was much like life?" said Andrea raising her glass. "I'm thoroughly seduced by the idea."

"A toast to life," said Morgan, touching his glass to Andrea's. For a moment, they held each other's eyes. "May our tomb yield up its secrets of life and death."

"I can see I've persuaded you, Dr. Jenner," said Riccardo, pleasantly surprised by the playful opening in his boss's demeanor.

"Hardly, but I do like the images," responded Morgan. "I'm ready to be surprised."

"I must say," said Marco, "your theories are appealing. But I'm afraid I need more evidence."

Justine set a dish of *Castagnaccio*, chestnut cake, in front of Marco.

"My favorite! Did you get the chestnuts from Caldine?" he asked.

"The festival in October. Maria ground them into flour," replied Lucrezia. Turning to Alessandro, she asked, "And how is the fashion business? Do the stars still want your shoes?"

"Stars and politicians, business tycoons and musicians. And women of great taste, of course. Like yourself," said Alessandro. "Business is good. Thank you. The rich rarely experience the vicissitudes of changing markets."

"I've heard that the Italian fashion industry is in trouble," said Marco. "Is it not so?"

"Not in sales, professor, but we are losing our center. As an industry we no longer have *raffinatezza*, refinement! The industry is pandering to the *ragazzi di strata*—the street urchins! When I see my shoes walking down the street on a woman who looks like a trollop, my heart, it stops!" Everyone registered surprise at the refinement of Alessandro's rage.

"You've certainly hit a nerve, Marco," said Morgan to the startled *museo* director. "Tell me, Alessandro, is Italy no longer the guardian of patrician ways?"

"Surely, Italy is still seen in France as a generator of style. Italian names still carry the profession," offered Andrea charitably.

"Miuccia Prada picked up her Miu Miu show and moved it to Paris. Traitor," pronounced Alessandro, staring at his chestnut dessert. Andrea's generosity failed to calm him.

"The media, the Internet, they're polluting the minds of youth who no longer are proud of tradition or loyal to country," said Lucrezia casually, cutting into her chestnut cake without looking up.

"That's the most conservative statement I've heard from you in years, Mother," said Justine, astonished. "Many people—and not just youth—think that Italy is old-fashioned and unable to move into the future." Did Lucrezia's support of Alessandro suggest they had a more intimate relationship than she was aware of?

Lucrezia blushed. "Coffee?" she asked, ignoring her daughter's charge. Three of the guests nodded.

"We are old-fashioned to an extent, Justine. To an extent," Alessandro admitted grudgingly. "Clearly we need to strike a balance, but the Ferragamo family is convinced that we also need to raise the standards, the sensibilities, of our youth."

"And you, Alessandro, are not part of the family?" asked Morgan.

"In spirit, but not blood, Dr. Jenner. Italy is a tribal society run by blood and favors," he said bitterly. "I perform many favors."

That's quite an admission for a mature man, thought Justine, looking from Alessandro to her mother, who looked away. The slightly embarrassed guests ate without speaking for several minutes. Nightingales could be heard in the silence, their song floating in on the chilling night breeze.

"I have a challenge for all of you," said Marco, finally breaking the tense silence. "Saturday next, I'm co-hosting a costume ball at Villa San Michele. A benefit for the *museo* foundation. Each of you is invited to come in costume that most closely represents your idea of the Etruscan afterlife. What do you say?"

"You're on," replied Morgan enthusiastically. "Andrea, will you still be with us?"

"I'm afraid not," she replied, and rose to help clear the dishes.

CHAPTER 10

———— ⧈ ————

Synchronicity is a meaningful coincidence of two or more events, where something other than the probability of chance is involved.

—Carl Jung, psychotherapist

---

*W*HO WILL BE THERE? *Dante's Beatrice? Machiavelli? Grand Duke Cosimo I de' Medici? In Florence, these characters never die. Surely, I can expect them to make an appearance,* thought Justine as she pondered her costume for Marco's masquerade. *Who will I be in the Etruscan afterlife? An angel dressed in gauze and lace? A goddess? Lilith with her snake? Who am I most like? It may be easier to pretend than to figure out the answer to such an impertinent question.*

Lucrezia had suggested that Justine search for costume ideas in her grandmother's old trunk in the attic. She hadn't even known such a trunk existed. *How strange,* she thought, *as interested as I am in historical artifacts.*

Justine walked to the spare bedroom at the far corner of the second floor and peered up into the narrow, winding stairway to the attic. She took the steps two at a time, feeling a rush of impending discovery. As she reached the top, her head popped through a canopy of cobwebs. Freeing herself, she noticed narrow ribbons of light from cupola windows dancing in the dust across piles of old furniture, probably seventeenth-century Italian. An Egyptian harem scene, brass tables, rolls of tapestries. Three table lamps, parchment shades imprinted with Gregorian chants. Small end tables of various sizes with mother-of-pearl insets. The astringent smell of mildew assaulted her. *What a find! When the time comes, I can furnish my apartment with these gems.*

In the darkest corner of the room sat the target of her hunt: a large trunk bound with leather straps. The switch by the staircase lit only a single bulb, so she drew out the flashlight in her pocket. Kneeling, she lifted the hinged brass lock on the trunk and creaked open the heavy lid, causing the fabrics inside to draw up in the air current like rising bread. She stared hungrily at the feast before her. *History in a box*, she thought.

She propped the flashlight on a nearby table and carefully began to remove each item: a wedding dress in white satin with puckered lace, browning with age, a velvet cape with a maroon satin lining. Petticoats of gauze and cotton, a black woolen suit with a long slim skirt. Tucked along the edges of the truck in tissue paper were nylons with back seams, lace handkerchiefs, and hatpins in padded jewelry boxes. *Where are the hats?* A fringed drawstring bag held a string of pearls.

She sat back on her heels. *Will Amir come to the masquerade?* She would tell him, encourage him, ask him. *Yes.*

Justine leaned back into the trunk. As she withdrew the sack of pearls, a fine lace shawl cascaded to her knees, the frayed edges catching on a thin splinter of wood arising from the floor of the wooden trunk. Lifting it ever so slightly, she patiently untangled the aging lace so as not to snag it further. For several moments she stared at a slight crack in the edge of the lifted, displaced bottom panel. *What?* She furiously began to empty the remaining garments from the ancient trunk. Red garters, a blue satin camisole, a white peasant blouse with drawstrings . . . *Ah, just a stiff paper lining*, she thought, running her hand across the lining, curdled by age.

A voice from the foot of the stairwell cried out, "Justine, are you up there?"

"I'm here."

"It's Amir, he says it's important."

Justine laid the clothes from the trunk carefully on the seat of the old rocker and hurried down the stairs, excited to hear Amir's voice. But what could he want?

"My grandfather's dead, Justine. Ibrahim is dead." His voice was tight, constrained.

"Ibrahim El Shabry?" Even though he was in his late eighties by now, she was incredulous.

"Yes," he said simply, his voice hoarse.

"What happened? Do you know?" Justine could hear a light sob over the wire.

"Apparently, he fell down the stairs in the Rare Books Library. You know how unsteady he was. The cane and all."

"Have you told Dad?"

"Yes."

Justine was quiet for several moments, suppressing her welling emotion. Amir was quiet also. Wrapping the phone cord around her fingers over and over, she looked at her mother. Lucrezia had not seen Ibrahim for years, but he had been her first lover, a lifelong friend, and a colleague to both her and Morgan.

The morning light began to whirl in Justine's line of vision. "An accident?"

Amir was slow to answer. "I don't know. We knew he was risking his life when he gave you the copy of the codex. And he knew too much. Nothing would surprise me."

"Will there be an investigation?"

"Our family will see to it." He hung up.

She reached for her mother, drawing her close.

CHAPTER 11

—⊗⊗⊗—

... and that is the true Etruscan quality: ease, naturalness, and an abundance of life, no need to force the mind or the soul in any direction.

—D.H. Lawrence, *Etruscan Places*

THE VILLA SAN MICHELE began its glorious life as the monastery of St. Michael the Archangel in the fifteenth century. It seemed only fitting that Michelangelo served as artistic midwife, designing the imposing façade and loggia of stucco, crowned with lions' heads. As Justine drove her Spider up the steep winding road to the front entrance, she once again admired the most romantic hotel in the world.

Her daily runs took her across the high path behind the Villa and into Fiesole, but tonight she was a guest at the benefit for the Etruscan Museo Foundation—an ethereal guest in white gauze, her grandmother's long lace shawl, a tiara, and satin in places that could not be seen. A lively Etruscan ghost.

At the last minute, she had decided to live eternally in the Etruscan world, floating in the firmament with her friends. *Ibrahim and D.H. Lawrence and Grandmother Laurence*, she thought. *The afterlife will be as I wish it to be, if it exists at all.*

A young man in a white tuxedo opened her door as she gathered layers of white into her left arm and stepped from the car, revealing silver slippers with Aladdin curled toes. His gaze met hers through the small openings in her silver mask, a fleeting, sensual moment. She smiled and handed him the keys.

Gliding up the rose-lined pathway toward the hotel, now owned by the Orient Express, she imagined Michelangelo beside her, explaining his designs: Gothic arches, nine supporting Ionian columns, ochre tile roof, high Renaissance art.

The lobby entrance was surprisingly small for such an imposing structure. Royal Egyptian armchairs lined one side of the lobby; Persian carpets accented mahogany desks with modest table lamps. Ancient statues and romantic period paintings adorned the sienna-colored patina walls.

A tall, upright lion walked toward Justine. Taking her by the arm, he led her toward the loggia. Her arm felt the warmth of his golden fur, his scary saber teeth nearly touching his chin. Justine shivered at this unknown creature with abundant fur.

"Amir?" she finally asked, unsure. The giant head nodded assent.

"You look beautiful, Justine," the lion mumbled.

"I didn't know you were back from Cairo. And the funeral."

"Just last night. An excellent service, fitting for a man of my grandfather's status. My parents are doing well." Now side by side, pensive, they stared at the city of Florence spread out below.

Justine placed her hand on the lion's paw and left it there. "Amir, I'm so sorry. I know how much you loved him. And I loved him. He was so wise, so dedicated to Egypt."

"I did, yes. More than I knew. I'm sorry that I had to fly out quickly; the Rome airport is so near to the work site. As you know, our services are immediate. Without an autopsy."

She pondered whether to follow up on her suspicions. Turning to the immense face with liquid black eyes, she began, "Amir, I . . ."

He interrupted her. "I share your fears, Justine. I wouldn't be surprised if he were pushed down the stairs. As you'll remember, they curve and are quite treacherous."

"Yes," was all she said, pausing for a deep breath of the evening air, allowing herself to be momentarily distracted by the fresh scent of lemon. "I think there is substantial evidence that he was in danger."

The massive head turned toward her; he held her hand firmly.

"There you two are," accosted their host, Marco de Marco, hardly recognizable inside a mythical creature costume—part snake, part lion, part dragon. "I've been looking for you. Won't you join us in the garden?" He took Justine's hands into his own, kissing one, then the other, and drew her toward him.

She smiled and took the arm protruding from the chest of the Chimera. She glanced back over her shoulder toward Amir. "I'm coming to Cerveteri tomorrow. We can talk then."

Justine and Marco walked through the arcade, followed by the lumbering lion. Far below, a lavender mist moved in from the Arno, mingling with the earthbound sky of lights flickering throughout the valley. In the garden, candles and lanterns softly lit round tables with linen cloths elegantly set for the glorious and grotesque gathering in conversation.

Near the southern ledge of the garden stood Lucrezia, Morgan, and Alessandro, who wore a tuxedo with tails and a black felt fedora. He appeared not to be playing the game. Lucrezia, on the other hand, was stunning in a gold lamé gown caught in the twine of a huge cobra whose ferocious head looked out over her right shoulder. Morgan wore a leopard body suit with wide whiskers, small ears and two fangs. *A cobra and a leopard—my parents.*

Seated with a view of the valley below sat Riccardo, attired in a shirt with white flowing sleeves, a leather vest, and a red sash. A hefty hat with a huge red feather shadowed his rakish eyes, which peered through a red mask. Justine admired his playful spirit. She'd liked him from the day they'd met in Cerveteri.

Marco liberated three glasses of champagne from a waiter's tray and handed two off to Justine and Amir. "Here's to the afterlife you desire," he said. Justine knew that Marco was still unconvinced that the Etruscans viewed the afterlife as a welcome experience, but he was a gracious host.

"Here, here," all of the guests replied, caught up in the spirit of the moment, although deep sorrows plagued Amir and the Jenner family.

"Now," Marco began, "each of you must explain to us your vision of life ever after." He turned first to Riccardo, who was fondling his red feather.

"I've always wanted to be a pirate," exclaimed Riccardo. "Pirates may have been scoundrels—and still are—but they probably enjoyed life. Hanging out on tropical gardens with tawny, raven-haired beauties. As Morgan knows, I have a penchant for romanticizing. That includes death."

Suddenly, without warning, Morgan exploded, his body stiffening, the leopard prepared to attack. "Damn romantic! Is nothing sacred to you? Death is no laughing matter," he snarled, then turned away, his tragic features cartooned by whiskers and ears.

No one spoke. Riccardo stared down, then whispered, "I'm sorry, sir." That was all. He knew about Ibrahim and his death.

Justine stared at her father with a mix of pity and affection. She understood that her father's outburst had little to do with Riccardo. Of course, she also knew that Riccardo wouldn't understand, be able to separate himself from Morgan's grief.

Lucrezia's eyes glistened with moisture.

Alessandro, clearly discomforted by the confrontation, yet willing to attempt a rescue of his friend and host, took a deep breath and launched in. "You may be wondering if I'd decided not to play our little game," he said. "*N'est-ce pas.* I'm dressed for the eternal party . . . champagne . . . sparkling conversation . . . elegant surroundings . . . everlasting romance . . ." The last word seemed to catch in his throat. He lifted his glass and winked at Lucrezia, who appeared not to notice.

"But a fedora?" challenged Justine as she moved toward Riccardo, intent on comforting the young historian.

"A lasting tribute to Humphrey Bogart. Forgive me, I have my Hollywood obsessions," said Alessandro, laying his forefinger on the rim of his hat and bowing to the group.

Justine smiled and raised her glass to the Bogart aficionado. "And Mother," she invited, moving forward to stroke the head of the cobra. "Tell us about your friend here."

"I am Lilith, the first woman," Lucrezia responded, thrusting both arms in the air triumphantly, careful not to spill her remaining champagne. "All-powerful. Never submissive. Unsatisfied as the wife of Adam, I turned myself into a cobra and seduced Eve, giving her a mind of her own. And death? Somehow I can't talk about death tonight." She looked intently at Morgan.

Morgan noticed tears welling up in her defiant eyes. He took her by the arm and moved her out of the circle. "Let's go sit in the garden and talk about Ibrahim," he said softly as they walked away.

Alessandro and Justine watched them go. Justine wondered how much love remained between her parents and whether it might ever rekindle. Alessandro, his nostrils flared with what appeared to be jealousy, must be wondering the same thing.

Soon after, Amir found himself sitting quietly on a wrought iron bench near the edge of the garden. He removed his headpiece, held his champagne glass with both hands, and stared down at the valley below, his face drawn tight at the temples, a shadow of grief sweeping across his damp eyes. Justine sat down beside him and placed her hand on his furry paw. Neither spoke.

A small chime drew guests toward the villa's archway. Inside the Loggia Ristorante, a six-course dinner with accompanying wines awaited the distinguished donors. After the sumptuous meal, an auction of donated art and artifacts commenced. Each auction offering secured a price beyond its apparent worth, and Justine speculated about the provenance of some of the treasures. Perhaps someday they would be of interest to the Italian Carabinieri.

And as for death? It wears many masks.

At 5:00 a.m. Justine awoke with a start, her blue satin camisole clinging to her breast. She stared up at the ornate molding and forced herself to breathe. What had she been dreaming? Lions and snakes and . . . Ibrahim. She forced herself to get up. Why, she wasn't sure. *Would Ibrahim be dead if it weren't for me? Probably not. If I hadn't found the wretched codex . . .*

She shook her head to loosen her feelings of guilt, remembering Nadia's comments that her guilt was hungry and she fed it with whatever she could find. Justine refused to take on such a heavy burden, but this morning the burden of guilt was intense.

Justine walked unsteadily into her bathroom and stepped into the primitive shower that had been scaffolded over the claw-foot tub. While the hot water caressed her back, she imagined Amir's hands all over her, moving the suds across her skin. Reluctantly, she climbed out of the shower, dressed, and headed downstairs to the small study where she had set up her laptop.

She scrolled through her email with alternating irritation and disinterest until she spotted a familiar address: NadiaM@yahoo.com. *How curious. She was just on my mind.* Justine conjured up an image of her Egyptian friend. Middle-aged, short, and full-figured, Nadia had an agreeable face whose animated features registered each new idea. Nadia had the energy of a much younger woman—and she needed it for her work with the Community Schools of Egypt, where she and Justine had briefly worked together.

> **My dear Justine,**
>
> Wishing we could meet for coffee this morning. So much to tell. I know you have heard that Ibrahim El Shabry died in an accident in the Rare Books Library. Fell down the stairs. We were all deeply saddened by this tragedy and pray for his family. You were so close to Dr. Ibrahim and must have taken the news quite hard. I saw Amir at the service and he told me you knew. I can only apologize for not contacting you sooner.
>
> I have some news. In addition to my UNICEF work with the Community Schools for Girls, I've begun working part time with UNESCO. The site at Cerveteri is part of my assignment and word has reached my office that the archeological team there is having some problems. The local superintendent thinks that personality differences may be slowing down the work.
>
> Could I impose upon you to check out the situation? See what is causing conflict among the team members? I hope to be able to get over there sometime this year, but not right now. I understand that this is a delicate situation because of your dad, but if you could just fill me in with a few details I would be most grateful. Much love, Nadia

Justine leaned so far back in her chair that it almost slid out from under her. *Spy on Dad? That's the way he would see it. Yet similar issues trouble him. Can I address the problem from both sides?* She hit the Reply button.

Dear Nadia,

    I do hope that you are well. It has been a long time—I am mutually responsible for the sketchy communications.

    I appreciate that you understand the grief that my family and I feel at the loss of Ibrahim. He was a friend, mentor, colleague—and so much more. We will miss him.

    Dad has mentioned some of the same problems at the site to which you allude. And he has asked me to work with him. I believe he is interested in mending fences as much as possible. I had already planned to assist with team effectiveness, so I'll see what I can do. But you will need to rely on communications from the superintendent or Dad directly, rather than from me.

    As you know, I am persona non grata in Egypt now, so I hope you'll plan to visit us here in Fiesole—or perhaps we could meet in Greece.

Fondly, Justine

                         ℘

"What's happened?" Lucrezia's beautiful complexion seemed even more radiant without makeup. Painted toenails crept out from beneath her blue kaftan.

"What makes you think something has happened?" grinned Justine. "I'm going to Cerveteri. I told Dad and Amir I'd be along this morning."

Ignoring her daughter's question, Lucrezia said, "I know. You said you were going to Cerveteri today." She took Justine's cup out of her hand, refilled it, and placed it on the table with a dish of blackberries and yogurt. Then she motioned for her pacing daughter to sit down. Lucrezia knew Justine well, but was prepared to be astonished, which happened less often than she liked.

Disregarding the maternal gesture, Justine walked to the window and stared into the garden, watching Prego loosen the soil around the pansies. Her thoughts returned to Prego's revelation that boots and fear had filled the villa during the war. Justine's left eyebrow arched as she drew her fingers into the shape of a tent and touched them to her lips.

"You have that perplexing expression on your face. Somewhere between a Cheshire Cat and an aging philosopher."

"I received an e-mail from Nadia." She sat down to enjoy her blackberries and described the message from Nadia. "I *was* perplexed. She asked if I would observe the goings-on at the dig and report back to her. I think I've decided upon my approach. After all, resolving the tensions there would be helpful all around." She told her mother of her return message.

"That's reassuring. I would hate you see you and your father caught in a vise between Italian and Egyptian authorities."

"Exactly. But I must tell Dad that I know about the superintendent's concerns. He will blow off steam for awhile."

"Predictably." They both laughed.

Within the hour, Justine had packed, dressed, and made ready for the lengthy trip to Cerveteri, which, as her mother had reminded her, she had planned to make anyway. Tossing her bag in the back of her Spider, she turned and walked toward the garden, looking for Prego.

"Prego. Good morning," she said, finding him still on his knees, rocking back and forth as though he wasn't sure he could get up. She considered whether to offer a hand, but thought better of it.

"Good morning, *signorina*. You go on trip?" Prego struggled to his feet and brushed the dark soil off his knees. Placing both hands in his pockets, he looked up at Justine, striking a familiar stance and squinting into the morning sun.

"Back to Cerveteri, Prego. To see Dad. When I return, we'll talk."

Concern darted through the crevices in his aged face.

CHAPTER 12

—⌘—

We are dying, we are dying so all we can do is now to be willing to die, and to build the ship of death to carry the soul on the longest journey.

—D.H. Lawrence, excerpt from *The Ship of Death*

Vladimiro ai Bastioni was as empty as it had been the last time Justine and her father had eaten there. When she opened the door, the succulent aromas sparked memories of their earlier conversation about feminism. That night with Amir. On the long drive from Fiesole, she had rehearsed several conversations she wanted to initiate with her father and Amir about Ibrahim and her work with the team. By the time she saw her father's relaxed smile at the far end table, she had decided that her best tack was to be direct and honest about Nadia's message. *How novel*, she mused. *There was a time when I wouldn't risk conflict with Dad, especially if there was any hint of criticism.*

As soon as Justine sat down across from her father, he began his wine ceremony with a treasured bottle of Brunello di Montalcino. She observed his methodical moves without comment. And then, unexpectedly, it was he who spoke first. "How confident are you that Ibrahim's death was not an accident?" he asked without looking up.

Surprised by his abruptness, Justine paused before answering. *How confident am I?* "'Confident' is probably not a word I would use," she said. "'Suspicious' is more like it. In those last few days in Cairo, Ibrahim told us the whole story of the theft of the codex, including the involvement of the Supreme Minister of Antiquities, then he somehow managed to give Amir the copy to bring to me. Both Ibrahim and Amir knew it was risky."

"I've got people in our Egyptian Embassy looking into the case, and Amir tells me the family is working with the authorities." He reached for her hand. "This was a painful loss, Justine. He was like a father to me."

"I know, Dad." Justine took his hand in hers and squeezed. "It must hurt a great deal. I knew him for less than a year and I came to care about him more than I might have imagined." She held her father's wounded gaze and wondered how she would handle his death. Not well.

He patted her hand and withdrew his own as the restaurant's chef and proprietor approached. It was not in his nature to have another man think him sentimental. "Here we are, honey. Vladimino will tell us what we want to eat." He smiled at the rotund Napolitano. "By the way, Amir drove back to Rome this afternoon. He needs to return to Cairo."

"Trouble?"

"Not that I know of—but he's going to ask some hard questions."

Justine just nodded.

"*Signorina. Signore.* Welcome, welcome back. You are both well?" The corpulent man had the head and mane of an opera singer. "Tonight we will eat *zuppa di pesce* and *Calamari Ripieni.* Fresh from Sicily."

"Sounds wonderful," said Justine, without asking what *ripieni* meant. She wondered how Vladimino managed his delicacies with such large hands, and his inventory with so few customers. When he disappeared into the kitchen, she turned to her father.

"Dad, I received an e-mail from Nadia Mansour early this morning. You'll remember that she and I worked together on the UNICEF project in Egypt. Well, she now has some responsibility for the oversight of a few UNESCO sites, including the one in Cerverteri." She picked up her wine and moved it toward her lips, watching him over the rim of her glass. "I told her I would be working with the team. What would you think if one of my duties is to communicate on a regular basis with Nadia? Just an e-mail once in a while. She won't be coming to Italy this year."

Morgan's eyes narrowed. "What does she want to know?" He was suddenly alert.

Justine saw her father's defenses rise. Understandable. "She just wants to be assured that the team is working well with the local authorities. No big deal. Routine." She released her breath slowly, awaiting the inevitable.

Morgan slammed down his wine glass, splashing some of the ruby liquid onto his hand. He reached for his napkin, "Bitch! The local superintendent has given Nadia reason to think that there are tensions in the project! But now that Amir is working with her, things are fine. This is my team. I'm a professional. I know what I'm doing and I don't need interference." His fist came down on the edge of the table, spilling his wine again.

Justine ignored most of his questions—and all of his anger. She paused while he again wiped the red wine off his hand and attempted unsuccessfully to salvage the white linen tablecloth. "Dad, relax. I think she'd just like to know if *you* are satisfied with how things are going."

"'Satisfied' is a strong word, Justine. Riccardo is a hopeless romantic, but a good worker. The local crew takes too many breaks and insists on wine with lunch. And Della Dora is qualified but picky. Can't stop asking questions. But now that Amir is here, things will be different. A competent man. Soon we'll get some research assistants and that will help too."

"Della Dora?"

"The linguist, a new hire from the University of Bologna. Quite a scholar, renowned in fact. He agreed to come out of retirement for this dig. But sometimes I think he has his own agenda."

Apparently, Andrea refused his offer to work as a linguist with the team.

Vladimino arrived with two clean napkins and the succulent seafood dishes. With characteristic drama, he took his time placing the dishes on the table. Bowing lavishly, he kissed his folded fingers and said, "*Buon appetito!*" Morgan managed a weak smile.

As soon as Vladimino was out of sight, the lines on either side of his mouth tightened and the veins in his temples throbbed. Justine felt an urge to rescue her father swelling up in her chest. She wanted to change the subject, but resisted her maternal impulses. "Any hunches about what this is all about? Why the superintendent is causing problems?"

Morgan turned toward his daughter. His eyes and mouth softened. "You're not going to let go of this, are you? Or tell me what business you have in this matter."

"None. No business whatsoever. I just thought you might want to hear it from me so you could nip it in the bud." She slowly ate her chowder and waited.

Morgan lifted a little white bundle of stuffed squid onto his plate and began to carve. "When our team meets, the conversation is all over the place," he said. "Riccardo's hopes are unreasonable. Della Dora just asks questions. The three local team members, Adamo, Donatello, and Fabiano—sound like actors in an Italian opera, don't they?—so far they have little to contribute, especially after lunch when they've insisted on wine. Amir will help me straighten this out. Lately he's been preoccupied with family affairs. But, right now, no one seems committed to the mission of this project anyway."

"And what is that mission, Dad?" said Justine between spoonfuls.

Morgan paused, his fork suspended in the air. "The mission is"—he searched for the right words, and a chunk of crusty bread—"we are searching for a tomb or tombs that could provide information challenging current theories about the Etruscan civilization—its religious and governing practices, the development of its language, its origins."

"So what's your plan to get everyone on board with the mission?"

Morgan threw her a dart with his eyes, looked exasperated. Then he met her question with one of his own. "Okay. Dr. Anthropologist. What can I do to bring this team together?"

Justine was astonished. Her father had never asked for advice before. For several moments, she struggled for the right tone and words. "Successful teams fully understand their mission. Their members understand their roles—their contribution to the mission. Each member is encouraged to share his or her ideas, and each one is listened to. Problems are handled by the group."

"Sounds reasonable, but what if the ideas are bad ideas? Why do I have to listen to bad ideas?" His voice had an acidic quality; he ran his fingers through his hair.

Justine laughed, responding to the words rather than the tone. "Dad, it's important to make people feel that they've been heard, respected."

"Respected. Ah, yes," said her father, sliding back in his chair. "Tell you what, honey. Come with me to the team meeting in the morning. Gather your own data. If you can bring this team together, you've got yourself a job. I'll be going out early, but I'll come back and meet you for coffee and we'll go together to the damn meeting. Okay?"

"Okay," she said, pleased to be asked. "Under the clock tower?"

"I'll be there by nine." Rising with his hands firmly on each corner of the table, Morgan bowed to the chef and his daughter and left the check on his running tab.

⁊

It was 9:00 a.m. Justine sat under the indigo and gold fairytale clock tower at the west end of the Piazza Risorgimento. She sipped her cappuccino and wondered who was more nervous about the impending meeting: she or her father. She considered her presence there risky for both of them. The young waitress hurried to the table, her dress very short, its faded, appliquéd roses swaying from side to side. Justine raised her voice so that her order for another cappuccino and a croissant could be heard above sirens in the distance.

By 9:15, Justine had finished her coffee, but her father had not appeared. *Unlike him to be late,* she thought. *He probably lost track of time at the dig site.* Several minutes passed before her mind cast back to the sirens. They had come from the east and faded toward the north. She threw down five euros, grabbed her backpack, and ran.

Justine sped east through clothes-lined alleyways. As she raced toward the Necropolis of the Banditaccia, her speedometer read 75 km/h. Parking outside the necropolis, she sped through the fields of tumulus and jumped the low-lying fence into the area of her father's dig. Ambulances were parked nearby. An older man wearing a button-up shirt and khaki pants belted high on his waist rushed toward her.

"You must be Justine," said Delmo Della Dora, introducing himself. His broad forehead was framed by a full head of graying, curly hair; large brown eyes jumped impatiently. Wrinkles began at his hairline and ran down, crowning the bridge of his nose. "I'm afraid that your father is still down there. And Adamo. The roof has collapsed, bringing the tombs from above into the freshly dug area. I'm sure he'll be all right. Riccardo is down there now." His calm voice denied the urgency of his words.

Justine grabbed Della Dora's extended hand and turned toward the deep trench encircling the tumulus. She headed for the open ditch as Della Dora unsuccessfully reached out to stop her. Heart pounding in her chest, Justine slid twenty feet down the rough ladder to the bottom of the trench, landing with such force that the air was nearly forced out of her. She shook her head and breathed deeply.

Riccardo Chia moved his open hands rapidly across the wall of rock and soil searching for softness, a possible point of entry into the area that now imprisoned Morgan. About a third of the chambers had collapsed into the newly dug-out area. The smell of damp earth was palpable. Riccardo worked like a madman, realizing that no oxygen could reach his supervisor, although there could be a small pocket of air around him. But how long could that last? There was only a slight chance that Morgan was still alive.

Suddenly, Justine was at his shoulder. Riccardo looked up at her, hoping she couldn't read his mind or his face. He did not slow his furious search for a way in. "We have a bit of a problem, Justine," he said in an anxious, restrained voice. "Wait upside. *Prego.* I fully expect the rest of the ceiling to collapse at any moment."

"Sorry," she said simply, shaking her head from side to side. "How are we going to get them out?"

When she said "we," a flash of disappointment moved across his sweating face. "This whole place could go at any moment!" Riccardo yelled at her. "*Pronto!* Get out of here!"

Staring at the wall of soil as though she expected an opening to magically appear, she stood her ground.

He stared helplessly at Justine for a split second. Realizing that getting her to safety was a lost cause, Riccardo changed his strategy. "Go! Tell the men upside to get as many two-by-fours as they can find. And get me a drill. And a pipe. Fast."

Riccardo's commands animated Justine. She ran halfway up the ladder on the far side of the trough and barked orders. "Two-by-fours. A drill and pipe. And tell the paramedics to get an oxygen tank down here. Make it quick." Everyone sprang into action. The boards began sliding down into the trough, followed by Fabiano, who passed them to Riccardo. Donatello ran, desperate eyes darting this way and that; he returned quickly with a drill from his pickup. Medics raced forward with an oxygen tank in tow.

The roar from the floor of the tumulus above collapsing a second time jolted Justine's mind back to the moment of the earthquake in St. Sergius. Now, this moment, gray dust burst forth from the opening in the tomb like steam from a boiling kettle. She shuddered and screamed as she ran toward Riccardo who was being buried alive. "It's collapsing!" The opening was now completely closed. Fabiano held half a board; the other half was caught in the debris.

"Shovels," yelled Donatello, panic surging through his voice. "Shovels!" As they arrived he threw them into the trough. Justine and the two men started to dig furiously in the area of the blocked entryway.

"Too many shovels," Della Dora insisted, realizing that the diggers were getting in each other's way. Justine and Fabiano pulled back, looking around desperately for an alternate route. Della Dora began furiously waving both hands over his head.

Deep inside the collapsed cavity, ten feet below, in a space thirty feet across, two remaining survivors were separated by soil and granite. Each struggled to stay alive. Morgan stooped in a three-foot-high space formed by two broken columns that had fallen from above. He shined his small flashlight around the moist earth, desperately searching for even a hint of an opening, until he realized, helplessly, that there was none. The narrow beam of light landed briefly on a granite edge situated on a flat plane near the bottom of the debris just beyond his reach. Morgan tried repeatedly to reach the granite tip, but further movement was impossible. His light flashed on a booted foot extending from under the collapsed beam.

He tried frantically to reach the body, who he thought might be Adamo because of the unique steel toe on his boot, but he couldn't move his right leg, and his short supply of air had to be conserved, would soon be gone. He felt around for a piece of lumber with which to dig, but found none. He drew short, shallow breaths, using as little of the precious oxygen as possible, his calmness that of a man who had been in tight spots before. Four feet away, on the other side of a wall of stone and soil, Riccardo sat up under a teepee of two-by-fours. The mud in his eyes blinded him, and his skin felt hot and clammy. He couldn't move, but didn't know if anything was broken. Like Morgan, he knew air was at a premium. He drew shallow breaths even as his heart began to beat rapidly. He knew he must regulate his blood pressure and breathing.

Riccardo was usually fearless. He had free-soloed Mont Blanc and risked a fatal fall on the cobblestones of Siena while riding in the Palio. But this was different. If his asthma kicked in, he knew his chances of survival would diminish quickly.The man with the waving arms, Delmo Della Dora, spoke urgently. "Through the top tumulus! Go in through the top!" Della Dora was now racing up the stairs, surprisingly agile for a man in his early eighties. Earlier they had dismissed going through the existing tumulus for fear of causing the floor to collapse further. But now that the top tombs had fallen through, this option became worth testing.

Justine and the men holding shovels stared at one another. Without speaking, they rushed for the ladder and moved toward the front of the tumulus, crossing on the single board that served as a bridge across the trough into the original structure. Della Dora was already inside. "It's still fragile," he said, standing on the stone rim just short of the collapsed area. "See here. There's a gap between the debris and the remaining floor. I'm afraid it is too dangerous to walk on."

Justine looked up at Della Dora for a second time. *Rational in crisis*, she thought. "Then we won't walk on it," she promised. "Span a few boards over the opening and hand me the drill. I can inch out there. Where do you think they are?" The question was directed at whoever had an opinion.

"Dr. Jenner is near the front." Fabiano pointed a few feet ahead of where they stood. "And Dr. Chia must be a few feet behind. We don't know about Adamo. There, maybe," he motioned.

Donatello nearly fainted, put both hands on his forehead, but recovered in time to plug the drill into a generator in his truck. "Adamo! Adamo!" he cried, and carelessly handed the drill through to Justine, who was already six feet out on the planks, suspended three feet above the debris. Distance was not the issue. If she were to fall, she could cause the debris below to pack tighter around the men, robbing them of whatever oxygen remained. She lay on her stomach, digging as much debris as possible away with her right hand. Shifting from her stomach onto her left shoulder and hip, she took the drill, propped it at a right angle, and began to drill. *Too much vibration!* she yelled silently. *My God—even if they're still alive, I'm going to kill them!* "How long do they have?" she yelled out to the men behind her.

"*Dipende. Dipende,*" said Fabiano. "Maybe no time. Maybe hour." He nervously rolled a cigarette but didn't light it.

"Let us assume an hour, *piu o meno,*" said Della Dora, feigning confidence.

"Yes. Thank you," said Justine, her courtesy offered without thought.

For Justine, and everyone else in the vicinity, eight minutes of drilling seemed like an eternity. "Hand me a longer bit," she said, "and the pipe." She raised her left forearm to wipe the hair out of her eyes.

Donatello handed her a fifteen-inch augur bit, while Fabiano created a sling on the end of a long board so that the pipe could be righted if Justine was able to force it into the hole. Twice the pipe fell with a sharp thud onto the soil below. "Careful!" yelled Donatello, heavy perspiration dripping from his brow.

"I'm through!" shouted Justine finally. "I've broken through." She handed the drill back to Fabiano and tried to steer the end of the two-inch pipe into the hole, lowering it slowly. She succeeded on the third try.

"Dad!" she yelled into the pipe. "Are you there? Dad! Is Adamo with you?" Only silence met her entreaties. She desperately called out again. Below, Morgan grabbed the pipe and began digging soil out of it with his forefinger. "Justine? Is it you? I'm afraid Adamo is gone."

She paused and quickly turned to glance at Donatello, who had heard that his brother was probably dead. He collapsed, head between his knees.

Justine paused, moisture welling up in her eyes. "Are you all right down there?" she asked, her lips brushing the pipe as she spoke. "Are you getting enough air?"

"The air's coming through," her father said in a stronger voice. "But I can't move my right leg."

"Can you hold on, Dad? Riccardo's down there too. Nearby, we think."

"Sure. I can hold on for quite a while." Far less confident than he let on, he forced his voice into normalcy.

Justine turned toward the men and said in a steely voice: "Give me the drill. I'm moving forward a few feet."

The fire department had arrived during the pipe-rescue of Morgan. They took over the more difficult rescue of Riccardo, and the unearthing of Adamo's body. Much of the collapsed tomb had to be excavated before the three men could be extracted. By the time Riccardo was freed, he was in the throes of a severe asthma attack. Morgan was unconscious. Adamo was confirmed dead.

CHAPTER 13

Upon this gifted age, in its dark hour
Rains from the sky a meteoric shower
Of facts . . . they lie unquestioned, uncombined,
Wisdom enough to leech us of our ill
Is daily spun, but there exists no loom to weave it into fabric.

—Edna St. Vincent Millay, 1939

A PALE LIGHT SHONE THROUGH from the nurses' station halfway down the hall; otherwise, the only lights and sounds in Cerveteri hospital were electronic flashing eyes, racing green lines on heart monitors, the purr of oxygen tanks. Justine dozed uncomfortably in a straight-backed armchair. When her father was dug from the rubble that afternoon, his condition had been worse than expected. Even though a small stream of oxygen had entered through the pipe into the space where he lay captive, his body oxygen level had been at 82, a result of his shallow breathing. The unbearable pain of multiple leg fractures ushered him in and out of consciousness. Justine and his doctors awaited signs of brain damage.

Down the hall, Riccardo Chia struggled in the aftermath of a severe asthma attack. "We found him just in time," the medic had reported. "His face was blue."

Justine shifted in her chair. It was nearly 5:00 a.m. When she had arrived the day before, Nurse Elena had taken one look at her muddy khakis and powdered, matted hair, and led her by the hand to the shower in the nurses' quarters. Anna, the proprietor of the inn where she was staying, had brought a change of clothes from Justine's room there.

She had called Riccardo's family members, many of whom were to arrive that day. Once reassured that the surgery on her father's leg had been successful, Justine had called her mother. Della Dora had driven to his daughter's home in Rome. Adamo's body had been taken to the family home in a western suburb; Donatello and Fabiano had followed.

The world felt ominous to Justine despite the morning's insistent light. What had she said at dinner two nights before? Anything for which she wished to make amends with her father? She didn't think so. She rose and walked to her father's bedside. Morgan's face looked younger under the oxygen mask. Its lines had relaxed in the absence of consciousness.

His eyes moved beneath the lids, then slowly opened, closing and opening several times, registering in quick succession recognition and pain. The corner of his mouth drew itself into a forced smile. "When did you learn to use a drill?" he asked simply, reaching for her hand.

Justine gave way to tears that had been on call all night. Her body shook with sobs of relief as she leaned over and kissed her father on the forehead. "Yesterday," she said haltingly. "Yesterday."

Morgan tried unsuccessfully to turn toward her, surprised that his right leg was suspended above the bed. "What's going on down there?" he asked, motioning to his leg with the arm unencumbered by an IV.

"Two fractures," Justine said flatly. "You were in surgery until late last night." Her body shuddered in the aftermath of crying. She blew her nose and rubbed her eyes.

"Prognosis?" he asked without affect, although his eyes expressed both gratitude and anxiety.

"The surgery went well. In a few months, you'll be as good as new. You'll be on crutches for at least six weeks, then a cane for a while . . ."

"An archeologist who can't walk. Damn. How is Riccardo? Adamo?" Then he was quiet, a flash of misery contorting his facial muscles.

"Yes, Adamo is dead. Riccardo's down the hall. The second collapse buried him too, and he was having an asthma attack when we found him, but he's going to be all right. There's a slight concern about the stress on his heart." Justine relayed Riccardo's actions, including his insistence on staying in the tomb even after it became clear to him that another collapse was imminent. "Everyone was a hero yesterday, Dad. Della Dora is with his daughter in Rome."

Morgan pondered his unwillingness to take Riccardo seriously—and his condescension toward the other team members. Remorse and embarrassment swelled like a wave, obliterating lighter thoughts. Tears hovered on the rim of the oxygen mask and slowly rolled down either side of his face.

Justine immediately regretted that she had told him so much. The screen attached to the heart monitor registered steep peaks and troughs.

The heart dance slowed. "Wish Amir had been here," he whispered.

Justine wiped his cheeks and eyes. "Now, get some rest. It's barely dawn and you have all the time in the world. I'll be right here." She turned toward the waiting chair.

"Justine." His voice was insistent, yet somehow tentative.

She turned and started back toward the bed. "Yes, Dad?"

"I was scared," he said almost inaudibly, as though he wanted to shield the world from this truth. "I was scared and kept thinking about your experience in the Cairo earthquake. We've never really talked about it."

"I was terrified, Dad. I was sure I was going to die. Nobody knew where I was."

"Fear is a natural human emotion. If you live your life fully, you can't avoid it."

"I know that now. But the nightmares won't go away. Very Kafkaesque, no rules, no boundaries. Unpredictable. Sometimes I'm drowning in deep, rushing water. On other nights, someone I love is buried alive." She smiled meekly and ruffled his hair.

He winced at her description. "It will help to talk it out, honey. We'll be there for each other . . ." He squeezed her hand, then released it as he fell back into deep sleep.

"I still need you—always will," she whispered into his ear.

Justine was unable to go back to sleep, so she sat staring out the tall window as the rising sun backlit undistinguished gray stucco buildings. She had thought modern civilization had bypassed the ancient town of Caere, now Cerveteri. The efficient surgical team and well-trained nurses had negated that idea.

A shadow cast itself across the black-and-white tiles. Justine turned, expecting the night nurse, but found instead a male figure standing in the doorway, leaning against its frame. She stood up and walked toward him.

"Amir? Amir!" she cried. "Thank god, you're back." Justine threw her arms around him. For several moments they held one another tightly, then she gently pulled away.

"I'm sorry I wasn't here. I should have been here," Amir said.

"But you're here now. That's all that matters. It's been horrible. Riccardo may not pull through."

"How is your dad doing?"

"Doing well, I think," she said softly, drawing Amir to the bedside. "His breathing has returned to normal and there doesn't seem to be any sign of brain damage. The leg will take several weeks to heal. But he was his old self again this morning." Justine stood at the foot of the bed, absentmindedly pulling errant hairs back into a ponytail.

"It was my fault," said Morgan when he awoke and saw Amir beside his bed. "I had the local engineer examine the site and he assured me that the ceiling would hold. I should have known better than to trust that sup and her team of merry men."

"So you didn't erect a temporary ceiling in the cavity?" asked Amir. His question bore no judgment. He had long admired his grandfather's old partner, and he was grateful to be working with Morgan on the Cerveteri dig.

"No, we didn't," said Morgan, embarrassed by the carelessness inadvertently implied by the question. "And Adamo's death is on my head." He choked up and looked away. "Damn, it's good to have you back," he said, sounding like a lost boy.

Embarrassed by the emotional response from his mentor, Amir changed the subject. "Justine texted me." It was clear to Justine that he regretted the question about the temporary ceiling. "She says you're your old self again."

"This leg will slow me down for a while. Damn it." Morgan stared at Amir with fatherly affection, the boy who had always hung around their excavation sites, asking question after question. Ibrahim had always bragged about his oldest grandson. The young man was nearly thirty years old now—not exceptionally tall, but with the rugged good looks and black eyes that had made his grandfather the Don Juan of the international set decades earlier. It was for all of these reasons—and memories—that he had hired Amir on this dig. Now he was the only vital connection to Ibrahim.

Justine returned with two cups of coffee. "No, you can't have one," she said even before her father asked. "Nurse Antonia is right behind me with the breakfast tray and she's going to check your vital signs—sans caffeine."

Morgan pulled off the oxygen mask. He spoke softly, with a raspiness caused by his dry throat. "Amir. Justine," he said in a conspiratorial tone, "There's something down there. Before my flashlight batteries gave out, I saw a granite edge situated on a flat plane at the bottom of the debris. If it was part of the tomb above, it would have fallen at an angle." His eyes betrayed excitement, as did the heart monitor.

"Take it easy, Dad. Please relax. We can talk about this later," insisted his daughter.

"*Si*, Dr. Jenner. No talking. Eat now." The matronly nurse set his breakfast tray on the side table, swung it over his waist, and reached for his pulse. "Did I tell you to remove your oxygen mask?" she demanded. She stuck a thermometer in his open mouth.

"Shall we take a walk?" Justine asked Amir, eager to leave the room. She knew he didn't like watching his idol being bullied, even by his nurse. "I could use a bite to eat."

Morgan's eyes pleaded with them not to go.

Justine chose to ignore her father's appeal. "We'll be back soon," she said. Taking Amir by the arm, Justine headed for the stairs.

"Tell me what happened out there, Justine," said Amir when they had stepped through the automatic doors and into the crisp morning air.

As she steered him toward a small coffeehouse near the hospital, Justine narrated the events of the previous day, highlighting the selfless actions performed by everyone involved in the drama. The death of Adamo, the near death of Riccardo. Her own actions she downplayed.

Amir remained silent, rolling the information over in his mind. As they arrived at the café door, he touched her shoulder. His gaze was full of compassion. "I will ask the same question we asked about my grandfather's death about the collapse of the tomb: Was it an accident? In both cases, I'll find out."

The pair took a table by the window. Only one other person was in the sterile room, a rotund man of about fifty. A ball cap lettered with PALERMO shadowed his bearded face as he stared into his coffee.

Justine was shaken. "I don't know if the collapse was an accident. It's probably a result of Italian carelessness rather than intent. However, there has been conflict between some of the local authorities and the team. I saw Dad checking the durability of the frame, I'm sure he didn't notice anything suspicious."

"I talked with the superintendent last week and assured her that nothing would happen without her go-ahead, and that she would be the first to know if anything turned up. I think she was reassured," said Amir. "I can't believe she's behind any foul play."

"A generous concession—but wise. I know that the local authorities who have been here for generations don't want to be shown up by an international team, but weakening the ceiling would be a criminal act, not professional jealousy."

"Exactly." He stared out the window for several moments before saying, "I'll check it out . . . Now, let me tell you why I accepted your father's offer. We've hardly had time to talk . . ." He turned to order coffees and croissants.

Justine blushed slightly, then smiled.

"After Zachariah was murdered and grandfather was implicated in the theft of the codex, and you and Andrea were expelled, I just couldn't stay in Egypt. At least, not for a while. I'd taken a leave from the museum just before your father called. Call it fate, God's plan, whatever—it was a message from the gods." A lock of curly hair fell over his eye as he leaned forward to take a bite of croissant.

Justine remembered again why she found him so attractive. "I am so deeply sorry about your brother and grandfather." She paused and reached for his hand. "So it wasn't about us?" she asked innocently, not sure whether she wanted to hear his answer.

"That was the frosting, as you Americans say." He paused to let the rumbling of two garbage trucks subside. "Unplanned," he continued. "I suspect I might have ended up in Italy even if your father hadn't called. I had submitted two UNESCO applications for projects in southern France and Spain, too."

Amir raised his coffee cup with both hands. "It was a difficult time. I felt unsettled, confused."

"Well, I'm glad you're here," she said with pronounced sincerity. "And so is Dad." She paused again, turning to find her small purse. "We'd better get back."

✑

The hospital hallways were unusually quiet except for an urgent voice over the intercom announcing, "*Codice Blu. Codice Blu. Secondo pavimento.*" Justine began to run. Amir followed. They took the stairs to the second floor two at a time. At the top of the stairs, a guard attempted to block their passage. Amir politely said, "Excuse us," and pushed through.

Justine demanded of anyone who could listen, "Who is it?!" She was ignored.

As she stepped into her father's quiet room, Morgan pointed east along the hall, his eyes portraying the panic that Justine felt. When Justine and Amir reached Riccardo's room, two physicians and three nurses crowded around his bed; other hospital personnel stood blocking the doorway. Justine recognized the young doctor who was securing the defibrillator cups onto Riccardo's chest. Another person adjusted the dial and lever on the machine. A flat line on the heart monitor told the story.

Justine and Amir stared helplessly through a window into the room. Justine pushed on the glass with both hands, fingers spread apart. The room began to darken and her legs began to grow numb. Amir put his arm around her shoulders to steady her.

For some minutes the doctors continued to alternate mouth-to-mouth resuscitation with jolts from the defibrillator.

"He's dead," Justine whispered. "Riccardo's dead."

Several minutes passed. How long had it been? Six, seven, eight minutes? The blue line started to move again, like a ribbon being picked up by the wind.

CHAPTER 14

—∞∞∞—

Our efforts are like those of the Trojans. We believe that with resolution and daring we will alter the blows of destiny, and we stand outside to do battle.
—Constantine P. Cavafy, Greek poet

J USTINE DROVE HER FATHER to Cerveteri on a crisp April morning in his Mercedes SUV. Her Spider was too cramped for his leg brace, and she found, to her surprise, that she enjoyed the power of the larger car. She had steered away from them, considering them too ostentatious, too expensive to operate. Four hours of driving and two stops at lavish autostrada centers for food would give her plenty of time to share her thoughts with him: about Andrea, her need to get an apartment. Amir? Perhaps.

As daughter and father drove from Fiesole through Florence, they marveled at the new apartment buildings and small tech industries that were spreading out from the city like a giant, flowing skirt. By the time they'd reached highway A1, Justine was ready to venture into more delicate subjects.

"What do you hear from Andrea?"

Morgan braced himself. He had noticed that his daughter was becoming increasingly frank with him. "Andrea's called every other day or so. She can't get away from Paris until next week," explained Morgan patiently. "Why do you ask?"

Justine hesitated. "She and I have some unfinished work to do on the codex and on the article we're co-writing for *Archaeology*, so I'd just wondered when she's returning. She e-mailed me to get reports on your recovery, but no commitment to return as yet." She drove in silence for a while, her eyes focused on the chaotic traffic. She finally added, "I came to know Andrea fairly well in Egypt. We spent a great deal of time together."

"And . . ." he prompted. He wasn't going to make this conversation easy for her.

"She had a tragic love affair many years ago. Her fiancé was tortured and killed in Algeria. She told me she hasn't had a grand passion since." In the glare of the morning sun, Morgan couldn't read his daughter's expression, for which she was grateful.

"She told me about Francois," said Morgan. "If this conversation is intended to warn me about Andrea, you needn't bother. I'll make my own decisions regarding my love life, honey. You don't have to worry about your old dad. I've had a few relationships since your mother, and I can assure you, I'm not that fragile."

Justine continued, seeming to disregard his remarks, "Andrea can be secretive, even manipulative. I've come to love her, but I'm not naïve about where I stand with her."

"I'm not naïve, either, Justine," snapped Morgan. The conversation was over. He turned away from her and watched the countryside open into rolling green hills punctuated with columnar cypress. So different from the scraggly cypress in Carmel, he noticed.

"An espresso?" Justine asked, not waiting for his answer, pulling over at a rest stop. Nor would she resist the temptation to dawdle inside and give her father time to cool off. Where better can one enjoy browsing and find the works of Alexander Dumas and books like *Madame Bovary* and *Moby Dick*, as well as prize cheeses and decadent chocolates, than at stops on an Italian autostrada?

Twenty minutes later, Justine returned with the coffees and *Madame Bovary* under her arm. They drove in silence for several miles. Morgan sipped his espresso more slowly than usual. *Is he angry? Or just making me suffer?*

Morgan finished off his coffee, folded the small paper cup, and carefully placed it in the trash satchel hanging from his glove compartment. "I thought Nasser was your 'grand passion' in Egypt," he finally said, "but there is something between you and Amir. Want to tell me about it?"

Touché, Dad. She decided she would. "While I was working in Egypt, there was tension between us. I respected him—and he respected me, I think—but he kept making these clumsy attempts to protect me. Well, not always clumsy.

And I thought there was sufficient evidence to think he was involved in the theft of the codex. Eventually, I realized he was trying to protect his brother . . . and his grandfather."

"Then Zachariah was murdered."

"Yes . . . and his grandfather—"

"—may also have been murdered."

"Yes. I'm sure of it." She paused and drove silently for a while. "After Amir saved my life, we became a team of sorts, trying to figure out what was going on. There was no romance, no . . ."

"You weren't lovers."

"Not then . . ."

"But now?"

"Now, we'll have to see. I would say we've started down a new path."

"Amir is a good man, at least as far as I'm concerned. Neither your mother nor I would be unhappy with Amir as a son-in-law. But would you marry an Egyptian?"

"Probably not. For the same reason that Mom didn't. I'd worry that the tradition of unequal relationships would set in sooner or later. That's not what I want in a marriage."

"But your mother made the wrong decision anyway." Morgan grinned and looked away.

Justine laughed. Her father had been overly protective of her mother. And he'd certainly tried to dominate her. *So much for cultural stereotypes.*

With no connecting highway between A1 and the western coast, the drive around Viterbo and Tarquinia took an additional curvy hour. They were now in the province of Lazio—what had been Etruscan territory. Cypress, olive, and apple trees lined the roadway, and small signs occasionally indicated the presence of Etruscan tombs nearby. They rejoined the highway at Tarquinia, where the hills vanished and the landscape rolled out flat down to the Tyrrhenian Sea. They turned east into City Centro and headed toward the hills that held the old town of Cerveteri.

"That isn't the base of a sarcophagus," declared Morgan with the enthusiasm of a novice. Having been helped down the ladder by Fabiano, he stood inside the empty cavity that had imprisoned Riccardo and himself only a couple of weeks before. Six broad beams now supported a newly erected ribbed ceiling. Quite different than when Amir had come out there right after the collapse and discovered the ancient beams partially sawed through. He'd photographed the evidence and handed it over to the Carabinieri. He squinted at Donatello, who still stood vigil with his grieving family.

Justine and Amir had heard Morgan hint at a possibly remarkable find. But it was Della Dora, the elder team member, who asked, "Then what is it? It's flat and framed like a base with the sarcophagus missing. I don't quite see . . ."

"It's the top of a step, isn't it?" Amir asked. "The top of a step," he repeated.

"Exactly," agreed Morgan, pleased to let the younger man announce the tentative conclusion, especially after what Justine had told him about their relationship. Patting Amir on the shoulder, he leaned fully on his right crutch, which was slowly burying its rubber foot in the soft floor of the cavity. "Look at the top more closely. It doesn't have the usual anchors for the walls of a sarcophagus. And notice the almost smooth ridge. The surface shows wear as though it has been walked on." He switched his crutch to his left side, supporting his weight with his left foot and leaned over to brush a layer of fine dust off the piece of granite.

"Then the tomb is below us!" exclaimed Justine, stating the obvious. "The find is below."

"I'd say so," Morgan grinned. "More digging is in order." He turned to Della Dora, who beamed with pleasure as though he could see Tut-like treasures in his mind's eye.

"We might yet find the truth about the Etruscans," declared Della Dora, his dimples deepening as he furiously took notes.

"And what truth is that, Professor?" asked Amir, fully attending to the older man, whose cheeks were flushed with both the rising heat in the sauna-like enclosure and the thrill of the hunt.

"The origins. The language. The prevailing theories have never satisfied me, *non sono credibile*," replied Della Dora. "I'm not naïve enough to propose colonization. The evidence doesn't support the uniformity of a colonization movement. And while the communities had much in common, much also *era molto fortuito*, randomized, serendipitous . . . unique."

"I favor provocation," said Morgan excitedly, still staring at the upper step.

Squatting to get a better look, Justine looked up, brushing her hair behind her ear. "What do you mean by provocation?"

"The Villanovans, if they ever existed, might have evolved from the Neanderthals or been very early immigrants from the north. We know that civilizations don't evolve at a steady rate. They can have setbacks—wars and natural disasters, for example. And also great leaps forward," said Morgan.

"Ah," said Justine. "Great leaps forward—provocations—can arise from immigrants with new ideas; an invention; a drastic change in weather; a compelling, unresolved need, such as figuring out how to fish for mysterious creatures . . ."

"Exactly. It could be a case of self-creation," ventured Amir. "The development of a society can be accelerated through its simultaneous employment of new ideas."

"*E' possibile*," said Della Dora, his knowledge of quantum physics oozing back into fading memory banks. He stopped writing and his eyes filmed over; an internal dialogue now demanded his attention. "The interplay or interdependence of new ideas merging into something entirely new."

"Very possible," agreed Morgan, listening carefully, even as his eyes searched the ceiling. "Do you think this ceiling will hold for another level of digging?"

"I do, sir," said Amir. "If anything, we were overly conscientious in building it. It will probably be here a thousand years from now, unlike the original." He caught Morgan's steely eyes. Amir had told Morgan and Justine that one of the original beams had been partially sawn through. They were being circumspect with the information until they could get to the bottom of it. Who would benefit from a collapse of the tomb?

"Well, I hope it won't take all that long to finish this project. *Sono gia anziano*, I am already an old man," declared Della Dora, moving his flashlight back and forth across the ceiling.

"No time to lose, then. Let's dig!" said Morgan, hobbling toward the opening.

⌒

Riccardo was sitting under a nearby sycamore tree when they emerged from the trench surrounding the tumulus.

"Hello!" Justine yelled as soon as she saw him.

"We missed you, *caro amico*," said Della Dora, cresting the top of the stairs after Amir helped Morgan to the top. Everyone walked toward the man seated casually under a sycamore.

"Soon we'll all be back at work, toiling away on our historical quest. Right, Riccardo?" Morgan laid his arm across Riccardo's shoulder.

Riccardo stepped out into the sunlight as Justine approached him and placed a hand on each of his shoulders, pulling him toward her. She hadn't seen Riccardo since he had left the hospital to recuperate at his family home. After a prolonged hug, she stood back and surveyed him closely.

He couldn't miss the shock that flickered through her eyes. What she saw was a much older and wiser man, with luminous eyes and a deep sense of peace. "You're different," she said simply.

"*Si*," Riccardo responded. "I died in there."

A slight breeze swayed the branches above, and dust from the tumulus rippled across the field. Everyone stood still, mesmerized by a scene that none would ever forget.

Justine waited with Riccardo while the others slowly walked back toward the unrevealed tomb. There was so much she wanted to know.

No words were exchanged as the two friends sat close together under the swaying sycamore. Blood-red poppies danced whimsically nearby, as though responding to an unseen conductor. The sweet aroma of fresh barley, somewhere nearby, entered their nostrils.

Riccardo knew what Justine wanted to know: what it was like to die. "My mother was there with me, when I was dying. She told me, 'Not yet, my son.'"

Justine's eyes held his. "She sent you back?" She paused in invitation. "Tell me everything."

"As a priest, I heard stories about near-death experiences and attributed them to deeply held Catholic beliefs about the afterlife—the tunnel and light, ecstasy, the presence of family members, a welcoming Jesus. I was skeptical— but I can't deny what happened to me."

She breathed deeply, exhaling slowly, in no hurry to hear what was coming.

"Do you know how long my heart stopped?"

"The doctors said less than ten minutes."

"Ten minutes," he repeated in a flat tone. "Yes . . . I felt . . . as though my soul opened up and I understood everything. Such clarity. Some force was touching my face, soothing me. The sense of peace was overwhelming. *Tranquillita di spirito.*"

"Where were you? In your body?"

"Someplace else. I was unaware of my body. My self was my consciousness, cradled by overwhelming love. *Amore. Amore.*" Riccardo sat quite still, embracing the verdant surroundings. "There is more you need to know about me now," he said. "When I left the priesthood, it was so I could be myself. *Mi. Io stesso, unicamente.* I would no longer hide my sexuality within the comfort of the Church. Or protect my father from the truth, for he had sent me there." Riccardo's voice became harsh, intense: "'You are the chosen one, Riccardo. It is you who will be our family's contribution to the priesthood. It is right, my son.'"

"It wasn't your choice? Nor your mother's?"

"It made sense, you see. With my asthma, I couldn't work with the vines. But history, not God, was my first love. My mother knew that too."

"Your death experience brought you back to the Church?" Justine felt a profound curiosity.

"When I left the priesthood, I didn't abandon my faith. Dying only strengthened it, but I have no intention of returning to the cloth. I can do more on the outside."

"Yet you are different now . . ."

"*Si,* my dear friend. I can now see more clearly. Accept myself more fully. God doesn't make mistakes; He made me as I am. With this experience, He has removed any lingering doubts, and the shame I felt. I am whole."

Justine's mind spun back to the revelation that Jesus had a twin sister, Elizabeth, in the codex. She had died and was buried just outside Cairo. *Religious leaders in Egypt insisted that God doesn't make mistakes . . . but why would he bring Elizabeth into the world only to take her away three short months later? Is Riccardo right—that God doesn't make mistakes?* She reached for her friend with open arms, pulling him into an embrace. After several moments, she rose and offered her hand. She whispered, "I feel your joy."

He accepted her hand, walking with her toward the tumulus.

CHAPTER 15

⚊⚊⚊

In the beginning is Goddess and Goddess is One Source of All Things. And She creates Her Self from Nothing And out of Nothing She comes by Magic. And the Goddess is filled with Joy and Love And She takes great pleasure in Her Self And out of Her Self She makes Her Self And the Self She makes is Woman.
                                                    —Shekhinah Mountainwater

---

"THE MAREMMA, the rugged coastal region of southwestern Tuscany, encompasses part of southern Tuscany and part of northern Lazio, including the province of Viterbo on the border. The poet Dante Alighieri in his *Divina Commedia* places the Maremma between Cecina and Corneto, its modern name Tarquinia. It was traditionally populated by the Butteri, cattle breeders who until recently rode horses on exquisite leather saddles with horns often tipped with silver." Justine paused in her reading of the travel guide to Amir. They were speeding south from Florence toward Santa Fiora. "I'd like to see one of those saddles," she said.

"We'll see what we can do," he grinned. Amir had convinced her to accompany him to the Maremma in search of the unusual tombs of Sovana, particularly the Tomba del Sileno. He was somewhat surprised that she'd agreed to join him. "Read some more," he urged gently. It wasn't the travel information he wanted as much as to hear the sound of her voice.

"Okay," she consented. "Endowed with significant natural and environmental resources, the Maremma is today one of the best tourist destinations in Italy, a region where ancient traditions have survived and Tuscan culture is preserved. It is being promoted as a destination for agritourism." Justine observed Amir's striking profile for a moment. *Would he have any reason to know what agritourism means?* "That means farms that offer lodging to the public. Sometimes they have great gardens," she editorialized, and wondered about

Miranda's spring garden east of here. Silently searching the text, Justine skipped ahead. "Cows and wine. Oh, here we are: 'The hills of the Maremma can be divided into three areas: the area del Tufo (literally, "the tuff area"), the Colline Metallifere (literally, "the hills of metals"), and the hills on the border with the Siena region. This is the heart of the Etruscan Empire.' I don't find anything here about the Tomba del Sileno."

Amir steered Justine's Spider into the Villa Narsi at Santa Fiora, a glorious period mansion reminiscent of Lucrezia's home in Fiesole. A small stone chapel huddled close to the west side of the main house. They had planned for Justine to drive Amir to Cerveteri on Sunday afternoon and then go on to Rome. Friday and Saturday would be spent in this exquisite villa turned bed and breakfast, as guests of the proprietors, Suzanna and Max. She had been told about the villa and hosts by her friend Carolyn.

Suzanna escorted Justine through a brick archway, up mahogany stairs to the front bedroom on the second floor. "We'll gather for wine and *bruschetta* in an hour or so. Will you join us?" She smiled invitingly. Suzanne had porcelain beauty. She seemed guarded—or was she shy? Clearly not Italian.

"We'd love to," Justine answered for both Amir and herself. Suzanna allowed a flicker of satisfaction to express her pleasure and drew the heavy wooden door closed.

Amir had planned for them to share a room, but she'd insisted on getting her own room. He was disappointed. Justine turned to survey her room and the view. Arched wood casement windows with heavy shutters framed a vista of rolling southern hills scattered with homes with ochre roofs. A large bed with a black-and-white plaid cover, deep-red Oriental rug, small antique desk, and towering armoire furnished the generous room sparingly. She ruffled through her suitcase looking for *Madame Bovary* and shook out the white blouse and slacks she had brought for evening wear. Justine lay diagonally across the bed, the muted afternoon light sweeping across her shoulders, illuminating the pages of her recently acquired classic. Although her own experiences were markedly different from those of this eighteenth-century woman, she could understand the age-old conflict between reality and romance. Flaubert's portrait of marriage left little room for heightened expectations. Did satisfaction destroy desire, as he claimed? She grinned as she pondered her own experiences with desire, her conclusions melting away into sleep.

Why aren't I sharing a room with Amir? She enjoyed moments alone, and also sensed that she wasn't entirely ready for such intimacy. That first wild night with Amir at Anna's had been an accident of desire, although she didn't regret it. She just needed time.

✐

"Maremma, the most genuine and intimate part of Tuscany," pronounced Max, the quintessential Italian host, pulling out a large map of the region. He paced the spacious, well-equipped kitchen with a cigarette in one hand, the other hand waving through the smoky air with a conductor's flair. He was well along in his travelogue with Amir when Justine joined them. Her contented companion sat listening intently, a glass of red wine in one hand, the other anchoring the corner of the regional map.

Max paused to take in Justine, stunning in white linen and chunky silver jewelry, hair brushed loosely over her shoulders. Burgundy lipstick was her only makeup. "*Ciao*," he said. "We're talking about your trip tomorrow, to the heart of the Etruscan empire, and which route is best: Sovana, Sorano, Pitigliano. The tombs in the archeological parks are distinct, although they are all built into the tufa mountains."

"So unlike the tumuli of Cerveteri." She paused, leaning toward him. "If you don't mind, Max, perhaps we could open the door behind you. A little circulation." The smoke was a long-hanging cloud in the massive kitchen.

"Forgive me," he said, immediately smothering his cigarette in a nearby ashtray and opening the door. Max reluctantly looked at his wife, who flashed a disapproving glance. His smoking was a frequent bone of contention with the couple. Suzanna found it particularly distressing when his smoke bothered their guests.

Justine wasn't sure how to interpret Amir's expression. *Admiration for my directness? Displeasure? Embarrassment brought on by my criticism of our host?* "Thank you," she remarked easily. "You were recommending a route for us tomorrow?" She reached for her glass of wine and sat down beside Amir.

Suzanna placed a plate of warm tomato *bruschetta* on the table. The pungent aroma of fresh garlic and simmering olive oil filled the air.

Max added a small board of pecorino and olives to the simple, delicious feast.

"I was telling our hosts that I am an archaeologist and that you are an anthropologist," Amir said to Justine. "They asked the difference." His dark, handsome face posed the question as he reached for the cheese board.

Justine felt playful, and decided to make sport of the difference between her profession and Amir's—and her father's. "Archaeologists are satisfied with the 'what,' but anthropologists want to know 'why.' We are the real mystery solvers." She winked at Amir. "Take the mystery of the Anasazi of the American southwest. They disappeared from Mesa Verde hundreds of years ago, and no one really knows why. Meteorological computer programs suggest it was probably a change in weather patterns." Justine was about to launch into her own theory but paused to give Amir his opening.

"You make archaeologists sound rather dull. We're as interested in the 'why' as you are."

"Of course you're curious," Justine said coyly. "You ask yourselves, 'Now what museum would be interested in this rare artifact . . . and what would they be willing to pay for it?'" She winked at Suzanna, who laughed unreservedly.

"Women!" declared the amused Max. "We are slaves to their charm." He patted Amir on the shoulder and picked up another cigarette, waving the unlit prop in the air.

Amir held up both hands in surrender.

"Archaeologists examine material remains," Justine continued. "For their studies, anthropologists don't have to dig as far . . ."

"Or as deep," interrupted Amir, beginning to get the hang of the game.

"*Toccato! Buona storta*," quipped Justine, raising her glass to Amir while reaching for a second piece of lumpy red *bruschetta*.

"Ah," said Max, putting his arm around his wife and squeezing gently. "Good partners. An olive?" he asked, glancing at Amir.

A carpet of white daisies and gold poppies welcomed Justine and Amir into the ancient Etruscan necropolis north of Sovano. More than a hundred tombs, many accessible to visitors, lay along the edge of the tufa mountain. Following their host's directions, they had driven south nearly an hour from Santa Fiora. One of the most famous tombs in the area was the Tomba del Sileno, the one they had come to see.

"The tomb was discovered fairly recently," Amir explained as they climbed toward the tomb. "It has two peculiarities: it's the only circular niche tomb in the area, and it was intact with all the funerary items, urns, and cinerary remains, which of course are now in museums in Tarquinia and Rome. A kind of King Tut's tomb—all the riches still present."

"I've seen a mold of the balding Silenus in Baltimore," replied Justine, slipping her arm through Amir's to scramble up the uneven stones leading to the entrance. They halted their ascent, staring at the entrance of the tomb. "A mythological creature, half-man, half-beast, with pointed goats' ears, a large, bulbous nose, and an animal-skin cloak knotted under his long beard."

"That's him. I'd recognize him anywhere," Amir agreed, placing his hand on her waist to escort her into the darkened tomb. Like kids on a treasure hunt, they entered through the tufa arch. The once-lavish tomb was now an empty, circular room with dove niches near the ceiling.

Holding a flashlight in his left hand, Amir slowly ran his right palm along the rough surface that housed undiscoverable secrets. Justine mimicked his actions, as though they were reading Braille together. Several minutes passed.

Standing close to Justine, his torch lighting her face, Amir announced: "Not much left to see, but I love being in here, imagining it in its full splendor. Smelling the lingering scents."

"How do you think the sarcophagi were laid out? Rectangular cases in a round room seem awkward." The light accentuated Amir's angular features now and then, and Justine felt the warmth of desire seep into her body. Her eyelids lowered ever so slightly.

Amir moved closer to her, shifting the flashlight beams toward the perimeter of the tomb. They stared into the dark for several moments. "These sarcophagi were the short ones, no more than a meter or so long. They contained incinerated remains," he said softly.

"It is unfortunate that DNA can't be extracted from ashes," she observed. "By the way, thanks for sending me the report on the extracted DNA from Mary's comb." In the same crypt, and in nearly the same place where the codex was found, Amir and Justine had discovered a yellowed ivory comb with lotuses carved across the top. Mary had sketched the comb herself into her diary, a gift from her husband, Joseph.

Outside, the sun was directly overhead; oak shadows encircled the two of them. "I'm afraid you were right," she said. "The data don't tell us much. European Haplogroup H2a2, not uncommon in the Mediterranean."

"I have the comb, Justine. Smuggled it out of Egypt," he said in a low, conspiratorial tone, despite their being alone.

"Oh my god, Amir! You are in one hell of a lot of trouble!"

Amir laughed. "And how about you? Little Miss Righteous. Carrying the codex out of Egypt on your lap?"

"A copy, I must point out," Justine grinned and snuggled into his arm. His skin was alive to her touch. Disappointed with the bareness of Silenus's tomb, yet heady with anticipation, Amir and Justine moved further along the path.

Justine found a moss-covered rock and sat down, staring in wonder at the crumbled tomb façade bearing carvings of a lion, a slithering snake, a ram. The most stunning feature, the image that captured her full attention, leaned upright against the mountain: an angel with a fully spread left wing, its face worn away. The erect body emerged from the bottom of a tufa tunic, feet wedged into mammoth snake coils wrapped symmetrically along the embossed wall. "Now this is more like it," she exclaimed. "I wonder when images of angels first appeared? Certainly before the Christians."

"Long before," said Amir, joining her on the mossy stone, "but no one really seems to know exactly. Angels appeared before the Jews as well, in Persian and Sumerian art—even the Zoroastrians had angels. I guess man always dreamed of flying." A lock of hair fell onto his forehead as he tilted his head toward Justine. He drew a sketchpad and pencil from one of the pockets in his Australian outbacker slacks.

I want him to turn around and take me in his arms . . . "Women dream of flying too . . . adventure is an aphrodisiac," she said, scooting over to give him more room on the stone.

Amir looked up from his drawing and smiled in appreciation of her flirtatious demeanor, but resisted the urge to draw her closer. "Since no people have been found without some semblance of religion, perhaps men *and* women always imagined a messenger, some creature to communicate back and forth with the gods."

"I assume so," she gently conceded. They sat in tense silence for several moments as though waiting for the other to move. Justine continued, "Notice the snakes. They show up in the worship of Gaia, as well as in the hands of the Minoan Snake Goddess and in Hindu imagery."

"And in the temples of Mithraic mysteries throughout the Roman empire. The ability to shed their skins gave them an opportunity for rebirth, which promised a new beginning, a form of fertility," explained Amir. "I understand there is an amazing Mithraic collection in the basement of St. Clement. In Rome."

Justine nodded and vowed to visit that collection.

"So what do you think all this means?" he asked.

"Well, we can assume that the Etruscans came from a goddess culture. Their deities were female, their governance and symbology. The least we can claim is that men and women were equal partners, partners in reciprocal relationship with one another. This is just further confirmation. The question is still: which one?"

"Exactly."

Justine smiled. "Dad will resist any notion of a goddess culture, unless evidence hits him on the head." She watched Amir sketch, wondering what evidence her father would accept. Imagining a culture ruled by women was outside of Morgan's conceptual framework. Amir added the last flourish to the angel's wings, then his warm black eyes gazed up into hers.

"Amir." She broke the spell. "What would anyone have to gain from causing the collapse of the tomb?"

"I don't know." His voice shifted into a low, cautionary tone. "I can't believe the superintendent would deliberately hire someone to damage the tomb and kill people in the process. Too dangerous. I found Donatello moody and distracted, but why would he kill his own brother? I suspect it was meant to scare us off, not kill us."

"For what purpose? But there may be other forces that we aren't aware of. The Mafia, for instance." They were quiet for several moments, afloat in an array of unknowns.

"Or their charge might have been to slow us down, discourage us enough so that the international team would stop work, then a local den of thieves could take over and benefit from whatever we found," she said.

"The reverse of the Luxor tombs," Amir reminded her. "In that case, the locals got there first."

"Except for King Tut," she reminded him.

Amir grinned and nodded. "There is a parallel there. Tut was buried underneath Seti's massive tomb. Whatever we find, it will be deep below the primary tombs. No matter what their objective, we must be careful. The superintendent has ordered guards to watch the site around the clock."

"That's reassuring," she said, turning her head to the path ahead.

They soon entered an intimate tufaceous gorge cut into the hillside. The ceiling of undulating stone looked like a roaring river frozen in place. Moss hung from the oak roots clawing the cliff above.

Justine pressed her body against one wall, looking upward through the narrow opening to the oak branches and patch of azure sky above. Amir braced himself with his right hand on the wall near Justine's head, leaning forward to see what she saw. He turned slowly toward her so she could feel his warm breath on her hair, repressed energy radiating from his tight body. He looked down, finding her eyes, his pupils dilating, mouth moist. Justine felt her own mouth go dry then dampen with desire as her trembling body grew warmer.

Amir turned more fully toward her now, his chest pressing against hers. He kissed her eyes, his penetrating lips and tongue moving to her ear and neck. His arm encircled her waist and drew her to him. Lips brushed, then pressed together fully, hungry for the embrace so long desired.

The lovers lowered themselves onto the moist grass between the boulders, helping each other loosen their clothing without relaxing their kiss. Amir rolled onto Justine in one flowing movement, rocking rhythmically, grasping desperately at her body. It was Justine who cried out first, followed quickly by Amir's deep-throated release.

They suddenly began to hear human voices, soft at first, then growing near, a group entering the gorge not far from where they lay. The presence of others made them grasp each other more tightly at first, then rapidly pull their clothes up over their sweaty bodies and jump to their feet. They looked at each other anew, surprised and slightly embarrassed. They started to laugh.

Still laughing occasionally, as though rediscovering their sexual selves, Justine and Amir returned to Villa Narsi. After they cleaned up, they set out for town, climbing the hill then turning into a narrow alley headed for Al Barilotto on Via Carolina. Pasta had never tasted so good.

CHAPTER 16

We look back and analyze the events of our lives,
But there is another way of seeing, a backward-and-forward-at-once
Vision, that is not rationally understandable.

—Rumi

WHY DID I BECOME an anthropologist? Justine mused as her feet pounded the damp path to the rim of the Fiesole hill. Spring rains had left the foliage glistening in the early sun. Water droplets clung to the leaves of the apple and fig trees. Turning east, she tried to recall the moment she had staked claim to her future profession. It had been an observation by Philip Noble, her first anthropology professor. "Ritual connects the conscious with the unconscious mind," he'd said. She was hooked.

But there were times, like the present, when she was disappointed in her chosen field. In this instance, it was anthropology's avoidance of death that she found appalling. Except for funerary practices, anthropology shied away from the topic. "How do you take notes when people are in anguish?" she had argued with herself, defending classical anthropology's avoidance of death and near-death experiences. "Death anxiety," Noble had called it. She considered whether the Etruscans viewed death as an initiation into a glorious afterlife. Then she recalled the horror of the day the children had been killed in the devastating earthquake outside Cairo, Ibrahim's murder, and Riccardo's sudden death, then revival. She stopped running. The weight of these thoughts was crushing. Her legs felt leaden, and in any case, she had reached the end of the path. Thirty feet below, a narrow road wove through the woods near the Maimo restaurant. Justine pulled her shoulders back, entwined her fingers behind her, and stretched. Droplets of rain fell from an apple tree above and ran like tears down her cheeks. She shook her head vigorously and headed for home.

Justine kicked off her muddy running shoes and grabbed a towel hanging on the back porch, rubbing her moist hair, then her feet and legs. She sat on the side bench for several moments, thinking about death. Taking a deep breath and releasing it slowly, she thought, *Am I coming to terms with death as a form of rebirth?* A strange sense of calm washed over her.

Justine stepped into the warm shower, allowing the shampoo suds to embrace her, cover her like whipped cream. *Why did I become an anthropologist?* she asked herself again, and nearly froze in place. Then, as though her curiosity had kicked in, bolts of energy ran through her body. Out of the shower, she wrapped a towel around her head, pulled on a T-shirt with "Napa Valley Triathlon" printed on the back, snapped her khaki shorts, and raced from her room. Headed for the attic.

As she ran, her own family anthropology flashed through her mind. Her father's profession as an archaeologist and her chance to nose around in the Egyptian fields with him as a child. Her mother's Egyptian heritage; her father's descendence from Lakota ancestors in Nebraska. Then, at the University of Illinois, her chance to do her residency with the Hopis in Arizona. If she hadn't favored cultures, she would have undoubtedly been an archaeologist. But her questions were different from her father's. Her compelling interests were the relationships among people.

Finally, Justine knelt in front of the still-empty trunk, its contents tossed clumsily on a nearby chair. She carefully lifted the loosened slats up, one by one, to reveal the stiff paper lining, she'd seen before. Instinctively she felt—she knew—there was something hidden in this mothball-smelly heirloom. Something secret. She peeled back and removed the stiff, yellowed paper lining. Sitting back, she drew a pocketknife from her shorts, using her fingernails to extract a small blade. One by one, she loosened the slats and lifted each of them from the bottom of the trunk, bracing them against a nearby chair. She enjoyed stretching out the process, tantalizing herself until she was feverish with the hunt.

As she'd expected, with the removal of four slats, there they sat, the treasure of her hunt: three bundles of letters tied with blue satin ribbons, browned by

time, thin and fragile. She sat back on her heels and stared. *Letters. To whom?*
From whom? Several moments passed; she was flushed with excitement, but
forced herself to wait longer. Then, lifting each bundle with the tenderness of
a new mother, she placed them on the floor beside her while she reconstructed
the original scene. Each slat and the paper lining were put deftly back in place,
the clothes folded and repacked, ready for another generation.

She rose to her feet with the three bundles in her arms and made her way
back down the stairs and across the hall to her room, where she placed the
light burden on her bed. For several moments she just stared in wonder. *Who
are they to? From? When? Why?* she asked herself again, as though she could
tease out the answers in her mind's eye.

Making sure the door was firmly closed, she sat cross-legged on her bed
and reached for the first bundle. Opening the first letter as though it would
crumble in her hand, she noted a date in the upper right corner. *Thank god,
they are dated—unlike the codex. March of 1928.* Opening the top letters of
each of the stacks, she discovered the earliest date—February 24, 1927—and
began to read.

Villa Mirenda, 24 February 1927
Madame Hassouna,

When I met you last evening I found myself at a loss for words. You
were kind to smile patiently while I found my speech. You probably
think me irksome. Other than meeting you, I found the party a bore.
Too many aimless Americans. No sense of history.

We are in Florence for the spring. Would you consider tea? I would
like to know more about your beloved Egypt.
Your humble servant, David

The letter seems rather routine, and this David a bit of a bore, Justine thought.
*Yet it must have been written to my great-great grandmother requesting a cour-
tesy call.* She picked up the next in line.

Villa Mirenda, 3 March 1927
Madame Hassouna,

Tea was most pleasing. I must visit Egypt before the English silence
the exotic pulse of the ancients. Tell me you will join us again soon.

What do you think of Huxley's new book? I'm afraid I must tell him
the truth, poor fellow. Perhaps you might help me find the words.

I will send you a copy of my newest. I am being criticized for the
political ideas—when will critics learn that I don't believe everything
my characters say? What a burden. You might find the piece heavy, but
I would like to know what you think.

Yours, David

Ah, he treats her as a fellow intellectual, Justine mused. *Capable of critiquing
Huxley. He must have been speaking of* Brave New World. *David seems to be
some sort of political writer himself, and seeks her ideas there as well. A respectful
friendship seems to be in the making.*

Villa Mirenda, 22 April 1927
Madame Hassouna,

I was gratified and surprised to receive your letter of Sunday 19. We
would be pleased to come to dinner.

You liked Huxley more than I did. I should ask you to write to him
for me, diplomat that you are. Please don't find me unkind. I cherish
truth and tell it directly, but too often I offend tender sensibilities. Hux
endures me, good man.
I travel to Cerveteri and Tarquinia with my patient friend this
week. I find the Etruscans a fascinating race. I felt an instinctual

sympathy when first I was in their presence—as I experience with you. They lived with a pagan sense of the flow of the cosmos and their place in it—so of course the Romans had to stamp them out two thousand years ago. The porpoises they drew in their designs are the same porpoises I wrote of four years ago, the same dance of life that is in everything they did, either in life or in art—for them no difference, as there is no difference for me. Where others see a bastard and primitive art, I see the flow of life, flowers of red and black decorating their black bucchero ware, whether flowers or porpoises, dancing in naturalness, free and spontaneous, connected to the earth, an ever-present religious connection, which was their Elixir of life. Niente paura, as you like to say—nothing to fear. The Etruscans lived in the highest religious state, which is the state of wonder. I proclaim myself, and you, dear girl, Neo-Etruscans.

You are right to find a space to write. I find privacy essential, but my dear wife says I should live alone.

Have you noticed the gardens? Roses and lilies in full bloom. Nature is my chapel, a sanctuary for the soul.

Yours, David

Justine placed the letter on her lap. *A state of wonder—how inspiring. The Etruscans. Huxley. A writer? All clues point to Lawrence . . . D.H. Lawrence! Written with such glorious language and abstractness. Clearly the writer respected Madame Hassouna. But "David"? As far as I know he never called himself "David." Perhaps I am overanxious, projecting—it must be another writer named David.* And which Madame Hassouna? Her great-great-grandmother? Her great-grandmother? Whomever it was, she was married. Risky business, this. Justine picked up the next letter and began to read, feverish with excitement.

Villa Mirenda, 1 May 1927
My dear Isabella,

Thank you for a lovely evening. Your husband was most gracious. We were disappointed that he was called away and could no longer regale us with stories of the Orient since the painful partitions of 1919. Frieda insists we go to Baden Baden next week.

Yours, David

Isabella! And Frieda! My great-grandmother and D.H. Lawrence? Is this even possible?

"What are you reading?" asked her father, leaning against the doorframe of Justine's room, crutch in one hand, right leg suspended in air. Since the accident at Cerveteri, he had been convalescing in the room down the hall. Lucrezia was not thrilled with the arrangement.

Startled, Justine slyly drew a pillow over the top of the letters. "Dad. I didn't see you there." Hadn't she closed the door?

Morgan knew that look of wide-eyed innocence when his daughter had something to hide. "Love letters?" he grinned.

"As a matter of fact, they probably are, but I'm not ready to share them," she said mysteriously, winking at her surprised father.

"As you wish," he said, staring at her for a time. His tan was fading, and there were a few new wrinkles around his mouth. The recent ordeal had taken its toll on this usually resilient man. "Help me down to lunch?"

CHAPTER 17

——&&&——

If we want things to stay as they are, things will have to change.
                    —**Prince Fabrizio in Lampedusa's** *The Leopard*

JUSTINE WAS BACK IN ROME, staying in a friend's apartment near the eleventh-century courtyard that led into the Basilica di San Clemente. She entered through a nondescript side door. On her morning run, she had toured this small residential community, Celio. It was crowded with apartments, banks, enotecas, corner grocery stores, laundries, and sumptuous villas from another era. The enclave sat in a triangle just east of the Coliseum, the site of her appointment with Andrea, who had suggested they meet in the stone tribute to Pope St. Clement, the third successor of St. Peter. Even though she was confident that Andrea would be late for their appointment, Justine had decided to arrive early so that she could tour the site and find the Mithraics Amir had told her about.

She stepped into the nave of the Basilica, twice reconstructed since the maniacal Emperor Nero burned Rome in 64 CE. As she entered, a nun sitting at a table near the entrance offered a small booklet with maps and text entitled *St. Clement's Rome*. Justine bought one and walked toward the altar to view three black nuns fingering rosary beads, an Italian family of five, a dozen elderly women in housedresses and black scarves, and two suspended old men awaiting communion as an aged priest in white with a green satin sash brought wine and bread to a younger priest, also in green satin. The children's eyes darted around the room as they pulled at each other and shuffled their feet, uncomfortable in such austere surroundings. *The same the world over*, she mused. *Church is the preoccupation of the old.*

Justine observed the proceedings for several minutes. Beside her, another voyeur, a young woman in shorts, held a Nikon camera. Balancing the open booklet in one hand, Justine surveyed the gold-embossed ceiling, the marble tile floor, the altar under a triumphal arch, and the cathedra on the podium for the presiding bishop. Nearby was the martyr's tomb. She glanced again at the little circus of practitioners and yearned to know what made Rome tick.

Justine's attention was drawn to ten frescos on either side of the nave that depicted the legend of the martyrdom of St. Clement. According to the apocryphal story in the booklet, Clement was persecuted for spreading the word of Jesus Christ. First he was forced to work in the mines of the Crimea during the reign of Trajan, and when he converted the soldiers and his fellow prisoners, the Romans bound him to an anchor and threw him into the Black Sea. The waters magically receded, revealing an angelic tomb encasing Clement's body. Soon, angels extracted the martyr from the watery grave and buried him on a nearby island. Justine wondered if Pope Clement had been mistaken for this daring man. *So which man is buried in this tomb?* she mused. *Perhaps neither.*

Justine walked to the eastern portion of the Basilica and descended the worn marble steps into the fourth-century remains of the former edifice. More like a cave than a church, the underground catacombs were connected by steps to narrow passages weaving through chamber after chamber, a maze often halting abruptly at dead ends. A musty smell filled her senses. The stunning, dark portrait of Jesus taking the wrist of Adam to rescue him from Limbo could barely be seen in the muted light. *Was Jesus compelled to rescue any worthy person who had died before He arrived on earth?*

The tomb of St. Cyril sat near the center of the room. To its right was the bust of the great benefactor, Cardinal O'Connell, Archbishop of Boston, who served as the Titular of St. Clement from 1911 to 1941. Much before that, as religious persecution in Ireland grew, she read, the basilica was handed over in perpetuity to the Irish Dominicans in 1676.

In one of the halls, a large reversible stone slab was suspended in air. Pagan inscriptions appeared on one side and Christian inscriptions on the other.

Why hadn't the Christians eradicated the pagan inscriptions, as they had in so many other places? Undoubtedly, the inscriptions could be construed to Christian meanings, as when the pagan holidays became Christian holidays to capture the ceremonial habits of the people.

Finally, Justine found the steps that led down into the first-century church. Lowering her head, she carefully contorted her body through the narrow passageway into the lowest catacombs. Some chambers ran east and west, parallel to a central area that might have served as the center of worship. After Amir's description of the Mithraic Temple in Sovana, she was increasingly excited about what she would find. Justine found one of the marble benches facing the carved stele depicting Mithra, his cape flying and head turned away as he slay a bull. Alongside, a raven, a snake, and a scorpion, signs of the Zodiac.

Justine could understand how Roman soldiers might have been captivated by these symbols of Christianity, with their emphasis on loyalty, obedience, and victory over one's enemies. The guidebook suggested that Mithra had been brought to Rome by soldiers returning from battles in Asia Minor. Since people at that time believed the earth, rather than the sun, was the fixed center of the universe, worshipping the Zodiac just didn't make sense.

"He was born of a virgin birth, you know." The rich male voice behind her resonated with a fine acoustical clarity. Justine started, then turned, but failed to distinguish any human form in the dark cavity. "Who are you?" she asked, more bewildered than afraid. But she knew even before she asked. The deep, resounding voice was unmistakable.

"Actually, Mithra emerged from an egg-shaped rock, bringing with him the notion of life after death in the star-filled universe above."

Justine stood and walked toward the voice. "Mr. Blackburn. What a surprise," she said, her voice tense with sarcasm. "Surely this isn't an accidental encounter." He was stalking her. But why?

"I don't take you for a naïve woman, Dr. Jenner. I thought I'd alert you to a small legal maneuver that has been initiated. You might be brought before a magistrate for colluding to steal treasured artifacts." The meager light barely caught his boyish features and self-satisfied grin.

"Theft? Me?" she exclaimed. "I find that highly amusing coming from the thief of the recently discovered Egyptian codex." Justine could feel the flush of anger rise in her chest.

"You wound me, my dear. Your charge is unfounded. Yet if I were to confess my transgressions, they would be almost irrelevant in the overall scheme of things—would they not? Men—and must I add, women—still dally with these obscure religious myths. How is that different from Mithras here? Whether it's a bull or a windmill, men play at finding meaning where there is none. History moves forward, yet nothing really changes."

"Where do you find your own meanings, Mr. Blackburn?" Justine folded her arms in front of her and anchored her feet a foot apart. She quickly recognized the predictable stance and relaxed her arms.

"In small moments of beauty, I suppose, Dr. Jenner. A Ming vase. A Berber weaving. A silver Mayan cup. A lovely woman's smile. Or in the beautiful discourse that is more rare than emeralds, yet can even be found among the servant girls at the grindstones. So much to appreciate."

Justine froze in place. Where had she heard that phrase about discourse and emeralds and grindstones? Her eyes squinted, yet she paused only a moment before returning to her main point of interest. "So why steal the codex? The object itself offers little beauty." She kept her voice unemotional now rather than accusatory.

"Ming vases are expensive. And, at my age, so are beautiful women," he said. "I will also admit to an unpleasant little habit of ego. I like to beat the Egyptian Supreme Minister at his own game. After all, he was the first to remove the codex from his safe. Stole it from himself, you might say."

Justine could not help but smile at Blackburn's frankness; she hoped fervently that the shadows would mask her amusement. Yet she also knew that his charm masked sinister intentions. Blackburn would stop at nothing to get what he wanted. But what did he want now?

❧

"I had a devil of a time finding you, Justine," charged Andrea as she entered the hall. "Who were you talking to?" Andrea moved into the temple as though the space was hers alone. A straw purse hung from her yellow gauze–draped shoulder; a sun hat was clutched in her hand.

Justine realized that Blackburn had disappeared. "It was Blackburn. He had some news."

Andrea's face paled in the meager light, her lips pursed into a slit. She was suddenly older.

Justine noticed the sudden change in her friend's demeanor, yet proceeded to relate her conversation with Blackburn. *I'll have plenty of questions at dinner.* "He said *I* might be accused of being a thief!"

A flicker of regret swept across Andrea's face as she sat looking at the relief of Mithras. Absentmindedly, as though she hadn't heard Justine's news, she asked, "What does the bull signify?"

"The ending of the Age of Taurus," Justine offered, as though it was self-evident. "So what do you think? Is it possible that I would be brought up on charges regarding the codex?"

"Possibly." She said almost too quickly. "Depending on what Egypt has offered the Italians. You'll remember, the antiquities crowd here got a taste of blood with the Marion True case." Reservedly, Andrea reached out to Justine and gave her a reassuring hug. "I'm sure you'll be okay."

"But why me? Surely Blackburn has the original; I only have a copy. A bit ironic, isn't it? Why in the world didn't the Carabinieri pick up Blackburn when you reported his whereabouts?" she demanded. *Did she report his whereabouts?*

"You're better press, *chérie*," Andrea was quick to say. "An American whose father is a well-known archaeologist working in Italy. And the Italians have a love-hate relationship with the notion of UNESCO heritage sites like Cerveteri. After all, it was you who found the codex. On the other hand, it could be a little game that Blackburn is playing with you. He must know that you asked me to alert the authorities about his whereabouts."

How would he know? Does he have friends in the police force as well? "I suppose so." Justine's body relaxed slightly, imagining that all this could mean nothing at all. She took a deep breath and let it out slowly. "Did you fly in last night?"

"A couple of days ago," Andrea said with characteristic nonchalance. "I drove in from Cerveteri this morning."

Ah, she's taunting me again about her affair with Dad. Well, I'm not going to give her the satisfaction of seeing me overreact again. "So, any new interpretations of the three codex pages I gave you?" Justine asked innocently, as though no other topics bore weight on her mind.

Andrea looked up, amused. "*Oui.* Quite illuminating," she managed to say. "The entry was a kind of note or reminder to someone else—to her nephew John, perhaps, the man who became John the Baptist. Before she died, she asked that she be returned to her family's original home in Lydia, an area near Ephesus. As we know, John was beheaded before she could return, but we think someone took her there after her son's crucifixion. Perhaps the Apostle John."

"That's extraordinary!" Justine exclaimed. "Ephesus. I've heard that there's a site near there called Mary's House. Well, if she wrote that note in the diary when Jesus was just eight, I would say two things: she had a premonition about her son's fate, and she didn't expect to leave the diary behind."

"Perceptive, Justine. The family must have left in a hurry. It does confirm her intent to return to Ephesus."

"Indeed it does." Justine exhaled slowly as the new information sank into her consciousness. *The wonder of it. Mary was a real woman, with concerns and doubts like the rest of us. Much like myself.* "Let's go have some tea. It's cold in here."

CHAPTER 18

—∞∞∞—

"The world is full of obvious things which nobody by any chance ever observes."

—Arthur Conan Doyle, *The Hound of the Baskervilles*

THAT EVENING, Justine and Andrea sought out the Hostaria Romano. It was a lot like most Roman trattorias, which seemed to follow unwritten rules: The bread must be stale, the room must be bright like a high school cafeteria, the wine should be a dry house red, and the waiters should be grumpy old men. The menu must be Cucina Romana, traditional Roman cooking that remained impervious to change since the days of the Caesars. The only fresh features should be local, seasonal ingredients.

Justine realized that she could live in Rome for a lifetime and not find this restaurant, self-promoted as the home of the best antipasti in Rome. Tucked away down a small street off Piazza Barberini, it was staffed by waiters old enough to remember that the establishment was once a stronghold against the Nazis. Baroness Miranda, who had a habit of charming Italians out of their most closely held secrets, had recommended it.

Andrea and Justine ordered bruschetta and an antipasto of local cheeses, cured meats, small marinated fishes, and a few nondescript, crunchy fingerlings. The dry red wine was eventually delivered to their table by a white-haired waiter with a drooping mustache and four small glasses: two for the water, two for the wine.

"Mother called an hour ago," reported Justine, appearing relaxed in white slacks and a black silk blouse, her flaxen hair pulled back into a makeshift ponytail. "An envelope of what appear to be legal papers has arrived for me at the house . . . this red wine has so much tannin I can hardly move my tongue."

Andrea found Justine's unperturbed façade unconvincing. "You seem quite calm, given the circumstances. Did Lucrezia open the envelope?" Andrea waved a piece of bruschetta in the air, the sensual aroma of toasted bread, garlic, and fresh tomatoes saturating her senses.

Actually, at first Justine had panicked, felt her stomach wrench into a knot, but since then she had permitted her attention to move to a different kind of hunt, one that sharpened her instincts and evoked her scientific curiosity. "I asked her to open it while I held on. The letter and supporting materials are from the Florence magistrate's office: a 'request' to appear for an interview regarding some missing artifacts. I had her read key parts to me. It was very vague, although it does hint at possible extradition." This last word stuck in her mouth.

"To Egypt? If so, that means the Egyptians have requested the inquiry. Do you want me to come with you? I could arrange it."

"I think I would. And perhaps a representative from the American Embassy. And possibly Riccardo, since he knows a great deal about the Italian legal system. I'm sure Dad and Amir will insist on being there." The elderly waiter approached their table with bowls piled high with marinated sardines, breaded onions, sautéed eggplant, a tangy celery salad, mushrooms and baby artichokes, potato croquettes, and firm ricotta. "No salami?" Justine teased in her broken Italian. He didn't smile.

Both women stared at the antipasti that was intended to be the first course. They laughed. Andrea picked up a sardine by its greasy tail and asked, "Do you think Blackburn had anything to do with it?"

"I'm sure of it. How long have you known him?" Justine cut off a piece of the ricotta and placing it on top of her bruschetta.

Andrea was silent, staring hard at the sardine held suspended in her fingers. "How did you know?"

"A little proverb about conversations and emeralds and servant girls . . . you used it at the dinner party in Fiesole. Blackburn used it today in San Clemente. How long?" she demanded.

"About fifteen years. We were lovers for a while. A few seasons. Then we ended it."

"Too much alike?" Justine asked in a solemn tone.

"Justine! You're accusing me of some sinister actions—I'm wounded." Andrea paused. "Yes, we were too much alike." She laughed. Not light and joyful, instead derisive and indignant.

"And now, Andrea? Are you working together?"

"No, Justine, we are *not* working together. We have stayed in contact, but that is all. I was not involved in the theft of the codex, if that is what you're suggesting."

"But you knew where his shop was. And you asked me to visit the shop and confront him. Why?"

Andrea nodded and returned to the panoply of food before her. "He wanted to meet you."

So she is still doing his bidding. What else is she involved in? The theft of the codex itself? I know she didn't steal it, but what other essential role might she have played? In spite of these troubling questions, she decided to believe her for now. Justine took several deep breaths and a sip of the high-tannin wine, and gazed at Andrea with guarded affection. "I see," is all she said.

Andrea appeared released, liberated from her near capture as a would-be villain. She continued on as though nothing had happened. "There are many possibilities besides Blackburn. You're sure to be the target of the director-general, the Catholic Church, other Christians, and the entire nation of Islam ..." She grinned at the absurdity of her statement, although it was not far from the truth. Omar Mostafa, Director-General of the Supreme Council of Antiquities in Egypt, had an ego that stretched from Cairo to San Francisco. A favorite of *National Geographic* and *Discovery* television, as well as American museums, he did not take kindly to losing something as important as the diary of the Virgin Mary. Especially when he had assured Islamic and Christian leaders that the most provocative of the findings would not see the light of day. Now he had lost control of any translations that could be made public.

"What is that other old proverb? Judge me by my enemies? I seem to be in season," Justine lamented, savagely stabbing a mushroom.

CHAPTER 19

—◦◦◦—

... in all matters of emotional importance, please approach the supreme authority direct!

—D.H. Lawrence, excerpt from *Intimates*

THE HEAT OF SPRING had already closed in on Rome when Justine escaped to the north, although Fiesole offered little relief. The drive back from her visit with Andrea had been especially tiring. She had chewed over the conversation with Blackburn and Andrea and the delivery of the potentially threatening legal papers to her mother's home. *Is it possible that I could be extradited to Egypt to stand trial?*

Her secret cache of letters from the trunk and the adventures of her great-grandmother, Isabella, awaited her at home. A worthy diversion from the stress of other realities. She sat cross-legged on her bed, daydreaming of life in Fiesole in 1927. Where had she left off?

... Frieda insists we go to Baden Baden next week. Her three children are there and we usually stay with her sister, Else. But this time we will stay with friends, Edith and Charles Stein. The Steins are respectful of my need for solitude to write there, as long as the weather isn't damp. Tea before we go?

Will you and your husband be in Fiesole through the summer? We are certain to return to Villa Mirenda by early autumn, or be off to the ranch in Taos. Please write. Your letters feed my restless soul, my sympathies are aroused by your voice.

Yours, David

He is making love to her in the words he used in his literature to describe those most haunting of emotions—"restless soul," "aroused sympathies." It can be no other than Lawrence. Justine's forehead felt hot to her own touch . . .

> Villa Mirenda, 27 May 1927
> Dear Isabella,
>
> I still find myself mesmerized by your thoughts on the Prophet Jesus, who needn't be divine. Perhaps the followers of Mohammed are right. Why would God need an earthly son? Indeed. I've just painted a piece on the resurrection and am working on a story called The Escaped Cock, named after a queer little toy that Brewster showed me in Volterra. I hope you'll approve. In it, Jesus tires of the old gang and sets out to find Isis.
>
> We are eating our first cherries and fat asparagus and beans. The garden here is glorious, so abundant. Is your garden lush with good eats and whimsical flowers? Wisteria wraps her legs around the olive trees. I am provoked to paint and capture this spring on canvas.
>
> It is getting humid. Not good for my bronchials. We may return to the ranch by August. Not sure as yet.
>
> Enjoy Egypt, dear Isabella, and write soon. Ciao, David

My great-grandmother Isabella, Muslim follower and scholar. Did she convert from Coptic Christianity for her husband—my great grandfather Ahmed? Not surprisingly, issues that concern Muslims in Cairo in this century are not so different than those she spoke of eighty years ago. "The Escaped Cock" must have become "The Man Who Died," an immensely provocative short story. Isabella might not have had anyone else in her life who treated her as an intelligent woman—one worthy of the attentions of a famed author, to be sure. *What would that have felt like? So seductive.* Justine picked up the next letter.

Irschenhausen, Germany, 13 September 1927

Dear Isabella,

I found your letter from Egypt enchanting. Your descriptions of the ancients bring them to life for me. Surely they must have known the Etruscans. And your etchings from the railing of the lighthouse in Alexandria offer the breath of fresh air I crave. I crave you as well. Write as often as you can.

We went into Munich for my birthday—an old man in my forties now, you know. I'm afraid the depression is making life difficult for the Germans, even Frieda's family. And the little clown they call Hitler marches in parades. We sneer at him over our aperitifs.

I don't require much, a small amount of food, a little wine, a place to write. And letters from my Isabella.

It is nippy now, autumn can't be far off. Winter comes too quickly here.

We are sure to be back in Italy before October leaves us chilled to the bone. I will soon see you in your Egyptian frocks and golden jangles, eyes made vivid with charcoal.

Tante bella cose, and love, David

She stared at the letters for a long time, as though waiting for the characters to step forth from the pages. *D.H. Lawrence, D.H. Lawrence,* she repeated over and over to herself, the mantra holding her awareness. And the little clown. Little did Frieda's family know what would happen in the following decade, but by 1931 she would be secure in Taos with her Italian lover and Lawrence would be dead of tuberculosis.

Justine was still in shock that such letters existed—were even written. And hidden in her grandmother's attic, no less. *D.H. Lawrence. David? David*

Herbert. Signing this last letter to my great-grandmother with "love." Where was my great-grandfather? Did he know about Lawrence? Did she love both men?

Lawrence, the very man riveting attention on theories of the afterlife, whose visits to Cerveteri gave special meaning to the village where her father was digging. More than a coincidence? *Many cultures believe there are no accidents. What do I believe? So amazing—events that seem related but are obviously not caused by one another. What are they caused by? Is cause and effect too Western an idea?*

Grandmother Laurence might say that the two men were drawn to Cerveteri by the hand of a deity. Mother might relate their interest in the Etruscans to Jung's collective unconscious. But Dad would probably say that this household has always welcomed the renowned: Picasso, Stein, Pound, Berenson, Stark, Lawrence. She paused and gazed out the window. *I think Dad has it right. Florence, like Cairo, is a small town, especially where expatriates are concerned. Yet . . .*

"May I talk with you for a moment, Prego?" Justine motioned to the two chairs in the center of the garden.

Prego eagerly obeyed, relieved to have the opportunity to sit down. He stepped aside to let her precede him to the small patch of grass bordered by rosemary, hydrangea, and boxed topiaries. They sat in the wrought iron chairs facing each other.

"Prego, you remember so much about this home. Did you ever hear your family talk about visits from a man called D.H. Lawrence? A famous writer." She spread her booted feet and leaned forward, elbows on her thighs, hands clasped.

Prego fidgeted for a few moments, taking his hands from his pockets and folding them in on each other, covering his dirt-encrusted fingernails. "*Si, signorina.* My mother, she was impressed by his gentlemanly manners. Hid his books under her bed, sometimes beside the flour bin in the kitchen. I find them. One time Mama took the stick to me for reading *Lady Chatterley.*"

Justine smiled warmly—the adventuresome boy, the cautious man. "Did she ever tell you that she knew the author?"

"No, but I think she did. Mama. She talk about him, what he wear. Once, when she prepare tea, she say he like *limone* only."

✍

Justine felt the rhythm of someone's breathing nearby. She turned, expecting to see her mother leaning against the doorframe. "Riccardo? What brings you here?"

"Maria told me I could find you here. I thought you might need my help. With the Italian legal system and all." He smiled. *Almost handsome*, she thought, surprised.

Justine stared, always pleased to see him, yet somewhat annoyed at being torn away from the lives of Isabella and D.H., or David, as she now called him. She tightened her robe around her, overlapping the fabric to diminish its transparency, and carefully gathered the letters, crawled off the bed, and placed the bundles in her drawer. She hugged him warmly. "What do you have to tell me? But first, how are you feeling?"

She noticed how his muscles moved smoothly under his loose linen shirt and pleated tan slacks as he walked across the small room and sat in the antique rocking chair, resting one ankle on the opposite knee. "I'm doing fine," he said finally. "Very well, in fact. Your dad told me that you have been summoned to the Florence court in a few weeks. What about? If I am not being impertinent."

"Never," said Justine, smiling. She described the discovery of the codex in Egypt, its theft from the office of the Supreme Director of Antiquities, and her escape to Fiesole with the copy. "I did find the codex during the earthquake, and I do have the copy," she said. "Perhaps I'm being charged with possession of the copy." She sat back on the bed, since Riccardo occupied the only chair in the room, and absentmindedly began to braid her hair.

Riccardo's eyes formed into giant orbs. He was stunned. He had spent enough time in the priesthood to know how reverent the Virgin Mary was held. Considered untouchable. He was not entirely immune himself to the aura of the Holy Mother. "I can understand the intrigue such a story could create in Italy. All we need to launch an inquiry is a hungry functionary looking to make a power move. But this story . . . well . . . well, it would invite conspiracy theories. Italians like to be in the game." Riccardo leaned forward with his elbows on both knees.

Justine looked like a little girl propped up on the bed with pigtails. "In the game?" She knew what "in the game" meant, but wanted to hear an Italian's explanation.

"We like to play with the big boys," he went on. "Appear to be experts. Our prestige as a nation depends on it. You'll recall the case of the 'Italian Letter' documenting the discovery of yellow cake uranium in Niger. The very letter that Bush used in his State of the Union speech. False, all pretense, in order to be in the game."

"I remember it well." She shivered, suddenly aware of the lengths the Italians might go to in order to indict her.

"In any case, if real evidence is razor thin, we Italians will embellish it. You were there and now you are here. That's enough to raise suspicion."

Justine swung her long legs off the end of the bed, picked up her jeans and T-shirt, and headed into the bathroom, leaving the door ajar so they could continue the conversation. "I can understand the hysteria that could accompany the discovery of the Virgin Mary's diary, but mustn't they have some sort of case?"

Riccardo rose and leaned against one of the four bed posters, facing the bathroom. He imagined Justine gracefully slipping out of the flimsy robe and stepping into her tight jeans. He was intrigued by beauty, the aesthetics of movement—and there were even a few moments when he wished he were interested in women. "The lack of legal safeguards here provides gaping holes for power to occupy," he said, raising his voice a little. "Let me put it this way. You are involved in finding and interpreting the codex. It disappears and so do you. Your famous father is here. Your mother. Probably a family ring of black marketers."

Justine was still laughing when she stuck her head around the doorframe. "If it were not me being accused I would find this delightful. The stuff movies are made of." She stepped back into the bedroom in jeans and T-shirt, a hand relaxed high on the doorframe. "What can I expect now?" she asked.

"In Italy, justice is about the person rather than the crime. That's the good part in this case."

"What does that mean??"

"You don't appear to be a dangerous person." *Especially right now*, he refrained from adding. "That's the first thing. The court may decide during your first appearance that the evidence is scant. It depends on how adamant the prosecutor is, how much he has at stake. But the Florentine court is quite sophisticated in such matters. Hundreds of years of dealing with precious art. And, of course, you will have the representative from the American Embassy with you. If he is respectful and contrite, you could walk out of there a free woman." With his left hand still holding the bedpost, he swung around and sat on the edge of the bed next to Justine.

Neither spoke for several moments while she pondered what she'd been told. Whose football was she? An ambitious Italian prosecutor's? A customs bureaucrat's, out to make a name for himself? She looked directly at Riccardo with a self-conscious smile, realizing that she had left him hanging while she succumbed to her own ruminations.

"How is the dig coming?" she finally asked.

"We're into the new tomb," he said excitedly. "Right now we're trying to sort out and catalog the objects inside this amazing room. Your dad found a gold filigree earring just yesterday." He paused. "I must get back."

Justine realized that he had made the four-hour-plus drive just to talk with her about her legal dilemma. Gratitude washed over her tanned face. "Can't you stay for lunch?"

He shook his head.

"Please tell Dad to call me the minute you know anything about the tomb. And Riccardo, thank you very much for coming here."

He kissed her extended hand and left the room.

As she watched him head for the stairs, her cell phone rang.

"Justine. We think we've found something interesting. Come," said the urgent voice on the other end of the line. That was all. Amir hung up.

Annoyed yet enticed by Amir's taste for the dramatic, Justine turned and ran to the top of the stairs. "Riccardo. Wait. I'm coming with you."

CHAPTER 20

‒◦◦◦‒

Egypt did not contain me. I crossed three continents.
I was honored upon the Tigris and the Tiber as well as the Nile.
I sailed beyond the Mediterranean, and flew north with the Roman eagles.
From the mists of Britain to the sands of Arabia, I was the universal Goddess,
And you who are not of the blood of my birthland may still be my children.
—Jezibell, Poet, Actress, Belly dancer

THEY HARDLY SPOKE. Hours sped by as Justine and Riccardo imagined what lay ahead in the archeological find and took turns driving his Maserati as the other pretended to doze. The call had told them little, really, but both knew that a cavern deep below the original tumuli in Cerveteri had been discovered and that there was something there. Each felt the suppressed excitement of impending discovery. Without asking, Riccardo pulled in at the autostrada way station at the Orvieto exit.

Justine set a large cappuccino in the cup holder and tore off pieces of a croissant, feeding it to Riccardo as he drove. Now well into the trip, she finally dared ask, "So, what do you think?"

Riccardo laughed. "After all this time I thought I'd hear a more complicated question." He reached over and pulled one of her pigtails. For the first time since she'd left home, Justine realized that she was indeed wearing pigtails. She held them in the air and grinned. "I considered asking whether lavish tombs brimming with treasures would offer up answers to all the unknowns about the Etruscans—but thought that was a bit much."

"I prefer the first question, the answer to which is, 'I don't know.' *Dipende.*" He managed a lopsided grin, glanced into the rearview mirror, and moved into the left lane to pass three cars, speeding the sports car to 120 km/h.

Justine stared straight ahead, methodically loosening her hair.

No one was on hand to greet them when they drove into the back entrance of the necropolis site at Cerveteri. They scrambled down the first ladder into the deep trough and moved to the inside of the initial level of excavation, the one where Morgan and Riccardo had been trapped weeks earlier. Justine could hear Riccardo's breathing shift; he was beginning to struggle for air. She turned and took his hand as they reached the top of the second set of stairs, and felt the muscles in his hand relax as they stepped into the narrow passageway leading to the cavern below.

At the bottom they found Morgan, Amir, and Delmo staring at a corner of the dished-out cavern lit by three overlapping electric torches. The newcomers edged their way through, eager to discover the source of fascination.

Justine slowly began to identify the focus of the converging lights. Two alabaster women sat erect atop a sarcophagus about two and a half meters in length. The women faced each other from opposite ends of the lid, their legs lying alongside each other's. One bare foot of each woman extended beyond the ripples of cloth that were wrapped tightly around slender midriffs. Their faces were beatific, yet amused, staring at one another through almond-shaped eyes with affectionate, unabashed daring while somehow managing to glance at an imaginary audience as well. Their hair, swept upward and back, cascaded down their backs and adorned one bare shoulder; a large broach secured their gowns at the other shoulder. One arm of each woman extended forward, holding her open palm toward the other. Their left hands lay flat on their laps, gripping a lotus flower.

Justine stood thunderstruck by the scene before her. *Such strong, confident women, so in command of their world. Were they lovers? Friends? Related in some way?*

Morgan's slowly exhaling breaths whispered in the stillness, "This image. What can it mean? These women have a stance of power, of command." No one was listening.

Mythical images, in carved relief, adorned the outer walls of the sarcophagus. Justine could distinguish the large wings of a sparrow hawk, waves symbolic of water, lotus blossoms, ducks. She placed her hand on Riccardo's forearm, moving the light beam to focus it directly onto the embossed base.

The woman bearing the wings came into focus, her headdress a majestic crown. Golden bands braceleted her upper arms, and her body was tightly bound in the skin of a reptile. To her right, the Scorpion Goddess, and on her left, Hathor, balancing the sun disk between her horns. Below the winged Isis, an undulating river bore the dismembered body of her husband, Osiris—a leg here, an arm there, a torso floating facedown. A long-necked cat looked up with adoration.

Justine gasped. "It's Egyptian!" she exclaimed. "Egyptian." Her face was flushed, her wide eyes caught by the perimeter of the flashlight beam.

Her father finally acknowledged her presence. "Or a culture heavily influenced by Egyptian mythology," he said more calmly. "Did you just arrive?" His face warmed, acknowledging his daughter and her thrill of discovery.

"With Riccardo," she said absently, unable to draw her eyes from the image of Isis. "Hello, Amir. Delmo."

Amir turned, took two steps toward her, and smiled. "Quite a find. Yes, quite a find." For so long he had felt imprisoned by his work at the Egyptian museum, trying to make sense of their meager Greek collection. This was his first real discovery experience.

Even in the dim light, Justine could see Amir's face, flushed with excitement. She wondered how much of his excitement was stoked by memories of their time together in the caves at Sovano. Right now it didn't matter.

"Professor Delmo Della Dora, what do you think we have here?" asked Morgan without taking his eyes off the sarcophagus.

Delmo, the distinguished retired linguist from the University of Bologna, was fixated on the sarcophagus and paying no attention to the crowd behind him. Reluctantly, he acknowledged the question and the man who asked it. "At this point we can only describe what we see: two sculptured women, somehow connected to one another, seated on an alabaster sarcophagus embossed with Egyptian goddesses. When can we remove *questo maledetto coperchio*?" he exclaimed, pointing to the sarcophagus lid.

What will we find inside?! Their corpses bound as mummies? Jewels? Literary remains? Explanations of this early culture? Justine was speechless with wonder.

Spotlights planted around the rim of the cavern illuminated the sarcophagus, their electrical cords trailing down the ladders more than fifteen meters from the rattling generator above. A fifteen-kilogram hand winch had been lowered into the lower tomb by three ropes held by local hires. Cleaning the caked soil from the sarcophagus had taken days of tedious work; small brushes, trowels, and shovels were scattered around the floor alongside equipment for removing the lid. Two soil sifters leaned against the damp wall.

A large oak table, the same height as the sarcophagus, stood on jointed legs in front of the massive coffin. The team had reached the decision that sliding the lid onto a table was the safest approach. Justine's cotton T-shirt, wet with perspiration in the sauna-like cavern, clung to her back and chest. She clutched an armload of gunnysacks. The dense air caused everyone to breath more deeply, fresh air in short supply.

Fabiano and Riccardo stood on either end of the sarcophagus with crowbars, ready to pry open the lid. Placing the bars along the edge and slowly maneuvering them back and forth, they inched along as though carving into a glacier. An hour passed. Sweat dripped from every pore. Finally, tiny cracks appeared between the lid and the base. Moving the crowbars more quickly now from side to side, the team was able to gently lift the lid a millimeter and insert a cable from each end, sliding the coiled wires toward the middle.

Justine wedged her gunnysacks into the narrow spaces as the team parted thousands of years of settlement. The two men gently clasped a steel cable over the padded laps of the two women, and Morgan stepped forward to attach the cables to a steel hook on the outer side of the lid, careful to avoid breaking off one of the women's extended arms as the cables became taut. Amir attached the hook to a new line of cable and ran it across the oak table to the hand winch, which was situated three meters out front.

Justine watched Riccardo closely, alert to his breathing, any uptake in his asthmatic response. Their eyes met and she motioned him back up the stairs to find fresh air. He shook his head, refusing the leave the scene.

Morgan, Fabiano, and Riccardo removed their gloves in order to get a firmer hold. They managed to slowly turn the wooden handle of the winch, causing the cables to tighten against the swinging hook. The others stood ready on all sides of the lid to steady and guide it to the table.

The giant lid groaned and creaked under the demands of the winch before finally giving way to glide, in jerks and starts, toward the table. The two ancient women moved gracefully through the changing light as though dancing a minuet, excited to be discovered. Justine stood, mesmerized, as the two were guided away from the sarcophagus itself and gently came to rest on the well-padded oak table. Morgan stepped forward, bowed slightly as though honoring royalty, and unhooked the cable, drawing it away from the lid. Amir unfastened the other cables.

Silence honored the moment. Then, as though on cue, everyone stepped to the sides of the colossal sarcophagus and peered in. They were nearly overcome by the escaping stench of ancient death, of mold and decay. What they saw left them all speechless.

CHAPTER 21

─∞∞∞─

All truths are easy to understand once they are discovered; the point is to discover them.

—Galileo Galilei

MOMENTS PASSED. Riccardo moved the lights closer to erase the shadows, to shine light on the persons within. Two mummies lay side by side, heads at opposite ends, nearly mimicking the pose of the women on the lid, their bodies wrapped with wide swaths of cloth. Their uncovered heads revealed hollowed eyes and leather-like skin pulled tight around now-protruding teeth. Long, steel-gray hair fanned outward as through recently ruffled by a spring breeze.

"What the hell!" exclaimed Morgan. "I've never seen anything like this!"

Justine let out a low whistle, as though she had been holding her breath for several moments. "Magnificent! The find of the century, Dad. The Italians will be jealous."

Morgan pondered her last statement briefly, then reconfigured his face into one of extreme pleasure and excitement. After all, discoveries like this came once in a lifetime, if that, although Morgan has been more fortunate than most. The library at Machu Picchu had been an extraordinary find, and the reason he was hired for the Italian job.

"*Bella dente*—nice teeth," Delmo observed enthusiastically. "Couldn't ask for anything better than this! Everything worth knowing can be found in good teeth." To this seasoned scientist, yellow, rotted teeth were glorious indeed.

Amir and Riccardo spoke almost simultaneously. "This is unlike . . ." Riccardo stopped, permitting Amir to continue.

"I've seen nothing like this in Egypt," said Amir, nodding to acknowledge Riccardo's gracious withdrawal. "Unless the wrappings are linen, of course. But uncovered, intact heads. Never."

"Certainly between the hair and the teeth roots we've got good DNA samples," suggested Justine, wildly pondering the fate of these two elegant women.

"The teeth, possibly, but not the hair. The follicles couldn't have survived this long," said Morgan, both deeply tanned hands gripping the side of the sarcophagus. "We may have original Etruscans here."

Delmo's slightly raised eyebrow could barely be seen in the shadows where he now stood. "*Pazienza*, Morgan," he insisted. "We must not jump to conclusions. These women could be Villanovans."

"We must bury these ladies in proper graves," said Fabiano finally, crossing himself. "It's the right thing."

Justine smiled at Fabiano's innocence. These women would never be hidden again.

It was dusk when Justine and Amir walked away from the site. He slipped his hand into hers, and she turned unconsciously to assure herself that no one saw her hand pocketed into Amir's. She wasn't sure why—or if—it mattered.

She had alerted Riccardo that she would be riding back to Anna's with Amir. They slid into the front seat of Amir's rented Jeep for the short ride back to Cerveteri, where Justine expected to rent a room for the night.

Anna's small hotel, also her personal home, surrounded a courtyard large enough for a half-dozen cars. The stucco building faced the western valley and newer part of Cerveteri. Richly waxed wooden beams supported white stucco interior walls. Anna was nowhere to be found. Justine knew by now that the lovely proprietor often went off for the day to shop, leaving the doors open.

Justine followed Amir up the back stairs to his room, kicked off her shoes, and sat casually on a small wooden box under the window. Too dirty to sit anywhere else. He stood by the four-poster and smiled at her. "What would you like for dinner?" he asked. "I could get some bread and pecorino. Wine. We could stay in."

"If I can clean up a bit, I think I'd like to return to Ristorante Vladimiro ai Bastioni. As you'll remember from your first night here, they boast the best Napolitano seafood outside of Rome. Dad and the others will be there." She thought she would find sanctuary among the others since she was unsure how an evening alone with Amir would go. Besides, she had abandoned Riccardo, who had generously driven her from Fiesole.

Amir looked disappointed. He didn't want to share her with anyone, including her father. "It will be a crowd. I was hoping for . . ." Amir was reluctant to say, "We haven't been together since we made love in the grass at Sovana," although he knew that she understood.

"I realize we haven't really talked since Santa Fiora." She smiled. "I think I'd like to take a shower. May I borrow a clean shirt?" Pulling her T-shirt, smeared with wet clay, up over her head, she accepted the white shirt that Amir grabbed from the armoire and headed for the shower. She turned on the water and left the door ajar.

Amir slid into the narrow shower stall behind her, his naked body pressing against her back and buttocks. She didn't flinch as his hand reached for her breast, the other encircling her waist, pulling her toward him. He kissed her neck and shoulders. Trembling in his grasp, she arched her back to press more fully into his body. Shampoo floated down her shoulders and onto his chest, silken flesh sliding smoothly together. Justine turned around slowly as Amir picked her up, her legs encircling his waist. He entered her effortlessly, leaning both of them against the shower wall to keeping from falling. She cried out once, burying her face into the nape of his neck.

Amir stepped out of the shower first, leaving Justine to luxuriously finish shampooing her hair. Several moments passed as she let the warm water caress her and reflected on the joy of Amir's caress. Then she quickly stepped out, grabbed a towel, and bent to brush the dust from her jeans. Rubbing her body and hair vigorously, while Amir watched, she slipped into her jeans, tucking in the white shirt, permitting its long tail to serve as makeshift underwear. "Shall we?" she asked, heading for the door, her wet hair forming into ringlets.

Amir had to scramble to get ready.

At dinner, Morgan looked from Amir to his daughter, noting the flushed countenance of the two lovers. Everyone around the table sensed what had transpired, and that knowledge had a discomforting effect on everyone but Riccardo, who was pleased for Justine—and for Amir.

Morgan broke the awkward silence by reviewing the culinary choices for the evening. There were few, since the chef invariably decided what his guests would eat. Tonight he offered a choice between fish and wild boar, cauliflower and aubergine. As always, the wine list was extensive. Although this was Morgan's domain, he made no selection; instead, he nodded to Riccardo, the son of a famous vintner.

Delmo joined them late. He pulled out a chair next to Justine and explained with only a hint of apology: "I needed a rest," he said. Age had freed him from most social protocols. "Have you ordered?"

"You'll eat what we've ordered, my friend," said Morgan playfully. "*Orate alla Romana* and *Insalata di Rinforzo*. Riccardo has decided on Brunelli."

"Ah, the gilthead bream fish is one of my favorites. But cauliflower?" challenged Delmo, looking especially debonair with a high-buttoned, newly ironed plaid shirt and glossy hair.

"So, what do you think of our great discovery?" Riccardo asked Delmo, clearly bursting with the excitement of the day.

"Hard to tell," he responded. "But one thing we can agree on: it's unlike anything we've seen. The rolled linen used for wrapping the bodies seemed like that of the Zagreb mummy in Egypt. Then there's the rolled parchment we found alongside the two women. It excites me the most. And, of course, the mitochondrial DNA options are incredible." His passion mounted as he spoke.

"And the Egyptian goddesses carved into the sarcophagus," Justine exclaimed, "This find could turn upside down everything we thought we knew about the Etruscans—couldn't it?"

There were nods around the table, but no one answered her question.

Instead, Amir asked, "What happens next, Morgan?" He reached for Justine's hand under the table. She pulled away gently, resisting any display that might signal possession.

"There are firm protocols. First thing in the morning we'll notify the local superintendent's office, then the lab in Florence . . . and Francesca at Villa Giulia. She needs to know. Possibly Barbujani at Ferrara."

"Too many people, I think, sir. Are you sure you want to announce the find so broadly, so soon?" asked Riccardo. "Could get messy."

"You may be right, Riccardo. What do you think?" Justine asked her father.

Morgan turned to the younger Italian. "Riccardo has a good sense of the scientific community here. Such an observation could be made in the US or Egypt as well. Okay, let's just start with the superintendent's office and the lab."

"I'm afraid we can expect the local office to put a freeze on the work until they've done their inspections. Perhaps I should keep the parchment with me for safekeeping." Delmo turned on an unusually charming grin. "Molto *delicato.*"

Morgan knew that this offer was highly irregular. He also knew that Professor Della Dora fully understood the implication of what he was asking. Morgan stared at the elder linguist for some time, slowly sipping his Brunelli.

Justine watched her father with unveiled curiosity, knowing that he had landed in hot water over an archeological dig in Egypt when he had withheld a stele, an ancient stone slab that suggested an alternative story of the Exodus. Then it had disappeared.

"Very generous of you. We wouldn't want anything to happen to such a treasure." Morgan had just consigned the scroll to Delmo.

Amir and Riccardo looked surprised.

Justine narrowed her eyes. *You're on dangerous ground again, Dad.* "What he means, Professor, is keep it safe until the inspectors get here. Right?"

Delmo looked like a young boy who had just lost the boxcar derby. But at least he knew that he would have the scroll to himself for a few days.

Morgan smiled with gratitude and embarrassment. He nodded, then busied himself, extracting some small bones from the bream.

The following day, Justine took the train back to Fiesole. Riccardo needed to stay at the site. Amir had offered to drive her, but she'd declined. She needed time to think, rightfully concerned that he might expect that their new intimacy would naturally lead to marriage. *It might start with equality,* Justine thought once again, *but would Amir want a more traditional Arab marriage later on?* Her mother had prepared her for the danger inherent in relationships with Arab men.

After a full day of travel, she stepped into her mother's kitchen and picked up a note:

Dear Justine,

Alessandro and I have gone to Lake Como for a few days. We'll be at the Grand Hotel Villa Serelloni. Will be back in time for the hearing.

Love, Mom

CHAPTER 22

⸺⸎⸻

Love is the flower of life, and blossoms unexpectedly and without law, and must be plucked where it is found, and enjoyed for the brief hour of its duration.

—D.H. Lawrence

ONCE AGAIN JUSTINE sat cross-legged on her bed, her mauve robe tied loosely around her waist. She held the legal papers from the Florence court in one hand and a bundle of D.H. Lawrence's letters in the other. She glanced down at the appearance date on the legal papers—three days away—and threw them on the floor. Then she sought refuge once again in the long-silenced, unfolding drama of her great-grandmother. Reading the letters had become her secret obsession. She was sure now that her mother had never seen these letters or she would have shared this treasure with her.

> Villa Mirenda, 28 February 1928
> My Bella,
>
> > The Martins are leaving today, thank the goddess. They hate Italy. They have a peculiar stiffness, like cutout dolls. Seem unable to breath deeply or turn their heads in the presence of beauty. Why do we host them, you might ask. You see, my darling, they host us in New York. Tit for tat.
> >
> > Your presence in my life is the fresh air of the mountains I love so deeply. What is it you are feeling? I must know. Your letters are so careful, while I want to sit on top of San Francesco hill and sing your name to the birds. When first we met I felt an instant and holy

sympathy and that is how we connect to those who are meant to reflect our lives back to us. That is one way we express ourselves—by instinctual sympathy with those to whom we are drawn, as I was immediately drawn to you, dear soul. The meaning of this intuitive connection may never be fully revealed. Never have I been in the presence of a woman who allowed the quiet space inside my chest to flourish uninterrupted.

Will you go into Florence this week? There is a lovely little exhibit at Dante's home. You know the church nearby? Where he saw his Beatrice? Perhaps I would see you there?

Amore, David

Justine stared out her window, focusing intently on two hummingbirds circling the feeder, suspended in space by their wing beats, as though frantic with passion. *Have I felt such intense emotion for a man? Been so enveloped in a connection that treasured my identity?* Unsure, she turned to the next letter.

Villa Mirenda, 7 March 1928
My dearest Bella,

I regret that you are feeling closed in, suffocated. Virginia Woolf insists that women need a room of their own. Women are born with creative souls striving to free themselves, to release their voices into an undeserving world. Do you have such a room? A small corner? I do suspect, my Isabella, that you may never become a real writer, for you are not sufficiently detached, separated. Even so, writing clears the soul. Best you not be stigmatized as a writer like me. A lonely business, that.

You tell me that my vitality is beautiful. I am at a loss to understand this. Vitality is not my frequent visitor. Only when I am with you, my lovely muse.

What think you of Mussolini? Have you met him? Power is obsolete, you know, but this little manikin ignores history. The rich families pander to him. Order! Order! That is all they care about, as long as their jewels and wine and fashions are protected.

Frieda likes him, but then she likes Baden Baden. Someday leadership will die and be replaced by a tenderness of reciprocity, such as we have.

Amore, David

Justine laid the letter down on her folded leg. She wondered how she'd react if someone, even someone she loved, told her she'd never be a real writer. It would anger her so—she might not write again. She knew that Virginia Woolf thought Lawrence a misogynist. History holds many opinions about that charge. *How patient Isabella was with him. Was she a good writer? Has mother stashed away some of her poems?*

Villa Mirenda, 13 March 1928
My dearest Bella, my muse,

You are angry with me. I'm sorry that my comment about being a real writer hurt you. But you have a much greater gift ... kindness, losing yourself in another, tolerance for stupidity. Writers are selfish. They turn inward when they ought to turn outward. I will always tell you the truth, my love. Even though truth often gets me in trouble. Do not let my flares of honesty terrify you. And never doubt that you will write lovely poems.

London will be printing John Thomas and Lady Jane soon. They want to call it Lady Chatterley's Lover, and of course they cut out some of the passages I find most endearing. The English are such prigs. I am printing the unexpurgated edition here in Florence, but it won't be ready until autumn. I don't want to lose one word of the tenderness you evoke in me. Of phallic consciousness, that sensitivity to others. I can see the pink blush on your cheeks, but know that you secretly obsess about love as I do.

We may need to travel to America when the prudish version comes out. Publicity. America and Italy may be the only markets. Leaving you even for a short time consumes me with sadness. But I do want to get to the ranch.

My health continues to bore me. Coughing fits and weakness from time to time. The rains will surely stop soon. Love, David

So, he apologized. Quite inadequately, I would say. Isabella was a patient woman, yet the love and regard she found in her affair with Lawrence must have over-shadowed any slight to the ego. Was it an affair at all? These love letters serve as an affair, even if it were not sexual.

Villa Mirenda, 18 March 1928
My dearest Isabella,

Huxley is coming next week. His wife Maria is a lovely soul. I hope you will be able to meet them. He wants me to read his latest. I don't know why he is so daring, he knows what a harsh critic I am of his fantasies. But we have good talks and he is interested in my ideas and my letters. Don't gasp, my Bella, I shan't part with yours.

I wandered about to my Etruscans with Brewster again, set on finishing the book sometime this year. All of my writing has been an expression that leads toward the state of perpetual wonder I feel in the presence of the Etruscans—and with you. My Lady Chatterley has been awakened to wonder, as was the gamekeeper of my very first novel. And when I was standing in the presence of these Etruscans I knew at once that I was one of them. In Tarquinia, the tombs are painted like caves in New Mexico, but more like Egypt, I suspect. How did these ancient peoples come to think so alike? Almost enough to make you believe in some divinity. But I've not weakened in that regard. The religious are bores. Like scientists, and for similar reasons. They both rob life of its mysteries.

I suppose this may be the last letter before you leave for Egypt. How long will you be gone? I already ache for your return. Write from Cairo.

Arrivederci, my love. David

Justine changed into her running clothes and headed down the back stairs. Lawrence's thoughts on the Etruscans were as refreshing and new as though he were speaking today. *How does life manage to echo the past?* It was almost too much to take in. At one moment she is in an Etruscan tomb, and the next reading letters written decades ago by a brilliant writer who could infer truths unimagined by others.

She headed northwest across the Fiesole hills, behind Villa San Michele and up through the Aurora restaurant terrace. The flora that usually captured her attention remained merely a blur; she was conscious of little except the sound of air moving in and out of her chest.

She crossed the main square, crested the hill, and approached the Zona Archeologica of the Etruscan Museo. She entered with the season pass she had pinned to her shirt. Only when her feet touched the edge of the Roman bath did she become truly aware of her surroundings. Her feet found station in deep green grasses and red poppies. Olive, cypress, pine, and mulberry trees surrounded the massive zone of Etruscan, Roman, and Longobardi ruins laid horizontally next to each other. It looked as though it was one architectural site when in fact it was three, created over a thousand years. She turned to face the Etruscan temple of Menrva. Here she sat down.

Menrva, ancestor of the Roman Minerva, sister to the Greek Athena. What do you have to say this morning? Offer me some of your wisdom. Help me to under-

stand the plight of Isabella. *Courageous, intelligent muse to one of the world's great writers. What was it like for her, a young girl bound by tradition, culture, physical control?* She wondered if—hoped that—she had inherited some of Isabella's traits, temperaments, and gifts, although Justine knew that compared to Isabella, she was as free as the raven atop the temple in front of her. *Could she possibly comprehend Isabella's world?*

She knew she shared a need for independence and sovereignty with her great-grandmother, grandmother, and mother. Justine knew she came by her extraordinary drive for freedom naturally, as well as through the unmistakable influence of these remarkable women. Hasn't she always known this? *But why, then, was Isabella drawn to Lawrence's despair, that spiritual cage that denied him joy in almost every situation he encountered—except in love with her? Perhaps Isabella needed to be the conduit of his convictions, his hopes, that the long convalescence that occupied his mind and body would someday end. Do all women want to rescue?*

Occasionally, when plagued by self-doubt, Justine wondered if her need for freedom at the sacrifice of a committed relationship was the result of selfishness, inevitable in an only child. She couldn't discount that possibility, or that self-centeredness was part of the mix of her character. *Or am I just too hard on myself? Would a man even ask himself if the need for autonomy is selfish?*

Justine smoothed her hand across the temple wall, wondering again what Menrva would have advised. "*Don't take yourself too seriously,*" Menrva whispered. "*Talk to your mother and decide how to deal with the letters.*"

"And leave my feelings behind? Just move on?" There was no answer.

"And how is your conversation with Menrva going this morning?" asked Marco, standing in front of her now, bemused by her preoccupation. His familiar Outback hat shaded his eyes.

She hadn't noticed the *museo* director's approach. *How long has he been there?* She laughed. "She advises me wisely as usual, Marco. How are you this beautiful morning?"

"I understand that your father has made quite a remarkable find in Cerveteri," he said. It wasn't a question.

"True," she replied, wondering how much to reveal. "A sarcophagus with two alabaster women," she hesitantly offered.

"Your father asked me to come round to the lab in Florence tomorrow. He seems quite excited."

"I'll be joining you." She relaxed now, knowing that Marco was in the inner circle. "Will the mitochondrial DNA studies be done there?"

"Yes, and some in Barcelona. Professor Barbujani from Ferrara is joining us, I believe. Good man." Marco stood with one foot on the edge of the temple, his khaki outfit seeming best suited for big game hunting.

Clearly her father had not taken Riccardo's advice to keep the circle of participants small until more was known. *So like Dad to rev up the drama, involve more characters, then stay on the sidelines to watch the spectacle unfold. After tomorrow, rumors of the new find will fly across Italy.* "I've heard, and I'm eager to hear your observations on this find. It's really quite stunning."

Marco tipped his broad brim further back on his forehead and gave her a measured look. "You've certainly piqued my curiosity."

Without acknowledging his comment, she said, "Got to run." She took off back up the hills toward the *museo*, wishing her mother were back from Lake Como.

CHAPTER 23

⚬⚬⚬

You can be great only if it is your destiny.

—Andrea Bocelli, Italian singer

IT MIGHT HAVE BEEN a lovely April 10th in Italy, except for two things: the heat rose to 30 degrees centigrade, and the city was celebrating the anniversary of the death of Luciano Pavarotti, the King of the High Cs, whose first performance was in Florence. A nation still mourned; a world grieved.

From the days when young Luciano watched movies of Mario Lanzo and mimicked Mario's singing in his bedroom mirror in Modena, he believed that singing was his destiny. After all, his father, a baker, filled his shop with high Cs as well as the aromas of warm baked bread and pastries, while Luciano's mother slaved away in a nearby cigar factory.

Born October 12, 1935, Luciano lived life fully, as all Italians dream of doing. No stage was too large or too small. Toward the end of his career, he formed the operatic trio Three Tenors, performing with Plácido Domingo and José Carreras in concerts that brought the world of opera to many new aficionados of the art form.

Upon the death of a Great One, as is always the case, all had been forgiven. His indulgences and forgotten lines, his debasement of his art by singing with Sting in Mostar. Pavarotti was remembered for his disarming charm, resilience, and Midas touch. "If you turn on the radio and hear someone sing, you know it's me," he had claimed.

People were still mourning, even enjoying mourning, Luciano Pavarotti, their Italian hero, a man larger than life, charismatic, flamboyant, and preciously irresponsible. Italy had lost one of its own, and in so doing, a piece of itself.

It was on this auspicious anniversary that Justine walked into a Florence courtroom. The judge asked for a moment of silence.

She felt an inexplicable sense of calm as she looked around the courtroom. She had decided to experience this event as an anthropologist "sitting in the balcony," distancing herself from the proceedings so that she could more objectively watch them unfold. She would rely on her well-developed skills of participant-observer to survive.

Justine noted that the room had worn wood paneling, dull lighting, and peeling red leather chairs, lending an austere feeling to the setting. The judge, a man in his mid-sixties, wore a faded Armani suit and had a full head of graying blond hair. Several red blotches on his forehead seemed the result of recently burnt basal cells. Yet his searing chocolate eyes were youthful and intelligent.

Beside Justine sat Julia Scarpetta, an attorney from the American embassy. An attractive woman of Italian descent, Scarpetta was the daughter of Brooklyn parents whose Italian ancestors had immigrated to the states in the '20s. Riccardo and Justine's father sat just behind her. She hadn't heard from her mother in the several days since she'd read the note about her trip to Lake Como with Alessandro. Would she show up? There was no prosecuting attorney.

Justine had little reason to be calm. She was worried about her mother and had learned from Scarpetta that, if convicted, Egypt could extradite her from Italy. Although she had been assured that was unlikely, Justine knew that Italy was trying to avoid the return of certain Egyptian artifacts from the Vatican and Giulia museums—strong reasons for granting Egypt its way in her case. She wished that Amir was here, but he had been called back to Egypt to help settle his grandfather's estate.

The judge cleared his throat and read the charges. "Dr. Jenner, you are being charged with leaving Egypt in possession of a rare artifact that you supposedly discovered. The codex is described in the brief as being around 2,000 years old, an artifact considered priceless, yet of unproven value to the country of origin." He turned several pages over as though to find the reason for the "priceless" designation. "This alleged theft constitutes international grand larceny. A serious charge. Egypt is requesting extradition of you, Dr. Jenner, as well as return of the codex."

"If I may, your honor." Scarpetta was speaking. "When my client, Dr. Jenner, was expelled from Egypt in November of last year, she did not take the codex with her and is thus not in possession of said codex." She chose not to refer to the copy as "the codex."

"Why was she expelled?" the judge asked suspiciously.

Justine listened keenly and let her eyes roam the ancient courtroom where Dante Alighieri had been tried and sentenced to burn at the stake for taking bribes. A social democrat, a White Guelph, he had supported the Pope, but not enough for Pope Boniface VIII, who had outsmarted him. Justine looked for signs that Dante had once been in the room, but remembered that he had not attended his own trial, seeking exile instead, never to see his beloved Florence again. *Maybe that's what I should have done!* Dante died in Ravenna—700-plus years ago.

"It's a long story, your honor. I'm going to ask Dr. Jenner to explain." She turned to Justine expectantly.

The judge motioned Justine forward and the clerk stepped to the side of the witness chair.

Justine walked slowly to the stand, holding the eyes of the judge in her gaze, and settled herself into the oversized wooden chair. She straightened her skirt as she sat down and began, "In April of last year, your honor, I visited the crypt under St. Sergius in Old Cairo, the crypt where the Holy Family was said to have rested during their flight into Egypt. That was the morning of the big earthquake . . ."

"I remember. Go on," said the judge placing both elbows on his desk and drawing himself forward, ready to hear a long, undoubtedly dull, story. He decided to focus instead on Justine's full lips and amber eyes.

"During the earthquake," she continued, "an ancient codex fell from the wall and landed at my feet. It turned out to be Mary's diary."

"Which Mary?" interrupted the judge.

"The Virgin Mary, also known as Mary of Nazareth, mother of Jesus, your honor." She paused for effect.

"The Virgin Mary! Now I've heard everything. You brought me here for this foolishness?" he demanded. "Clerk! Why wasn't I told of this?" The clerk—a short, rotund man with a nose that sloped toward his upper lip—shrugged. The judge grimaced. "Continue."

Justine explained that a team of investigators had been formed under the leadership of Professor Ibrahim El Shabry, and that after carbon dating of the patina, leather, and parchment, the date of the codex had been set at around 10 CE. After months of analysis of the writing and surrounding events, the team had concluded that the Virgin Mary was indeed the author.

"Incredible. *Non può essere possibile.* But why did you steal it?"

"I didn't steal it," said Justine evenly. "I found it." She turned her head, tucking her chestnut hair behind her ear.

The judge softened his voice, striking a less accusatory tone. "I see that the brief charges you with stealing the only remaining copy of the codex."

Now, I am guilty of that charge. She continued to smile innocently.

"Apparently the original was stolen earlier. Is that right?"

"Correct, your honor," affirmed Justine. "The original was stolen from the office of the Supreme Director, Omar Mostafa, reportedly by a man named Robert Blackburn. He was arrested and imprisoned, but is now living somewhere in Rome. The copy was in the hands of Professor Ibrahim—who, I believe, has been murdered."

It was as though everyone in the room took a deep breath at the same time. Scarpetta stood rigid. Justine had named the thief and made an accusation of murder in the same statement.

Justine calmly turned and looked at her father and Riccardo. They stared back at her, wide-eyed. It was not as though Morgan didn't agree with his daughter's analysis of the situation, but he believed there was too little evidence to make the claim of murder.

"We'll leave conclusions of murder up to the Egyptian authorities," said the judge, surprisingly unruffled. "And we'll refer your statement about Blackburn to the Italian *consigliere*. But I still haven't heard why you supposedly left the country with the copy."

"Dr. El Shabry, who was the principal investigator on this project, loaned it to me so that a linguist from the Sorbonne and I could write an invited article on the entire discovery for the journal *Archaeology*. I was asked to leave the country because the contents of the diary were controversial, especially since strife among the faiths was accelerating. Churches were being burned."

"Do you know where the copy is?"

"Yes, I do, your honor."

"Dr. Jenner, I appreciate your candor. But please—where is it?" demanded the impatient judge.

Justine fidgeted with the papers in front of her, whispered to Scarpetta, stalled. She had asked her mother to place it in the family safe in Fiesole. *Where is Andrea?*

"You will tell me where the copy of the codex is being kept or I will hold you in contempt of court." The judge's pen pecked at the papers in front of him.

Riccardo leaned over the railing and whispered rapidly into Scarpetta's ear. She immediately stood. "Objection, your honor."

"What is your objection, *Procuratore*?"

"The charges today relate to my client's behavior in relationship to said codex. She need not reveal the name of the person currently in possession of the copy."

"Fine," said the judge, his voice heavy with sarcasm. "We'll let the Egyptians deal with this case." He shuffled through his papers again; his face relaxed slightly. "The extradition order is here somewhere . . ."

"Your honor. Permission to approach the bench," said Lucrezia, suddenly seen to be standing in the aisle in her best white Valentino suit.

The judge looked up mid-sentence, clearly surprised by the request and the woman making it. "Creta . . ." he murmured, quickly correcting himself, "Ah, Mrs. Jenner. Yes, you may approach the bench."

Justine glanced at her father, who looked perplexed and miserable. The lines around his mouth tightened, his temples flushed. The presence of his former wife clearly also caused distress to one of Italy's most respected, *married* judges.

Justine felt sympathetic and amused.

Lucrezia walked toward the judge and placed both hands on the front edge of his elevated desk, moving her chin forward so that it nearly touched the desk as well. The judge stared at her with the tenderness of a young boy look-ing at his first love. He stood up and leaned forward. Lucrezia whispered in his ear.

He paused and blushed. "*Sì, sì*, I comprehend," is all he said, his face falling. "Case dismissed."

CHAPTER 24

... you must never show partiality to any person in a case, you must listen equally to low and high, you must not be afraid of any man—for the judgment is God's.

—Moses, Deuteronomy, 11.17

"So, WHAT DID YOU whisper to the judge?" demanded Justine as she and her mother settled into kitchen chairs back home in Fiesole.

"I simply reminded him of our delicious weekend in Venice and asked if he had ever told his wife," admitted Lucrezia, small crows' feet near her green eyes wrinkling as she grinned.

Justine took a deep breath. "I assume this was after you left Dad—not because you left him. Did Dad know before today? I saw his face." She walked to the refrigerator and withdrew a bottle of *limoncello*, pouring them each a small glass.

Her mother paused, searching for the answers, rifling through the fallen leaves of her marriage to Morgan. How much did he know? She wasn't sure she remembered. Should she reveal the distress of those personal doors now being pried open, doors that her mother and grandmother had passed through before her? Those doors had begun to loosen when she went away to school in Alexandria, and later at the American University in Cairo. It was her own history she had shuttered away when she met and married Morgan.

Justine contemplated the relationship she assumed her parents held between them when she was a young girl. She had been stunned when they'd divorced during her first year in graduate school in Chicago. If she hadn't gone to Berkeley, so near home, for her undergraduate years, it probably would have happened even sooner. Her presence had obviously kept them together. She had grown up thinking she was part of a happy family. Lies.

Secrets. *Now what?* Each woman reviewed her hurtful history in silence. "What happened at Lake Como?" Justine finally asked, topping off both of their glasses with the lemony liquor.

Lucrezia stared at her daughter and exhaled gently, relieved to focus on the present. "I was astonished. Alessandro proposed," she said easily. She had been freed by her decision to not keep things from her daughter. *Most things*, she corrected herself.

Justine almost choked on an olive pit. "Proposed? Really, Mother? But are you really that surprised?"

"We had an agreement. Alessandro knew that I wasn't interested in marriage, and he wasn't going to venture into forbidden territory—at least, that's what I thought."

"So you told him no?"

"Not exactly. I told him I'd think about it."

"Now it's my turn to be astonished."

"Would it be such a bad thing? He's a fine man, very attractive—and I could have all the Ferragamo shoes I want." Lucrezia's eyes sparkled as she laughed.

"You're joking, right?" Justine said lightheartedly, amused that the *limoncello* was beginning to affect her speech. She rose and walked to the refrigerator again, pouring herself a glass of ice water, which she drank while leaning against the stove. "What about your line dancing rule?"

"Ah, yes. Wait until your husband dies and then do what you've always wanted to do. Free yourself to dance."

"Exactly. Won't you be afraid of losing your freedom again if you marry Alessandro?"

"My freedom is important to me—but I may be up for another adventure." Lucrezia stood and joined her daughter, standing close enough to touch shoulders. She leaned around, examining Justine's eyes. "What do you think?"

Now it was Justine's turn to laugh. She put her arm around her mother's shoulders. "You didn't ask me what I thought when you left Dad. Why now?"

"This is woman to woman. Not mother to child."

"Then I'll give you my honest opinion, woman to woman. I realize that—"

"Are you girls ready?" asked Morgan, leaning into the doorway, very dapper in his black turtleneck. "Champagne is waiting, and we have a lot to celebrate."

Justine and Lucrezia looked at one another. Girls indeed.

∽

It was still too cool to eat in Aurora's garden in the evenings, so Lucrezia had reserved a table for seven in the corner of the voguish dining room. Andrea and Riccardo were already seated at the table when they arrived.

So now you show up. "I thought you intended to be at the trial today," Justine charged Andrea.

"I am so sorry, *chérie*," confessed Andrea, her eyes darting from Justine to Lucrezia, then Morgan. "My plane was late. A bomb scare in the airport." She stared at Justine through an arrangement of yellow chrysanthemums atop the gold damask tablecloth and fumbled for a cigarette, which she didn't light. A larger walnut table of pancetta, cheeses, wines, and red candles stood nearby. Tensions adopted the colors of the feast before them.

Two walls of windows faced columnar cypress on the crest of the southern hill. Morgan lifted the chilled champagne bottle out of the silver bucket and poured each of them a glass, but said nothing. He seemed preoccupied. Poured mechanically. Was it the trial? Andrea? Or his ex-wife's secrets?

"Riccardo tells me it went well . . ." Andrea began. Justine noted that her lower lip was trembling slightly. "I am sorry to have missed it."

"It did go well." *No thanks to you.* "So I offer the first toast to my mother," said Justine. "Thanks for rescuing me today, even if you had to use blackmail. I think the judge was ready to put me on the next boat to Egypt." Justine smiled, her pulsing temples tensed. "I'm sorry you missed the party, Andrea. You would have found it fascinating."

Andrea stared at the chrysanthemums, picked up her champagne, and fingered her cigarette case. She began whispering to the waiter, whom she apparently knew.

Morgan's eyes narrowed as he turned toward his ex-wife, "And what did you say to the judge today, Creta?"

"I'll never tell." Lucrezia winked seductively so as to suggest that the whispered message referenced an earlier assignation. Which, of course, it did. As usual, she was stately and beautiful in white and a jacket of East Asian ramie. Even if she didn't want Morgan back, she had a strong competitive streak.

The muscles around Morgan's mouth tightened. He looked away.

The subterranean tensions in this room could be cut with a butter knife, Justine mused, and changed the subject. "What will happen now, Riccardo? Am I still in danger?"

"Not likely," Riccardo replied calmly, which was his wont. "The Italian authorities will stamp the case closed and they'll report to the Egyptian embassy that the codex copy is not in Italy." He never dressed for dinner, which reinforced his casual demeanor.

"But what if the original codex is in Italy?" *I assume that Blackburn has already negotiated an outrageous price from his buyer.* "Wouldn't it be embarrassing if it turned up?" Justine rose slightly to remove her beaded jacket as she spoke. While it was too cool to sit outside, the inside was warming up.

"It would, indeed," admitted Riccardo. "Let's hope that the transaction involving the actual codex takes place someplace other than Italy."

Andrea rose and excused herself. "*Le toilette*," she grinned.

Justine watched Andrea walk away. "Well," she finally said, holding her empty glass out to her father. "More champagne, please. We do have much to celebrate, including our two women of the Egyptian sarcophagus." She lifted her glass first to her father, then Riccardo, then her mother.

Amir appeared across the room, having just returned from Cairo.

"A bomb scare delayed you?" Justine asked innocently.

"What?" Amir appeared puzzled, and placed both hands on the empty chair next to Lucrezia.

"Nothing. How is the investigation going?" she asked.

"Regarding my grandfather or the Etruscans?" he asked, seating himself and reaching for his empty glass. "I'd prefer to talk about the Etruscans right now. The Egyptian authorities are running after their tales. The Etruscan DNA and patina studies will be ready any day now. Here's hoping for a few stunning revelations of early secrets that shake up these Italian archaeologists."

Justine found him more edgy than usual. Undoubtedly he was tired, since this was his third trip back to Cairo in a short time.

"Secrets, indeed," replied Lucrezia, her voice slurred slightly. "So many secrets. What people think they know about the Etruscans is just theory."

"Not entirely, Lucrezia," said Marco, seating himself in the seventh chair. "We know a lot about them that is uncontested." He placed a napkin on his lap and reached for the antipasti.

"Such as?" she asked. "And welcome, dear friend."

"It's an honor to be invited. Morgan filled me in on today's court proceedings. There is much to celebrate," said Marco, smiling and nodding to each guest. "And as to your question about the Etruscans, Lucrezia, most scholars believe that they were indigenous to this area. Their language is definitely not Indo-European, but it is fairly well understood now because they adopted the Greek alphabet in the early part of the seventh century BC . . ."

"All right, my good man, you've convinced us for now," interrupted Morgan, not ready for a long treatise.

"I've only just begun," grinned Marco. "I could go on . . ." But he resisted.

"Enough for now, my friend, let's consider what we don't know or what is contested," suggested Morgan. "As you know, I take issue with the assumption that the Etruscans were indigenous."

"And where does Egypt come into the picture?" asked Justine. "The linen on the famous Zagreb mummy with Etruscan writing opened that question, but now with the carvings on the sarcophagus we've just found, an Egyptian connection can't be ignored." She realized that she was repeating herself.

"Granted," said Amir, graciously, "but 'indigenous' doesn't deny the influence of other cultures through trade and exploration. Look at what the south Saharan trade routes did for Timbuktu."

"I would say that the connection with Egypt is irrefutable, regardless of how it took place," insisted Justine, who knew a great deal about Isis and the significance the goddess held for the whole of the Mediterranean. *After all,* she thought, *Isis paved the way for acceptance and adoration of the Virgin Mary.* "Everything is connected," she asserted the obvious. "And now, shall we order?"

The waiter, whom Justine recognized as the same young man who had flirted with her mother on the terrace during their last visit, stood near Lucrezia and watched as she described the restaurant's new chef. "He's from Basilicata, in the arch of the boot, as Alessandro would say. May I?" She turned to the eager young man. "We'll have the *Pasta con Peperoni, Crushi E. Mollica Fritta* with plenty of goat pecorino cheese, *Fagioli di Sarconi, Focaccia al Pomodorini*—please bring that first." She turned back to her guests. "You'll find that the *Peperoni di Senise* in the pasta has a smoky caramel tang. You'll enjoy it."

"Basilicata produces only one local wine," Morgan offered. "And it ranks at the forefront of the best-known and appreciated Italian reds. It's called *Agliano del Volture.* Do they have it?"

"None other," replied Lucrezia, nodding to the young waiter to bring the wine, although she had decided to stick with water. The limoncello and champagne had been quite enough.

"*Aglianico*," added Riccardo. "The name of the original grape is a corruption of the word *Hellenic*. In fact, there are no native grapes in this region. The plant was brought over by the Greeks when they settled the area in pre-Roman times, making it among the oldest grapes in Italy."

Andrea returned to the table, placing her phone back into her purse. Her cheeks were flushed. She sat down quietly, without the usual fanfare.

CHAPTER 25

—⊶⊷—

To be a *choicemaker* in the third phase of life means that what you choose to do or be must correspond with what is true for you at a soul level. What you do with your life is then *meaningful*; it is something you know in your bones, at your core, in your soul.

—Jean Shinoda Bolen, *Goddesses in Older Women*

"I'M THINKING OF GETTING married again. What do you think?" asked Lucrezia of her houseguest and friend, Andrea. "Justine has reservations." Her daughter had not told her what she knew about Andrea and Blackburn, and was reluctant to do more before she knew the extent of their involvement.

"Has she said so?" asked Andrea cautiously, surprised that Lucrezia would consider such a move. "Alessandro? The Ferragamo guy?"

Lucrezia sat on one of the stools at the long counter, her white kaftan trailing behind. She grinned at the stiffness of Andrea's manner, a woman who rarely hesitated to voice her opinions or feel comfort in her own skin. "No, she hasn't said so in so many words . . . and, yes. That Alessandro."

The two women heard the back door open and watched as a sweaty Justine stepped into the kitchen. She picked up a towel, dried her face, and flung the towel around her neck. She'd had a late night with Andrea, but hadn't mentioned Lucrezia's possible marriage. Or Amir.

During their late-night discussion, Andrea pointed out that the previously indecipherable section of the codex copy, which she worked on when she was in the villa's guest bedroom, revealed Mary's desire to return to her grandmother's homeland in Lydia before her death.

"Is the coffee ready?" Justine asked, landing on the stool nearest her mother.

"We were just talking about marriage," ventured Andrea, pouring Justine a cup of coffee from the Melitta.

Justine took a sip of the warm, thick mixture her mother called coffee and grinned at the two women. "Whose?" she teased. "Andrea, are you getting married?"

"Not me, *chérie!* Not my style."

"Oh, then it must be you." Justine directed the comment to her mother, her smile fading. She couldn't hide the fact that she held strong opinions on the subject of the possible marriage. "What are your thoughts about the proposal today?"

"Well . . ." her mother began. "While I wouldn't want to lose my independence, traveling and dining with a man can be very pleasurable. I rediscovered that at Lake Como. Alessandro is a pleasing companion, a considerate lover. Not too predictable. Interesting, still curious. Then there is the part about growing old together. That's important to Alessandro, much more than to me . . . I'm feeling pressured to make a decision."

"It's not like you to respond to pressure, Creta," said Andrea. "And what makes you think that marriage with an Italian would be an equal partnership? Italian men are coddled by their mamas—and they expect the same from their wives, not so unlike Egyptians. Don't get me started on the lack of Italian women in government or that buffoon Berlusconi."

Lucrezia found a trivet and extracted cinnamon buns from the oven. The scent of cinnamon wafted through the room. "But women won't put up with these conditions for long—things are changing in Italy," she said. "I respect Alessandro and must take his feelings seriously. But I must also consider where I am in my life and what it would mean to live each day with a man, sharing a bed, a closet, perhaps even a bathroom." She looked uneasy as the daily events of married life unreeled before her eyes. "At fifty-eight I'm becoming a crone, my dear friends, nearing the third chapter of my life. I'm pretty set in my ways."

Justine liked being considered a "dear friend" as well as a daughter. But she also wondered how much Italy was like Egypt and how soon things would actually change for women. She feared that her mother might be headed for a repeat of her experience with her father.

"A crone? Isn't that an offensive term for an older woman?" asked Andrea, wrinkling her nose as though a rancid smell had overcome the cinnamon-sweet of the cinnamon buns.

"No," replied Lucrezia. "The writer Jean Shinoda Bolen—a friend of mine—uses the term. She defines it as a wise elder who understands herself, who makes choices true to that self."

"Jean is a Jungian," added Justine, "so she insists that to be a crone is to understand your archetype, who you truly are."

"I like that," Andrea relented, walking over to Lucrezia and placing her hands on her shoulders. "So, *chérie*, does 'croneship' make your decision more clear?"

"I think it does . . ." Lucrezia leaned forward and kissed Andrea on both cheeks, then lavished white cream cheese frosting on the still-warm buns.

Justine winced as she watched the display of affection, for she had grown increasingly uneasy with Andrea's secrets. She sensed that she knew her mother's decision, and she turned her attention to Andrea. "How are things going with Dad, Andrea? All kidding aside."

Andrea was taken aback, but quickly recovered her natural aplomb. "As you both know only too well, Morgan is a charmer. A challenging companion, conversationalist." She chose not to include "lover." "A little devious, *n'est-ce pas?* I've seen a few undesirable flashes of jealousy. He calls too often and asks too many questions," she added. "But a dear. We all sacrifice for the men in our lives, don't you think? They can be such boys."

Mother and daughter let slow grins curl across their lips, then began to laugh.

"What's so funny?" Morgan asked, standing barefoot in the doorway.

Dad has a gift for appearing at inopportune moments.

"Ah, Creta's cinnamon buns!" he exclaimed.

Justine watched her parents, their games predictable. *Yet some fates are not so well known—or known at all.* She pondered the fate of Mary of Nazareth. *What happened to her? Why did she leave the diary behind? We'll probably never know.*

EPHESUS, APRIL, 27 CE

The journey of Mary of Nazareth was difficult. Summer storms heaved the sea, dragging her ship off course. The voyagers from Palestine had been two days without water. Yet the splendor of the great city awakened their senses and enlivened their step. The Ephesians welcomed them, for they had an abundance of all things. As the financial and cultural center of the world, Ephesus provided its inhabitants with such abundance that compassion came easily. There was enough for all: running water for drinking and bathing, foods and wines, silks and jewels. The poorest among the Ephesians were without want. All could find shelter. None were turned away.

This was a city so tolerant and diverse, even a Jew such as herself would have nothing to fear here except her own memories, which would haunt her for the rest of her years. Mary and John, her son's disciple, and their companions entered the city through the Magnesia gate and came into the agora. On the northern side of the square, a mammoth basilica housed the city courts. The square itself boasted grand stone religious and civic buildings. Doric columns, fountains, and marble statues, one of the daring Artemis, stood guard before the public baths, gloriously surrounded by porticoes paved with mosaics. The eternal flame of Ephesus reflected in Mary's astonished eyes. Never had she seen such wonders. Turning right at the bottom of the Street of Curetes, Mary and her companions faced the most astounding of vistas: the Temple of Artemis, goddess of the hunt, the largest and most glamorous temple in the world.

Some months later, Mary reflected upon her time living in Ephesus while John built her house on Bulbul Dagi Mountain. It was one of those incredible evenings, the glow of sunset framing the mountain. Her new home stood behind her. Light balmy air filled her lungs with buoyant energy; bursts of sweet hyacinth and honeysuckle filled her senses.

Ahead, at the base of the mountain, the great city stretched out across the valley and west to the sea. Fifty tall torches along Harbor Street radiated a veiled lavender glow over the Grand Theater and Temple of Artemis in the distance. Mary had come to admire Artemis, as she had Isis those long years ago in Egypt, known to her as a fiercely independent goddess who fought for equality and fairness. *Ephesus is Artemis's city*, she thought.

Mary rose, smoothed the front of her favorite faded blue tunic, and walked slowly to the western door of her new home, built solidly of local stone. She carried an armload of kindling that she placed in the central hearth, lighting a fire for tea and warmth in the evening ahead. Near the southern window, crowded near a sink with running water, a loom stretched tight with a blue and lavender weaving. Behind the hearth, a small alcove and altar adorned with one of Joseph's prayer cloths led into a smaller sleeping area where Mary spent her restless nights.

She walked to the sturdy wooden table and cupboard that held her supply of tea, bread, honey, dried fish, onions, salt, and Arabian spices, along with ceramic dishes, glassware, and a pitcher, often filled with milk from her goats. She placed her tea in one of the copper pots that hung nearby.

Daily, her companions brought fresh supplies, and twice monthly she managed to take her weavings into the agoras in the city below. As a woman of forty-seven summers, her knees often complained as she made the climb back up the mountain. Yet she delighted in market days that gave her a chance to remember such days with Jesus in Egyptian markets, those days when she was the teacher and he had so many questions. "Can only some women write?" he had asked one day as she purchased papyrus for her diary. "All women can write if they are taught how," she had told him. "Just as you were taught to read and write." As was his way, Jesus was quiet for several moments. Mary realized then that she was the only woman he had seen writing. So curious and reflective was her son. *My diary. Such a loss. If only I had brought it from Old Cairo—had not left it in the cave wall with the comb from Joseph. I could pull the stories of Jesus to my chest.* Her eyes moistened with lost.

On that last day in Jerusalem, when she had sat in anguish witnessing her son's death, Jesus had thought of her, saying to John, "See your mother. Keep her with you." It was John who had brought her to Ephesus that summer, afraid for her welfare. She was eager to leave Palestine, to escape to her ancient family home, the home she only knew from stories told by her Grandmother Faustina.

Now John tells her of a new religion and a man called Paul. Of efforts to make her son divine. Jesus would not have been fond of a movement that glorified him. His mission, Mary knew only too well, taught love and tolerance, forgiveness and compassion, not deification. Fortunately, Paul, with the blindness to women he revealed in his letters, would not arrive in Ephesus from Rhodes until the summer of her death. Mary died peacefully, painlessly, on August 15th, in the year 53 of the current era, as her community was preparing for the Ephesus Wine Festival, which would take place on the 19th of that month.

CHAPTER 26

Pope Alexander I to his daughter Lucrezia: "Do people say that I am both your father and your lover? Let the world, that heap of vermin as ridiculous as they are feeble-minded believe the tales about the mighty! You must know that for those destined to dominate others, the ordinary rules are turned upside down and take on entirely new meaning. Good and evil are carried off to a higher, different plane."

—Caroline Murphy, *The Pope's Daughter*

FERRARA, THE GLORIOUS Medieval and Renaissance city in northern Italy, has so preserved its historical center that, like the necropolis at Cerveteri, it is designated a UNESCO World Heritage Site. Situated on the Po River at the mouth of the ancient Etruscan Po Valley, Ferrara is considered one of the greenest cities in Europe, and it is a bastion of the arts. This urban oasis is walled by one of the oldest defense systems in Italy, made of sinuous red brick, and embraced by lush gardens. The city boasts the great Castello Estense, surrounded by a moat, and houses great cathedrals, public buildings, museums, and the ornate Teatro Comunale opera house, symbols of the influence of the extended Este family that ruled Ferrara for more than three centuries.

In the late fourteenth century, Ercole I, an ambitious son of the Este family, petitioned Pope Alexander I for a ducal title, a designation in keeping with the family's growing wealth and properties. "I will make you a duke, a title to be held by the family in perpetuity," responded the Pope—but only if Ercole would promise that his first-born son would marry the Pope's illegitimate daughter, Lucrezia. This promise did not prove to be an onerous burden. Lucrezia was a remarkably stunning woman with flowing blond hair, although as a former wife, twice over, and mother of an illegitimate child born in the

Sistine Chapel, she did not come into the marriage unsullied. It was thus that the young Alfonso d'Este wed Lucrezia Borgia.

Lucrezia became the flamboyant Countess d'Este and reigned over the further glorification of the city. She also worked tirelessly as a sponsor of the Clares, an order of Franciscan nuns dedicated to supporting the poor and homeless. Well-schooled in her father's Machiavellian ways, Lucrezia was politically devious. She was accused of having poisoned her abusive father and of being unfaithful to her husbands. Lucrezia Borgia died during the birth of her eighth child.

Justine's mother took delight in the machinations of her namesake.

On the morning after their arrival in Ferrara, Justine, Delmo, Amir, and Morgan left the Hotel Europa on Viale Cavour in Morgan's SUV, following their host, Guido Barbujani. The party turned left onto Corso Martiri della Liberta, passed the Castello Estense, and entered the Piazza Cattedrale, which was crowded with students, stylishly dressed though pedaling bikes. Turning right onto Cortevecchia, Morgan turned left off the piazza into a narrow street of shops, and then left again into the narrow Via del Turco. They parked, as instructed, across from apartment house five.

"I appreciate your willingness to meet here this morning, Justine. I needed to get the new *frigorifero* delivered before leaving for Sardinia," Guido said as they stood together in his kitchen making tea. A population geneticist, evolutionist, and novelist, Guido taught at the University of Ferrara and was a sought-after consultant. A man in his late forties, Guido had hair made nearly platinum by streaks of silver and gold and startling green eyes that matched the lightweight turtleneck sweater he wore carelessly with worn jeans.

"When you said your *frig* died," said Delmo, standing nearby, "I thought you said your priest had died." He frequently had difficulty hearing his younger colleagues.

Guido laughed heartily. "Even such an unfortunate event wouldn't have changed my schedule, I'm afraid. I come from a long line of anarchists. Once, in a fit of rage about Catholicism, my grandfather posted a sign on the church door that read, 'Bankrupt!'"

Delmo laughed at himself and lowered his aging, yet surprisingly fit, body into a kitchen chair to become a silent observer.

"Bankrupt? An apt term. Your grandfather must have been quite a spunky character. Are you very much like him?" Justine asked, noticing humor lines fanning out from under Guido's long lashes.

"The spitting image," he grinned. "I can be quite irreverent and often difficult."

"You must have been an exasperating kid," Justine said, staring into his eyes with a challenging expression. "Is that how children behave in Adria?" She found him much more attractive than his photos on the Internet.

Guido wondered how—and why—she had learned where he was born. "Most Italians have a strained relationship with the Church," he said. "Even so, I'm sure that I often embarrassed my mother." His platinum hair caught the morning sunlight filtering through the casement window.

Where had she seen that grin before? For a moment she lost her train of thought. "My mother has green eyes," she said finally. "Her name is Lucrezia." She opened the darkened refrigerator and found a can of milk. Mildewing cheese assaulted her nostrils. She quickly closed the door, smelled the contents of a small can of milk, and poured the remains into a miniature, hand-painted pitcher.

"Ah, another Lucrezia Borgia with green eyes! My mother insists that the green eyes make me Etruscan. I'd like to think she's right. Sugar?"

"So would I," Justine said, taking the sugar bowl from his hand and placing it on the tray. She couldn't think of anything else to say, so she picked up the tray loaded with cups and started toward the living room.

"Can I help?" Guido asked, brushing against her shoulder and placing his tanned hand over hers on the tray handle.

They stood for a moment, gripping the tray. She felt the warmth of his body. "I think I have it," she said, a little breathless. "Why don't you carry the tea?"

The three of them made their way into the living room, Justine with the tray, Guido with the sacred pot of tea. Delmo, carrying his oversized notebook and newly acquired cane, trailed behind the bearers of libation. "A temporary tool," he'd insisted. "Those ladders at Cerveteri are getting the best of me."

" . . . for each thousand years, that would mean almost four hundred generations," Morgan was saying to Amir. "The two women of the tomb have been on a long time-travel journey."

"And that translates to greater chances for substitutions—and for technical difficulties," added Amir.

"Substitutions?" asked Justine, placing the tray in front of the two men.

"Substitution of one nucleotide for another, in other words, mutations, the markers on the evolution tree created by mtDNA," offered Guido. "Such substitutions can be the result of internal evolutionary changes in the species or environmental changes. Either way, the result is nearly the same."

"Ah," said Justine, slipping into the overstuffed chair facing the divan, crossing her long legs, covered in denim that was tucked into brown leather boots. She had brushed out her hair, which draped over a yellow silk blouse. "I understand mtDNA, lineage, and mutations . . . but remind me, how does mitochondrial DNA work?" She paused, a spark of mischief in her eyes. "Chemically, I mean."

"A little 101, Professor, if you please," said Morgan, who was eager to renew his relationship with Guido. They had worked together on Crete in the late '90s. On this dig, their work together had begun when the Cerveteri samples from the women in the tomb were brought into the Florence lab and a duplicate set sent to the University of Barcelona.

"If you like," said Guido, bowing slightly toward Justine as he settled back into his white denim divan. "Mitochondria are structures within cells that convert energy from food into a form that cells can use. Each mitochondrion contains thirty-seven genes, thirteen of which are involved in cellular respiration, meaning that they remove electrons from organic compounds like food and pass them through a series of electron receptors that convert them into energy." He turned to Amir, "Is that right?"

Amir nodded in agreement. The conversation was interrupted by the clamor of a lumbering delivery truck filling the narrow street below.

"Ah, my *frigo*," Guido said, acknowledging the arrival and then turning his attention back to Justine. He remained seated, knowing full well that it would take a while for the men to wrestle the refrigerator up to the third floor.

Amir raised his voice to command his host's attention. "But what do the chemical aspects have to do with the functional uses of DNA, Professor?" He was well acquainted with the archeological uses of DNA, but not necessarily the chemistry.

Justine slid forward in her chair, preparing to pour five cups of tea. She knew the preferences of everyone in the room, except Guido, toward whom she silently lifted the sugar bowl and raised an eyebrow.

Guido shook his head. "As you know, Amir, mitochondria contain their own DNA, which is what we use to reconstruct genealogical trees. In a dead body, most DNA will be in bad shape, but since each cell contains a lot of mitochondria, each contains several copies of its own DNA. By working on mitochondria you have a better chance of finding some intact DNA fragments. Nuclear DNA is still difficult to type, and there is a high risk of contamination . . . that is, of reading the DNA of somebody else, an archaeologist or a biologist who happened to touch the specimen, rather than the specimen's DNA." The clamorous knock of a fist on the apartment door prompted Guido to get up and greet the two heavyset deliverymen.

"So you can expect the roots of the teeth of these two women to still possess mtDNA and perhaps some nuclear DNA?" questioned Justine, watching Guido closely, his body moving comfortably within his comfortable old sweater and close-fitting jeans. She quickly turned toward Delmo. "I know that nuclear DNA has very different properties than mtDNA. Right, Delmo?"

Guido was now laughing with the two panting deliverymen. He smiled encouragingly at Delmo, his longtime mentor from Bologna.

"Nuclear DNA exists within the nucleus of the cell itself and is like an individual fingerprint," began Delmo, pleased to assume his favorite role. "Unique." He made a circle with his thumb and forefinger and pointed to the center. "On the other hand, mtDNA is not necessarily unique, but is more likely to remain consistent within and among populations over time, interrupted only by mutations. Nuclear DNA is the result of the influence of both parents." He paused. "How am I doing, Guido?" As he became more animated, his cane fell to the floor. He promptly kicked it out of the way, just in time to keep the deliverymen from tripping as they wheeled the refrigerator toward the kitchen. An expression of disdain for his temporary handicap washed across his face.

"Excellent," Guido nodded, standing by the kitchen door. "The notion of 'consistent within and among populations over time' is key here. And it's important to obtain more than one sample from a region, the area where most substitutions occur. Multiple samples give us the sequencing pattern, or haplogroup."

"So, what can we expect to learn from the DNA of these two women?" asked Justine.

"Two things, hopefully," said Guido, pausing to sign the bill of sale and provide a small gratuity to the men. "One, are these two women related? And two, are they related to other samples of lineage from Italy or elsewhere? MtDNA will tell us that."

"Why don't you explain what mtDNA tells us about lineage?" invited Morgan.

"Explain it as you would in one of your novels," interjected Justine.

"Ah," said Guido, laughing softly as he pulled his chair into the circle. "Since we're looking for markers, or patterns of mutation, let's say that a mutation is a paper clip on a long, lovely, blue satin ribbon."

Justine grinned and recalled the lovely blue satin ribbons on the Lawrence letters. Guido began to spin his metaphorical web. *Nasser*, she now remembered. *His grin reminds me of Nasser.* She was stunned to think that her intense physical response to Guido might be connected to her Egyptian lover. She forced her attention back to the conversation.

"For instance," Guido began, "suppose we have some credible samples from the Phoenicians and the Lebanese. If the paperclips match up, that would strongly suggest that the former are somehow the latter's ancestors. Is that what you meant?"

"Exactly, professor," Morgan said. "Well done. But what use are your 'paper clips'? Can we date these women through mtDNA?"

Amir interrupted. "Actually, no." He walked across the room and leaned against the wall facing Morgan. "Dating will need to come from the carbon dating of the linen, parchment, and sarcophagus patina—but it's quite feasible. This isn't the first time such products have given us a historical map. In Egypt—"

"And, fortunately, these two are women," said Guido. "We biologists prefer women, at least their remains." He immediately regretted his interruption of Amir.

"Why the preference?" Justine asked, glancing at Amir. *Does he realize what is happening to me?* Her eyes reflected an inner fire, as well as the morning sunlight.

"MtDNA comes from the female and is handed down through the female only, my dear," said Morgan. "Oddly, mussels and fruit flies are the exceptions. Right, professor?" He didn't wait for an answer. "MtDNA in males that might have been passed on to future generations is either destroyed by the egg or early on in the embryo. Males retain their own capacity for developing energy sources, but they don't tell us much about their ancestors. You must know this is difficult for me to admit, since I'm often deemed a misogynist."

"Not always, Dad," laughed Justine. "But don't try to pass that trait off as DNA-related!" Her playful eyes moved from one man to the other, "So what do we know about our two women?"

"Amir?" invited Morgan. "I think you have some preliminary findings." He had become aware of the preliminary report from Barcelona that morning.

"I do," said Amir, walking across the room to his valise. "The Barcelona lab has not sent us the results, but if they confirm what we found, it would seem that the two women are close relatives, maybe even sisters."

"Sisters?" piped Justine. "I guess we shouldn't be surprised. They certainly look alike. How helpful is it that they are sisters?"

"The information is more solid," offered Amir. "We need to confirm the results by two independent laboratories, that is the rule of the game. But if the results are the same, these efforts will have been very helpful," he concluded.

Guido nodded, glancing from Justine to Amir. He squinted. "When will we have the final mtDNA information, Amir?" Then he asked a second question of Delmo. "And the translations from the linen and parchment?"

"In other words," added Justine, "when will we get the full picture?" She sensed that Guido had become more distant, had smothered the sparkle in his eyes.

"I would expect to have our translations ready quite soon. Within the week," said Delmo.

"And the other data," offered Amir, "at about the same time."

Morgan's face flushed with both consternation and excitement. "We may finally have the story of the Etruscans!" he exclaimed, his controlled demeanor turning ebullient.

"Or whoever they were," added Justine, stretching her arms in the air to signal her interest in bringing the conversation to a close.

"Come," said Guido, standing again as though she had signaled him by raising the flag at the start of *Il Palio*. "Let us go eat . . . then I will feed my new *frigorifero*. Ferrara food. *Cappellacci di Zucca*. We call those little dumplings Venus's belly button. Then *Salama da Sugo* and our infamous *Comacchio* eel . . ."

Amir looked as though a mild nausea was moving through his body. Like most of his countrymen, he was attached to his native foods and not adventurous in the culinary arena. Justine wondered if there were other arenas in which he was not adventurous. Ones she didn't know about.

"Wines?" asked Morgan, predictably.

"The excellent appellation wines of Bosco Eliceo," said Guido with pride. "The only grape that will grow in the sandy soils near the Po River."

"And of course your world famous *Coppia Ferrarese*," added Delmo. "Breads twisted like a fisherman's rope, originally created by none other than Cristoforo of Messisbugo, the master of banquets at the Este Court."

Guido nodded, picked up his hat and a woven cardigan that reminded Justine of Hemingway, and started for the door.

At lunch in the delectable local restaurant near Guido's apartment, Justine noticed two Senegalese going table to table, selling leather accessories. What struck her most markedly was the invisibility locals accorded these attractive, youthful men. Unlike the seething tension regarding immigrants beginning to boil over in Castelvolturno and Rosarno, Ferrarans appeared not to notice them. Over Delmo's obvious disapproval, Justine engaged the young men in conversation and bought herself a red leather belt. When she didn't haggle over the price, Guido smiled in approval.

After lunch, Guido returned to the university, Morgan set out to investigate the hydrology used to regulate the nearby canals, and Delmo returned to the

Europa Hotel. Amir and Justine decided to visit the Municipal Palaces and the salon of Lucrezia Borgia.

∽

"You were very silent during lunch," Justine said to Amir, but her eyes were elsewhere. She was examining the panels of cupids and sirens adorning the salon as though she expected them to come alive and join them in conversation. Columns, supported by carved female figures known as caryatids, divided the room. Sebastiano Filippi's grotesques blended the fantastic with the realistic throughout the ostentatious room. *What is Amir thinking?*

The silence in Lucrezia Borgia's salon, devoid of other visitors, was compounded by Amir's quietness. "I was thinking of my grandfather," he said, reading her mind. "If he hadn't become involved with the codex, he would still be alive."

Justine turned, cringing, scrutinizing his expression carefully. His facial muscles were relaxed, his pupils enlarged, reflecting the abundant golden threads of a nearby tapestry. Amir's head was cocked to one side, waiting. Words nearly failed her. "You're blaming me? Because I insisted you take me to see him? Take the codex to him?"

"No, of course, not. Perhaps it was fate. Everything evolved naturally from the first time you told me you needed to visit him. He was your father's mentor . . . and he found his final challenge in the codex."

"You wouldn't be connecting the events unless you thought it was murder," she said, reaching for him, touching his cheek with her cool palm.

That errant ebony curl fell over one eye again as he placed his arm around Justine's waist and led her to a nearby bench, where they sat facing each other. He didn't answer. Then, his eyes narrowed as he asked, "Would you ever consider marrying me?"

"Are you proposing?"

"No," he said firmly. "But you know I've loved you since we worked together in Egypt, and our recent relationship has deepened that love. And expectation."

She was taken aback with his paradoxical response. *Yes, he loves me; no he is not proposing. He is afraid of my answer.* "Tell me what our life together would be like."

He received this question as a good sign. "A home. Children. Pleasure of each other's company. Travel . . ."

"My work?" she interrupted, one eyebrow raised.

He responded quickly, "By all means. Yes, your work. Very important." His face drew tight around his cheekbones and temples.

He is almost irresistible. "Where would we live?"

"In Egypt, most probably," he said simply.

"I'm *persona non grata* there. You know that."

"After the Italian court's decision in your favor—and with time—the whole incident about the Virgin Mary will slide into history. Besides, you'd be married to an Egyptian," he said with unabashed pride. He was floating into this fantasy.

"I still have to learn what freedom requires of me. I also need to know what compromises marriage will demand."

"I wouldn't expect you to compromise, Justine. I don't think that's your *forte.*" He managed a grin.

She smiled at his insight, feeling no need to defend herself. "You wouldn't expect it now, perhaps not next year or even the next. But eventually, I fear, you would give in to the pressure of your family's expectations. Your culture."

"My culture is changing, Justine. In spite of evidence to the contrary, women are leading their own lives, getting divorces, setting new rules. Besides, I'm a modern man."

"Understanding the effects of your own culture, Amir, is like a fish trying to understand water. I'm afraid that culture is stronger than individual will . . ."

"Stop being an anthropologist for a moment. We are two individuals, not one of your textbook cases." Any tentativeness that he'd expressed earlier was gone. He also knew that this stance was losing him ground.

Justine permitted her moist eyes to admire the garlands of festoons framing Amir. Her friend. Her lover. She gave him a long, measured look, her eyes growing moister. *Is he right? Am I swimming in my own generalizations?* "That may be a fair appraisal," she finally said. "I won't discount it. We are friends, we've been lovers. Can that be enough for now?"

"Enough for now," he said, a grin spreading across his classic Arab face. He winked, as though to say, "I'll wait."

She reached out and pushed his ebony curl back into place, tightened the sash on her cashmere coat, and motioned for him to walk with her out into the cool, darkening afternoon. Parallel clouds of moisture formed in front of them. Before they reached the door of the café across the street, a rack of newspapers arrested their attention.

Blazed across the front of the *The International Herald Tribune* was the headline: "Virgin Mary's Diary Surfaces in Rome." *La Repubblica* put it a little differently: "*Scoperta: diario della Beata Vergine - una truffa! - secondo il Vaticano.*" Discovery of the diary of the Blessed Virgin a hoax, according to the Vatican.

Amir's body seemed to shrink inside his heavy wool jacket, his facial muscles tightening into a mask of devastating distress. *Slide into history? Mish mishkilla, no problem*, he thought miserably.

CHAPTER 27

—❦—

The history of men's opposition to women's emancipation is more interesting perhaps than the story of that emancipation itself.

—Virginia Woolf

ONCE AGAIN, Justine found herself running on the path above the San Michele, the breath clouding in front of her partly obscuring the frosted olive and cypress trees. The events in Ferrara were heavy on her mind. Guido's charm. Amir's near-proposal. New data on the two alabaster women. Andrea. *Who is Andrea?* The missing codex. How was she to make sense of these threads of the tapestry, to construct a meaningful pattern? A décollage, to an anthropologist. A type of collage that tells a story. *Amir says that we create narratives and revise them as more data become available. So right.*

After reading the blazing headlines in Ferrara, the fate of the codex demanded her full attention. Since its purchase by the Mycenae Foundation, the contents had been splattered all over the Italian media. She knew without it being said that the Vatican's ire had been aroused.

Justine stepped onto the porch of her mother's house, shaking out her hair and taking off her snug jacket. She sat on a bench and removed her running shoes before taking the back stairs up to her room, dropping her clothes around her in puddles of black lycra, and slipping into the warm shower. She shivered as the soothing water traveled down her cold back, remembering Amir's hands enveloping her breasts, her stomach, her thighs. But for now, there was something she had to know.

❦

Once more she was Kim Novak in *Vertigo*: tailored grey suit, black heels, a golden bun at the nap of her neck. Elegant and simple makeup, arched eyebrows, mauve lipstick. She wrapped her beige cashmere coat tightly around her, walked unnoticed to her car, donned her sunglasses, and headed for Florence. Thirty minutes later, she found a parking spot on a side street just off Piazza del Duomo. *Astounding.*

Justine stepped into the elevator and pushed the button for the second floor of the Mycenae Foundation. Liberally funded by a number of deep-pocket sponsors, the Foundation was known to be very loose about provenance when prize artifacts came their way.

Justine walked to the reception desk and waiting patiently while the young women in bright red lipstick finished filing her ragged fingernail. She glanced up and straightened her posture. "May I help you?"

"Yes, you may. Thank you. My name is Dr. Justine Hassouna and I've been commissioned to follow up on the recent sale of a certain item referred to as the 'Cairo Codex,' which information unfortunately seems to have been released to the media."

The receptionist stared at her. "Just one moment, please." She left the room quickly.

Justine waited patiently, checking inside her black leather purse to make sure she had brought along the cards she'd made with her pseudonym, attorney at law title, and fake address. She casually walked to the modern orange divan and was ready to sit down when another woman walked up to her. It had been less than three minutes.

"Dr. Hassouna?" asked the woman without blinking.

"Yes." Justine held out her hand.

"May I be of service? I'm Ms. Ansaldi, Assistant Director of the Foundation. I understand that you had a question regarding the Egyptian codex."

"My colleagues and I were surprised to find that information about this remarkable artifact had been released to the press. This seems premature." Justine's voice was stern, indignant.

Ms. Ansaldi blushed ever so slightly, embarrassment quickly subsiding, replaced by a thin bravado. "An unfortunate occurrence I can assure you. Someone in our lab, we suspect . . . So, what may I do for you?"

"I am told that you have a couple of petitions of transfer yet to be signed. Has Andrea, Dr. LeMartin, taken care of those?"

"I believe that Dr. LeMartin has taken care of those." She consulted her iPhone calendar. "Ah, yes. Just last week. Is there a problem?"

"Perhaps not. I'm sure that everything is fine . . . except for the leak, of course. I'm sure I'll receive my copies from Andrea today or tomorrow. Thank you." Justine turned to leave. Nausea rose in her stomach.

"Is there anything else?"

"Well. Since I'm here, I have been trying to reach Mr. Blackburn. Mr. Robert Blackburn. Has he already left for Sicily?"

"I don't know a Mr. Blackburn. Now, if you'll excuse me."

Justine's eyes were still moist, her breathing labored, when she sought refuge in the Lawrence letters. She could hardly believe that it was true: Andrea had betrayed her. Betrayed her profession, and the trust others held in her. *Yet I suspected, didn't I? Why else would I enter into such a masquerade?*

Her gray suit was thrown across the chair; her hair was loose on her shoulders; her black leather shoes squatted in the corner. Somehow, she would find wisdom in Lawrence and Isabella. What would she do about Andrea? Clearly she was the go-between in the sale of stolen artifacts. How long had this been going on? Had her partnership with Blackburn involved some of the most valued of lost treasures? Even the Gospel of Judas? *Should I call the police? Am I in danger for knowing too much?* She picked up the next letter and began to read:

> Hotel Beau Rivage, Bandol, 13 January 1929
> My Dearest Bella,
>
> The length of our separation steals my strength. Too long, my dear muse. How am I to write without your letters in hand? Frieda has friends about who fawn. Disgusting habit. Let them find their own pretender to some throne.

I will go to the ranch when the weather warms. Then to Villa Mirenda. The bronchials are still a nuisance. Doctors want to putter with me. Friends too. I have finished The Escaped Cock. Will send a draft to you by the next post. I think of New Mexico so often, the exotic innocence, the cave on the Kiowa trail. Did I ever tell you that I set the ending of The Woman Who Rode Away in that cave? It's about Mabel, you know. But my mind wanders.

Remember the lovely little apartment near Dante's house? I will let it again when I return. I can write there once my wits are about me.

Frieda and friends are off to Sanary-sur-Mer tomorrow. Wish I could reach out and touch you, my love. We must see each other.

Love, David

I know that his plans to return to the ranch never materialized. Because of his tuberculosis, he couldn't get a visa. But the lovely little apartment near Dante's house? Did he let it that winter? Justine reached for the next letter and, hopefully, the answer.

Hotel Beau Rivage, Bandol, 2 February 1929
My dearest,

My memory of our stolen days are medicine to my soul. Your body gives me heat and sustenance, you feed my very being. I have never experienced such tender fire. Intimacy without feeling you would own me.

Ah, so they did consummate their relationship. Sometime in '29, at least. Soon before he died . . . how weak he must have been . . . A deep sadness gripped Justine, making her shiver yet also feel feverish.

I'm feeling better, although it changes from day to day. Can we dream of a life together? I know you say it is not possible because you are Egyptian and being with another man would be unforgiveable, even though your husband was chosen for you. Have you no right to also choose? To be free of the shackles imposed by others? My own freedom has been largely stolen by this damned consumption that saps my breath and energy. I don't know how to free my own body. Here we are my darling, two prisoners marking time.

You ask about Frieda. Yes, she would be disturbed if I left, but only because she had lost a possession, not out of passion for our marriage. She insists on winning, even as she entertains her lover in Baden Baden, and now some Italian peasant as well, I suspect. I'm afraid I have devised a weakened sort of dependency on Frieda. But I must fight this darkness in me.

Love always, David

How devastating it must have been to give up his muse, his love, to be torn be-tween desire and duty. Could he have left Frieda? Would Isabella have dared to leave her husband? Unthinkable in those days. How painful this affair of the hearts—for both of them. Justine lifted her hair from her perspiring neck and twisted it into a temporary bun. *Is freedom always an illusion? Did my great-grandfather love his wife? Was he a good man?*

Since the day Justine told her father about the letters, he'd pressed her to let him read them. She wasn't sure why she'd resisted his entreaties, perhaps be-cause she hadn't told her mother as yet. *What am I waiting for?* She picked up another letter and lovingly fingered the texture of the eighty-year-old enve-lope. *How many hands have held this treasure?*

Suddenly, her eyes alighted on an oddity: the postal stamp on the letter read "Grand Central Station, NY, May 3, 1929." *But he wasn't in America after '25. How was this letter mailed?*

Hotel Principe Alfonso, Palma de Mallorca, 3 May 1929
My dearest Bella,

My American editor arrived this morning. He had promising and troubling news about Lady Chatterley. Otherwise he is an old woman. Martin and Huxley conspire with this quack who calls himself a physician. They wring their hands about my health, insisting that I return to high dry air, but that a New Mexico trip would be too difficult right now. I need to get back to the ranch. Next spring perhaps. With you?

I've enclosed my new poem, "How Beastly the Bourgeoisie Is." Tell me what sensations it evokes. Do you think that my stanza, "Full of seething, wormy, hollow feelings, rather nasty"—is a bit too hateful? Too strident? Men are such empty vessels, my dear. If only we could feel as you do.

We were in Paris last month with the Crosbys. They will probably print The Escaped Cock and Lady Chatterley given time, and if he can hold himself together. A queer fellow. His wife, Caresse, is all right. But Paris is not. A dark, hateful blanket has descended over this glorious city and they cry out for someone to blame.

Enough of me. I did so love your poem. Do I see hidden symbols of our devotion? Optimism abounds, nature and its children thrive. How do you manage to stay afloat in this miserable life?

Am sending this letter with Hux to mail from America. Can't trust the mails in Europe anymore.

All my love, David

Justine pursed her lips and read on.

Hotel Principe Alfonso, Palma de Mallorca, 4 June 1929
My dearest Bella,

Wish I could get to Taos. The dryness and that dreary American doctor could offer some reprieve from this damned malady. Tuberculosis, they're calling it now. Brewster tells me to try deep breathing and Buddhism. Since we found the Etruscans together, he is a good friend, but the way of Buddha takes him into foreign ways, I'm afraid.

I'm calling my little book of poetry Pansies. It will be out this month. Somehow I'll get a copy to you. Let me know what you think. Your beautiful eyes see beneath the words. I did a drawing of myself to send along. Don't know if you'll like it, I look a bit long in the tooth. But sanguine.

Hoping to get to Florence next month. Will be staying at the Lungarno Corsini or Hotel Porta Rossa. My hands yearn to touch you.

Lilacs are gone. When I can't do this writing, I'll surely take up gardening. What do you say?

Love, David

He shared with her as an equal, a colleague, as well as a lover. A relationship to be coveted. Justine folded the letter and carefully put the stack back into her drawer. She was now rationing herself, stretching out the joy of reading, as though each letter influenced her identity, told her more about who she was.

The joy was short-lasting, as her gut tightened once more with the tragedy that was Andrea. *What will I do now??*

CHAPTER 28

⁓

What is it that women most desire?

FLAMES FROM THE CRACKLING fire reflected in the hanging copper pots and teakettle in Lucrezia's kitchen. *My favorite place*, thought Lucrezia for the hundredth time, tying her white cotton kaftan more tightly around her. She turned toward the door as Morgan stomped into the room, disheveled and frenzied. His sweatshirt announced, "Dig Deeper. Come to Crete."

"She dumped me, Creta. Just like that. A little note. A note!" he exclaimed, plopping into an antique wooden chair by the French country table. It creaked as he relaxed his large frame.

Lucrezia walked to the long granite counter, opened a translucent jar with a blue ceramic lid, and pulled out two almost-warm chocolate chip cookies. She placed them on a napkin in front of Morgan. "Are you surprised?" she asked gently.

"Of course I'm surprised. Why wouldn't I be?" He took a bite and registered pleasure. "I'm dashing. Handsome. Some women think I'm quite a catch."

"Humility was always one of your best attributes, my dear." Lucrezia could not help but find her former husband charming and frequently amusing. This morning, she also found herself empathizing with the father of her only child.

"Milk?" he asked. "You understand, Creta, that I'm devastated."

"And embarrassed." She restrained the smile that had begun to form on her lips.

Morgan shrugged, and reluctantly repeated, "And embarrassed. Justine warned me and was cautious about getting Andrea's full participation in the Cerveteri project. Now everyone will know."

"Andrea can be discreet when she wants to. In this situation, I suspect that she will be. Because she's working with Justine on the codex and the writing project, she's in the center of something new, even for her. A group that includes a former—may I refer to you as former?" Morgan grinned weakly. "Former lover, a longtime friend and former wife of her lover, a young colleague who just happens to be the daughter of her lover . . ."

"I get it, Creta," he interrupted, looking pained. "You can stop the recitation."

Lucrezia was quiet for several moments. She turned her back to Morgan and poured herself a cup of coffee, then continued without turning around. "You knew who she was, Morgan. Like me, only more so. More independent, certainly more experienced in affairs of the heart. More secretive. Where did you think this would end up?"

"To tell the truth, Creta, I thought I'd changed enough to make this work. And I thought she was enamored enough with me to tolerate my rough edges. I made a real effort to listen, not to talk over her. I wasn't demanding. Well, less demanding than I've been in the past . . ."

"What about jealousy? How did you react when she was around other men? Or when she couldn't be contacted immediately? Or when she broke an engagement?" Lucrezia turned and looked straight into his cobalt blue eyes.

He winced. His temples flushed. "Damn it, Creta. What do women want anyway?"

"I'll tell you an old story, my friend. Just relax. Sit still. Have some more milk." She placed the cookie jar in front of him.

"This is the story of Sir Gawain and Lady Ragnell. Do you know it?"

He shook his head.

"Well . . . one day, as the story goes, King Arthur returned from the northern lands after an encounter with the fearsome Sir Gromer, and told a most troublesome story to his young nephew, Sir Gawain. It seems that Sir Gromer had agreed to spare Arthur's life if he would return within a year with the answer to the question, 'What is it that women most desire?'"

"Ah, yes, what do they desire?"

"Be patient." She continued, "Sir Gawain assured Arthur that together they would find the answer, but after almost a year, they failed to do so. King

Arthur turned to the grotesquely ugly Lady Ragnell, an animal-like sorceress, in desperation. She agreed to give him the answer if Sir Gawain would willingly marry her. 'Impossible!' raged Arthur.

"But he related the demand to his generous nephew, who promptly agreed to marry Lady Ragnell."

"Amazing sacrifice," exclaimed Morgan, reaching for another cookie.

"Well, Morgan, his uncle's life was at stake. What could he do? So Arthur reluctantly agreed to accept his nephew's sacrifice and received the answer from the fiendish lady. When King Arthur related the answer to Sir Gromer, he was enraged because the answer was correct: 'What a woman desires above all else is the power of sovereignty—the right to exercise her own will.' You may not be surprised that the hideous Lady Ragnell, upon her marriage to Sir Gawain, turned into a beautiful damsel."

"Of course she did!"

"Ah, but the story does not end there. The now-beautiful lady informs her husband that he has a choice: 'I can be beautiful at night or during the day, not both,' she explained. 'Which do you prefer?' Lucrezia sat down beside her former husband. "Which would you prefer, Morgan? What would you say?"

Morgan thought for several moments. "A Solomon's dilemma, indeed," he said. "I guess I would choose the day, when she would be seen both by me and others. I would hide from her at night." He grinned at his cleverness.

Lucrezia sipped her coffee, watching Morgan closely over the rim of her cup. She continued, "The wise Sir Gawain pondered the question, dropped to his knees, took her hand, and replied: 'It is your choice to make, my lady.' 'You have broken Sir Gromer's wicked spell,' she told him excitedly. And the now continually beautiful lady and her young knight lived happily ever after. Women still desire free and conscious choice above all else, Morgan."

Morgan's eyes narrowed. "Why didn't you tell me this story years ago?"

"Because there was more involved than my sovereignty, wasn't there? More between us that couldn't be repaired."

"You mean our son?" An expression of pain washed over his handsome features.

"Our son. Yes," she said.

"I was in graduate school. The opportunity to work on the excavation in Guatemala was an extraordinary offer. I really had no choice," he pleaded.

"But you didn't have to insist that I go with you. I was in my second trimester and not feeling well. I realize that a great deal of the responsibility lies with me, Morgan. But I was young, naïve. I told you that I had a premonition that we might lose the child, but I let you choose. I shouldn't have."

Morgan dropped his head toward the table, enfolding his arms across his sunken chest. "Justine doesn't know, does she?"

"No. Justine will never know," she said. "I put the blame, but not the pain, behind me some time ago. The folly of youth. We were both responsible." She walked behind him and put her arms around his neck and hugged him for several moments.

"Do you think it could ever work for us again, Creta? It might be worth a try," he said repentantly. "Justine would be pleased."

"No," she said releasing her grasp on his shoulders. "Too much has happened between us. We're different people now."

Justine leaned hard against the wall in the hallway outside the kitchen. Tears streamed down her cheeks. Her labored breath came in short spurts.

As Morgan walked to the door and slowly turned around, Justine shrank back into the shadows in the hall. "The letters, Creta," he said. "They are by one of the world's greatest writers. They deserve to be made public. They must be published. Give Cambridge a call."

Lucrezia did not pause or turn around. "Never," she said.

Justine placed her hand over her mouth to muffle a gasp.

CHAPTER 29

A free bird leaps on the back
Of the wind and floats downstream
Till the current ends and dips his wing
In the orange sun rays
And dares to claim the sky.

—Maya Angelou, *I Know Why the Caged Bird Sings*

THE ELDERLY MAN BENT into a question mark moved slowly around the corner from Piazza dei Donati onto via Santa Margherita, then stopped at the heavy wooden door to the stone apartment building. Justine followed. Standing before the door with his iron key in hand, he tilted his head awkwardly to let his eyes travel the full length of Justine's body, regarding her with a mixture of appreciation and fear.

She had encountered this expression once before when she'd gotten out of a car in Morocco to talk with a short Bedouin. Smiling, she backed up and waited for the man to enter the building and close the door. She wanted him to know that she actually belonged here now, so chose to use her own key. Stepping into the darkened hall, Justine permitted her eyes to adjust to the absence of light and locate the stairs.

It was almost evening now, and the medieval Torre della Castagna nearby blotted out whatever meager winter light had remained over the piazza when she had parked her Spider and walked the short distance around the House of Dante to number two. She slowly ascended the two flights of stairs to the second floor and found another key on the same chain, the one belonging to her new apartment.

Justine stepped into the open space that would be her living quarters in the months ahead, placed her satchel against the east wall of the living room, turned on the lights, and explored her new home. Now she noticed the predictable signs of neglect: peeling, discolored wallpaper and baseboards, warped doors that didn't quite close, two small holes near the corners of the living room floor, undoubtedly eaten away to host mice. The one bedroom was larger than her own in Fiesole, which wasn't saying much, but the kitchen was a disappointment. She would miss her mother's lavish cooking area and the opportunities it offered to visit while cooking together. The white and black tile in the bathroom, three squares missing, told of '70s modernization. The two closets were adequate; the one in the entryway she would use for guests and her running clothes. The living room was spacious enough, with a small fireplace that looked as though it hadn't been used for a century. Her furnishings, a motley collection of antiques, a few prized discoveries from her mother's attic, and several items from IKEA, would arrive tomorrow. Unwelcome mildew made her throw open the two windows, which she fairly easily unstuck. She stood and surveyed the apartment once again. At least it was hers.

Returning to the living room, Justine turned off the lights, pressed her back to the east wall, slid to the floor, and sat there lotus-style. Outside the western window, a lit glass box rose and fell—the modern elevator attached to the Casa de Dante. Not really the house of Dante Alighieri. This house-museum had been built more than a century ago at the location of the thirteenth-century home of the famous poet. But she could pretend. Others did.

She was momentarily transfixed by the glass elevator, then allowed her eyes to close and her mind to mull over the past two weeks. Her mother had been disappointed, but not surprised, when she'd announced that she was moving to this apartment next to Dante's house. "The apartment let by D.H.?" her mother had asked. So she had been told.

The conversation she'd overheard between her parents had increased her desire to create some distance from them. Everyone had secrets, she knew. She also knew that secrets ate away at relationships. She opened her eyes and noticed that the magic box had stopped on the third floor, probably to pick up staff at the end of the workday.

Marco De Marco had persuaded her to accept a new job at the Etruscan Museo in Fiesole. While her father had originally asked her to work with him, an appropriate niche never seemed to materialize, even though she had remained on the team. Fortunately, Marco didn't see conflicting loyalties there. The trip back up to Fiesole entailed a challenging commute, but Guido had convinced her to buy a Vespa, which she could wheel into the lobby of the apartment house. She had rented a nearby garage for her car.

Justine had seen Guido twice in recent weeks. Once when she'd delivered new samples to the Florence Museum of Archaeology lab on Piazza Santa Maria Maggiori. Another when he came for dinner in Fiesole. She was still mesmerized by his green eyes that stared so intently into her own, his spirited manner, his playfulness. He had asked her to dinner tonight and had arranged to pick her up at her new apartment.

The chilly air, as well as her own reservations, caused her to shudder. Andrea. Amir. Her parents. She had e-mailed Andrea asking that she bring the full translations of the codex with her on her next visit. While Justine had the copy of the codex, the translations were with Andrea, and she couldn't write the *Archaeology* article or carry out the next phase of her plan until she had the translations in hand. After that, she would confront Andrea.

She pulled her satchel toward her and extracted a small CD player, placed her laptop computer beside her, and removed a CD of Gregorian chants from a side pocket. She sat back again and closed her eyes as the melodic ascent, descent, and repeat of the solo cantor, and the chorus, calmed her. Soon a trance/calm permeated her consciousness, her muscles relaxing to the chanting vibrations that seemed to use her bones as tuning forks. Serene colors flooded her mind, now cleared of chatter. Quiet descended like an angel's silk blanket. Street sounds gave way to ethereal voices.

In these moments of altered awareness, recurring dilemmas began to refigure themselves into understandings. Justine reflected once again on her desire for independence and what it had required of her. She had always framed it as "freedom from" . . . freedom from parents, from male domination, from cultural expectations. Now she realized that, for her, real freedom was recognizing self-imposed expectations. How many of her decisions in the past had been about pleasing others? Or about fear? Fear of displeasing others, of being controlled by others? But she was different now. Matured. In charge of her own life.

Justine slid her hand into her satchel once more, reaching for the small bundle of remaining letters, leaning back, chants accenting Lawrence's words . . .

> My Isabella, I arrived last night, after a brief stop in Forte dei Marmi, a sea town near Lucca. You know it? A gay little place. So happy to be back in Florence, for I can feel you nearby. I needed to escape the interminable Prussian atmosphere of possessive, insistent women— except for you, my love, who never lays claim to my soul and therefore owns it. I am not afraid of you; I am not afraid when I'm with you. Women are capable of causing men agony and you have no such will, my love . . . I watch the sea swallow the orange orb, casting golden ribbons across my bare feet. Such a glorious sight that I was imprudent. Should be up and around in a couple of days. Will you join me at the little apartment near Dante's?

This apartment? My own communion with Isabella and Lawrence? By not laying claim to one's soul, do we therefore win the souls of others? Only mutuality, reciprocity work, never fear? She didn't desire ownership of anyone, and would not grant license to her own. She read on.

> I want you to have my Dance sketch. If I can retrieve it from England, I will leave it in the Dante house. Know that it is yours. Remember when we lay under the lemon tree in your yard and blew the delicate swords of lion's teeth from the dandelions into the warm air? Such a rare day—alone on the grass.

Justine's eyes darted around the room, searching for the sketch that surely hung in this room. She grinned at herself. Had she really expected it to still be hung on the wall?

> . . . I recall meeting Georgia and Ansel Adams briefly at a party hosted by Mabel in New York, back in '25, I think. As you know, Georgia is a painter, mostly of landscapes I believe. And sensuous flowers. Adams

photographs similar subjects. At first I thought, another boring evening with the "realists." Then Georgia said, "Nothing is less real than realism . . . it is only by selection, elimination, emphasis, that we get to the real meaning of things." I began to see my writing as the personal and physical landscapes that I've selected. That's also how I evoke my inner visions of the characters that inhabit my writing! They spring from my intuitive consciousness. A palette of sorts. Colors and shapes, contours. New metaphors abound.

Transmutation was surely at hand. Personal, professional, cultural. "Nothing is less real than realism?" *Look below the surface, Justine.* She reached over and turned up the volume on the Gregorian chants, pulled a green crepe dress and brush out of her satchel, and headed for the bathroom.

Three hours south in Vatican City, Rome, two officials in flowing robes, one red, one black, sat in the parlor of the Roman Curia, the official offices of Pope Benedict XVI. The elegant room was adorned with rich burgundy, leather, and gold. The back wall of bookcases held the treatises of St. Constantine the Great, the Letters of Paul, and volumes of decisions made throughout the years by the Holy See. "The pontiff is concerned about this diary business," said the deputy cardinal, stretching his gnarled hand out from his flowing scarlet sleeve and touching his left ear, a habit signifying that his anxiety level was elevated. "What do you think is behind it?"

The cardinal's subtle signals did not escape the sensitive young bishop. "A young woman trying to make a name for herself," he replied unconvincingly.

"The Maecenas Foundation for Ancient Art doesn't pay five million euros for a document unless there is substantial verification of its authenticity," insisted the cardinal, settling himself into an armed leather chair.

"When we heard of the impending purchase, our press release was quite clear: 'Scoperta: diario della Beata Vergine - una truffa! - secondo il Vaticano.' We declared the diary a fraud. But I will look into it further, your Excellency."

"I remember the headline, Bishop Juan. A delaying tactic at best," said the deputy cardinal, clearly unimpressed. He grasped the mahogany arms of his chair. "If such a diary exists, the Vatican, not Egypt, must have it."

CHAPTER 30

—

"My course is set for an uncharted sea."

—Dante Alighieri, *Paradise*

JUSTINE AND GUIDO stepped out through the heavy door of her new apartment, and she motioned for him to turn right from the small piazza into the narrow cobblestone street leading to a small church. Justine tried the locked handle. "This is where Dante first saw Beatrice."

Guido finished her sentence, "His great love, an unrequited love." He placed his hand gently on her shoulder. "The worst kind," he said.

Justine wondered if he had been wounded by an unresolved passion. "You know the story . . ." It wasn't a question.

He took her hand and they began walking toward the end of the street. "Where are we going?" He had asked her to choose a nearby restaurant, so she had consulted her mother, whom she considered an expert on Tuscan cuisine.

"Mother suggested the Restaurant Enoteca Pinchiorri. The Chef, Annie Feolde, is a friend of hers," she explained, taking great care that her heels didn't catch in the cobblestones. She wished she had brought a flashlight.

They approached the elegant restaurant at Via Ghibellina, number eighty-seven. Lights from the columned villa entrance of sweeping arches emitted a glow that flooded the alleyway and the stone buildings nearby in cinematic radiance. More formal than Justine would have liked. She would have preferred a more intimate place.

"Good evening, Professore Barbujani," said the maître d', escorting them to a table adorned with pink linen and situated under a portrait of Renaissance dancers. Guido nearly knocked his head on a hanging potted plant. The location afforded them privacy, although they were the only ones in the room at 8:00 p.m. Indecently early for dinner in Italy.

"Stunning," he said as the green crepe dress appeared from under Justine's cashmere stole.

Justine looked down at her attire. "Thank you," she said casually. "You've been here before."

"A couple of times with my friend David Caramelli from the University of Florence. He loves the place. Great food, but a bit straitlaced."

"We could go somewhere else," Justine offered as she observed the stiff waiter in formal attire, "although my mother and your friend may both have good taste. I say we give it a try."

"Excellent," he agreed, glancing at the wine list. "They have some of my favorites. A good list."

Justine nodded with pleasure at his assessment; her eyes moved to the Renaissance dancers. "A lovely painting, so elegant and graceful."

"It reminds me of some of my father's paintings."

"Were you close?"

"We were. He was a scientist and often shut himself up in his lab, but when he was with my sister or me, he was fully present. Do you know what I mean?"

"I could say the same of my parents. I felt them stoking my curiosity."

"That's the kind of parental attention I plan to provide for my own children." Guido let his voice drift lower, realizing that he had entered personal territory, territory that he wasn't ready to explore.

This wasn't the direction she wanted the conversation to go either. "You know, Guido, I've been thinking a lot about the sarcophagus we found in Cerveteri," she said. "What kind of culture do you think could have produced it?"

He was comforted by her abrupt diversion. "As you know, sarcophagi, at least later on, were manufactured. We don't know if this one is unique. It may be one of many that look exactly alike. Remember the 'married couple' sarcophagus—the one in the *museo* at Cerveteri? There are many of those," he said.

"Granted. But no one has ever found a sarcophagus quite like this one—right? I think it reveals the presence of a goddess culture."

"Does it?"

Even as he asked the question, he dismissed it. "Sarcophagi were usually adorned with mythology narratives. Perhaps your goddesses are merely an aesthetic expression—décor. Nothing more."

"Perhaps," she said. "But I think there is ample evidence that the role of women in Etruria was significantly different than those in Greece—and then Rome. More equal, more independent, more partners than subordinates."

"Inferential at best," he said, studying the wine list closely.

"Inferential? Let me see . . . just what kind of evidence do you require?" She smiled. *He doesn't need to please or agree with me—or seduce me, for that matter*, she mused, relishing the confrontation.

Guido now studied the sparks in her amber eyes and her smile. He was amused and aroused, yet before he could respond, the sommelier was at their table.

"I prefer reds," she said simply.

"I would recommend a local Tuscan wine—Le Pupille, a lush, raspberry-scented red." He stared directly at her lips as though to find the color of which he spoke. "Would you like to take a look?" He placed the menu in her hand, which she quickly laid on the side of the table.

"No, I trust your judgment—in regard to wines, at least."

Guido ordered the Le Pupille and returned his attention to Justine, eager to pursue the conversation.

Anchoring her palm on her chin, she asked, "What do you think of D.H. Lawrence's *Etruscan Places*? He certainly supports the idea of an Etruscan goddess culture." She anticipated that he would not be enamored by Lawrence.

"Quite a romantic, D.H. A novelist, not an anthropologist. I'm afraid that much of what he had to say has been discredited. But I appreciate his adoration of the Etruscans. He seems to have identified with them in a mystical way."

"Romantic, undoubtedly. That's what Pallottino said." *That's what Dad says.* She pronounced the name of the Nazi archaeologist slowly, as though the syllables were pointed darts.

Guido looked up quickly. "Ah, Mussolini's old pal. I would not like to be seen in his company."

"Nor I. Do you consider yourself a romantic?" She continued without waiting for a response. "I'm persuaded that Lawrence was more right than wrong about the Etruscans. He brought a literary eye to his study—sometimes art can tell us what we can't see otherwise. I have an associate at McGill University who says that D.H. Lawrence got it right." She didn't feel free to tell Guido about the Lawrence letters. She still cherished her secret, holding the letters close as though releasing them would be like liberating a small bird before it had wings. And she had yet to consult her mother, who she now knew was strongly against public exposure of the letters. Why, she couldn't imagine.

"Yes, I can be a romantic, but I reserve my flights of fantasy for my novels," he said, pouring the ruby liquid into her glass. "As a biologist, I think it's unlikely that many of Laurence's observations are accurate. I'd say he projected his own desires for a peaceful death onto his subjects." They held each other's eyes. "Shall we order?" he asked.

Justine nodded. *Half a romantic*, she mused, lifting her glass unhurriedly toward her lips. "I like the image: fellow traveler of Lawrence!" she said, studying the menu. "Mother says that one of Annie's specialties is Tuscan tomato-bread soup. And wild boar . . ."

"Ah, *Pappa al Pomodoro* and *cinghiale*. That's what we'll have, then. We can share." He nodded their readiness to the waiter.

After Guido had ordered the desired dishes, Justine reached across the table and touched his hand, wanting to draw his attention back to the tomb—and to her. "What do you think of our investigative team?"

He clasped her hand and held it for just a moment. "Sometimes managing a diverse team like yours can be difficult." Then he released her and slid back in his chair. "I was at a conference in London two years ago and the linguists there told us they were forbidden to talk about the origins of languages. Can you imagine? That should be their primary function. Otherwise, what good are they?"

Justine placed her abandoned hand into her lap. "Linguists can be a society unto themselves," she said, thinking immediately of Andrea. "I've encountered similar precautions—sensitivities—with regard to human origins and race—"

"'Sensitivities' can be a euphemism for cowardice," he interrupted. "Science stops where political correctness begins. Take evolution, for instance—"

"Ah, a favorite bogeyman of the Far Right." It was her turn to interrupt; she leaned into the table and suspended her glass in midair. "How does that play out in Italy?"

"Same as in the States, I suppose. Although the Catholic Church is not as intent on resisting evolution as some evangelical churches are. It learned its lesson with the Galileo disaster."

Justine laughed at the antiquity of the example. She crossed her legs and smoothed out her crepe skirt in preparation for a story. "When I was in college," she began, "my friends—most of them ex-Catholics now—became concerned for my soul, so they arranged for me to talk with the priest who ran the Newman Center. Charming man. He told me that God had used evolution to create life; then, when animals evolved into man, He instilled a soul into every human. A convenient story."

"Ah, *si*. It's the soul that separates us from lower animals."

"Do you believe that?"

"I don't think there is such a thing as a soul. Whatever needs to be explained about humans can be accounted for by this magnificent brain," he said, pointing to his temple.

"Neither do I. Even though I occasionally worry about my own." She laughed at her own contradiction.

Guido joined in her obvious pleasure. "So what evil acts have tainted your soul?"

"Not a great deal recently, but I did get kicked out of Egypt last year."

"So I've heard. Were you guilty?"

"Guilty of finding the Virgin Mary's diary—the codex—yes. Guilty of insisting that the findings come to light? Absolutely. Perhaps even guilty of contributing to religious strife in the Middle East." She breathed in deeply, aware of the savory aroma of the arriving *cinghiale*, which blended pleasantly with the masculine muskiness of her dinner partner.

"That's quite a burden to carry," he said, his green eyes surveying her shoulders. "I've picked up a few things about the Virgin's diary from your conversations, but I have to admit I'm incredulous. Skeptical, actually. No one even knows if Mary ever existed."

"You don't believe it?"

"No, I don't."

"Well, I can assure you it's true. The article that Andrea LeMartin and I planned to write was accepted by *Archaeology*. Moreover, the original diary has been purchased from the black market by the Maecenas Foundation."

"Planned to write?"

"It looks as though I'll be writing it on my own . . ." She left it at that.

Guido raised and eyebrow and paused. "Impressive, but no DNA, I'll bet."

"Just a comb found in the same niche! I have a copy of the DNA report."

"Hair in a comb isn't of any use a couple of millennia later. No chance."

"You'd be surprised. You *will* be surprised. Dried hair follicles were present in the comb and the lab in Alexandria was able to extract small amounts of mtDNA," she insisted. "I know it sounds incredible."

"Probably polluted data. Some labs are sloppy. You must be cautious around me, Justine. My forte is unearthing frauds. The Shroud of Turin. Or the head of Petrarch. The head doesn't belong to the body, you know."

"It doesn't surprise me that the linen shroud with the image of a suffering Jesus isn't legitimate. But how did you ever convince the priests in the Cathedral of St. John the Baptist that their Petrarch's head was a fraud?"

"Whoa . . . I didn't say that I'd convinced the Church that it was a fraud." He laughed. "That's beyond the abilities of any scientist. That would take a miracle."

"I will be careful around you." Her lilting laugh softly filled the corner of the room. "You're a skeptical man. Perhaps too skeptical for your own good. I'm afraid I don't harbor many subtleties."

Was that a warning? he appeared to ask himself, refilling her glass. "Yet I detect an air of mystery."

"Intentional," she said. "All the better to lure you with . . ." Justine grasped her glass and ran the forefinger on her left hand around the rim.

"Are you seducing me?" He smiled broadly, his mouth slightly open. "I surely hope so."

∽

She awoke in a dreamy, misty light the next morning in her new queen-sized IKEA bed. Their lovemaking the night before had been languorous, each touch adding to the arc of sensuality. Now she watched him sleep and wondered at the veil of innocence that blanketed most sleepers. Her mind began to spin once more. She had given little thought to hurting Amir when she dove headfirst into this tryst.

Guido slowly opened his eyes, stared and her, and said casually, out of the blue, "Getting a divorce in Italy is difficult." He let the statement just sit there.

So did Justine. He need not be cautious, she didn't desire to own him.

CHAPTER 31

—⊷⊷—

To live is so startling, it leaves very little time for anything else.

—Emily Dickinson

A͟FTER TWO BOWLS of Cheerios, Guido left for Ferrara around nine. Justine took a shower, grabbed her phone, and jumped back in bed.

"Miranda?" Justine asked, leaning against her grandmother's ancient headboard with the delicately painted angels peering over her shoulder.

"*Pronto*. Justine?? It's been a long time!" Still sweaty from exercising her favorite bay horse, Miranda had just come into her stone farmhouse, the lovely Il Pero, just outside of Arezzo.

Justine imagined this delightful English baroness transplanted into a historic and tastefully restored farmhouse with her husband, Baron William, and their two daughters. "I've followed you on Facebook and joined your fan club. But now I need to talk with you directly. Remember the night we had dinner with Andrea at Harry's Club?"

"How could I forget! What a grand time we had," exclaimed Miranda, peeling off her leather gloves.

"You were quite knowledgeable about the case against Marion True, the former director of acquisitions for the Getty. And how the Italian legal system dealt with the provenance of ancient artifacts."

"One of my hobbies. The case against Marion has been settled, you know, but not the case against the Getty. The Italians are determined to get the Getty Bronze returned . . . but how can I be of help?" She sat down, balancing the phone between her chin and shoulder, and removed her leather boots, wiggling her toes.

Justine could almost see the Baroness Miranda, her blue eyes broadening into near circles. "You'll remember that we told you about the finding of the Virgin Mary's diary? Well, that's finally coming to a head . . ."

"I know! I've read the headlines," she said, nearly breathless. "Fascinating. When I saw you in Rome, you and Andrea were searching for a certain Blackburn. Is he the man who sold the codex to the Mycenae Foundation?"

"I'm certain of it, but there's more to the story. Miranda . . .won't they come under the same scrutiny about provenance that other museums and foundations have? Why aren't they worried? Why would they pay so much?"

"Remember, the approach of that particular foundation is to shepherd the science and bring the results to publication, as they did with the Gospel of Judas. Then they'll return the artifact to the country of origin. In this case to Egypt, probably the Coptic Museum. So they might not have to concern themselves with provenance."

"That doesn't make sense, Miranda. Without provenance, their publications could be discredited." *The foundation has information that I haven't anticipated.*

"Strange, isn't it. I imagine they place their scientific methods—and good intentions— above professional protocol and the law. Like the Vatican."

"Unless they had assurances of provenance from a highly regarded professional, like a linguist. What do you think the authorities would do if they knew who the thief really was? The person or persons who sold them the artifact?"

"Probably look the other way."

"Ah," said Justine. She now knew what she would have to do. She would have to handle Andrea in her own way.

"What about the Vatican? It's up to something," said Miranda.

"Any hunches?" She admired how Miranda could anticipate issues that hadn't formally surfaced. Justine told her so.

"I suspect that the Vatican may not let the diary leave Italy."

"Could it do that? Does its power supersede the law?" Justine was incredulous, but not surprised.

"Many consider its power the law. I'm sure it'll try for an injunction, and the courts would be sympathetic. Every judge is Catholic, if only in name. So the answer is probably 'yes.' But remember, I'm not an attorney."

Justine grinned. "You're a barrister by intuition and information, Miranda. This business could further aggravate the friction between the Muslims and Catholics over the rightful ownership of Mary's diary."

"The Vatican could claim that since Mary and her son were the genesis of the Church, that historical provenance trumps geography."

"Clever thought. And either Pope—Catholic or Coptic—would have good reason to bury the diary's contents. *Che sarà, sarà.*"

"*In bocca al lupo!* Good luck," replied Miranda. "Keep me informed and come see my new kitchen when you can."

"I'd love to! And may the wolf die, my friend. *Crepi,*" laughed Justine, wishing her some Italian good luck in return.

Justine considered her usual durable clothes and shoes in the morning, but discarded them in favor of her linen slacks, a lavender silk blouse, and simple gold loop earrings. *Almost a uniform,* she thought as she regarded herself in the full-length mirror behind her bedroom door. She allowed herself comfortable walking shoes, for she planned to see Florence anew this morning. As an official resident now, she wanted to visit *her* city. And consider her planned approach to the Andrea problem.

And she wanted to visit Caravaggio again. She still cherished vivid memories of Rome's Chiesa di San Luigi dei Francesi, where she'd first met the Baroness Miranda and felt the thrill of experiencing Caravaggio in an intimate, well-lighted setting. This morning, that hunt would take her to the Uffizi museum, repository of the greatest collection of Italian Renaissance art.

Justine made her way through the narrow streets of small shops buried in stone walls, down Via del Proconsolo to the glorious Piazza della Signoria, then northwest from the Piazza toward Via Calimaruzza. Once again she was struck by the fondness Europeans project for their old cities. So unlike America, where inner cities are relegated, run-down, to the poor, those without resources to sustain shops, theaters, museums, and historical architecture. Thankfully, that trend of neglect was beginning to reverse itself in cities like Oakland and New Orleans. Soon, Via Calimaruzza emptied into Piazza di Mercato Nuovo, the pathway to Via Porta Rossa. A slight left at Via de Tornabuoni would take her to the Palazzo Spini Feroni and Salvatore Ferragamo.

Justine had been frugal since coming into her Grandmother Laurence's trust at the age of twenty-five. The funds had allowed her the freedom to educate herself thoroughly—at least in the academic sense—as well as take some time off between jobs. To secure and furnish her own apartment. It was not that she sacrificed unnecessarily on her linen slacks—or shoes—or silk blouses—but . . . she had grown up as a fat child, which forever casts a shadow over self-image. It wasn't until she put on running shoes that her life began to change. She arrived at Ferragamo.

Encased in a centuries-old stone building, the mammoth windows of the original, and still most glamorous, of the Italian clothing establishments provided a museum-quality showcase for the world's most chic fashions, embracing generously spaced red leather purses and chunky gold belts, leather coats and cashmere. Each item was, indeed, a work of art. Then she saw it: a full-length buckskin suede coat, matching knee-high boots, tan leather shorts, and a cashmere turtleneck sweater clasped by a gold belt.

"Justine!" cried Alessandro when he spied her in the shoe department. As a store manager and now partner, he projected a stunning figure in his deep blue Alfani suit, ivory shirt, and matching ascot.

"Alessandro. Hello." *Mom's tastes in men certainly lean toward elegance. But haven't they always.*

"Shopping for a special occasion?" he asked.

"Not really. I'm considering changing my style—taking on a more modern Italian look," she said, pointing to the stylish boots.

"If you need any help, we have a few excellent fashion consultants in the store. I'm more of a businessman myself."

"I'm doing fine, thanks," she said. "How's the shoe business?"

A slight redness moved through Alessandro's temples. Then he laughed. "I certainly let my hair down at your dinner party, didn't I?"

"A bit," she grinned, holding his gaze. She liked his directness.

"Too much good wine." He let the topic drop, shrugging off the momentary embarrassment. "Come by my office when you're finished? Say, how about lunch?"

Justine graciously turned down his lunch invitation, but stopped by his office on the way out. She wasn't quite ready to become adjusted to a new father. Thirty minutes later she stepped out of Ferragamo with her new attire, feeling reassured that if her mother decided to marry Alessandro, he wouldn't be a poor choice. There was something very real and playful about this man.

Turning on her new heels, she made her way along the Arno to the Uffizi, her wandering gaze taking in the many small boats on the shimmering silver surface. Guido had erected a firewall this morning with the comment about divorce. He seemed so familiar to her—more familiar than their brief time together warranted. Then it struck her: D.H. Lawrence. Guido. So much alike. Intensely sensuous, romantic, yet skeptical and satirical. She felt a little melancholy.

Justine climbed the few steps into the Uffizi—formerly the offices of Cosmo de Medici—paid the entrance fee, and asked where she might find the Caravaggio Room. Glancing down the long, narrow internal courtyard opening onto the Arno, she reminded herself that this unique haven for great art had existed for nearly 500 years. Although the niches between piers were filled now with sculptures of famous artists of the nineteenth century, she wondered who had filled them originally. Heading for Room 43, Justine stopped briefly to view Michelangelo's *Holy Family,* thoughts of Mary flooding her mind. Everywhere she turned in Florence, she was there: the Virgin Mary carved or painted, captured as a passive yet compassionate saint. *If Florence only knew the real Mary . . . independent, reflective, an intelligent teacher of her legendary son. The Church certainly could not have denied the idea of strong, unconventional woman then.*

"Which do you prefer?" the male voice asked, almost reverentially. "*The Sacrifice of Isaac* or *Bacchus?*"

Resisting the desire to look at the visitor, since she already knew who he was, Justine said, "I prefer *Bacchus*, but *The Sacrifice* is truer to Caravaggio—the personal anguish felt by the artist, a child orphaned by the plague, his use of light, the heart-wrenching choice . . . a profound historical moment."

"Well said. My choice as well," Blackburn said. "Life is often a reflection of Caravaggio, is it not? You are confronted with a 'heart-wrenching choice.'"

She paused for several moments. "Andrea."

"Andrea. I understand you paid a visit to the Foundation. Clever. Although you now possess information that you don't want."

Justine's laugh was sardonic. "You're quite right. A profound complication. And Donatello?" She took a wild guess.

"Some young Italians get carried away, exceed expectations. Have profound regrets."

"Like the loss of a brother?" In the suffused light, Justine observed Blackburn's every movement, each expression. She had the confirmation she needed. It had been Donatello who had partially severed the supporting arch in the tomb. She gulped and struggled to maintain her composure. *But why?* "Why sabotage the investigation? Surely no treasure had been found as yet."

"Yet the find was imminent . . . and we—my colleagues and I—weren't ready." His left temple twitched—he had said more than he intended. "What are your plans?" he asked.

Ready? Ready to carry out another theft? "I am sorry, sir, but I don't intend to share my plans with you."

"Unfortunate. I might have been helpful."

Justine dismissed his offer. "What will happen now?"

"With the codex? Nothing, I should think. Absolutely nothing. We have the euros safely deposited in Geneva," he replied. "The Foundation has the codex. Nearly everyone is happy."

"You and Andrea must be quite happy. The euros in Geneva. The resolution of the current heist. What's next? The statute of David?" She turned to gaze at the man she remembered all too well: tall, with an impish manner, protruding belly, startling blue eyes. A flash of consternation moved across his face as he limped away. "She will regret the loss of her friendships with your family: you, your mother, your father."

"Very true. And the Vatican is not happy."

"Ah, yes, the Vatican. Troublesome institution, the Church. Always poking its nose into perfectly reasonable business transactions." Blackburn's eyes glistened with humor now, as though the Andrea business was forgotten. "The Vatican will vie for this codex. I'm not sure it will be successful, but the matter is out of our hands now, yours and mine."

"No remorse?"

"Remorse, my dear, is for those who believe in a hereafter, an earthly hair shirt designed to prepare the way, seeking acceptance from a demanding god." He slowly rose and walked away.

Justine watched him go. His gait was slow. He favored his right leg, hardly the countenance of an international art thief. After his confinement and torture in Egypt, she felt less compunction to "bring him to justice." She considered the irony of her own situation, that state of affairs that seems deliberately contrary to what one expects. Her eyes returned to Bacchus, and the salacious expression on the face of the Roman god. She realized that, like Bacchus, Guido and D.H. were often amused by the subtle verities of life that escape more ordinary mortals.

Justine stepped back into the sunlight of the Piazza della Signoria and stood still for several moments to admire the larger-than-life statues of Dante, Machiavelli, and Vespucci. She remembered the murder witnessed by Lucy Honeychurch in *A Room with a View.* The novel had been in the back of her mind since Alexandria. *Am I only a witness? Or am I going to untangle this web of mysteries?*

On her return to Via Alighieri, she purchased a strawberry gelato and relished its sweet coolness on her tongue while she considered her next step.

Back in her apartment, Justine grabbed a cup of coffee and sat down at the computer. She would deal with Andrea first, then contact her father about Donatello. Her fingers sat on the keys for several moments. She expected that

Blackburn would e-mail or call Andrea immediately—or not, depending on the game he wanted to play.

> Hi Andrea,
>
> I know you will be leaving for Florence shortly, and I just want to remind you to bring along the full translation of the codex. I know you have a couple of passages you want to verify, so we can sit down with the codex copy still in the family safe in Fiesole. The team meeting has been moved back two days; we need more time to process the data. Eager to see you. Best, Justine

How would Andrea play it? Would she refuse to come to Italy at all? Act as though nothing had happened? Acknowledge that she'd been dealing with the Foundation, but concoct a story to explain her contacts? *Who knows.*

Ping. Another e-mail. *Could it be Andrea so quickly?* She checked the screen—it was from Guido, with an attachment.

> Hello, Justine,
>
> I enjoyed our evening last night. Dinner was delicious. I am sending along a little surprise: the DNA report on the two women of the tomb. I think you'll find a reason for this gift. Love you, Guido

Excitedly, she opened the attachment and began the download and print. While the pages were printing, she had time to think: "love you" is like "love ya," and is certainly not "I love you." She had interpreted their morning interactions correctly, yet she still found herself infatuated with those lovely green eyes. A "reason for this gift," indeed. A consolation prize.

Justine jumped up, walked quickly to the ancient wooden file cabinet, and found the file labeled simply, "Mary's DNA." Alone in the house, she spread out both sets of data on the table in the sunroom. Haplogroups the same. Not surprising. Then she went deeper, into matching genes and mutations, those metaphorical genetic paper clips on the blue ribbon that Guido had talked about in his apartment that day.

In spite of the sun streaming in through the high windows, the blood drained from her face, her limbs went immobile. As moments ran into minutes, she vigorously massaged her arms, shuffled the pages of data, and placed them carefully into separate files.

CHAPTER 32

Peripheral vision: what is seen on the side by the eye when looking straight ahead.

—New Oxford American Dictionary

ON THE FOLLOWING DAY, a day scheduled for the full team meeting, Florence was buried under a frosty blanket, the last stab of wintry cold in early April. Even so, the city was warming to the spectacle of the country's upcoming election. To the unpracticed eye, Rome's glamorous mayor, Franco Rutelli, would appear to have the edge on the crude, yet wealthy and amusing, former Prime Minister Silvio Berlusconi. Although no stranger to scandals, Berlusconi had utilized his nearly exclusive ownership of Italian media to keep his peccadilloes and shady business dealings mainly out of public view.

Nevertheless, Justine was betting on Berlusconi. Italians had a penchant for choosing unseemly characters for their dysfunctional government, since Italians had little interest and virtually no trust in politicians. Life was local; the people had turned inward during the Baroque period, and never resurfaced. The gems of life resided lovingly in family, the land, the Church, history, art, wines, cheeses, and pasta.

She turned on the radio in her toasty car to hear Berlusconi's Mediaset criticizing the Vatican for seeking an injunction to keep a certain codex from being returned to the Coptic Museum in Cairo: "Vatican contradicts own position on the proper ownership of ancient artifacts." Mediaset had duly noted the Vatican's dramatic defense in the earlier case against the Getty—and concluded with a proclamation from a representative of Forza Italia, Berlusconi's party: "We cry hypocrisy!" In turn, leftist Rutelli, hardly a defender of the Church, charged during an interview with Rome's *La Repubblica* that Berlusconi was out to bring down the Vatican.

Justine rolled her eyes. The election was less than two weeks away: April 13th.

"Where's Andrea?" Morgan asked his daughter.

"She couldn't make it this morning—complications at the Sorbonne," was the simple answer, *or lie*, which Justine addressed to those seated at the oval table in the conference room of the Florence Archeological Museum. Justine had not received a response from Andrea as yet, but knew she had received her e-mail; otherwise, she would have been at the table this morning. Delmo and Morgan had invited Andrea to be here today, but Justine had steered her toward a false date. She needed more time to deal with the fallout of Andrea's deception.

Justine paused, assuming a most professional demeanor, which she realized might be a little difficult in a leather motorcycle jacket over a tangerine sheath. Although her father was the team leader, he had asked her to begin with her new—although not her newest—discovery. Seated around the table were the key players of the investigative team: Morgan and Delmo, Marco, Amir, Riccardo, and Guido. The closed report, loosely bound in dark green backing, sat in front of each of them. A few members, including Justine, had already pored over the mtDNA and carbon-14 results; Morgan declared that they were ready to share the major revelations from the Cerveteri tomb.

Justine launched in, "Our story begins with an Icelandic volcano eruption. Hekla 3. In 1159 BCE. Devastating ashen rain and abrupt climatic changes warmed the earth and increased its acidity—the lands became unusable."

"Herodotus insisted that it was the battle at Troy that caused the Etruscans to scatter. Not so?" Morgan asked, smiling at his daughter, whom he hadn't seen much of since she moved into town. In fact, it was Amir who had told him that she was investigating the Icelandic volcano.

"Troy, then a part of Lydia, was indeed destroyed, but not by soldiers in a Trojan horse," said Justine. She unzipped one of her eight jacket pockets to extract a pen and opened the report. "The dark sky and raining ash must have been more frightening than a mammoth horse. They understood war. But not this." Since the 2007 earthquake in Cairo, Justine had been studying how natural disasters affected cultures and migration, using the facilities at the Fiesole museum.

"The story sounds a little far-fetched, Justine. Iceland is thousands of miles away. What evidence is there?" asked Guido, narrowing his eyes. During their time together, she had said little about her inquiries—even though he had shared with her the mtDNA data yesterday.

"Greenland ice cores. Irish and Turkish tree rings . . . let me find the section." Justine opened one of the pages of the report marked with a Post-it. "A radiocarbon date secured from ice cores shows volcanic activity about 4,000 years ago. A more precise method of dating volcanic deposits of recent age is, of course, tree rings. Anomalous growth patterns are detected among the annual rings of trees growing at the time the deposits were embedded. Trees that were injured but not killed by flying rock particles and mudflow may have a sequence of narrow rings beginning at the time of impact." She looked up expectantly.

"You're referring to 'cross-dating,'" said Marco, finally taking off his wide-brimmed hat and setting it on the desk behind him. A crease appeared across his two-toned forehead. "The matching of ring-width variation patterns in one tree with corresponding ring patterns in another. Fairly solid evidence."

"Exactly," replied Justine, nodding toward Marco, who had been highly supportive of her investigation. "Thank you. There is also a small lake above Sardis in Lydia in Western Turkey that deepened drastically between 1200 and 1100 BCE. Another sign of significant shifts in the earth's crust."

"As our two women occupying the Cerveteri tomb tell us," said Delmo. He patted the report in front of him, which contained the translation of the papyrus scroll found in the tomb, as well as the historical, geological, and mtDNA analyses. "Migration from Lydia would have begun about that time. Listen: 'Summer snow everywhere. Difficult to bring. To see. My eyes fail me.'"

Riccardo nodded, mesmerized by these ancient words, as though they were written that very day. "It's widely accepted that peoples throughout the

Mediterranean were on the move then. The Sea Peoples were raiding and plundering. The Palestinians moved south. Eruption of the Icelandic volcano could have contributed to the migrations."

"I'm convinced of it," said Justine. "It would not be the first time that an eruption reconfigured the map."

"But there was no wholesale migration into the Italian peninsula," added Guido. "That we know of, anyway. I've always been convinced—like you, Marco—that the Etruscans were indigenous to Tuscany. Although we now have mtDNA evidence that there might have been connections between the Lydians and the Villanovans, ancestors of the Etruscans, thousands of years before. Everything we thought we knew is being questioned."

"Thousands of years before, you say . . . ?" began Justine, almost in a whisper. "That would coincide with the volcano, and small-scale migrations of the Lydians could have accelerated the evolution of the Etruscans." She scanned the room and returned her questioning eyes to Guido.

"Such a theory is credible," he agreed, holding her searching eyes as he spoke.

"Small groups," interrupted Amir, "even a few individuals, may have come into the area and provoked dramatic advancement. Of course, they would have had to gain the trust and respect of the locals. I've found that such jumps in development can just as often be explained by the zeitgeist."

Justine paused, gazing down at the report. "I do realize that zeitgeist can be explained as a collision of several emerging ideas that ignite advancement," she said warmly. "But in this case, I'm suggesting that these women from the tomb may have had knowledge that others didn't have."

"Let's back up a bit and start at the beginning," suggested Morgan, irritated. His face told Justine that he thought she was wandering astray. "Delmo . . . tell us about the translation process that you undertook. I understand that the linen wrappings weren't that useful. Read us more."

"Right," said Delmo, looking up from the report at the mention of his name. "The strips of cloth had other uses before their application as body wrappings: partial messages, bills of sales, lists of products ready for market. Much like the wrappings on the Zagreb mummy in Egypt. But the scroll, now that's another story. Hieroglyphics and Phoenician, a bilingual document. A true gift."

"Phoenician was derived from hieroglyphics, isn't that right, Professor?" asked Amir, whose khaki uniform was nearly identical to Morgan's, telling Justine how much their relationship had deepened during their recent work together. Morgan watched Amir with a paternal gaze, concerned about the young man since the mysterious death of his grandfather. "I know of other ancient documents containing more than one language. For instance, I'm aware of the Pyrgi Tablets—the three golden leaves recording a dedication to the Phoenician goddess Ashtaret. Found near Cerveteri, in fact. And, of course, our own Rosetta Stone."

"Well, 'derived from' is probably too definitive, Amir. The Phoenician language made use of Egyptian hieroglyphs, but the two systems were actually quite different. Hieroglyphics are primarily made up of *ideogrammme—ho domenticato, come si dice in Inglese?*" Delmo asked, turning to Marco.

"The English word is 'ideograms,' *Professore*. Both come from Latin by way of Greek," explained Marco, who, like the other men in the room, held extraordinary respect for the retired Bologna professor's advancement of linguistics.

"*Si, si,*" continued Della Dora, "you must forgive an old man who sometimes forgets the names of his own children. In hieroglyphics, each ideogram depicts an idea, but in Phoenician we have an alphabet and each symbol represents a unit of sound. The symbols are letters that together build words—the first known alphabet of Western civilization. Phoenician is derived from hieroglyphics only in the sense that the Egyptian 'glyph'—that is, symbol—for 'bear' is simplified by using a single stroke to represent the letter 'b'." He paused only briefly to mask his breathlessness; having ditched his cane, he once again felt like a man of action.

"Now, back to your question, Amir," Delmo continued. "It is much more difficult to write or read hieroglyphics. Only the well-educated members of the highest classes were able to learn it—even in Egypt. Remember that after the Rosetta Stone was found it took scholars many years to completely translate it because it was sometimes read from left to right, right to left, or even up and down. Phoenician acted as a cross-reference, since most traders could read Phoenician. They were indeed the middlemen in the Mediterranean. Peoples like the early Etruscans could learn to write any spoken language by using the letters of the Phoenician alphabet."

"Enough of the technical linguists, Delmo. Give us some more words. What do they actually tell us?" Morgan raised his hand as though to gently halt Della Dora's recital. "What is the story here?"

"Let me begin—with your permission, Professor," Justine said, reaching to her right to place her hand on Delmo's shoulder. He reached up and patted her hand. A respectful affection had grown up between the two since he had consulted her on her knowledge of Egypt.

"It's a remarkable story," she began. "Assuming that the volcanic eruption and its effects on Lydia had caused the migration, this is a story of the history of the two women on our tomb. Del gave us an example earlier of winter snow, listen to more: 'The skies were dark and rains of gray snow covering the land. Goddess Artemis and the governing council of Lydia tell us we must have fewer on our land, so we set out for the land of the Pharaohs. One ship stopped in Lemnos, another in the Levant.'"

"Lemnos? Where the Etruscan stele was found?" Marco jotted several notes in the margins of the report. "Not sure how that would have worked . . . Etruscan traders must have returned to that island centuries later—after they had developed their own unique language." He was talking to himself.

"Just a brief historical note here," interrupted Riccardo. "Those who were left behind would return to prosperity about three decades later and establish the city of Ephesus."

"Fascinating," said Justine, pausing only briefly before she ask Delmo to read more.

"We women landed in the land of the pharaohs, where the rivers make a fan . . ." he read.

"The Delta!" exclaimed Amir.

"'. . . among the Israelites, where we lived for many moons,'" Delmo continued.

Startled, Morgan said, "The Jews must have remained or returned after the Exodus some 300 years earlier. They lived together loosely, yet we've seen evidence that the small band of Lydians seemed drawn to the moral principles of the Israelites. Perhaps the Torah gave the force of words to the practices of the pagans."

"Inscriptions from Deuteronomy in the *Etrusca Disciplina* may inform the Etruscans' contact with Israelis in the delta," said Marco, intrigued by the possibility that a pagan goddess culture with a Hebrew morality and the Phoenician language could have once existed in the same place.

"Exactly," said Morgan, who began to add his firsthand knowledge of the report. "The women of the tomb suggest that contact was made with the Egyptians and the Phoenicians. There's more, my friends. Patience." He lifted his open palms and framed his fingers into a tent, as though praying for indulgence.

Justine continued; this part she knew was difficult for her father to accept. "It seems abundantly clear from recovered artifacts that the followers of Artemis welcomed Isis into their pantheon of goddesses. And by the late tenth century BCE, trade with the Phoenicians and others of the Levant had lured the daughters and sons of these Lydian women into the Tyrrhenian Sea. These pioneering mariners were welcomed by the farmers of Elba, Caere, and Tarquinia, so they settled in the Caere Valley. Around 1080 BCE, it appears."

"Their own words tell us this??" queried Morgan, continuing to be amazed.

"Exactly," confirmed Delmo.

"No wholesale migration there," noted Marco, turning toward Guido. "We're clearly not talking about colonization or even an extensive influx of a foreign population."

Guido nodded in agreement and appreciation, noting that Marco shared his perspective on colonization.

"Perhaps these two sisters—we now know they are sisters, right?" Everyone nodded. "Perhaps they led these women and brought with them many gifts and skills from Egypt and their homeland, as well as knowledge of iron processing, which they learned from the Hittites," said Justine, fishing into one of her many pockets for some Post-its.

"Iron processing?? Are you sure?" interrupted Marco. "We've suspected that they learned that skill from the Celts."

"That's what they tell us," added Delmo, back in his element. "The papyrus made it clear they also brought skills in hydrology, divination, and a willingness to experiment with governing. Here is a description of the early use of divination. These two women may have even worked with locals to form the first city-state. That's not clear, but it's no wonder they were revered."

"Are you suggesting that the development that peaked during the Orientalizing period in the eighth century BCE may have begun with these two sisters?" asked Riccardo, incredulous. "Several hundred years before the Greek influence became dominant?"

"I share your skepticism," agreed Guido. He had developed a warm relationship with Riccardo, who shared his interest in fine wines and Raphael.

"When they adopted the Greek alphabet, the Etruscans retained the Phoenician habit of writing from right to left. Yet how they 'invented' Etrurian from Phoenician is still unclear," said Delmo, unbuttoning his tight collar, which he usually wore closed. Delmo's wife had died several years before, so he now felt compelled to starch and iron his own clothes, including his undershirts.

"So we have no other knowledge on how the Etruscan language was invented, or how it became isolated?" asked Marco, sliding back in his chair, clearly disappointed.

Delmo looked uncomfortable. "Forgive me, but an old man needs to wash his hands often," he announced, pushing back his chair and slowly rising.

"I think this is a good time for a short break," Morgan suggested.

"From what the women tell us on the scroll," said Justine, resettled in her chair, "we can speculate on the answer to Marco's earlier question: How *was* the Etruscan language invented? Let me test this out . . . perhaps the answer is fairly simple, as answers often are. We know—or we think we know—that our small delegation joined the Villanovans, and they had their own unique spoken language expressed through Phoenician writing. As the years passed, the two languages morphed into one. Communication with mariners from throughout the Mediterranean would require a highly utilitarian language. The Etruscans would have had to adopt—and invent—words. Right?"

"Language is a living process," insisted Delmo. "Over a few hundred years, the Etruscan language would have reflected great changes in grammar, the lexicon, and usage."

"Eventually, the Etruscans would have found the Phoenician alphabet wanting—it didn't have vowels, you know—and adopted the Greek alphabet instead," suggested Marco.

"Makes sense," admitted Guido, nodding to both Delmo and Justine. "Perhaps language is just another artifact of evolution." He grinned. "Yet a language that is a monolanguage, an isolate, has no known roots to other languages. Many mysteries remain."

Morgan was momentarily quiet, pensive. "Amir," he said finally. "What can you tell us about the mtDNA dating?"

Amir, who had worked closely with Guido and Marco on this portion of the report, quickly obliged. "We know that low levels of acid in the tomb's soil allowed fairly accurate carbon dating of the sarcophagus patina and linen wrappings—but most dramatically, from the women's teeth," he began. "The reports from both Barcelona and Florence suggest dating at about 1100–1050 BCE. Does this dating match with the mtDNA findings?" He turned toward Guido, his manner friendly, as though earlier jealousies had subsided.

"Close. Very close," Guido said, allowing his excitement to overcome his usual skepticism. "Date-wise, our data from the tomb and its inhabitants are a match."

CHAPTER 33

No greater symbol of harmony exists than a circle closing.

—Michael Grant, *American Southwest*

"MY MOTHER USED to dry tomatoes on our tile roof for the winter," offered Riccardo as he considered the pastas added to the limited menu at Rivoire, one of his favorite restaurants. "The house wine here is very good," he added. Two decisions were quickly made: pitchers of house red and rigatoni pasta with chicken and sundried tomatoes.

Built into the gray stone wall of the historic Piazza della Signoria in 1872, Rivoire was known for its magnificent hot chocolate, which made it a good pick for a cold day. But it was too chilly to sit outside with hot chocolate today, so Riccardo and Marco pulled two tables together just inside the entrance.

A dish of olives and crusty panini soon made its way to the table in the nimble hands of a boy no more than fifteen. Riccardo ordered wine, rigatoni, and salads for all.

Marco, a frequent visitor to Rivoire, nodded his approval.

"We have some incredible finds, my friends!" began Morgan as he swirled the ruby liquid around in his miniature glass. "There is little doubt now that the locals of Rasenna, later Etruria, paid homage to their glorious new residents by burying them together in a sarcophagus embossed with the likenesses of the goddesses Isis and Artemis, who delivered them to the land of Caere."

". . . and in a tomb recognizing their gentle passage into the spirit world, as D.H. Lawrence would argue," added Justine. Wedged into the narrow corner between Marco and Guido, she struggled to take off her leather jacket, her long legs stretching into the space between the two angular table legs. Marco placed his hands on her shoulders and completed the removal, folding and placing the jacket behind him.

Her father grinned at her attempt to slip in Lawrence. But he was relaxed, and made no effort to challenge his daughter.

"Gentle passage? Unlikely," said Marco. Glancing at the woman pressing against his shoulder, he continued the argument that had started a couple months ago at Lucrezia's dinner table. "I thought I'd convinced you that the Etruscans hardly expected a gentle passage into an afterlife."

Justine had bigger fish to fry, more pertinent news to offer, so she just smiled and let Marco's comments stand.

"They could have learned gentleness and cooperation, the value of reciprocity, from a goddess culture as well—don't you think?" Morgan asked, gazing at his daughter.

Justine stared back at him, incredulous.

"Did you think I was hopeless?" Morgan asked.

"Yes!" Justine exclaimed.

The scene slightly embarrassed Marco. Riccardo and Amir watched with fascination. Delmo fidgeted with his silverware.

Guido winked at Justine. "Men are teachable," he postulated brightly. "Even the early Etruscan men. As Morgan suggested, our findings here *are* incredible. We know much more about the origins of the Etruscans, at least a few of them, as well as the possible origin of their language," he said, his temples flushed with the excitement of a hunt well executed. "Where do we go from here?" The question hung in the air.

After the salads and rigatoni were delivered by an elderly waiter, Justine said nonchalantly, "I have another short report. This might shock you, but the mtDNA of Mary of Nazareth and of the two women of the tomb is a match."

Everyone looked up. "What do you mean, a match?" Amir asked sharply.

"Let me back up a little," said Justine. "In the diary, Mary tells us about Joseph giving her the comb. She even drew a little sketch of it! Right, Amir? And you were able to extract root fragments from the little artifact, the report of which you shared with me. We—Amir and I—discovered that Mary's DNA revealed that she was of Haplogroup J2, common to most Mediterraneans, including those in Anatolia. That didn't tell us much. So, it took the mtDNA from the two women of the tomb to confirm matching mutation patterns."

Guido stared at his plate as though the tomatoey pasta were alive. Sending the data to Justine had been professionally questionable. But the results had been worth it.

Justine watched his face, struggled to infer his feelings. "The last translations that I've seen of the codex confirmed that Mary hoped to travel to the family home in Ephesus before her death," said Justine, devouring her rigatoni. *And it might be the last we see of the translations. Andrea is clever.*

"Mary was Etruscan," Morgan whispered.

"Mary was Italian." Delmo had stopped, wasn't eating a bite.

Deep breaths of astonishment reverberated around the table, causing people in the now-crowded café to turn and look toward the small gathering of scientists. Refractions of light off the brass coffee urn and ancient mirror frame appeared psychedelic to the swimming minds around the table.

Guido was the first to recover his voice. "What does that mean? Better yet, what *will* that mean?" He held his half-full glass in midair with both hands.

"To the press? To science? The Vatican? The international community?" Morgan cast his questions into the air, letting them float there.

"What's important here," said Amir, "is that the two women of the tomb are *forebears* of Mary. So, we haven't found her descendents, we've found her ancestors."

"And?" asked Delmo.

"And," said Marco, fully in step with Amir's thinking, "that makes Jesus part Etruscan. A people nearly lost in the shadow of the Romans now move to center stage."

⁂

Yes, Andrea is clever, Justine said to herself once back in her apartment, sitting at the kitchen table. She opened the lid of her MacBook Pro.

My dear Justine,

> I want you to know several things about this tragic situation. I do love and value you and your family, especially your mother, whom I've known for years. Even though I suspect that I may never see you again, I will explain as much as I can. Soon after Francoise was tortured and killed in Algeria, I met Robert Blackburn. He was kind and empathic, and expected nothing from me. As the years went on, I was needy in many ways: for a sexual partner, as well as money. My teaching hardly provided me with an income suitable for traveling, salons, clothes. We became intimate. While I knew that he was involved in certain thefts, I turned my head the other way. But, as you know now, I was the go-between with the Foundation. I set the terms of the sale, completed the transactions, signed off on provenance.

Justine stopped and read the last sentence twice. *So, that's it. Respected linguist from the Sorbonne verifies provenance.* She felt a chill, and returned to the message.

> I so wish that you hadn't become so curious, Justine, and had left well enough alone. After all, the Foundation will be returning the original codex to Egypt after it confirms the translations and publishes the findings. And, you have the copy.
>
> As for our partnership on the article, and your receipt of the translations, I'm afraid that neither is now possible.
>
> Fondly, Andrea

"Shit! Shit!" Justine yelled at the computer as tears moved down her cheeks. *I don't have the translations! And—she's just confessed to accessory to antiquities theft in print. What is she up to?? Why would she do that?*

CHAPTER 34

—◦◦◦—

This is Italy, "where you can pull one string and it leads you to a garbled skein of interlocked groups of power."

—Carlo Lucarelli, Italian novelist

JUSTINE AND AMIR sat side by side on a stone bench in the Piazza della Signoria. As they left the Rivoire the day before, Amir had asked to meet with her. So this morning they returned to the same restaurant for a cup of hot chocolate.

"I must return to Egypt soon," Amir said almost stoically. "Family matters, new evidence in my grandfather's death. I think our work is done here for the time being, and the Ptolemic collection in the Egyptian Museum still needs work."

"New evidence of murder?"

"They're almost sure—but that's what we thought, wasn't it?" He turned his handsome face away. "Hardly a surprise."

Justine placed her hand on his shoulder and waited. His pain was palpable. "I honestly didn't think a conclusion of murder would come to light." *Is he also telling me that we are finished, that he is leaving me? Could I blame him?*

He turned toward her without acknowledging her gesture. "Our family is influential in Egypt. There was bound to be an investigation. And now a witness has stepped forward. He claims that Grandfather was pushed down the stairs outside his office. You remember how steep and winding the staircase is. It had seemed plausible to the authorities that a man in his eighties with bad knees and a cane could simply fall. Apparently, that's not the case."

Justine blanched. She stretched out her sandaled feet, placed both hands on the bench beside her, and dropped her head. *If I hadn't involved Dr. Ibrahim in the translation of the codex—a translation that I've now lost—this would not have happened. By giving me the copy of the codex when I left Egypt, he placed himself at grave risk. He must have known that.*

Amir stared at Justine's profile as though he knew what she was thinking. "They have a suspect, and I need to be there to support my parents. This business has been very hard on them."

"Will you return?" she asked gently, turning to regard his watchful eyes. Memories of their passionate lovemaking flooded her body.

"Do you want me to?" They watched the city awaken in front of them—children climbing on fountains, postcard salesmen moving among the sightseers, women in red spike heels stepping cautiously over smooth stones.

The blood returned to her face, turning it a pale pink. Their uncomfortable silence was punctuated by the chatter of tourists and the roar of motorcycles entering the piazza. "Of course I do." She paused. "Amir, I have something to tell you." She slowly unwound the story of Blackburn. Andrea. Her confession.

Amir stared at the pigeons in the square, watching their dance, their skittering feet moving rapidly across the smooth surface. Stabbing at crumbs lodged between the stones.

Justine followed his eyes, observing the lively puppetry. She waited.

"Andrea was very close to Grandfather. He admired her greatly. I came to know her as a young man." Wounded, yet not surprised. "Why didn't you tell me before? I could have been there with you, supporting your investigation."

Justine scrambled to understand her own motives, her unwillingness to share secrets. Even now, she would not tell him about the letters. "When I was a young girl, an only child, my mother and I would watch *National Velvet*. We watched it over and over because I loved it so. I named my doll Elizabeth, begged for a horse. I told my secret thoughts to Elizabeth. She kept my secrets close. It was safe."

"Safe from what?"

"Exposure, I guess. As an only child with preoccupied parents, I felt alone. I had no sense of whether I was normal—whatever that means . . ."

Amir turned toward her, his eyes moist. "You can trust me, Justine."

"I know that, Amir." Their eyes met, exchanging expressions of warmth, empathy. "Come with me to Miranda's," she said. "Then go."

∽

New York Times, April 11, 2008, International News: Rome. *The Italian high court has issued an injunction* that prevents the return to Egypt of an ancient codex alleged to be the diary of the Virgin Mary. The injunction was sought by the Vatican. Egypt will appeal it to the International Court in the Hague. Page 12.

La Repubblica, April 12, 2008. *Man's Body Found Near Piazza Navona.* Rome police discovered the body of an alleged black marketer, Robert Blackburn, in an alley near the antique district of Piazza Navona. A reputedly wealthy American citizen who has lived abroad for many years, Blackburn has been linked to dealings in foreign antiques involving underworld figures in Egypt and Spain, as well as Italy. Police say he was under investigation, most recently in connection with the theft of a codex alleged to be the diary of the Virgin Mary. The Vatican communications director offered no comment. On the eve of the election, Silvio Berlusconi was asked to comment during a news conference, but refused.

Il Firenze, April 14, 2008. *Berlusconi re-elected Prime Minister.* Silvio Berlusconi, uniting Forze Italia and The People of Freedom parties, will form a government with a gain of 141 seats in the Senate and Chamber of Deputies. Democratic Party candidate Walter Veltroni, the celebrity mayor of Rome, trailed by nearly 140 seats. Casini, with the Union of the Centre, lost 21 seats, leaving only 39 total seats under the control of the Christian-Democratic coalition. The election was called when the government of Romano Prodi fell in

February 2008 and the temporary appointment of Franco Marini proved unsuccessful.

"Did you know this guy Blackburn? The one whose body was found near Piazza Navona?" Riccardo asked. He was wearing a T-shirt supporting Veltroni and reading *La Repubblica* while sitting on the floor of Justine's apartment. His attention was diverted regularly by the arrival and departure of the glass elevator attached to Dante's house.

Justine was curled up on the couch in her pink pajamas reading the *International Herald Tribune*. She and Riccardo had discovered the item on the death of Robert Blackburn at nearly the same time.

Riccardo detected Justine's emotional shift. "Did you know him?" he asked again.

"Oh . . . no, not really."

He regarded her expectantly. "Meaning?"

"We've had several unexpected encounters in Italy. At least *I* didn't expect them—I'm sure he planned them. Blackburn was remarkably intelligent, charming, and totally amoral. I will miss him, in a way." She grew quiet.

Riccardo waited. Since his near-death experience in Cerveteri, he and Justine had become close friends. They didn't need to exchange words to communicate.

Justine placed the *Tribune* on the coffee table and sat back into a mound of soft, gold pillows. "And then there is Andrea. I don't know how she'll take Blackburn's death."

Riccardo raised a quizzical eyebrow. "Andrea? How would this concern her?"

Justine told him the whole story. Her history with Blackburn, involvement with the Foundation. Her e-mail. She raised her palms as if to say, "There you have it." A feeling of relief flowed through her. She was shedding secrets.

"Incredible. Have you told Amir—your mother? Your father? The authorities?"

"I've told Amir, but not my parents. They will both be disappointed and hurt that Andrea is not the person they thought her to be. Will the authorities do anything, even if I turn her in?"

"Probably not. Depends on their relationship with the Foundation and whether it would serve the purposes of the Vatican to bring Andrea to justice now that Blackburn is gone."

She shifted her posture and stood up, walking back and forth across the room to realign her thinking. "That's what Miranda said. 'Probably not.'"

He grinned. "If you live in Italy long enough you absorb a certain form of disillusionment, a resignation to non-action, letting justice slip away like a Chekhov play." He glanced at the elevator moving upward as he rose and moved to the couch, patting the space beside him invitingly.

She didn't answer immediately, but moved back to the couch and sat beside him, reaching out to push on the end of his patrician nose. "You told me in the lead-up to the trial that justice here is personal. So, if justice is achieved, it's through individual pursuit? Vigilantism?"

"Or redefining your notion of 'justice.' Either walk away or define it more narrowly. Like: 'Was anyone hurt?' The Mafia idea of justice ensures loyalty and family—all else is chatter," he said, pulling on one of her pigtails.

"What would you do?" She smiled, thoughtful.

Riccardo paused and drew his eyebrows together into that familiar shelf. "I guess I would be as straightforward as possible. Tell your parents. Write to the Foundation. Andrea has a lot to lose, even without prison time."

"Tell the authorities—whomever they might be?"

"Probably not . . ."

She stared fully into Riccardo's black eyes; a flicker of pain quickly washed across her face before her left eyebrow arched, a devilish expression replacing the pain as she tented her long fingers and drew them to her lips.

"I know that look. What are you up to?" He stood up and took her hand, pulling her into his arms. "Let's tango."

CHAPTER 35

—ᘓᕓᕽ—

Out of lemon flowers loosed on the moonlight, love's lashed and insatiable essences . . .

—Pablo Neruda, excerpt from *Ode to a Lemon*

JUSTINE AND AMIR sat together on the still-warm grass, watching the evening sky at Miranda and William Taxis's family farmhouse, Il Pero. He planned to leave for Cairo the following afternoon; she would take him to the Florence airport on her way back to her apartment. For now she began to weave a story.

"One evening," she said, filling her lungs with air so buoyant that she felt herself being lifted, her body touching lightly on the land, "the Etruscan goddess Menrva, yearning for the beauty of her Motherland, reached for her brush and, dipping it into a well of daffodils and cherries, began to paint the horizon." Her white cotton blouse ruffled in the slight breeze, the collar brushing against her tan cheek.

"And her sister, Uni," continued Amir, sitting with his arm around Justine, "chose cinnamon and charcoal, crimson and wine, painting with wild flourishes, her flaxen hair flying through the evening sky . . . the Etruscan sky." Inquisitive sunflowers bent randomly with the gentle gusts of wind.

"Ah," said Justine with soft laughter, her eyes filled with desire as she ran her fingers around the inside of his collar, "The sky welcomed their offers of beauty, but said, 'All things are temporary, my lovely friends,' as she dropped her ochre orb beneath the horizon and turned the sky to pumpkin."

Amir took her face in his hands, kissing her gently on the lips. "This is an Etruscan evening, my lovely, filled with mystique. The sacred evening when ancient lovers rediscover each other and know they are fated to be together for eternity."

Justine inhaled deeply, suddenly.

They stood and embraced for several moments, their shadows stretching toward the blood-red horizon.

As darkness fell, the two poets silently made their way back to the main house for dinner with Miranda and William.

Justine and Amir stepped through the mammoth wooden door into the main house and took the winding stairs to the loft at the top of the vast grey stone cavity. As though suspended in midair inside a cavern, the special suite hung like a stalactite from the ceiling. A bed with a hanging canopy of mosquito netting and a white linen coverlet occupied the middle of the small room. An oversized tub made from a wine barrel sat near the window. Between the two, an antique dresser and wall hooks held the few items of clothing they had packed at the last moment.

The couple sat on the bed and raised their arms dreamily as they lowered themselves back onto the bed, laughing from the pure joy of the evening, still young, still ripe for pleasure. They lay still, eyes holding each other's, breathing deeply in rhythm. Amir rolled over onto Justine, reaching for her extended arm, and pressed his fingers into hers while he kissed her lips lightly, her eyes, her neck. They made love languidly, savoring each touch, each sensation. She released control of the question of their future together and indulged in the joy of the moment.

Baron William Taxis opened the vast royal banquet room for the occasion. Haunting in its vastness, the stone fireplace, large enough to accommodate four people standing at full height, was adorned with a crossed Valiant Armoury Celtic sword and a Viking Francisca Axe. Huge iron chandeliers about the room held forty-nine candles, washed soft light onto the wooden table long enough for King Arthur's men. Miranda had covered it in white linen.

In Tuscany for their daughter's spring vacation, Adriano Panatta and his wife Gabriella had driven the thirty minutes from their estate near Cortona to Il Pero for the evening. The couples had met at the Saturday market in Arezzo.

As was fitting for their elegant surroundings, Justine and Amir dressed for dinner. On her simple black cocktail dress Justine had pinned an antique golden locket containing a picture of her Grandmother Laurence as a girl. Amir had chosen a tan sports jacket, a white shirt, and a burgundy ascot. Hand in hand, they made their way down the stairs, through the farmhouse, and up another set of stairs to the royal banquet room.

Individual salads of roasted carrots and beets tossed with walnuts, blood oranges, arugula, and a citrus vinaigrette sat before them. It was a recipe drawn from *The Lake House Cookbook,* by Trudie Styler—Sting's wife—a gift from guests on another visit. Gabriella looked down at her salad, glanced up, and caught Miranda's eyes. They both grinned.

"How did you come by your name—and your professional name, Adriano?" asked Amir, for even Egyptians knew that Adriano Panatta had been a renowned tennis player—but that didn't explain "Leone," the lion. Amir asked the question that must have been asked a thousand times before.

Adriano graciously responded, a fresh answer to an old question. "My parents were avid tennis players, and since our family name was Panatta, they named me after the famous tennis king—who just happened to win the French Open the year I was born. But my father often referred to me as the Little Leone because I had a full head of wild hair. Then, when I was just getting started in the music business, Amir, I decided to use only my nickname, Leone. Along with Sting and Bono—Madonna—single names had become the rage. While young people today rarely know of the tennis giant, a *leone,* a lion—everyone can imagine this majestic image."

"And now you're the most famous Italian recording star today," observed Justine, tilting her head and smiling broadly. "No longer a little *leone.*"

"Sadly so, after the recent death of my friend Luciano," replied Adriano, giving Justine an enigmatic smile.

"What was it like . . . singing with Pavarotti?" she asked.

"Sublime. He was so relaxed, larger than life. Luciano embraced his voice as a gift from God and was dismayed when it began to abandon him." Adriano held her glance for several appreciative moments before turning to William, fine lines of grief registered on his face, even a year on since Pavarotti's death. "And what do we have here, Baron?"

"Frescobaldi Lamaione," he said, holding the glass to permit the newly lit fire to evoke a brilliant ruby glow. "A hint of tobacco, clove, cinnamon . . ."

". . . a generous weave of tannins, not too much acidity," offered Amir, to Justine's surprise. Egyptians rarely had experience with fine wines.

"I'm fond of the fruitiness, can even forgive the tobacco leaf," added Gabriella, her blond hair lightly brushing a collar of lavender linen. Justine thought she looked sophisticated, but also delicate.

"We discovered this bottle of rubies when I asked our neighbor to give me advice on our vines. Glad you like it," said William, handing the bottle to Adriano so he could examine the label.

"Why don't you tell us about Il Tuscan?" asked Miranda. "Still picking your own olives?"

"I find it therapeutic living here, although we're not here often enough to keep me wholly sane. Gabriella's commitment to running does that." The couple exchanged glances suggesting that nearly twenty years of marriage and separate, demanding careers had not dampened the romance between them.

Justine had the fleeting sense of being a voyeur, a witness to an intimacy that warmed and pleased her. She turned to Amir and found him looking at her. They both smiled at the same time, then she picked up her fork and plunged into the inviting salad.

"I saw an Etruscan wall near your vines," said Amir, turning to William. "Quite a find. I would hope someday to have some land and a few walls of my own, but I'm not sure where. Someplace in the Nile Delta, I suppose."

Justine winced.

"We do cherish those walls," said Miranda, noticing Justine's reaction. Clearly, the couple had decisions to make. "We're reminded every day of the thousands of years that these generous lands have been expected to offer up treasures to intruders. Amazing, but hardly a sustainable practice."

"You've used the magic word, Miranda," said Gabriella. "I wish such respect for sustainable land was universal. The degradation of the environment is an international crisis. I'm not at all sure that the betrayal of the earth can be slowed enough to save our planet. Or that the betrayal of women can be rectified."

"As you may know," interjected Adriano, evident pride washing over his face as he watched his wife, "Gabriella has been working with the UN on a number of issues. She founded Women's World nearly twenty years ago."

"*We* started the foundation," Gabriella corrected. "He's so modest. The work is satisfying, even if progress is slow. We're making inroads with the rights and safety of women in many places, including the recent tragedies in Guatemala and the Congo, where rape is often used as a weapon of war."

"Me? Modest? What an accusation," Adriano teased, turning his attention to the hosts. Adriano's sinewy physique was tanned, and his full head of black hair framed a disciplined face with prominent cheekbones and a square jaw. "Tell me about this dish, Miranda. The sauce on this delicious *branzino*, or sea bass as you English call it—a family secret?" His intense, dark eyes met Miranda's.

"Not at all," she said. "It's a simple artichoke *caponata*—artichokes bathed in white wine, tomatoes, olives, and pine nuts—all lovely Italian ingredients."

Justine watched Amir discreetly now. As he ate. As he conversed with William or Adriano. His classless strength, confident shoulders, hands that claimed the air as he spoke. He was comfortable in his skin. *Would it be possible to have the kind of relationship with Amir that Adriano and Gabriella appear to have? Yet his comment about the Nile Delta troubles me.*

"What do you know about these Etruscans, Amir?" William asked. "Where did they come from? Mythology is so rampant here it's hard to get a straight answer." Side conversations ceased as all eyes came to rest on Amir.

"Your timing is excellent, William. We," he said, motioning toward Justine to include her in the response, "do have some new information about those rascals—isn't that true, Justine?"

Justine nodded gratefully and extended her open hand by way of invitation. "You tell the story . . ."

Bowing toward Justine, he began, "Well, our story started with an Icelandic volcano . . ." For the next ten minutes Amir spun a captivating narrative of the tomb of the two sisters; the destruction of crops by volcanic ash, causing the Etruscans to leave Lydia; their time in Egypt; their journey to the peninsula that is now Italy. The ideas they brought with them. The goddess culture. The other diners were enthralled and astounded.

"Etruscans can now take their rightful place alongside the Romans," exclaimed William, turning toward his wife. "And land with Etruscan walls will increase in value. We'd better reassess our investments."

"To the Etruscans!" declared Adriano, lifting his glass to lead a toast. The others followed. "Tomorrow I'll walk our acreage in search of Etruscan remains."

"All 800 acres?" Gabriella teased, "We'd better run." Turning to Amir, she asked, "Then D.H. Lawrence may have been right?"

Justine looked up in surprise. "What do you mean—Lawrence was right?" she asked innocently, without waiting for Amir to respond. Miranda stared knowingly at Justine.

"Well," continued Gabriella, directing her comments to Justine. "Lawrence speculated about the origins and culture of the Etruscans, the role of women, their view of death. Not the warriors that the fascists would have liked. Isn't that true?"

As though to give Justine time to respond, Miranda replied simply, "My great-grandfather knew Lawrence, at least for a short time in Rome. They were both there during the early days of Mussolini." She passed the basket of warm breads she had made especially for the American in their midst. "At first Lawrence was an admirer of the dictator, but he became disillusioned when he saw what he was up to. My great-grandfather spoke of a girl, a daughter . . ."

"A daughter?" Justine nearly whispered. "But Lawrence had no children, none that we know of . . ." The fire and chandeliers gave her skin the tone of alabaster white. She fell silent.

"It was an off-handed comment, Justine, rather hush-hush, I believe. Perhaps only a rumor, not to be taken seriously." Miranda gazed at her visitors one by one, fully noting that Justine looked pale and distracted. She would speak to her later; in the moment, though, she could appreciate the energy each guest brought to her table, as though to express, *This is turning out to be a rather remarkable Etruscan evening.*

Justine and Amir gazed at each other, eyes locking in desire. She knew that Amir would be leaving tomorrow for Cairo and she had no idea whether or not he would return.

As dinner drew to a close, Adriano began to hum the melody to "Fields of Gold." William picked up his guitar and the others moved wordlessly to sit on small upright logs near the fire. April evenings in the country could still be chilly.

CHAPTER 36

—⊗⊗⊗—

APRIL 19, 2008

> *La Repubblica*, Rome—**Gesù Cristo è etrusco**
>
> *New York Times*—**Speculation: Jesus of Nazareth is Etruscan**
>
> *Le Monde*, Paris—**Jésus, le Christ est étrusque.**
>
> *San Francisco Chronicle*—**Jesus Etruscan??**
>
> *Al Ahram*, English version, Cairo—**Christian Prophet is Egyptian**

A LTHOUGH THE TEAM should not have been surprised, they were met with crowds of flashing cameras, reporters edging each other out, chaos. Crowds outside held up conflicting placards. The persistent theme: *Jesus is Italian!! We were right all along! Jesus lives in the Vatican!!*

The team members stared at each other in disbelief. The Etruscan finds were being buried by the linkage to Jesus. Dr. Morgan Jenner, in cooperation with the Universities of Ferrara and Bologna, had called this press conference today at the Museo Archeologico in Florence. He had planned to calmly summarize his team's findings at the Cerveteri tomb and the tomb's connection to Mary of Nazareth. But this was not an atmosphere that lent itself to calmness. He could hardly be heard above the noise of the crowds drifting in from the streets and the flashing of cameras. Morgan turned to Justine, Guido, Delmo, and Marco and raised his palms as though to ask, "What do I do?" However, Justine knew that her dad was also in his element. His latest thrilling press conference had been in Cuzco after the discovery of a library at the base of Machu Picchu.

Delmo dragged up a chair and sat down. Justine scanned the crowd for weapons—just in case someone tried something crazy. She was relieved to find six Carabinieri entering the side door. Marco stepped forward and started to translate into Italian. Morgan and Marco glanced at each other and nodded.

One astute reporter asked, "Is there any connection between your discoveries and the death of Robert Blackburn?" Both Morgan and Marco ignored the question and called for another question. Perspiration appeared generously on the temples of both men. Justine was taken aback and noticed that the reporter was from the Egyptian newspaper *Al Ahram*. It was clear that this reporter knew of the connection between the thief of the original codex and Blackburn.

The next day, *The New York Times*, the *International Herald Tribune*, and *La Repubblica* covered the research in detail, including the discovery of the codex, or diary, in Cairo and the tomb in Cerveteri, the mtDNA results, and the lineage of Jesus of Nazareth. The media in Catholic countries emphasized the Virgin Mary's life along the Nile, literacy, and love of family. They did not report the most controversial revelations in the diary: Mary's sexual relationship with Joseph; Jesus' twin sister, Elizabeth; and the real reasons for the Holy Family's flight from Palestine after the birth of the twins, chased by Herod's son and his forces. Justine read of the eight-year duration of the Holy Family's stay in Old Cairo before moving back to Jerusalem, where Jesus was crucified. And of the Etruscans' lengthy stopover in Egypt. Thus the *Al Ahram* headline. *How do they know so much?*

"Aren't you going to open it?" asked Guido who, at 10 a.m. on the morning after the press conference, stood in Justine's recently transformed kitchen near Dante's home. The ancient casement windows had been pried open and framed with yellow gauze curtains. Daffodils sprang from a clay pot that swayed in the cool morning breeze. He had shown up early wanting coffee.

Guido's question caused Justine to momentarily abandon her hunt for the granola and eye the special delivery letter from the Vatican that had been lying on her kitchen table for more than an hour. "Can they excommunicate a non-Catholic?" she asked.

"Ah . . . there are many forms of 'excommunication,' but if you're Catholic, chances are you'll be thrown out of the church." He walked over to her cabinet, moved a container of whole grain rice, reached in with his large, tanned hand, and pulled out the granola. Opening the refrigerator, he asked, "Milk?" Guido had stayed in town the night before, but not with Justine. He planned to return later that morning to Ferrara to teach a class.

"A little." Justine pointed toward the pitcher. She hugged him briefly, and stepped back to pick up the letter. It bore an official Vatican stamp and had been delivered by a young man in medieval dress. She held the letter up with both hands, examining it in the light, as though to open it would be to succumb to its command.

Guido impatiently waited for her to open the letter. He was as curious as she. Reaching for two unmatched bowls, he poured a half-cup of granola for her and twice as much for himself, after which he crushed the empty box and placed it in the recycling bin under the sink. After the press conference the day before, he'd decided to stay in town for dinner with the team and give Justine a ride to work the following morning.

"We need to get on the road," he said, running his hand slowly around the back of her neck and up through her unbrushed hair.

Justine still enjoyed his small gestures of intimacy, although she had made it clear that it wouldn't go any further. She now felt committed to Amir—whatever that would mean. "Are you about ready?"

"I am. I just need my jacket." She walked part way across the room, suddenly spun around and demanded, "Give me that."

He handed her the envelope and she tore it open with trembling hands. She froze.

Guido gently lifted the letter from her hands and read it aloud:

"'His Holiness Pope Benedict XVI Bishop of Rome and the Apostolic See, The Vatican, Rome, Awards the Grand Cross of the Papal Order of Saint

Gregory to Dr. Justine Isabella Jenner, on this day of our Lord, 19 April 2008.' Impossible," he exclaimed. "This just isn't done for a non-Catholic. And a woman?" He sat down.

Justine's shock turned to excitement. "What does it mean, this Order of Saint Gregory?" She plopped down on a chair next to him, staring at the letter.

"I'm not entirely sure, but I've heard that it relates to a person's special meritorious service to the Church." He placed his forefinger on her nose and moved it back and forth, savoring the minute intimacy of the moment.

"This is crazy!" She jumped up and began to pace. "Of course we know what this is about. Mary's diary. Jesus. The Etruscans. But I'm not the most directly responsible for the ultimate find. Amir is." She turned to the second page of the document. "Ah," is all she said.

"But you did find the diary originally. And you may be a safer bet in this case: a woman is more sympathetic, less controversial. The Church would hardly give the award to an Egyptian when it has just secured an injunction to keep the diary out of Egyptian hands."

"So I'm the most likely recipient." She stood and stared into his eyes, although the gaze was distracted.

"You've got it. And being able to declare Jesus Christ is part Etruscan—therefore Italian—would be among the dearest wishes of any Pope," he said, gazing at Justine with a desire aroused by the fragrance of her lavender shampoo.

"Also quite a distraction from less desirable notoriety—"

"—the child abuse scandals in the States, Ireland, Germany." He paused as though saddened by his own remark. "Will you accept the award?"

"Will I accept it?" she repeated in a flat tone, lost in reading the details of the award document. She finally looked up. "Should I?"

CHAPTER 37

⎯∞⎯

"A secret's worth depends on the people from whom it must be kept."
Carlos Ruiz Zafón, *The Shadow of the Wind*

W ITHIN MINUTES, Guido was making his way back to his office at the University of Ferrara, and Justine was pulling on her running clothes. She called Marco to say she would be late for the planning meeting on the new Etruscan exhibit, a job she had undertaken recently. Working with her father had proven too complicated, although she remained on his team. Stepping into the narrow street, she turned right and began to run toward the east. She had decisions to make.

As Justine's feet pounded the pavement, she began to review the previous years—what had catapulted her into this place in her life. It had been exactly a year since she'd arrived in Cairo to begin work in the Community Schools for Girls and made her visit to St. Sergius. If she hadn't picked up that small book at her feet during the earthquake, she would still be working in Egypt. But then she would not know the true story of Mary of Nazareth and the story that would come as a relief to women the world over. The real Mary was a virtuous woman—but not a virgin mother.

But how would she write the story without the translations? There had been three linguists: Ibrahim, Andrea, and Isaac Yardeni, the Israeli scholar. *Is he still even alive? How complete are his notes? Does he have a copy?*

Her thoughts turned to Amir and Il Pero. His sexuality often overpowered her, his character and spirit enchanted her. *What would Isabella do?* While she was a modern woman at heart, Isabella had been bound tightly by two cultures: an Egyptian in the Italian world of the 1920s. Could she even find parallels in their two lives? Yet she also knew that women were more alike than different—hadn't she discovered that in the pages of Mary's diary? And Sappho's poetry, a testament to our commonalities. *For each of us, desire and intellect pushes at the constraints of culture.*

Justine awakened from her musings just in time to avoid the rearview mirror on a parked Mercedes. She'd nearly had her head lopped off; she pictured it rolling down the busy thoroughfare. Stopping on the curb and panting, she glanced into the mirror and noticed a man she'd seen cross the previous square. Was he was following her? Yes! But with distance enough so she couldn't make out his face. *Who . . . who is it??*

The man slowly but steadily gained on her, enough so that she now recognized him. Justine picked up her pace for the next block, weaving in and out of heavy foot traffic, behind cyclists, Vespas cutting in and out. Ahead, a city bus bound for Santa Maria lumbered carelessly down the middle of the street.

Justine veered in front of the bus, so close that her left shoulder touched the immense front fender. Then she heard it. A heavy thud, human screams blending with screeching wheels. She stopped and turned around, walking back toward the inanimate body. She stared at the dead man, took out her iPhone, and called 118 for emergency medical services. Her breathing was labored; she could hear her heart beating as though it would escape from her chest. She had killed a man. Not personally, but not entirely accidentally, either. Hadn't she just wanted to lose him—to scare him off?

Justine turned back toward her apartment, then pivoted her body toward Fiesole and began to run. For fifteen minutes she continued alongside congested traffic, ducking under overhanging tree limbs on the four-mile uphill journey. Turning right onto the short stretch of Largo de Vinci at the bottom of the Fiesole hillside, Justine ran close to the high stone wall until she reached the back door of her mother's home.

She was surprised to find her father standing comfortably at the kitchen window with a coffee cup in hand, his thick hair uncombed and shirt untucked. Her mother stood near the stove dodging bacon sizzle. Both were equally startled to see their daughter enter the back door, although they didn't allow themselves to show it.

Nonplussed, Lucrezia threw her daughter a hand towel. Justine caught the towel in midair and began to dry her hair with one hand. Both parents looked up expectantly. Justine regarded their non-expressive faces closely.

"I just killed a man," she confessed.

Her parents were speechless. Finally, her father rose and walked toward his daughter, taking her in his arms.

Justine began to shake, then she let her body crumple into sobs while her father held her.

Several moments passed before her mother took her by the shoulders and helped her into a chair. Lucrezia kneeled in front of her daughter. "Tell us about it."

Justine slowly described her distracted run through Florence, being followed, veering in front of the bus. The man's body. "I should have stayed to identify the body. I realize that now."

"You knew him? Who?" her father asked.

"Donatello," is all she said.

Morgan and Lucrezia stared at each other. He released a low whistle, as though expelling air caught in his lungs. "I notified the Carabinieri when you told me he was mixed up with Blackburn. And probably the Mafia. They still harbor the desire, you know, to project the Etruscans as the great warriors and founders of Rome. A goddess culture would certainly not sit well with them. But I'm more practical than that. There had to be money involved." He paused, as though reviewing the steps leading up to this moment. "I'll take care of it."

"Thanks, Dad, but I'd prefer to handle it myself." He gave a short nod. Justine took her cup of tea and stood gazing out the French doors, as though in a trance. Breathing deeply, she felt energy revitalizing her arms, her legs. Regaining her composure, she turned around and pulled the Vatican letter from her pouch and gave it to her mother, who read it in silence and handed it on to Morgan.

She was prepared for her mother to be skeptical and her father to be practical. Perhaps they would surprise her.

"What does Guido think?" Lucrezia asked.

Justine was caught off guard; her mother had no reason to assume that she was with Guido this morning. "He thinks I should accept," she said simply. "What do you think?"

"I don't trust them," began her mother, standing and walking around the counter to turn off the fire under the popping bacon, now burnt. "But then that won't surprise you. I can't understand their motivation. Since the injunction, they already have access to the diary—how will this help?"

"A distraction? An extended hand to America? Women? A display of modernism by appearing to accept the science verifying the discovery?" Morgan pressed his large frame against the south wall, and grew quiet as he pondered his own words. "But your thoughts are more sinister, Creta," he said invitingly.

Lucrezia's thin eyebrows moved together, her dark eyes coming to rest on her ex-husband's face. She pursed her lips. "Sinister? Absolutely. They've always got something up their flowing sleeves . . ."

Justine interrupted their speculations. The run could have cleared her head, although it was mottled by Donatello's death. "Here's how I see it. The Vatican could interpret my acceptance as supporting the seizure of the diary. An artifact that rightly belongs to Egypt. On the other hand, the award also means the Vatican is willing to risk going public with the existence of the diary, possibly ensuring two things: making it obvious they possess an Egyptian artifact and legitimizing the diary—codex—as an accurate historical document. I can't understand why the Vatican would want to do either."

"Astute, my dear. Why, indeed?" said Morgan, pulling his buckskin boots on over his stockinged feet.

Justine stared at her father's feet for several moments, then turned her gaze toward her mother, who had returned to her breakfast tasks. "What are the implications of a refusal?"

"A refusal would be a serious affront to the Church and to Italy, I'm afraid," admitted Lucrezia, gripping three plates so hard that her knuckles were turning pale. "The consequences might not be worth taking an honorable stand. Although you know my attitude: spit in their eye."

"I think your mother is right—with her first statement, at least. It's difficult to anticipate the results of a refusal. However, your integrity may require nothing less."

Justine winced at the Solomon's choice before her. Slowly removing her running shoes, she walked further into the kitchen and poured herself a cup of lukewarm coffee. She turned and faced her parents. "I have another tragic story to tell you." She took a sip of her coffee, deciding how to start.

Her parents stared, cups suspended in midair. Her mother plopped down on a kitchen chair as though to ask, "What now?"

She told them about Andrea. How she'd made the connection with Blackburn. Her visit to the Foundation. Her suspicions confirmed by e-mail, which she now extracted from her pants pocket. Justine handed the crumpled page to her mother.

Lucrezia slowly smoothed the message on the kitchen table, Morgan leaning over her shoulder. As she read, her eyes grew moist, the linings darkened into deep pink. She began to cry.

Morgan's body and face muscles tightened, eyelids narrowed. They both looked up.

"It can't be true," Lucrezia cried. "I've known and loved Andrea for twenty years, and all the while . . ."

"I knew there was something too mysterious, too exotic about her." Morgan straightened and stared out the window.

Justine imagined that her father had been desperate to find a credible reason why Andrea dumped him. That there had to be something wrong with her.

"And then there's the codex translations," Justine began.

Morgan turned toward his daughter, sternness flashing through his eyes, a lion ready to protect his daughter. "The codex translations?"

Justine reminded her parents that there were three major linguists involved: Ibrahim, who was dead; Andrea, who was inaccessible; and Isaac Yardeni, the elderly Israeli. "And I don't even know if he is alive."

"I know Yardeni. Good man. But I've heard that he's been ill . . ."

"I think I have a solution—to the translation issue, at least. I have to try," she said finally. Sliding onto the long bench, Justine placed her arm around her mother's shoulder and hugged her while she trembled, seeming to shrink in upon herself. Justine held her for several moments, then asked softly, "May I use your computer?"

CHAPTER 38

—⁂—

"It is easier to forgive an enemy than to forgive a friend."

—William Blake

JUSTINE'S IPHONE RANG, announcing "Unknown Caller." While she didn't usually answer an unknown caller, she was waiting—but waiting for what?

"Justine?" the aging voice asked.

"Isaac? How are you?" She put the phone on speaker, leaned against the wall of her apartment, and slid down to the floor.

"Not well, I'm afraid. An old man, ready for his maker. But I have something to tell you, and should have done it months ago. Before Ibrahim died, he sent me the translations of the codex. And a summary to the communication minister, I believe."

Al Ahram.

"He knew he was in danger," Isaac continued slowly. "He had been interrogated, told them nothing, but returned home a beaten man."

It was almost too much to process. Tears burst onto Justine's flushed face.

"Justine, are you there?" Isaac nearly shouted into the phone.

"Yes, I'm here," she whispered. "Your news is quite a shock. You must be deeply grieved to know that your dear friend had to go through such torture, such humiliation, in the country he so loved."

"*Toda rabah.* Thank you, I appreciate your compassion. Always have." Isaac started to cough.

"If there is anything I can do. Do you have some help?"

"My daughter is with me." He paused. "Shall I send them to you?"

"Yes, thank you. I would be so appreciative." Justine sat up straight, alert.

"Ibrahim sent me everything before he was killed. His notes, all of his translations, photographs."

"Do you have a pen?"

"Just a moment." His daughter came on the line.

"I'm ready to write down your address, Justine."

She gave Rachel her address. "Please, take good care of your dear father. *Lehitraot.*"

Justine sat still for several moments, allowing herself to be mesmerized by the lift moving up and down on the side of Dante's house. She was startled out of her reverie by a sharp knock. She got up and walked to the front door.

"Andrea!" Justine nearly cried. This was the last person she expected to see.

There she stood, as beautiful as ever, half-bangs over her high forehead, yet the lines around her mouth were deepened, and her eyes revealed profound sorrow. "May I come in?"

Wordlessly, Justine stepped aside and let her enter. They stared at one another as though remembrances of their friendship were passing between them, filling the quiet space. Several moments passed.

"Why are you here?" Justine finally asked. She didn't ask Andrea to sit down.

"I know this is too late—too late for our relationship, too late to make amends."

"Yes it is, Andrea. What do you have to say?"

"You know that Blackburn is dead?"

Justine nodded.

"I loved him, Justine, first as a lover, then as a friend and mentor."

"Sounds like Ibrahim, doesn't it?" Justine charged. "Lover, mentor, father. One man fulfilling all of your needs." She was unforgiving. "Is that where you were headed with my father?"

Andrea flinched, her face reddened, eyes darting across the room. She clearly hadn't seen the parallels. Finally, "I was afraid I was losing your mother's friendship. That's why I broke off my affair with your dad."

"I see. A little charity work?"

"Justine, can't you reconsider? Trust me again? I've resigned my work with the Foundation." She was pleading.

"I need to know, Andrea. Why did you confess in writing? In your e-mail?"

Andrea spoke softly, pushing her bangs away from her forehead like a timid child. "I trusted that you wouldn't hurt me."

Justine gulped, but was not derailed. It was too late for amends. *Besides, I'm probably being manipulated again.* "Where are the translations? The original codex?"

"The codex is with the Foundation. The translations are right here." She patted her briefcase.

Justine arched an eyebrow and drew her long fingers close to her lips. Her stare was steely. "Why was Blackburn killed?" She needed to fill in the gaps, put the puzzle together.

Andrea paused long enough to sit down, perspiration making her sculptured face glisten. "Robert had made a Faustian bargain."

"With the Mafia?"

Andrea nodded. "He was never satisfied—lived a fashionable life—always wanting more. I assume that he crossed them in some way. He never included me in the seamier side of his life." She paused and stared at the glass elevator for several moments. Up and down, up and down. "Could you ever trust me again?"

Justine gazed at Andrea with a mix of pity and affection and pondered her agreement with Isaac. Did she even need Andrea's translations, sitting within touch? She was confident that Isaac's daughter would send his notes and Ibrahim's translations. But what condition would they be in? Could she be sure that they wouldn't be intercepted? She shook her head to clear it. "Trusting you again is out of the question. As I'm sure it is for my parents, and Amir as well. We have all been deeply wounded by your betrayal." Justine decided right then that this abandonment, coupled with others in Andrea's life, was enough punishment. She would not report to the Carabinieri, nor send her letter to the Foundation. Not that pursuing a legal path would result in any satisfying resolution. *We may never know the whole story . . . About Donatello, Blackburn . . .*

Andrea gazed at Justine, eyes inflamed, and barely nodded before she turned and walked toward the door, opening it without further words.

Justine watched her go. Her chest ached as though she had run up a steep hill without stopping. She turned back toward her living room and glanced down. Andrea's briefcase sat where she had stood.

CHAPTER 39

—⦵⦵⦵—

"In a time of deceit telling the truth is a revolutionary act."

—George Orwell

JUSTINE STOOD STARING from just inside the Chapel door—behind her, her parents, and Amir, who had just flown in from Cairo. For a couple of days, he claimed. Guido was unable to attend, although she had invited him. He had read and applauded Justine's speech outline.

She scanned the ceiling, swarming with frescos of Christian dramas: Genesis, the creation of the universe, Adam and Eve's expulsion from the Garden, the cataclysmic finality of the Last Judgment, the spirited lives of Moses and Jesus. The scenes tiered in three massive layers nine stories in all, divided by horizontal cornices, the lowest scenes sketched into visual narrative tapestries. At the altar, a fresco by Perugino depicted the Virgin of the Assumption, to whom the chapel was dedicated. Effigies of early popes, from the greatest of papal persecution, stared ominously from niches.

Such are the traditional theatrics on stage in the Quattrocentro interior of the Sistine Chapel. Each sublime panel is electrified with life, animated with Biblical characters performing God's deeds, which take on new proportions depending on where each gazer stands in the vast room. A visitor to the Chapel may turn around quickly, startled by the illusion that one of these actors of faith is following him. Although these lively wall paintings were executed by many artists, including Perugino, Botticelli, and an exquisite star-flung sky by Piero Matteo d'Amelia, the room is considered chiefly the creation of Michelangelo. Even so, his Genesis disappoints many, for, like Mona Lisa in the Louvre, it is smaller than one would imagine and is not readily found, even though it is on the ceiling in the middle of the room. Yet as a woman who had last been there as a young girl, Justine found the Sistine Chapel a wonder to behold.

Lowering her eyes, she observed the Reverend Angelo Lombardi, the Vatican's Director of Communication and Protocol, making his way toward them. Behind him were members of the press, with cameras held discreetly at their sides. Justine made the appropriate introductions to Reverend Lombardi, whom she had met earlier in the day and who was now charged with leading the guests of honor across the marble mosaic floor toward an elaborate screen and the seated Pope Benedict XVI. The pontiff's snow-white hair fluttered from under a towering white and gold brocade mitra that appeared too heavy for such an elderly man. His matching cape was clasped together by a golden broach, a cross dangling from his chest. On either side of the Holy See, two middle-aged men in cherry red woolen gowns overlaid with white linen smocks, appearing ready to catch the hat, or the man himself, if need be.

"Your Holiness," said Justine, bowing deeply and shaking his extended hand, cool as untended clay. She looked directly into his clear, piercing eyes, and he responded, "Thank you, my child, for bringing the words of the Mother of God to us." She smiled, as did he. For a moment, she felt the sensation that there was a secret connection between them; what that meant she couldn't fathom.

The moment passed and the pontiff turned toward Morgan Jenner: "I know of your work, Dr. Jenner. Tell me about Cerveteri . . ."

Respectfully retreating from the private conversation, Reverend Lombardi nodded to Justine, indicating an end to the formalities and the invitation to talk privately. She caught her mother's attention and then walked alone with the Reverend to the center of the great room.

"That is quite a discovery you've made, Dr. Jenner," he said stiffly. "You must know that the Church is most grateful that such a treasure was unearthed. And the Italian heritage of the Mother of God and her Son is without price."

"Thank you, Reverend Lombardi. I was astounded myself. The Blessed Mary is a historically, as well as religiously, significant leader. *Lombardi's smile is artful and practiced*, she thought. *Patronizing and sardonic as well.*

"We have never thought of the Mother of God in that regard, Dr. Jenner," he said, his voice growing tense. He paused for gravitas, and to segue to a new subject. "You know of our injunction against the Mycenae Foundation."

Ah, here it comes. She nodded.

". . . Amazing claims in this codex. Yet we cannot deny the scientific confirmation of its physical origin. Such a treasured artifact belongs in the Vatican."

"I detect a somewhat cynical attitude toward the intention of the codex, yet I am attempting to remain neutral in regard to the injunction. Although I do have a personal preference for its eventual residence."

"You may assume that I—and my colleagues within the Church—take exception to a few of the claims. Yet we are overcome with pleasure in regard to Her direct relationship to Italians. That confirms the wisdom—long denied—of the placement of the Holy Church here, rather than Constantinople. Further, Catholics identify with her loss and take comfort in her love, which is a love only a woman can express."

"And yet the Church accords lesser authority to women than men . . . In any case, I see nothing in the diary that would detract from Mary's devoutness."

"The Holy Mother offers more than devotion. She is no ordinary woman. The Mother of God is a symbol of unattainable perfection. That makes her a saint. People revere what they themselves cannot achieve."

Justine's eyes once again sought the Genesis scene on the ceiling. God reaches out to Adam, below his feet is Eve. "An interesting observation, Reverend. It could also be said that humans revere achievement, often to the detriment of others."

"You will understand that we would not want to compromise the Mother of God's role in the Church. We feel that some information in her diary need not be made public."

Justine smiled with an innocence that could be interpreted as assent.

The Reverend examined her face closely, bowed with utmost courtesy and said, "If you'll excuse me." Assured of his victory, he turned and walked across the room toward a gathering of men in scarlet robes, leaving Justine standing alone in the middle of the Sistine Chapel.

She turned to observe American Ambassador Ronald Spogli approaching. A man taller by a few inches than Justine, with thinning hair. He wore a gray suit subtly enlivened by a lavender tie. Dark, full eyebrows dominated his otherwise pallid complexion. He smiled and extended his hand, which Justine clasped warmly.

"Great to see you again, Dr. Jenner. Washington is most pleased that you are accepting this award from the Vatican." He held his smile while his eyes, already close together, appeared to move closer beneath those bushy eyebrows. "We can use a little reprieve from the recent tensions. These unfortunate scandals have colored the waters between the United States and the Church."

"I'm gratified that Washington is pleased, Mr. Ambassador. I'm aware that our relationship with Italy has improved in the last few years," she said, stepping closer to heighten the intimacy of her remarks. "You are to be congratulated."

"Thank you, Dr. Jenner. If I've had a small hand in creating closer business and military relationships, I am most grateful for the opportunity. We have seen some major breakthroughs in economic development here. More entrepreneurship. We're optimistic that Italy is once again becoming an important partner. It has the world's seventh-largest economy, you know."

Justine hated to dampen his enthusiasm, but she needed to prepare him. "I should tell you that my acceptance speech is unlikely to please the Vatican." She smiled broadly as though to soften the effect of her words.

The Ambassador stared at her. "Should I worry?" he asked, forcing a smile of his own.

"Perhaps so," she admitted, placing her hand on his gray cashmere sleeve.

As Justine walked toward her parents, who were seated in the front row of chairs set up for the occasion, she saw the Pope rise from his throne-like chair and move slowly toward the lectern near the marble screen. Reverend Lombardi approached Justine once again, and they walked toward the stage. Pope Benedict XVI, surrounded by the gathering of gowns, nodded slightly toward Justine and stepped forward, standing just to the right of the lectern, now occupied by Cardinal Benedetto.

After welcoming the few dozen guests in the room and establishing the purpose of the proceedings, the cardinal began, "It is my honor, on behalf of the Holy See and the Holy Church, to present the Grand Cross of the Papal Order of Saint Gregory to Dr. Justine Isabella Jenner, esteemed American anthropologist, in recognition of her discovery of the sacred diary of the Virgin Mary, Holy Mother of God." Benedetto was triumphant, turning his best side to the flashing cameras. It had been his idea to make this unusual award to the American woman. A gesture toward the Americans was useful, the cardinal had reasoned.

Justine had been coached to step forward and accept the award from Pope Benedict, his powdered, fleshy face now non-expressive. Yet as he presented the award, his aging eyes registered mild affection. Much taller than the pontiff, Justine bent her head low so that the Grand Cross could be placed around her neck. She reached up and grasped the cross, holding it tight for few moments while observing the pontiff's pointed red shoes.

Justine graciously thanked the pontiff and turned toward the cardinal, whose huge, hanging golden cross glistened in the camera flashes. "May I say a few words in appreciation?" she asked.

Although caught off guard by her unexpected request, Cardinal Benedetto nodded his permission, comforted by the knowledge relayed by the Reverend that Dr. Jenner understood the vital role of the Holy Mother within the Church.

"Thank you," she said, stepping forward and placing both hands on the lower edges of the lectern erected near Mino da Fiesole's carved pulpit. She slowly scanned the room. Since her words were being broadcast, most members of the press stood a respectful distance away, although photographers had edged forward, eager to capture the image of the first American woman to speak in the Sistine Chapel. The stunning young woman in sapphire silk would make good copy the next day for *La Repubblica*, *The International Herald Tribune*, and the thousands of papers served by Reuters.

"First, I would like to thank the Holy See and the Holy Church for this great honor, and recognize a few of the special guests in this remarkable chapel— Ambassador Spogli and his wife, Rebecca; my parents, Lucrezia and Morgan Jenner; and my colleague, Amir El Shabry, the Egyptian archeologist most responsible for identifying the link between Mary of Nazareth and the Etruscans." All eyes turned momentarily toward Amir, press members silently shuffling for space to situate themselves closer to the Egyptian archeologist.

"In 1924," she continued, "my great-great-grandfather, The Honorable Baraka Mohammed Hassouna, was most honored to come to Rome as the Egyptian Ambassador to the Vatican. With him were my great-great-grandmother, Samira Hassouna, and their daughter, Isabella, my namesake. I stand before you today, the daughter of an Egyptian mother and American father, with great love and respect for Italy. So it is with great humility and pleasure that I accept the coveted Grand Cross of the Papal Order of Saint Gregory awarded in the name of the noble and humble physician of the soul who found peace in service to others. I honor this man who led an austere life despite his station in life and in the Church.

"Curiosity about and admiration for Saint Mary led me on a path that resulted in the discovery of her diary under Saint Sergius Church in Old Cairo on April 12, 2007, during a major earthquake. With this ancient codex, or diary, we discovered the Holy Mother's own voice and reflections, telling all of us more than we'd known about this remarkable woman of intellect and compassion. This diary is a testament to her efforts to teach the values of humanity and tolerance to Jesus." The pontiff shifted uncomfortably in his chair. According to Catholic theology, Jesus had no need to be taught these values, for he himself was always the teacher. The silence in the room felt impenetrable, as though seeking to resist the strain that was forthcoming.

"I have had the unparalleled privilege of learning some of the deepest desires of Saint Mary through the pages of her diary." Justine paused, noting the Reverend's sharp intake of breath. "The desires of Mary for women are evident . . . that they learn to read, to seek knowledge and freedom, to express their wisdom in raising their children. Taught by her Grandmother Faustina that inequalities are the source of evil, Mary, I am sure, would wish women to have equitable standing within the Church and society. Such standing would honor the life of Saint Mary. I am hopeful that the Church will continue to honor her by returning the coveted diary to its country of origin."

The collected gasp from the cluster of men to her right was audible across the room. "Once again," Justine continued with unwavering confidence, "I thank you, your Excellency, for this incomparable honor."

As Justine turned toward the pontiff, she noted that a flicker of fear moved rapidly through his eyes. Scattered applause traveled from sections of the room, pockets of silence were even more pronounced. The cardinal failed to step forward to escort Justine from the stage. She stood before him patiently, waiting for him to regain his composure. Cameras continued to flash; reporters scrambled for the exits.

CHAPTER 40

≈≈≈

There are no secrets that time does not reveal.

—Jean Racine, French Dramatist

"YOU WERE EXCEPTIONALLY confident today," observed Lucrezia. "I had no idea that you would speak with such aplomb and authority in the Sistine Chapel." She and Justine stood alone in the kitchen of the family home in Fiesole. Their exit from the Chapel had been hectic, the press for interviews nearly smothering all of them on their way back through the labyrinth of the Church. Amir had kissed her good-bye and headed for the airport. All he'd said was, "I'm proud of you."

"You'll need to be careful," said her mother. "As your dad observed, all hell could break loose." It already had.

Justine had decided to ignore the warning; after all, she'd been under surveillance for more than a year. She chose to respond to her mother's comment on aplomb and authority. "I have been inspiring and emboldened, Mom, by the examples of audacious women I've had. Great-Grandmother Isabella, Mary of Nazareth, and you. Women of daring and clarity. Isabella's secret life—in the '20s—a dangerous time for a woman to engage in sensuous communion with an infamous author. All of these women made courageous choices and in doing so, found themselves." She paused. "I assume you know I've read the letters."

"I do. I'm sorry I didn't give them to you myself. You see . . ."

"Yes?" Justine said empathically, gently, although she couldn't imagine that her mother had a defensible reason for leaving her on the outside. "Why did you keep the letters a secret from me all of these years? From an anthropologist?"

Lucrezia rose and walked to the refrigerator, took out a bottle of Perrier-Jouët Belle Epoque, grabbed two small crystal glasses, and returned to the table. Slowly pouring the clear, effervescent liquid, she topped off both glasses, then reached in her pocket and pulled out two letters as thin as filo. "I'll answer those questions after you look at these. Let's go in by the fire. You'll need to sit down."

Justine followed without a word. Champagne in one hand, letters in the other, she eased her sapphire dress above her knees and curled up on the floor. For several moments she gazed at the blazing fire as it shone in her crystal goblet, then set her glass down on the stone hearth. She began to read:

Hotel Beau Rivage, Bandol, France, 18 September 1929
My dearest Isabella,

Your news fills me with a joy greater than I've ever known. I was sure the fates had decided that I would never have a child of my own. Undeserving. With little to offer another. Still, I'm afraid that I might have to leave fatherhood to your fine husband. Does he suspect? Surely not.

This French doctor is as useless as the others. I overheard him tell Frieda that there was little chance of improvement. The air is damp here; all my strength goes to pulling in what oxygen I can. And writing what I can. I need you at my side, my darling, but know that is not possible. Even if you changed your mind and wanted to come to me, you shouldn't travel with little Lawrence in your womb.

I beg of you to consider these thoughts when raising our child. I wish him to have your lightness of spirit and innocence about the world rather than his father's cynicism. Give him freedom and choices early, and love without suffocation. Let him spread his wings wide. Protect him from the life of a writer! Terrible lot. And science and politics ... almost as bad. They steal away life's mysteries. But I digress. I am excited beyond words by our good fortune. My one regret in this short life has been the absence of a child of my own. And now that my child will be given life by the woman I truly love—what more could I want?

So, from me, a God-be-with-you. I have lived as vividly as I have written—and if I have left with you, dear woman, the seed of my deepest self, I die with gladness and fulfillment in my belly, worshiping the sun in yours. You have brought me a sense of peace that I have never known. How brief, yet how important, you have been to me. As if God said, "Wait!—there is someone you must meet."

A tear fell onto the letter. In spite of the fire, Justine shivered. "Grandma Laurence . . . she is?" At some level, she already knew.

Her mother just nodded.

"Miranda said there was word of a daughter. But I couldn't quite believe—after all, none of his biographers wrote about it." Justine turned back to the end of the letter.

If you need anything, my love, remember you can trust Lady Brett. She is living at the ranch. Stay well, and carry my seed with care.

I love you, David

Justine held her breath. Muted light from the setting sun flooded into the room, and in the distance painted the Duomo with a golden helmet. She was cognizant only of her pounding heart. *I'm the great-granddaughter of D.H. Lawrence. The great-granddaughter of D. H. Lawrence*, she repeated to herself.

"Frieda made it known that he wasn't capable of consummating any relationship toward the end. Biographers believed the myth—after all, it was credible."

Justine grimaced, rebelling against being defined by others. "Tell me about Lady Brett."

"Lady Brett was from a British royal family who idolized Lawrence. She followed him to Taos in hopes of joining in the establishment of an Utopian community."

"Which never came about . . ."

"Right. She was a strange one. Nearly deaf, she carried around a big trumpet of a hearing device and dressed like a Wild West show performer. Frieda couldn't stand her, but she was unwavering in her devotion to D.H."

"Umm," was all Justine said before picking up the second envelope. Different from the first—different stationery, thinner, more frayed at the edges. Frieda had written one short line across the top of the yellowed newspaper clipping, posted from Ad Astra, Vence. It read: "I knew you and Lorenzo were close. Frieda." Justine opened the article from *Paris Match* dated March 3, 1930. The headline read simply:

Celebre auteur D.H. Lawrence meurt a Venise.

"Famed author, D.H. Lawrence, dies in Vence, France."

Justine's cry was soft, almost silent. "How long have you known? About Lawrence? About the letters?"

"Since I was a young girl."

"But why reveal the information now?" Justine struggled not to sound accusatory, although she couldn't help feeling that somehow she'd been denied a vital dimension of her identity, her self.

"I tell you now because your father said you had the letters." She chose not to say: Because of your performance today in the Vatican. "You're a mature woman. It was time. It was time for me to break another promise in order to fulfill a more important one."

"Another promise?" Justine asked, staring at the last letter, rereading, "*As if God said, 'Wait!—there is someone you must meet.'*" It was difficult to tear herself away from Isabella and her dangerous liaison. Then, settling back against the wall, she gave her full attention to her mother. "Tell me the whole story . . . tell me about Isabella."

"It's a bit of a story."

"I have time."

Lucrezia sat down in the burgundy French provincial chair facing the fire and her daughter and held her stemmed glass in both hands. Although this moment had been a long time in coming, a scene she had rehearsed a thousand times, she searched for the right words. "As you now know, your Grandmother Laurence was named after David Herbert Lawrence."

Justine nodded.

"It's important for you to realize that our house was occupied during the war, first by Mussolini's thugs, then by Germans . . ."

"Prego said there were heavy boots. He's still fearful."

"Fear of the Nazis never goes away. Nearly 9,000 Jews were transported out of Italy. It haunts you forever. When Laurence was twelve—that would have been 1942—she overheard what was probably a casual conversation." Lucrezia's voice trembled. "As mother told it, she would fold herself into those massive velvet drapes," she pointed toward the northern wall of windows and the drapes, thinned by decades of dry cleaning, "and eavesdrop on the Nazis. On one occasion, there was a gathering of Italian Fascists and Nazis—Italy was still a member of the Axis powers. The topic of D.H. Lawrence came up, and a comment was made that he had been a frequent guest in the house. The renowned Italian archeologist, Massimo Pallottimo, was in the room . . ."

"Pallottimo?? In the room? The Fascist archaeologist who denied the validity of D.H. Lawrence's views in his introduction to *Etruscan Places*?"

". . . the very same. According to mother, Pallottimo commented, very deliberately to be sure, that there were rumors that Lawrence's mother was Jewish. You'll remember that the Fascists despised Lawrence because he had not portrayed the Etruscans as the majestic warrior forebears of the Romans. Your grandmother heard one of the officers say that Mussolini's mission was to return Italy to the greatness of Rome, and to rid the country of undesirable races. This conversation terrified her."

"But why? Did she know of her real connection to D.H Lawrence?"

"She did. Grandmother Isabella was distraught with guilt after grandfather died at the first battle of El Alamein at Mersa Matruh. Even though he was Egyptian, he'd managed to join the British troops in North Africa when Mussolini assured the Italian people that the fall of Egypt was imminent. So she chose to tell her daughter about her real father when she turned twelve. She must have felt very alone with her secret. And when she overhead the conversation, she mistakenly assumed that she was Jewish. She knew what that could mean. Jews were being exported from Italy on a daily basis."

"My god." Justine's face tightened with the pain the young girl must have felt. She trembled.

Lucrezia gazed at her daughter, appreciating her capacity for empathy, compassion. "Mother told me the story when I was fourteen. That would have been 1966. She was still frightened. She showed me the letters and made me promise never to tell anyone."

"Not even your own daughter."

"At fourteen, I had little sense of the future or what such a promise would mean. I would have told you, probably soon, but I'm just as glad that you found the letters yourself."

"So am I." Their eyes met with warmth and closeness. *Secrets keep us apart. Secrets have kept us apart.* Justine finally asked, "Why didn't the family leave Italy? After all, they weren't Italian."

Lucrezia shifted her eyes to the fire, took a sip of her champagne. "I know that seems reasonable now, but Egypt was dangerous then, and Grandfather believed his homeland would soon fall to the Nazis. That Alexandria—and probably Cairo—would soon be under siege. Here, at least, they were allowed to stay in a wing of their own home."

Justine was silent for several moments. Her eyes flooded with a mixture of affection and sorrow for her mother, for she knew that living with secrets whittles away at the soul. She rose and walked to her mother's chair, kneeling beside her, taking her hand. "The photo of Isabella on your bureau—she looks so sad, as though all spirit had been drained from her."

"The one in the fur stole?"

Justine nodded.

"It was taken in 1930."

"The year Lawrence died and Isabella was born," said Justine. "Almost more than one can bear." She imagined what it must have been like for Isabella to be in the arms of her husband while bearing another man's child. "Living with a lie day in and day out could twist anyone into an unrecognizable person—being careful about what she said, how she felt, her expressions of affection for her husband."

"The woman in the photo tells the story doesn't she? Of grief and shame and remorse."

"Yes." Justine stared back into the fire. *Grief and shame and remorse,* she repeated to herself. *Yet Isabella also knew pleasure and joy. She'd been swept away by a grand passion. And she'd been given a daughter, a legacy of her trust in love.*

She voiced her thoughts to her mother. Then, "Can such a love balance out the pain she was to feel later? I doubt that she regretted her affair with Lawrence."

"I'm certain that she didn't regret it. After all, it was so much more than sexual, which I doubt was very satisfying, given his weakened condition. Their relationship was spiritual and intellectual. She felt acknowledged as a woman. Someone worthy of being consulted and included in the pivotal decisions of his life. Lawrence's life."

Justine wiped the moisture from her eyes and smiled. *The great-granddaughter of D.H. Lawrence. What will this mean to me? How am I different because of this heritage?* "Where is he? My great-grandfather?"

"His ashes are buried in a chapel on his ranch, on the side of Lobo Mountain," said her mother. "A few miles north of Taos, New Mexico."

Where he wanted to be. From the pyramids to Italy's Tufo Mountains to Lobo.

The journey continues . . .

Introducing the third novel in The Justine Trilogy . . .

A RAPTURE OF RAVENS: AWAKENING IN TAOS

PROLOGUE

—⸎⸎⸎—

I will never forget one thing. In Winter time, when you go to Wounded
Knee, never dig deep into the snow. All you will do is find the blood left by
your family before me. Think only of them and say, it is a good day to die!
                                    —Tashunkala (Little Horse), SihaSapa Lakota

---

FEBRUARY 3, 2011

J USTINE STOOD AT THE FROSTED WINDOW in flannel pajamas, an Indian blanket
wrapped around her like a cocoon, curtains drawn to reveal an island of
lights on the Taos campus of the University of New Mexico, a half-mile away.
A shooting comet disappeared into a palette of stars, a mere sliver of moon
hung in the western sky. Barely 4:30 a.m.; she hadn't slept since Amir's 2:30
call. In another hour, the mantle of snow on the Sangre de Cristo Mountains
would turn pink in the early morning light.

Revolution Day all over again. She held her steaming coffee cup with both
hands, the noise of the television in the background. Without turning, she
listened to the sounds of men and women flooding into Tahrir Square in
Cairo. It was Wednesday.

All Amir had said before the line went dead was, "I love you, Justine. It could be
today. Then I'll be home . . ." *It could be today*, which could only mean one thing:
Mubarak was expected to step down. The revolution would achieve its goal: the end
to a brutal thirty-year dictatorship. Justine felt a tension in her gut—*Can it be so
easy? Can Mubarak be brought down in less than two weeks?* Perhaps, but not likely.

The possibilities were promising, yet she was gripped by deeply unsettling fears for Amir, his leadership role with the youth of Egypt placing him at great risk of being arrested. And she knew what that meant. The turmoil in the Middle East was unprecedented, clearly, so, perhaps none of the old rules applied. *This is a new game, in a new world bursting from the ground up, a popular revolution quickened by social media. But then what?* She knew that if Mubarak were removed, Egyptians would still have the military and Brotherhood, since no one else was organized. Perhaps with Amir's help, those who led the January 25th revolution would form themselves into a focused political movement. *Perhaps.*

Justine gripped the blanket more firmly around her chilled body and returned to the kitchen for the last dregs of coffee. On the couch, she curled her stockinged feet under her and stared at the screen. Tahrir Square was crowded with thousands chanting, "Down with Mubarak," arms flailing in the air, placards in Arabic demanding the president's resignation. The crowd throbbed like a singular heart beating in concert.

Her vision was captured by a familiar-looking figure in the throng. While the images were nearly indistinct, she recognized his gait, his posture, even his profile. *Amir!* She smiled involuntarily to see that he was wearing the Kokopelli scarf she'd given him for Christmas. *It must be Amir.* She couldn't be wrong, could she? He was facing west, toward the burned-out Hilton, leaning into a small group of four or five men.

From the edge of the screen, like the meteor, men rode swiftly into sight on sturdy Arabian horses and lanky camels, clubs swinging above their heads, then coming down to strike indiscriminately into the swarm of young people.

Suddenly, one of the camel riders rode in Amir's direction, charging with intent, as though he knew his target. Amir didn't see him coming. Justine jumped to her feet, spilling her coffee, turning over the coffee table. "Amir! Amir!" She was with him in the middle of the grassy square, screaming, warning him. Two men in the crowd pointed frantically and raced to pull the hoodlum from his camel, but too late. The club crashed against Amir's head. She imagined blood spurting into the electrified air. As the rider lifted his club for a second blow, he was pulled from his camel and beaten into the ground.

Bloody Wednesday had begun.

ACKNOWLEDGMENTS

The author and her husband, Morgan, in Vitero, Italy

IN *THE CAIRO CODEX*, I acknowledged the challenge of writing about a culture that is not my own. In writing *The Italian Letters,* I received the assistance of Italian friends who generously shared insights, personal perceptions, and scientific expertise. They helped me to understand the essence of being Italian, and without their expertise, this novel could not have been written. Even so, I am but a stranger in their beautiful land.

I wish to thank these many friends. The Baroness Miranda Taxis and her husband, the Baron William Taxis, made available their voices, beautiful estate, Il Pero, and sensitive feedback. Guido Barbujani, professor of biology at the University of Ferrara, lent his expertise on the Etruscans and mitochondrial DNA, as well as his editing expertise as a novelist. Marco De Marco, Director of the Etruscan Museo in Fiesole, provided insights into the Etruscan afterlife as well as photographs of the Zona Archeologica and the town of Fiesole. Francesca Boitani, Director of Il Museo e Villa Giulia in Rome, was the first to share her expertise on the history of the Etruscans. Guido De' Medici taught the marvelous cooking class at Badia a Coltibuono. Paule Beauchef Beretta of Veii, Italy, shared her intimate knowledge of Rome. Delmo Della Dora is an Italian-American friend who provided linguistic research, editing, and language additions, while appearing as a retired linguist from the University of Bologna. Robert Blackburn, friend, villain, and gentle critic, continued his misadventures that began in *The Cairo Codex*. All of these individuals lent their personas as fictionalized characters in this novel.

The research and editing for this novel was ably assisted by Mary E. Gardner, Rae Newell Meriaux, Carolyn Horan, Julie Biddle, Susan Clark, Jerry Burroni, Larissa Bonfante, Seymour Collins, Gary Thompson, Molly Buckley, Martinia Hücke, Thomas A.J. McGinn, Guido Sirolla and Suzanne Narayanan, owners of Villa Narsi in Santa Fiora, and sister-in-law Janet Todd. Playwright and Lawrence scholar Neal Metcalf assisted with the details regarding D.H. Lawrence and made helpful additions to the letters.

Invaluable feedback and coaching was provided by my supportive and talented writing group, composed of Judith Fisher and Ida Egli, who is also my editor.

My husband, Dr. Morgan Dale Lambert, fulfills my life and my writing adventures as supporter, researcher, and editor—as well as playing the role of the arrogant archeologist, Dr. Morgan Jenner, in this novel. I must point out that my Morgan is neither arrogant nor an archaeologist.

Linda Lambert, Ed.D.
Santa Rosa, California
www.lindalambert.com

ABOUT THE AUTHOR

LINDA LAMBERT, Ed.D. is Professor Emeritus from California State University, East Bay, and a full time author of novels and texts on leadership. During Linda's career she has served as social worker, teacher, principal, district and county directors of adult learning programs, as well as university professor, state department envoy to Egypt, and international consultant. Her international consultancies in leadership have taken her to the Middle East, England, Thailand, Mexico, Canada, and Malaysia. Linda is the author of dozens of articles and lead author of *The Constructivist Leader* (1995, 2002), *Who Will Save Our Schools* (1997), and *Women's Ways of Leading* (2009); she is the author of *Building Leadership Capacity in Schools* (1998) and *Leadership Capacity for Lasting School Improvement* (2003). *The Cairo Codex*, her first novel in a trilogy was widely acclaimed. It was the winner of the Silver Nautilus Award and the Bronze IPPY Award, 2014. She lives with her husband, Morgan, a retired school superintendent, in Santa Rosa, California.